About the Author

Louise Grace is a writer who loves to tell stories. She wants to be an award-winning author but hasn't quite got there yet, so has currently settled for being a broke university student instead. But she's been writing since she learnt how to hold a pen, which is a start, I guess?

That's about it…

…Oh, she won a story writing cup at school in Year Six. Hopefully after this book she'll have an award or something to add to this very short description.

Hopefully.

The Enchanteds

Louise Grace

The Enchanteds

Olympia Publishers
London

www.olympiapublishers.com
OLYMPIA PAPERBACK EDITION

A CIP catalogue record for this title is
available from the British Library.

ISBN: 978-1-80074-130-0

This is a work of fiction.
Names, characters, places, and incidents originate from the writer's
imagination. Any resemblance to actual persons, living or dead, is purely
coincidental.

First Published in 2023

Olympia Publishers
Tallis House
2 Tallis Street
London
EC4Y 0AB

Printed in Great Britain

Dedication

For anyone who has ever encouraged and supported me.

Prologue

If anyone was to be sat on a throne sculpted from the bones of slaughtered innocents and belong there, it was the malevolent psychopath, Atlas. The throne, which signified no sovereign power and was built only for egotistical needs, was the sole furnishing of the fortified chamber. It stood lonesome, in the centre of the room, the once white bones discoloured over centuries where Atlas had neglected to replace them. Smooth obsidian coated the floor. Its purpose lay not in creating an intimidating atmosphere but in concealing the blood of the countless people who had died across the slabs.

A single, high-standing window shattered the murk of the musky room with a shard of blinding light which, slicing across Atlas' face revealed a pair of soulless, black eyes. They were unsettling at best but a permanent characteristic to flaunt the evil that resided within him.

A broad shouldered, muscular, and malicious looking man, Atlas wore armour that tightly encased his figure; he lived in the anticipation of battle. His pallid skin was disfigured by plentiful battle scars; and his tangled facial hair deceptively hid his true age of several hundred millennia at least. But although the tyrant was feared by all unlucky enough to cross his path, his age came at the cost of fragility and illness. The powers he once possessed were slowly dwindling.

Screams broke the quiet in which he sat to scheme; they were muffled by a heavy titanium door but were clearly screams of agony. Whilst the noise didn't faze Atlas and instead made him sneer, the ensuing silence clearly captured his interest. He leant forward slightly, staring attentively at the doorway. Moments later, footsteps echoed outside the chamber door before a pause, as though whoever stood on the other side didn't want to come in.

Three heavy bangs penetrated the silence.

Atlas smirked.

"Enter," he bellowed. The door squeaked open, and light breached the darkness in which Atlas shrouded himself. He scowled. The man, specifically a doctor, who had appeared hastily, shut it, allowing the gloom to fall once again. His body trembled, stooped over, wide-eyed and his white beard would have perfectly complimented his scrubs had he not been covered in thick, fresh blood. He bowed and waited to be addressed.

"Well?" Atlas questioned, his stentorian voice rattling the doctor.

"Your wife is doing exceptionally well sire; she had a safe delivery. She is in excellent condition and—" the doctor fell at the force of Atlas' yell as he interrupted him.

"--I don't care about her!" He smashed his fist on the throne and the arm splintered under the pressure, loose teeth from the skulls bouncing down the stairs. The doctor watched them clatter to a stop. He knew his head could easily replace the crushed skull. Atlas growled. "What about the child?" For a moment, the doctor hesitated to speak, hunching his shoulders, and shrinking from Atlas' shadow.

Something was wrong.

Atlas clenched his fist tightly and the doctor instantly struggled to breathe, clawing at his neck as his eyes bulged. It was a great pleasure of Atlas to watch others suffer under his hand. When the doctor fell to his knees, Atlas spread his feculent fingers wide. The doctor swallowed air like he'd never tasted it before.

"The child is doing great sire," he stuttered. "It's a girl, um, very healthy."

"Enough!" Atlas roared. His thundering voice sent the doctor into a state of overwhelming terror. He whimpered as Atlas rose from his chair, the near seven-foot giant exhibiting his towering height and terrifying rage. His footsteps stridently pounded the floor and the doctor's heart hammered so loudly it nearly matched the sound.

Atlas knelt in front of the doctor and wound his hair in his hand, almost gently, but with malice intent. He drew so uncomfortably close that wisps swayed back and forth from his heavy wheezing. And although it was alarming when Atlas was loud, his threatening demeanour when he fell quiet was chilling. The doctor remained silent but exhaled sharply as Atlas yanked his hair back, forcing the two of them to lock eyes.

"Is she like me?" Atlas asked. The doctor was so afraid he couldn't speak to tell Atlas the truth. Looking down in humiliation he mouthed the word 'no' and shook his head. In the brief pause where they both made eye contact again, the doctor saw his death reflecting back at him.

He was going to die.

Atlas processed what he had been told. "You've failed," he decided, "and you've broken my chair." Before the doctor could protest, Atlas grabbed the top of his head and in a single swift movement, twisted his neck 360 degrees. A thud followed a horrendous crack and the doctor's lifeless body crumpled to the floor. The obsidian floors had again served their purpose.

As if killing a man tired Atlas, he groaned and showing his actual age, pushed himself slowly to a slumped, standing position. Conflicted, angry but most importantly worried, he backed towards his chair and with some amount of pain, lowered himself into it, grimacing as his old and frail bones struggled to move his weight. But he didn't show anyone this and so, composing himself, he regained his mighty statute and raised his voice once more.

"Daegel," he called. An unbearably obsequious servant bowed deeply on entering, in fidelity and allegiance rather than fear. Equipped with heavy weaponry, he prepared for whatever Atlas was going to ask. After a fleeting glance at the dead body, Daegel trod over it as though it was a daily occurrence and dropped to one knee.

"My lord?" he asked.

"Tell my wife to prepare for another child. She will keep trying until we have one capable of harbouring magic." He leant back on his throne, temporarily defeated but not giving up. The sycophant nodded readily.

"I shall tell her immediately sire. Is there anything else you require of me?"

"Dispose of this garbage -" Atlas waved a heartless finger at the dead body, acknowledging it now as nothing more than a pile of waste, "-but save the head. I need a new throne arm."

"I will, my lord," Daegel pledged. He grabbed the doctor by the leg, hauled his flaccid body over his shoulder like a bag of rubbish and went to leave. It was an average day for him.

"And Daegel."

Daegel tilted his head. "Yes, my lord?"

"The baby is useless. Kill it." Unlike a person with empathy, or even a shred of common human decency who would have refused, Daegel's wiry lips split into a grin of decayed teeth. He favoured the command over all Atlas had given him.

He left the room, leaving Atlas engrossed in thought. The door slammed shut and Daegel marched with intent through the corridor, not pausing as he twisted the head of the doctor from his shoulders and let the body drop amongst the bins.

As he rounded the corner, he shoved through the door of a juxtaposing sun-bathed suite, half unsheathing a broad bladed sword and ready to kill without remorse. The room bustled busily with nurses who, as Daegel appeared and nonchalantly dropped the doctors head on a tabletop, backed away in fear. He ambled through the room, well aware of the discomfort his presence brought, and approached a curtain, yanking it back to reveal the languid figure of Atlas' wife, Joplin, who seemed unsurprised but fearful of the rude intrusion.

Atlas was egregious to the core. Joplin had let him hold their first child. He killed it, claiming the fragility of a child's skull was unexpected. So, she had anticipated Daegel's arrival the minute the Atlas deemed the baby unusable for his cause.

"And what iniquitous task have you been sent in here to fulfil?" she asked him.

"You know what has to be done," said Daegel. Joplin, whilst being a devoted wife was now, above all else, a loving mother and not prepared to hand over her new-born, when she had already lost so many.

"Back away Daegel," she warned. Daegel stilled but made no attempt to leave.

"I'm sorry Joplin-" He wasn't, "-but it is Atlas' will and I shall see through his request." She allowed him a second longer to leave but his reprehensible shadow loomed closer over her bed. With heavy eyelids and a fatigued posture, Joplin clenched her fists and power flowed through her. She wasn't an Ancient; a centuries old demon, like Atlas. She was an Enchanted, a slightly lesser breed of magical being but still with monumental power. As was Daegel, but she could fight him and win. Her abilities surpassed his.

"You won't lay a finger on my child," she told him. The small baby who had seemingly sensed the mention of its being, started wriggling and crying amongst the wrap of blankets. Joplin tugged back the quilt and cupped its cheek in her hand. "You'll be fine," she whispered, kissing its forehead gently. She may have hoped that the endearing cuteness of her daughter may have swayed Daegel's opinion, but his nose crinkled in disgust, and he drew his sword fully. It became apparent he didn't care.

Bloodied sheets dropped to the floor as Joplin stood and although the nurses shook their heads, she gently placed her child in the cot and clutching her swollen stomach, prepared to stand her ground.

"Daegel. I'll give you one last chance to walk out that door," she growled. Daegel snorted at her insolence, confident in his combative skills and disputatious personality.

"Don't challenge me," he jeered. "You've just given birth. Your weakness is more evident than ever." His taunt didn't deter Joplin's defiance.

"If you believe childbirth to be a sign of weakness then you are greatly mistaken. You won't hurt my child. Ever." Daegel shook his head and raised his sword as the nurses spectated helplessly. He was cocky, his head filled with Atlas' praise made him overconfident. He chuckled as if to say, 'I know I'm going to win' and advanced, swinging his sword at Joplin. It was a clumsy swipe and she easily dodged it, but it meant that nothing barred Daegel from the baby. Rather than fight her, he lunged for the cot. Screeching like a banshee, Joplin grabbed his leg and yanked him to the floor, smashing his head against the marble tiles as a brave nurse wheeled the cot out the way.

He clawed at Joplin's eyes and so she shut them, but it gave him time to kick her in the stomach, followed by a calculated punch to the jaw. She screamed in pain as the chorus of 'stop!' and 'leave her alone!' from the nurses increased, although none of them dared to step in. He hit her again, curling his fist and smashing her nose to pieces.

She tasted blood.

Lots of it.

The sour iron taste filled her mouth and she spat at him rabidly, finding her feet as he leapt back, wiping the red gore from his eyes. However, rather than head for the baby again, Daegel remained with Joplin, colliding with her and wrapping his gorilla-like hands around her throat as hard as he could. Joplin grabbed his ear and yanked, and blood splattered across the floor following a horrendous sound of tearing flesh. Daegel howled but he grimaced and continued to strangle her. The pain was immense but the fear of answering to Atlas suggested an agony likely to be fatal.

Lashing out furiously, Joplin kicked him between the legs, but Daegel's armoured uniform meant she injured herself more than him and her foot bruised in mere seconds. She was losing consciousness, her ears were ringing, and she was seeing double if not triple but all she needed to render him harmless was to touch his skin for a second or two. So, rather than fight against him she grabbed his exposed wrist between his gloved hand and armoured arm as a last resort and coughing, yelled:

"Sleep!" Power surged from her hands into his body and Daegel's expression dulled. He went rigid, as though catatonia took hold and his eyes lulled back in his head. He thudded to the floor, unconscious.

In anger, Joplin snapped Daegel's wrist before letting go. It was an unintentional but well-deserved act.

The nurses swarmed around her like flies, helping her up as she gasped for air. She made the extra effort to trample Daegel's ear and it stuck like gum to the tiles.

"Get him out of here," Joplin commanded. She sank onto the blankets, eyes clouded with rage. She was a naturally graceful person but at this moment her appearance was inelegant and haggard.

"Here, my lady." One of the nurses pushed through the crowd of her colleagues with the mewling new-born and tried to put it in Joplin's arms but worryingly, she refused, seeking instead a tissue to tend to her fractured nose.

"Ma'am?" they questioned. "Your daughter needs you." Joplin shook her head. A single tear rolled down her cheek. She had to save her daughter, even if it meant giving her up.

"No, she isn't safe here. If Atlas finds out she's still alive he'll kill her himself." She looked at the nurses who were avoiding eye contact. None of them wanted the responsibility of the child, especially if Atlas found out. "Please." Joplin was in a position where it was not often that she had to beg. "Keep my daughter safe. Atlas doesn't understand he could learn to love something that isn't an asset to him."

"We can't take your child from you," the nurse holding the baby argued. It was gurgling happily but was also reaching for Joplin, its eyes wide in curiosity.

"I'm not giving you the choice." Joplin didn't want to abandon her child, but what choice did she have?

"But you'll never know each other." Joplin went silent. She allowed several more tears to fall and the baby curled its tiny fist around her finger as if to comfort her. But she didn't take her daughter from the nurse's arms. Like a completely different person, she wiped away her tears and bloody lipstick, straightened her posture and glared at the nurse.

"You will take her. Take her as far away as you can." The nurses couldn't go against Joplin's authority. "Take what won't be missed from the vault so she has wealth to her name and leave her on the doorstep of a loving family. The nicest people you can find. Make sure she's taken in. I don't want her ending up without a mother who cares."

"But you're her mother, you care," the nurse protested. Joplin's eyes bore into hers.

"You dare talk to me like that? Like I don't know what's best for my daughter!" Joplin yelled, demonstrating the anger her and Atlas shared. The baby began to cry lightly, and Joplin sighed, calming herself as a white hot pain shot through her nose. She remained brutally strong willed and buried all maternal instincts. "Goodbye, my angel," she whispered. Reaching her hands to the back of her neck, she unclasped a necklace from beneath knots of greying hair and tucked it into the folds of the blanket. "Now go."

"My lady, are you sure about this?"

"I said leave!" Joplin screamed. The nurse inclined her head and smiled a fond and brief farewell to her friends before hurrying out the room, checking behind her nervously as she fled. The last thing Joplin saw of her daughter was her crying in fear. She couldn't control her anger and the baby feared loud noises.

One of the nurses tentatively put her hand on Joplin's shoulder in an attempt to console her. Whilst Joplin hid her upset well, she had the temperament of a new mother, and her emotions were unruly.

"Ma'am, are you all right?"

No reply.

"You did the best thing you could." From down the corridor, the nurses froze as Atlas' voice was heard.

"Joplin. Come here now."

"Don't go ma'am, you need time to recover," the nurse urged, trying to lead her back to bed. Again, Joplin didn't answer. She instead moved towards the door, hunched in reluctance. The dead gaze of the doctor fell on her; he'd lied to Atlas to protect the baby and paid the price with his life. Joplin looked away shamefacedly. She gripped the door handle and paused, allowing herself a moment of reflection before smiling sadly at the nurse.

"I did the best I could do." But she'd failed to convince herself so, before she left the room on Atlas' command.

Chapter 1

Ebony didn't know she was going to kill everyone.

She would do it indirectly. But she would do it nonetheless, and the deaths of thousands would weigh on her conscience before the night was over.

But for now, she celebrated.

"Thanks to the extraordinary findings of the scientists aboard Transtar Labs research stations, we are one step closer to finding out what life could be lurking on the planets buried within the Helio Galaxy." A raucous applause arose from the spaceship's auditorium as the broadcaster recognised a year of hard graft. Molecular biologist Ebony Echnovarria stood with an aura of accomplishment amongst her colleagues; the corner of her eyes wrinkled, and she beamed as the cameras recorded the crowd. She'd never been on TV before.

Ebony's beauty radiated more in her cheerful personality and compassionate disposition than conventional looks. Of average height and shapely build, her ivory skin was accentuated by layers of curled, mousy brown hair cascading over her shoulders. The colour of her hair changed subtly between the summer and winter months and was yet to lighten. The corners of her mouth aligned with the angle of her prominent cheekbones, so she always seemed pleased, her plump lips curved into a slight smile. And in this situation, she most definitely had a reason to be smiling.

"And thanks to all your hard work and dedication, we can all head home two weeks ahead of schedule," the supervisor of their research sector declared. Clapping rose to cheers and Ebony squealed in delight as she was lifted high into the air on the shoulders of her co-worker, Jonah. 2592 had been a good year so far.

Champagne bottles were popped, and music flooded the room. White lab coats and smart blazers were carelessly discarded into a messy pile as scientists left the hall and inundated the huge lobby, the ceiling of which rose so high to the point that the disco ball hanging from the top had no effect on the crowd below.

"Congratulations Ebony," Jonah praised. He pulled up alongside a sofa as though it was a bus stop and leant down. Ebony hadn't noticed his towering height until she clumsily climbed off and could no longer see over the crowd of people. Thankful she'd chosen to wear a jumpsuit to avoid mishap, the two of them sat and Ebony sighed with the utmost content as she pulled off her heels and wiggled her toes.

"Thanks for the ride, Jonah." She removed two champagne flutes from the waitress who waltzed by, handing one to him. "Congratulations to you too." They clinked glasses.

"Cheers." He downed the boozy drink and flipped it upside-down like a shot glass onto the sofa. Ebony followed suit and they laughed giddily.

"You going to continue working on the ship after this?" she asked, making conversation over the loud music. Scratching his stubble, Jonah shrugged undecidedly as he eyed up another drink.

"Maybe. But the Homestead ship re-entered the Delta Quadrant of the galaxy recently; I'm going to visit my little girl first." He spoke with sincere affection.

"She'll be over the moon." Ebony was pleased for him.

"And you?"

"Haven't thought about it."

"No family to go back to?" Her and Jonah had known each other for a while, but the conversation of family had never come up. Ebony had no family to speak of.

"An overprotective robot," Ebony chuckled, "but Transtar are building a new HQ in Chane city, and I've been offered a job there." She announced it like it wasn't a big deal, but the opposite was true.

"Ebony, that's amazing," Jonah applauded but she brushed off his enthusiasm.

"Not really," she admitted. "I'd rather anything than sit in an office back on Drognir."

"But Transtar HQ?" Jonah reiterated. "That's a once in a lifetime opportunity. You'll be heading the biology sector."

"I don't know if it's for me. I want a life of adventure," Ebony replied.

Jonah's head perked up as the song changed. "How about a life of dancing?" He sprang to his feet and offered Ebony his hand.

She shook her head. "I don't dance," she declined politely. Jonah's face fell and Ebony couldn't bear to upset him. "But maybe later?"

"Deal," he decided. "I'll find you later for the dance of your life." Ebony laughed as he moonwalked towards the dancefloor, giving her finger guns before he spun around, and she watched his blonde mop disappear into the crowd.

"Crazy boy," she muttered fondly. After surveying the room for the closest exit to flee to when Jonah inevitably tried to make her dance, she wandered slowly along the window. Emphasised by sweeping lashes, starlight reflected in her sepia eyes as she watched the nebulas and galaxies before her. Adventure was tantalisingly close, but just out of reach. She had two rotations of her home planet left before she could leave Transtar and travel the stars.

The planet Aqua-B Solar orbited below the ship and Ebony watched, mesmerised, as the terminator line glided across the planet's surface; colonies waking for a new day as others prepared for their nineteen hour night. It was never really dark on the planet though; bioluminescent plants forbid it. When the haloed glare of the star struck Ebony, her eyes briefly flickered away, and she was engrossed by a rarer sight.

The window provided a view, not only of space but of the southern sector of the ship and more notably, one of the four major engines. But, in Ebony's vaguely knowledgeable opinion it didn't look to be functioning correctly. Ferociously spitting embers into space, she stared as it glowed.

Swaying out of the crowd of dancers, an inebriated Jonah appeared at her side.

"I know you hate dancing, but this song is an absolute tune. You cannot not dance." He pressed his palms together. "Please?" His best puppy dog eyes under any other circumstance would have convinced Ebony, but she ignored him.

"Does that look right to you?" she asked. He followed her gaze out the window.

"No." Jonah's lips pressed into a firm line to match the wrinkle on his forehead as he sobered up.

"Definitely not right," she murmured. Ebony pressed her hands against the glass. It was warm to the touch, almost uncomfortable. Soon they were part of a crowd of scientists who had left the dancefloor for closer examination of the irregular activity. The engine, a cool grey aluminium which usually didn't show a sign of heat, radiated an amber hue. Oxygen from the ship was fuelling a fire that flared into space and melted it from the inside out.

"The engine coolers aren't working." Ebony tried to take a step back but was trapped in an enclosure of people.

"How is that possible?" Jonah worried.

"I don't know," she said, "but nothing's stopping it overheating..." Ebony's eyes widened in fear. She struggled to finish her sentence as every breath felt like wind across a dry desert. With a shudder of the ship, the engine cracked.

People began to scream. A rampage ensued as they sprinted for the doors. Accidental hands shoved Ebony to the floor and she was unrelentingly trampled by others attempting to save themselves. Blurred shoes rushed by, and she curled into a ball as the sharp heel of a peep toe stiletto sliced her arm to the muscle.

"Ebony!" Jonah fought against the crowd and yanked her up, wrapping his arm around her shoulder as the two of them joined the rush.

An ear destroying bang exploded from the engines.

The ship lurched, throwing the inhabitants across the room and Jonah and Ebony were separated again. Landing across the dance floor, the wind knocked out of her, Ebony slid into a deceptively plush bar stool. She grimaced, clutching her arm as she heaved herself into a sitting position.

"Jonah?" Taking a sharp intake of breath, Ebony stood and inspected the state of the room. The party had come to an abrupt end; few people were on their feet and Jonah was nowhere to be seen. As the gravitational shield adjusted to the new angle at which the ship carried itself, Ebony rebalanced along with it. Blood was smeared across her arm in a messy streak and when she tensed, the wound spurted blood like a water gun. Grabbing a bottle of whiskey from behind the bar, she pulled the cork with her teeth and bit down on it harshly as she doused her arm with the stinging alcohol to clean the lesion. Saving the last ounce of liquid to calm her nerves, she spat the cork out, downed the Balvenie and grabbed a discarded blazer to tie around her arm, before searching the sea of injured people.

"Jonah," she called again.

"Ebony!"

Ebony whipped around and yelped as Jonah, with the bearing of a rugby player, barrelled into her and tackled her across the room. The disco ball, which was four times larger than she'd ever realised, smashed to the ground where she was standing not moments ago. Shards flew through the air in search of a target, but thanks to Jonah, Ebony wasn't one of them.

"Thank you," she breathed. Blood seeped through his ruined suit. "Are you all right?" Jonah didn't acknowledge the stain.

"Think so," he replied, patting himself down, "you?"

"Yeah." Ebony stood to face the window and was greeted with a death dealing situation. The engine had ruptured. The turbines were snapped from their compartment in the explosion. They were now hurtling towards the window.

"Jonah, get up. Get up now." Ebony hauled him to his feet, and they hobbled towards the exit, but another bang shook the floor, causing them both to fall again. One of the turbine propellers had collided with the window.

It cracked at an exponential pace, spreading across the glass like an infection. Ebony, paralysed, watched the cracks with wide eyes. Her fight or flight response failed. True fear wasn't what she'd expected it to be. The adrenaline kicked in and she could hear her heart thumping in her ears, but she still couldn't move and the anxiety that came with the fear, nearly crippled her.

"Ebony, come on!" It was Jonah who saved her again. He pulled her roughly away from the window until her feet worked on their own.

With a deafening siren, two feet thick steel shutters descended from the ceiling, but it was too little too late. Before Transtar's so called state of the art security system could even cover half of the window, it shattered and exploded inward across the crowd.

"Mayday, mayday! This is the Intergalactic scientific research station

Transstar Labs Inc. code 17-4, current location above planet Aqua-B Solar. Extensive damage to the Southern and Western sectors, ninety percent power loss to all engines. We are losing altitude. Only half the emergency ships are online and activated, the rest unresponsive or destroyed. Loss of life substantial, but unable to estimate death toll. The majority of the survivors are situated in the Northern sector, but we do not have enough escape pods. Requesting mass rescue immediately, I repeat, requesting mass rescue immediately." A distress signal echoed from loudspeakers across local space, begging for assistance. Ships crowded around the huge station that once sat firmly in the sky but was now plummeting towards Aqua-B solar on an unstoppable collision course. They were able to do nothing but sit and watch, collecting the deceased floating amidst the debris out of respect for not just those aboard Transtar, but for those on Aqua-B solar. Acid rain was common, but raining corpses was inequitable.

Inside, automated system protocols echoed through every hallway of the ship.

"Hull integrity breached. Collect an oxygen helmet as provided. Proceed calmly to your assigned escape pod. Follow all emergency protocol as practised. Emergency power initiated." The sirens wailed in anguish as flames engulfed the powerless vessel. Without warning, another explosion threw the mighty ship onto its side as though it were a mere dingy in an ocean storm and with a groan, the electricity failed.

There was a chorus of screams as red warning lights flickered on and rather than proceeding calmly to safety, the remaining crew members and scientists sprinted to escape pods with no thought for anyone but themselves. Black smoke billowed from the wreckage, each swell fighting for supremacy, to be the swirl that rose highest, engulfed the most. It was carnage. Emergency oxygen rapidly pumped through the vents accompanied unintentionally by smoke. It spread from floor to floor, marring perception where the red glow already made it hard to see, and making each breath smarting.

"Jonah," Ebony cried, covering her mouth with the jacket as she strained her tear stained eyes. She was unaware of how it had happened but the air from the sudden breach and force of the explosion had blasted her into one of the hallways. Emergency shutters had slammed behind her swiftly and so, despite an intense shortness of breath and flames stripping the walls of the ship to its bare carcass around her, she was still alive.

"Please collect an oxygen helmet as provided," the sirens preached again. The ringing in Ebony's ears was disorientating and looking to the end of the corridor, she stumbled as she rushed over to the remaining helmet. With bloody hands she reached out to grab it, but someone flung themselves into her side, knocking her to the floor. Her head collided with the shelf and she blinked rapidly as everything began to spin. The ringing in her ears intensified until suddenly the world went unnervingly quiet. She looked up at the rangy man. She could see two of him.

"I'm sorry-" She read his lips as he snatched the helmet, sliding it swiftly over his head, "-but I have kids at home." He sprinted off down the corridor.

Ebony rolled onto her stomach, watching as he sprinted away, but he didn't get far. A detonation of the backup engine threw him to the floor as a firestorm swept the corridor. Ebony rolled into a nearby room, wincing as flames shot by the doorway, singeing her arm hair. It took only a moment for them to subside and when they did, she peeped out guardedly. The man lay where he fell, barely a skeleton, with the oxygen helmet melted onto his skull. She wrenched her eyes away, cheeks bulging as sick rose to her throat. She swallowed it and hobbled over broken glass in her bare feet to escape the smell of burning flesh.

"Transtar," she said loudly and a band around her wrist lit up. "Search for life-signs on this ship. Ignore escape pods," she ordered. The band took a moment.

"Closest life form is precisely 429 metres away, located inside the Glassway," it said, its droning voice unaware of the urgency.

"Is it Jonah Pallius?"

"Jonah Pallius is precisely 412 metres away, located at the entrance of the Glassway," it told her. She exhaled deeply, shaking, but fuelled by the smallest shred of hope as she took off down the corridor.

"Jonah!" She yelled again, but each word was becoming more of a chore as her saliva blackened. An uncharred vending machine provided Ebony some comfort to lean on as she caught her breath and robbed the machine of a water pouch. But she relinquished the hydration to push on and find Jonah, stopping only when she ran into a group of people charging the opposite way.

"Escape pods are this way." A crew member reached for Ebony's arm as they passed without stopping. She halted them.

"Have you seen Jonah Pallius? About this tall, tanned, muscly—" she was abruptly cut off.

"--Sorry love, no time to look for survivors," he said, beckoning for her to go with them.

"Life forms found," the band said.

"Then-" Ebony dug her nails stressfully into her ash dusted hair, "-where's Jonah?" Her optimism for finding him alive dropped.

"Come on love," the crew member urged but she was adamant.

"I've got to find my friend." The bewilderment on their faces was quickly replaced by pity of her foolish hope and in spite of their protests, she continued her search.

Bodies decorated the corridors and Ebony tried to pace herself as she jogged, determined not to join them. Feeling light-headed was the least of her concerns however, as she entered an entirely glass corridor acting as a shortcut between the North and South sectors. It speared through space and was normally one of Ebony's favourite places, yet on this occasion, she floundered through in a daze and her heart dropped.

Freezing bodies floated lifelessly through space, forced around by the strength of the explosions riddling the main body of the ship. Ebony fought to hold in the first tear but once it broke free, others cascaded down her cheeks, soaking her chest as she watched the bodies of her friends and colleagues float past her. Swollen and frozen with faces contorted in pain.

Ebony couldn't hold it in any longer. As the head of a raggedy teddy bear floated by, she vomited violently.

There were children on the ship.

Panting, she rested her hands on her buckling knees and tried to calm herself, but wherever she looked, bodies haunted her vision. Then a thud on the glass caused her to scream and trip back. A body hit the window. The shirt snagged on the outside cable structures and slowly rotated, until its face was revealed.

Ebony's tormented sobs penetrated the nothingness and fell only on the ears of the dead.

"Jonah," she whimpered. His blue eyes had frozen over like a wintery lake. His expression was one of agonising fear and his mouth hung agape, where he'd tried to scream for help.

"I'm sorry," Ebony mumbled. She held her hand to the glass by his face, as if to comfort him. But he was knocked onwards and over the Glassway and she watched helplessly, as the corpse of her friend joined the countless others.

Ebony's hands fell limply into her lap. Her mind was so inundated with thoughts, she couldn't say anything of coherence, only mumble as she dragged her torso upwards and stumbled back across the walkway.

"Follow the lights to your nearest escape pod." The siren became more urgent as though it personally willed Ebony to safety. She could see from her vantage point as escape pods shot rapidly from the ships, full beyond the maximum capacity as people fled the massacre.

"Shit." The gravity of the situation began to sink in. Soon, all of the escape pods would be gone, and the ship would descend as a catastrophic fireball into the side of Aqua-B Solar. She would be abandoned and left to die.

Every moment counted.

Every movement was critical.

Heart beating through her chest, she picked up the pace and ran. Through the corridors, the man with the melted face served as a harrowing reminder of the danger Ebony was in.

Cold air flooded through a hole in the wall as the cabin's pressure slowly fell and Ebony continued to the pods. The likelihood of survival was plummeting. But at least if the ship ran out of oxygen Ebony couldn't burn alive. Right? She clung on to what little optimism she had left as the planet below was hammered by Transtar fragments. She could see ships who had heard the distress call hovering a safe distance away. None of them could see her. Flicking her wrist, Ebony looked at the band again.

"Transtar, where's the closest escape pod?" she asked. it beeped and a hologram shone from the band, mapping the ships interior. A green dot flashed profusely, locating the escape pod just through the door in front of her. The key card was ready in her hands, but she fumbled as they shivered uncontrollably. Eventually she swiped the magstripe and the door flung open, granting her access to salvation.

"Pod ready for take-off," the voice said.

"Wait!" Ebony started but the noise as the engines roared to life drowned her out like the buzz of a fly competing against a volcanic eruption. People, some Ebony would go so far as to call friends, saw her from the windows of the pod and offered looks of cruel commiserations. With survival instincts setting in, they turned a cold shoulder and did nothing to halt the pod and help rescue her. Ebony reached out a helpless hand as the pod shot from its bay.

Under normal circumstances, the air pressure of the room would have levelled itself out within a nanosecond, but the circuitry was destroyed and effortlessly, the wind from the open gate swallowed Ebony up and spat her into space.

She tumbled into the vacuum.

She wasn't able to stop.

She panicked as a burning pain devoured her insides and her blood boiled and her limbs swelled.

She exhaled deeply in an attempt to stop the air inside her rupturing her lungs.

She clenched her jaw as her exposed body was burnt by unfiltered cosmic rays and began to freeze over.

She squeezed her eyes shut to try and preserve her vision, as the training she'd been through told her.

But whilst she'd had training to know what to do to maximise her chances of survival in this situation, she was unconscious before she could put anything into practice.

Chapter 2

Ebony woke up in a bed she had never slept in under a ceiling she didn't recognise. Her eyes were gritty with sleep.

The beeping from the ECG that she was attached to accelerated as she awoke. Protruding from her arm were tubes flowing into bags of unpronounceable liquids. She had chemical hot packs tucked under her arms and was buried far within a mound of blankets.

The jacket wrapped around her arm had been removed and the wound cleaned and bandaged. It still throbbed a little, and bruises accessorised the matching white bandage and robe Ebony had been dressed in. Her eyes were dehydrated and she struggled to move them from side to side, as though they'd been frozen in place. She blinked repeatedly until she could bare to open them for a sustained period. Even when she could, she struggled to see. A harsh, white light was glaring down on her blindingly. With her limbs aching, she raised her arms to cover her eyes and that's when she discovered the handcuffs holding her tightly to the bed.

"Where am I?" She wasn't the type of person to make a habit of waking in an unknown place. The room she was trapped in was uncomfortably clinical; white walls, sterilised medical equipment and a single mirror faced her directly. An uneasy feeling rose within her that it was a two-way mirror.

She looked to the other side of the room and out of the window and in catching sight of a large ship rolling by all the memories flooded back to her like an electric shock. The blankets weighed tighter on her chest and Ebony lashed out. Her mind filled with the distressing recollections of the ordeal and reality blurred as her heart pounded from her chest. Her senses were overcome. Her ears filled with the echoing screams of the dead and all she could see was Jonah staring at her, his lifeless eyes burning into her soul, yearning to know why she didn't save him. What would happen to his daughter, who was waiting excitedly at home for him? She cried out, rocking the bed as she pulled against her restraints and a woman ran into the room.

"Ebony," she rapped sharply, grabbing her shoulders, and pinning her down. Ebony tried to kick out but couldn't and could only watch as the woman stuck a needle into her shoulder. She winced and watched a cobalt liquid drain into her. It could be anything. Anaesthetic? Poison? Ebony fought against the cold sensation travelling through her veins but as quickly as her panic gripped her, it was gone. The room stopped spinning and her chest rose and fell, progressively slower as she locked eyes with the woman who cautiously let go.

"Am I... dead?" Ebony asked, which earnt her a scoff. The stern-faced woman frowned as she straightened her sharp suit.

"No," she said, reaching for an eyedrop dispenser, "and surprisingly, you're relatively unharmed." Ebony was still drowsy and the medication she was administered was keeping her subdued, so she barely registered what the woman said.

"Oh." Her pupils constricted as the woman doused them in liquid, and she relaxed slightly.

"I'm Dr Feverfew. To confirm, you are definitely Ebony Echnovarria?"

"Yeeeaaaaah," Ebony's speech was slurred. She proceeded to lift her arm as high as it could go. "What are these for?" She beckoned to the cuffs that had worn puffy sores into her wrists.

"Simply a precaution," Feverfew said hurriedly. "You're in a Roamer orbital ship above the Nir planetary cluster. I have a couple more tests to run, then a few routine questions." She gestured to the machine on which Ebony was hooked up to.

"Why me?" Ebony's eyes fogged, as she recollected the nightmare she'd lived through. "And how am I here?" she asked. "I was sucked from the ship, wasn't I? How did you rescue me? And why did it blow up? And what tests are you running? Am I okay?" She rapid-fired questions but Feverfew raised her hand for silence and the authority she commanded meant that Ebony instantly quieted.

"So many questions," she scolded. "They'll be answered in due course. Can you stand?" Feverfew was kind to her, but her demeanour was of someone who clearly had better things to do than look after Ebony. Ebony wasn't sure but didn't want to inconvenience her any longer.

"Yes." She sounded confident but her legs wobbled like unset jelly.

"Come along then," Feverfew said, grabbing the tubes sunk into Ebony's arms. She yanked them out and whilst it didn't hurt, the expectation that it would cause her to flinch violently, and Feverfew rolled her eyes. The handcuffs were unlocked and Ebony stood, scowling. Following a few shaky steps, her determination to defeat the judging eyes of Feverfew helped her walk assuredly out of the clinic.

"In here." Feverfew's short hair bobbed in a cartoonish fashion as she opened a door to a new empty room with one lonely table, which Ebony was promptly handcuffed to despite protests. The walls were dressed in navy panels in keeping with the Roamer uniform, and another two-way mirror. Ebony shifted uncomfortably. Again, she sensed people watching her through the mirror and the camera in the corner of the room.

"Now what?" she asked.

"Someone will be along shortly. Be patient," Feverfew told her.

"Be patient," Ebony mimicked as she left. "How long for?" she called but it was the last time she would ever see Feverfew.

It was only two hours later when someone came in to talk to her.

"Ebony Echnovarria?" To the sound of a buttery voice, Ebony lifted her head from the table, yawning as she looked with hazy eyes at the Roamer who was taking a seat opposite her, his police badge worn proudly across his left chest. But past the orderliness of his uniform, the tufty black hair swept carelessly behind his ears and the dark circles beneath his eyes told Ebony he'd been hard at work but had clearly stumbled into one dead end after another. However, he looked pleased to speak with her, and Ebony was worried about how she could possibly possess the answer to his problems.

"How are you feeling?" he asked. He had an immediately kinder conduct than Feverfew, and Ebony felt like less of a burden and more of a human being.

"Like I've been thrown from a burning ship," she answered. The Roamer smiled kindly.

"You'll be on your way soon," he said. "I'm Lazlo, one of the chief Roamers on this station. I am obligated to read you your rights—"

"--I know my rights," Ebony said. Lazlo nodded slowly.

"Are you aware of the reasons as to why we've brought you here?" he asked, taking out a tablet for notes.

"Because I was on Transtar 17-4?" She took an educated guess.

"It's more than that," he said to her surprise. "You were the only survivor."

The only survivor.

Impossible.

Ebony shook her head at the erroneous information.

"I watched hundreds of escape pods take off, full of people," she said, matter-of-factly. Lazlo smiled sympathetically.

"It's hard to believe, I understand. But all the escape pods were destroyed."

"Not possible," Ebony argued. She was sure, absolutely certain, people had escaped.

Lazlo furrowed his brow, unsure of how much information to give. "I need to ask you some questions. Do you know what happened?" He was visibly perplexed, and Ebony suspected the Roamers didn't know much at all about the explosion, despite their critically acclaimed investigative skills. She put her head between her hands in frustration at the lack of material he was giving her.

"Some idiot didn't check the southern engine coolant and it overheated," Ebony deduced for him, tapping her feet on the floor impatiently.

"No."

She raised an eyebrow. "No?"

"No." Lazlo was laconic with his successive statement. "A suicide bomber laced the station with bombs."

"What?" Ebony's stomach lurched into her throat.

"Do you know why?" Lazlo asked and Ebony scoffed in disbelief.

"How would I know?" she asked. Lazlo quieted and was studying her mannerisms carefully. How only one eyebrow raised, and her bottom lip quivered as she tried to find the words to defend herself. Ebony felt compelled to sit as still as possible as he glanced at her shaking hand and buried it between her thighs which then began to shake instead. "I have no idea. We were a station focused on molecular biology, hardly a big target. So, unless someone was curious as to what flowers were in bloom in the labs, I don't know. Why?" The attitude she took told Lazlo her patience was wearing thin, and the Roamer hesitated to answer as he drew his mouth into a thin line.

"It's only a theory, but we think he did it because of you." Ebony's heart sank. The hope from her eyes faded.

"Me? No, I... no... Why? Why me?" she stammered.

"We don't know exactly."

"What proof do you have?" she whispered. Nausea didn't blend well with agitation, her mouth tasted like dry sand and beads of sweat formed on her forehead. She wasn't guilty of anything but in the presence of galactic police, she couldn't help the inexplicable fear that she'd done something wrong.

"We have a security video from before the explosion." Lazlo put his thumb to the interface embedded into the wall and it stirred with a video corrupted by static. "What you're about to watch might be upsetting. But you need to see it."

He pressed play.

"Hello there." One of the three men in the video spoke. It was a bird's eye view of the control deck of the ship. A man had marched in wearing a vest stacked with enough bombs to take down a small country and a detonator in each hand. The captain and first officer swivelled, the captain standing steadfast as the officer trembled behind.

"Who are you?" the captain asked.

"Captain Mulvaney, it's a pleasure to meet you." The terrorist bowed deeply into his sarcasm, his black mop of hair stroking the floor. "The name's Daegel. I'm looking for a girl," he snarled. "Ebony Echnovarria, is she on this vessel?"

"I'm sorry but we do not disclose passenger information from any Transtar Labs station," Mulvaney said, defiantly. Daegel looked at him, almost gleeful that he'd refused to give the information. There were no second chances offered; Captain Mulvaney's lack of cooperation was his first and only mistake. Daegel whipped his hand out and for a split second the video froze and then the captain was on the floor, blood and other bodily matter soaking through the clothes of his torched carcass. Daegel allowed himself a rewarding clap of exuberance at the captain's dead body. He approached the trembling first officer who, although scared, took a firm stance.

"What do you want with her?" he asked.

"I merely need to know if she's here," Daegel replied. The first officer's eyes darted to the camera. He looked directly into the lens as if to beg for help.

"As the captain told you, we do not disclose passenger information," he said with a quivering voice.

"The captain is dead. No one listens to dead men." Daegel's disrespect angered the first officer and he leant down, never breaking eye contact. Dusting off the cinders, he picked up Mulvaney's hat.

"If the captain is dead, I'm the new captain: Captain Pompeo," Pompeo said, placing the cap upon his head.

"All right, Captain." Daegel's foot was impatiently tapping the vinyl floor, in sync with Pompeo's racing heartbeat. "I'll play ball. Where is Ebony Echnovarria?"

Pompeo respected the dead captain. "We do not disclose passenger information from any Transtar Labs station," he reiterated. Ebony gulped, fearing the worst.

"You have balls, Pompeo." Daegel tossed the detonator carelessly in his hand. Ebony choked on her heart in her throat. She knew how it was going to play out, but somehow still hoped that he wouldn't detonate the bombs. "You've cost everyone on this ship their life."

"I'd rather you only take mine," Pompeo said bravely.

"On any other day I'd be delighted to oblige in your intimate, slow murder, but today, I'm aiming to kill the many, not the few." His words were chilling. Pompeo shouted and lunged forward as Daegel, with dramatic flair, lifted the button he was holding, locked eyes with the camera, winked and whacked it with all his might.

Bang.

The screen cut to static.

Ebony tore her gaze from the screen to Lazlo who was leant back in his chair, closely observing her reaction.

"That was the final recording from your ship," he said. "Do you know who Daegel is?" Ebony, who was beyond any other reaction other than blinking rapidly as she replayed the video in her head, shook her head.

"I've never seen him in my life," she assured, "I promise you. I don't know this man." Lazlo wasn't convinced and the evidence against her from the video was substantial enough for a conviction should he choose to charge her for the deaths of thousands.

"Are you sure? He certainly knew who you were," he pressed.

"I don't know who he is!" Ebony fought back tears. "Thousands are dead. Believe me, if I could tell you who he was, I would!" she cried, throwing her head against the table as she sobbed. Lazlo's expression changed; his face softened.

"I'm sorry for the hurt this must cause. But you must understand, you are the best lead we have for all these attacks." Ebony's face dropped. There couldn't be more bad news, could there?

"*All* these attacks? There have been more?"

"Your station was the fourth to go under in a matter of hours. And the videos from the last moments of the captain's deck all show this terrorist asking for you." Ebony began to sweat profusely. Was it her or did the room get hotter? Her surroundings swayed. She felt claustrophobic and flustered.

"How can he be a suicide bomber if he's bombed four stations?"

"Don't evade the question," Lazlo said, which really meant 'I have no idea'.

"I swear to you I don't know him." There was a brief moment's silence as Lazlo contemplated asking her more, but he decided against it.

"In which case, you're free to go," he said calmly. "If you think of anything we should know, however insignificant, let me know. We want answers for this unforgivable crime, and someone will be held accountable." Passive aggressive warning aside, he pressed a button on the table and an electronic contact card flickered into existence. Ebony held out her palm and it melted into it, and the information was downloaded to her band.

"I will," she said. Lazlo stood, undid her handcuffs, and drew from his pocket a sachet of cream for her wrists. With a well-meaning nod, he left the room, leaving Ebony to collect herself. After a moment, she too stood and left the room, cradling her own shoulders for comfort.

As she meandered down the corridor of one of the many Roamer space stations, with no idea where the exit was and looking like an escaped psych ward patient in the white gown, she appreciated how on high-alert everyone was. Each room, which normally would be dedicated to individual intergalactic criminals, had been stripped of all their information, the walls now decorated in this man, Daegel and his crimes. Her clothes were strung up and subject to meticulous scrutiny by several Roamers, and Ebony realised she would never get them back.

An atmosphere of melancholy swamped everyone who marched by, as there was an apparent lack of knowledge about Daegel. Her stomach knotted walking past the glass rooms filled with images of people floating dead in space, not to mention those killed when the stations plummeted onto nearby planets. The devastation was something not seen in recent history and the universe was glum in its wake.

A section of wall covered in close ups of Daegel caught Ebony's attention and she paused by it, staring into his face in anguish. Pinned to his chest was a badge. It was of no obvious meaning to anyone except Ebony, who, horror struck, gawked in incredulity as she noticed it for the first time.

"Miss, you can't be in here any longer, would you like me to escort you out?" A Roamer gently but purposely put his hand on the small of her back and Ebony jolted, as though his touch woke her from a dream.

"Of course. Sorry," she mumbled. The Roamer led her to the deployable Roamer taxis parked outside and opened the door of one to ensure she left.

"Have a safe journey, Miss Echnovarria," he said.

She gulped. "I hope so." Clambering inside, she pulled the belt around her as tightly as she could, gripping the door handle fearfully.

"Where to, Miss?" the driver asked.

"Drognir please, Chane city, sector seven." she said. As the ship took off, Ebony's stomach simultaneously lurched in fear. For the first time, she had a moment alone to take in everything. So many people were dead that she could hardly comprehend the situation but what chilled her more was her undisclosed link to the bomber, Daegel. With a sweaty hand, she discreetly reached down her gown and pulled out from it a necklace the Roamers hadn't thought to take. It was a silver chain with a delicate charm hanging from it, embedded with several jewels and an entirely unique pattern. Until recently, Ebony had reason to believe it was from an unknown family member to who the necklace originally belonged, left to her when she was dropped on the doorsteps of an orphanage. But the psycho, Daegel, was wearing the same thing. Not similar but an exact replica of what she was wearing. Normally, Ebony would assume coincidence, but the circumstances were too outlandish for it to be possible. She dropped her head into her hands, slowly manoeuvring it from side to side. The trauma of the day had reduced her to an emotional wreck.

"Are you all right Ma'am, would you like me to stop?" The driver looked back at her.

"No. No thank you," she said. She looked away from the driver's concerned eye contact and out of the window.

Drognir was one of the first inhabited planets, grown from humble beginnings in an empty area of the Milky Way. Ebony stared attentively at the planet she called home: a densely overpopulated world in terms of humans, robots, and buildings alike. The familiar skyline was an idyllic melange of interconnecting features, old and new; ceaseless streams of new and increasingly outlandish structures appearing. This time, yet another eccentric skyscraper strove to be the tallest and whilst the planet itself was arguably the smallest in the vicinity, embellishments such as these made it look mightier.

Ebony watched as larger ships jetted from the west of Drognir and headed towards the neighbouring planet, Farnir. They rotated in close proximity to each other and for those who worked on one and lived on the other, they waited to go to work at the times when their ship ride from one planet to the other would be shortest and work would physically be waiting for them right above their heads.

Ebony favoured the dystopian, cyberpunk aesthetic of the cities such as Chane where she lived. She loved how they looked so messy, but everything worked perfectly in tangent. If a new flight path needed to be created, houses wouldn't be demolished but alternatively built on stilts to allow ships to travel beneath, and roads were piled several storeys high for those who still preferred cars to travel with ease.

An amass of hologram advertisements, laser lights and boldly-lit screens cascading down the side of buildings overwhelmed the cities, lighting it at all times of day and night, and the streets were always busy with street vendors selling the new technological gadget. The interplanetary workers were transported in bigger ships, whilst the smaller ships dodged and weaved through the buildings whose tops couldn't be seen from the ground, and Ebony half-expected to get back and find something new built on top of her home in the four months she'd been away.

But that didn't play on her mind, and she focused on the situation in hand. Drenching her wrists in the lotion Lazlo had kindly offered, she dialled him.

"Lazlo, it's Ebony," she said.

"Ebony? I didn't expect to hear from you so soon. You have information?" Lazlo asked. Ebony hesitated, immediately doubting her action.

"He'll think I'm a part of this." She dreaded the idea of being held responsible for the death of so many. "What if I get blamed for this?"

"Ebony?" Lazlo asked suspiciously, as her end of the line fell quiet.

"Sorry, no. I realised I didn't thank you Roamers for saving me. I appreciate it." She quickly changed her reason for the call.

"Oh." Lazlo was surprised, if not somewhat annoyed she didn't have anything of use. "You're most welcome."

Ebony hung up. As her ship got further away from the Roamer station and closer to Drognir, Ebony decided not to call Lazlo ever again.

Chapter 3

The month of September had been solemnly quiet. Ebony had decided to demote herself to office work in Chane, a metropolitan on Drognir. It was decided in fear that if she got back on a ship, she would cause more deaths. Her office was in a supposed quiet corner of Transtar HQ, by far the most majestic building in Chane, even though it was only half-built, and she was disturbed only by the workers as they drilled metal crossbeams into the roof above her head. The lotus flower building climbed to the clouds in a daring architectural feat, funded by the multitude of experiments Transtar carried out, indelicately both ethical and unethical. The words 'Transtar HQ' were plastered on the side in case the building wasn't obvious enough already. It also had the number '7' written on it like most buildings in the district to show what sector of the city it belonged to. Number seven was the science sector, where megacorporation's ran the planet with illegally accumulated wealth far beyond the government's capabilities.

Each day dragged on far beyond the twenty-six hours it was allotted. Ebony kept the same regime. Arrive in the office at seven when the city woke up, pour herself a coffee which always tasted too bitter; it came from an old machine but the new one was further away. Then she'd busy herself with the virtual paperwork on her desk which competed in height with the skyscrapers around her.

At two o'clock every Tuesday and Thursday she would grin and bear mandated therapy sessions where she spent time convincing herself she wasn't an accidental murderer. And then, when the sun faded and shadow of Farnir loomed over Drognir, she would go home and binge whatever TV show the remote found for her first. Despite the monotony, she had to be thankful that since working in Chane, no further repercussions of the explosions had occurred. But the normality of day-to-day life didn't last for as long as she was hoping.

Ebony's thoughts wandered without direction or reign, and she had the short pleasure of leaving reality behind as she daydreamed, until someone banged on her office door.

"Echnovarria."

"Yes?"

"Andromeda mail for you downstairs," the receptionist informed her. Gratefully leaving her work, she stood uncomfortably amongst her co-workers as they took the two-minute lift to the ground floor. By now, news concerning the suicide bomber and Transtar ships had spread like wildfire and whilst the Roamers had tried to keep it quiet, Chane's reporters had once again bribed their way into a juicy news story, and it hadn't been long before the seamy name Ebony Echnovarria was circulating the Science sector with intrigue and exaggeration. With judging eyes piercing her back like knives as she left the lift, she hurried alone through the corridors of the postal shelves where deliveries too substantial to be electronically delivered or too organic in nature were left. A solitary letter sat on her shelf, an unusual use of paper considering the rarity and heavy fee. The feel of something so natural in her hands was rather odd.

Thud.

Ebony's skin crawled as a noise in the poorly lit room caught her attention. There was a creak, and she slowly lowered the letter, goose bumps rising across her arms. She had the unshakable sensation she wasn't alone. Still, glancing over her shoulder she could see no sinister shadow, no bomb wielding maniac, no psychopathic terrorist. Her mental state was fragile and too many times in the past month she had scared herself silly over a figment of her imagination.

"Ebony?" She flinched at the unexpected voice, but it wasn't there to harm her. The slender silhouette of her best friend appeared in the light cast by the doorway. She could tell who it was by the comforting smell of freshly baked bread drifting in with him; his office sat directly opposite the HQ café.

"Oscar," she said.

His eyebrows arched in a concerned look. "Didn't mean to startle you," he apologised with an amicable, crooked smile. His hazel eyes expressed concern; Ebony knew how worried he was about her without a single word shared between them.

Ebony settled herself. "You didn't. Don't worry."

"Hey." Another familiar voice, just as deep but less startling, came from the corridor. Oscar and Ebony were joined by two others.

"What are you all doing here?" Ebony asked.

"Bought you coffee darling," the girl, Stella, answered, holding it up. "Receptionist said we'd find you down here." She removed her glasses to wipe away the steam that had fogged them and a cluster of freckles were momentarily revealed over the bridge of her nose. Stella was short, but hosted a tall debonair personality which she'd used to get into the post room despite forgetting her Transtar ID.

Ebony took the coffee from her gratefully. "Thanks Stella."

"No problem." Stella crinkled her nose with a wink. The boy standing a foot behind spoke out.

"We're going out for dinner," Caleb announced. "Place called Benjo's has just opened. Rumour has it they've imported a fish called cod for the new menu and it's meant to taste-" Caleb blessed the air with a chef's kiss, "-delectable. You coming?"

Caleb was last to wander in, but Ebony had noticed him first. The third of seven children, the seventh finally being the girl his parents wanted, Caleb was an eccentric character built not of flesh and blood but of poorly timed humour. In all honesty, Ebony had forgotten what his original hair colour was. For the time being, it was piled atop his head in a bundle of less than subtle, ice blue curls. He had a cheesy grin you could never receive without replying with a smile twice as wide, and Ebony did so.

"Give me two minutes and I'll be there." She revealed the letter which had been crumpled in her palm.

"Paper?" Oscar arched his eyebrows. Ebony shrugged.

"We'll be outside," Stella said, linking arms with Oscar and Caleb and dragging them out as neither made an attempt to move. Ebony gave a singular nod and opened the envelope.

No return address.

'My dearest Ebony,

Words can't describe how thrilled I am to have finally found you. The burning of Transtar's ship lit you up like the ethereal light of a solitary star, and I am the black hole come to destroy it.

You have something of mine; something stolen from me twenty-one years ago: a key of immeasurable value. One Earth Day from the delivery of this letter, someone will be along to collect it, and in the days following, will subsequently be sent to collect you. Know this, if you refuse to return the key, or refuse cooperation, the consequences to you and your loved ones will be ongoing and severe. Death would be a mercy by the time I am done ripping apart your insignificant existences. I want that key and mark my words; I won't stop until I have it.

Best regards,

Atlas Sinclair.'

Ebony grabbed the shelves for support. Her stomach tied in knots and heart forced its way up her throat. She tried to reach the light of the doorway, stumbled, and the shelves crashed to the floor as she fell against them, spilling fragile parcels in all directions.

"Ebony?" Oscar called out. He rushed down the stairs, hastily followed by Stella and Caleb. "What happened?" he asked, holding his hands out to steady her. Without a word exchanged, she handed him the letter and Stella stroked her hair calmingly as her and Caleb read it over Oscar's shoulder. The expressions they wore contorted into further alarm as they read.

"He's waited twenty-one years for a key? Has he heard of a locksmith?" Caleb tried to lighten the mood with a jest, but the severity of the situation meant his comment was in poor taste.

"Not now Caleb," Stella muttered. Silence befell the corridor; Ebony stood trembling as Oscar handed the letter back, shoulder's slack. She held it tightly, knuckles whitening as her chest tightened in the musty room. Oscar put a hand gently on her shoulder, but it was abandoned in mid-air as Ebony leant back against the brick wall and slid into a slumped sit. Stella crouched next to her, offering all the consolation she could, but it wasn't much.

"Ebony." She rubbed her back soothingly. "Breathe." Ebony released a long puff of air, unaware that she'd been holding her breath as fresh air taunted her from beyond the room. Stella breathed with her as Oscar and Caleb paced in perturbation, crossing over each other in front of Ebony as they took deep strides.

"Who is he?" Oscar asked frantically, hands flailing about. "Ebony, who is Atlas Sinclair? Do you know him?"

"No," Ebony clarified, which made her wonder for the millionth time as to why people she didn't know were so intent on hurting her.

"So, this man, this… abhorrent monster, was responsible for the Transtar bombings?" Caleb asked.

"I'm not sure," Ebony answered into her knees. "I know what it says but the ships were destroyed by a bomber called Daegel."

"Could he have worked for Atlas?"

"Personal kamikaze pilot?" Stella added.

"But how does he know who I am?" Ebony cried. "Why is he looking for me?"

"I don't know." Oscar answered both questions unhelpfully. Ebony squeezed her temple as though it would pop some miraculous answer into her brain, or at least push the veins back in.

"I never stole anything."

"And why kill so many people?" Stella said. Ebony gulped. She scratched nervously up and down her shins.

"Collateral damage."

A cold breeze swept down the corridor. They found themselves missing the days that now seemed so dull: filling spreadsheets, collecting samples. They'd swap it for their situation instantly.

"You can't blame yourself for this," Oscar said but Ebony was already convinced.

"Thousands of people are dead." She tasted the salty tang of tears as they brimmed her eyes and overflowed down her cheeks.

"This doesn't fall on your shoulders," Stella reinforced, digging in her pockets for a tissue.

"How does it not?" Ebony sharply pulled away from Stella's delicate handkerchief dabs. "This psychopathic murderer has been searching for me and people have died in the process."

"It's a slight oversimplification," Caleb said.

"Parents are burying their children," Ebony told him. "So yes, it is my fault."

"Ebony…"

"I need some air." She hauled herself up and barged past her support system, not looking back. She was so confused. Why, like any normal person, could he not have looked for her online or asked around; why did he have to launch an attack on Transtar?

"Ebony!" she heard Caleb call but chose to keep moving, wrapping her jacket tighter around her. The sky was a uniform grey, gradually darkening as it clouded over and threatened to rain. It always rained when Ebony was in a grumpy mood, and she scowled as she stormed through the city. Chane's rain was slightly acidic and metal umbrellas were sold second only to phones. People's outfits were judged on how their umbrellas matched their shoes. Ebony pulled out her clashing blue one. Her mood worsened as the light drizzle became a torrential downpour and as she reached the lobby of her building, she stepped in a deep puddle, soaking her leg.

Sometimes, it was the smallest things in life that threw Ebony over the edge.

"Why?" She threw her hands in defeat as thunder rumbled above her, warning her to get inside. Rushing through the high rise in which she lived, she didn't stop to make conversation as she passed a neighbour and practically threw herself into her apartment, rattling the walls with the force of the slammed door.

Inside, with a frantic urgency that made it seem like she was committing a burglary in her own home, she searched high and low for a key. Yanking her clothes from the wardrobe, throwing drawers across the living room, and pulling dinnerware from the shelves didn't reveal anything of use. But as everything crashed haphazardly to the floor, it caught the attention of Ebony's humanoid assistant and friend, who until then had been enjoying a pleasant and undisturbed day reading about the robot uprisings in other parts of the galaxy.

"Ebony, do you require me to call a cleaning service?" He rolled over, assessing the state of the apartment he had recently tidied. "I can only see sixteen percent of the floor."

"Don't judge me, Esso."

"I am a robot; I am not capable of emotions such as judgment."

"You sound sarcastic."

"Never."

"I don't need a cleaner, thanks Esso," Ebony said, "but let me know if you find a key?"

"Of course," he said, walking away with the purr of his robotic legs. Ebony continued to dig, interrupted only once before she gave up. Esso handed her the front door keys which she owned, only in case the hand scanner she used to enter her apartment malfunctioned. Never in her life had she eyeballed such an innocent object as a set of keys with such hatred and she threw them across the room, bowling down a cup as she did so.

"Fifteen percent," Esso said. He was advanced enough to know not to say anything more when Ebony shot him a nasty glare.

"This is useless," she groaned, lying back amongst a pile of clothes. She lay there in defeat, disliking the odds of her ever finding this key. She felt the letter in her pocket, touched its papery envelope and wished she could burn it and forget about it.

Esso soon reappeared.

"Ebony, there is someone at the door. Would you like me to let them in?" he asked. She sat bolt upright.

"Who is it?" she panicked.

"Oscar." Her shoulders untensed and she nodded.

A moment later and Oscar was stood in the doorway, studying the mess. He leant against the frame; arms crossed.

"Love what you've done with the place," he said. Ebony looked at him with a pursed bottom lip and Oscar's eyes filled with sympathy.

"I couldn't find the key," she moped. Rather than help her up, he sat with her, lanky legs sprawled amongst the clothes. She rested her head on his bony shoulder.

"We'll bring an end to this Atlas creep," Oscar said defiantly. "No one threatens my friend and gets away with it." He squeezed Ebony's hand. "Caleb's gone to the post office to try and work out where the letter came from and Stella's gone to the computery to find out who Atlas is."

"And you?"

"Key hunter extraordinaire."

"Thank you." Ebony smiled gratefully. With an inward sigh to avoid showing Ebony his doubts at finding it, Oscar heaved himself up and held out his hands, a fake but convincing look of determination crossing his face. Ebony took them and wearily, they both continued to search.

After another despondent hour, they neglected to find anything helpful save Esso's spare hand and their search was drawn to a close with a buzz of Oscar's wristband. With the push of a button, a hologram of Stella appeared. It looked like she was in the room. The only way to tell that she wasn't was due to a white tint surrounding her body. It was a relatively new invention and allowed people to travel to nearby planets without actually leaving their own home. Once they were a hologram, they were as good as physically in the room, despite not being able to touch anything. Their physical body didn't move, allowing the hologram to roam its new space as long as the owner of the band allowed it.

"Find anything?" Stella asked. She looked at the mess and didn't comment.

"Nothing Stel. You had any luck?" Ebony asked and to no surprise, she shook her head.

"I can't find a thing," she complained, hands on hips. "Whoever Atlas is, he doesn't want to be found." It wasn't good news.

"Let's hope Caleb's had better luck," Ebony said. She tapped her wristband. A couple of seconds went by, and he too appeared.

"This guy is a complete nutjob." Caleb didn't even say hello. His frustration was evident as he trampled through the clothes. If he weren't a hologram, they'd be flying in all directions.

"What have you found?"

"The letter went through 38 different intergalactic couriers to try and loose the trail. Also, the courier who delivered it to Chane is in a critical condition back in Andromeda after being attacked by a man who, and brace yourself for this," Caleb warned, "a man who called himself Daegel. Beat him into a vow of silence so we're not finding Atlas through him."

"That's impossible," Ebony exclaimed. "Daegel was a suicide bomber." But she doubted the title he had been granted. After all, Lazlo had told her that Daegel had destroyed three ships prior to hers and unless the rules of death had changed without her noticing, he likely hadn't died on the ship.

It was a dead end. Ebony flapped her arms cluelessly.

"So, what now?" Stella asked.

"We could try a library?" Oscar suggested.

"Is there one on Drognir?" Ebony asked.

"And how would it help?" Caleb added. "The last physical book was written, what, over two hundred years ago? And with trees protected by the oxygen constitution, I doubt any would have been made for even the most elite of the universe in the past fifty years."

"All we can do is check," Oscar said. "After all, Atlas sent Ebony a paper letter. Maybe he's rich enough to be old fashioned."

"Anyone have any better ideas?" Stella asked. Silence confirmed they didn't.

"We'll meet you outside," Ebony said. The bands flickered off and Ebony and Oscar left Esso to navigate through the mess, as they exited the high-rise and ventured back out into Chane.

Chapter 4

The rain had stopped and steam rose from the sun baked stone paths, but Ebony was still under the weather. Heading through the busy streets, passed many splendid doorways and Benjo's from which radiated the most incredible smell and subsequently a long queue of people, they found a tiny, faux wood door nestled between a local diner and an office block. The sign above the door was made of chipped plastic, with faded, gold leaf writing that read, 'Chane library'. Compared to the flashing extravaganza of the luminescent diner sign next door, it was scarcely noticeable, but thanks to Esso's directions, they found it.

The door crumbled and cobwebs snapped as Ebony pushed it open. It appeared to be abandoned.

"Doesn't look like much." Caleb voiced his concerns wearily. But as Ebony led them inside, he ate his words instead of the cod he was so hopeful for. The library was a transformed, antiquated theatre, with never ending shelves of books lining where the seats once were. It was sunken far into the ground, the dilapidated state deemed too dangerous for elaborate performances and hence, dedicated to the preservation of uncared for history.

"This place is like a museum," Stella remarked as she admired the murals adorning the plafond. Paintings depicting fallen angels loomed over them and Ebony gazed in awe, feeling somehow protected by the pictures. The ceiling tapered to a point where a globe of Drognir hung, once golden and dazzling but now old and worn. As they strode down red-carpeted steps, an elderly gentlemen appeared.

"Visitors?" He planted his walking stick firmly in the ground as he checked out the group with a squinted eye. Well past retirement age, with wrinkles covering wrinkles, his jacket was nearly as dusty as the dust that lined the shelves, and Ebony could have sworn he had cobwebs hanging from his white beard. His appearance gave the impression he'd come from far in the past as most of the books had.

Ebony smiled warmly. "Hi. We're searching for a book on someone called Atlas Sinclair," she said. The librarian's eyelids creaked wider.

"Atlas Sinclair." He stroked his beard clichély. In his head, he rustled through the knowledge collected from years of lonesome reading. "I don't think I've ever heard of such a person," he said. Nevertheless, he guided them through cramped bookshelves and onto a balcony overlooking the main stage.

"This is a good place to start," he offered. Once reserved for newer books, the law banning the destruction of trees had left the shelf desolate, and there were few books to hunt through.

"Thanks," Stella said.

"I hope you find what you're looking for," the librarian said kindly, shuffling out of the room as he left them to search around.

Oscar ran his thumb along the books. A musty copper dust rose from the spines. He picked one at random. "Let's get searching."

Three hours had passed; the longest three hours Ebony had ever endured.

"Please tell me someone's found something," she asked, as she slammed the seventh musky book on the desk, coughing as a cloud of dust flurried into her face. She didn't bother to feign interest in the eighth, leafing through before discarding it like all the others. They'd quickly abandoned the new books, whose contents mainly documented self-centred billionaires who wanted papered bibliographies made about them. It was a boring and fruitless read, so they'd gone to the historical figures section in hope of finding at least a relative of Atlas as a starting point.

"I have found bugger all," Oscar said from his position on the floor in the middle of a circle of books.

Caleb yawned, "absolutely nothing." He stretched and dropped a book from the top of the shelf rack he was lying across and it landed in front of Ebony, who screwed her eyes shut from the added dust. It was clearly as riveting as the ones she had gone through.

The books Caleb was reading were written in foreign languages and despite his fluency in only two, he could understand them like he was reading his native dialect. Caleb was a cybernetically enhanced human. Still ninety-five percent human but with several technological advantages, one eye was the original dove feather grey, whereas the other was a cyber eye to improve his impaired eyesight. It glowed softly with a silver rim, translating the unknown words as he read.

Stella emerged from the bookshelves suddenly, majestically gliding in a wheely chair with a glimmer of hope in her arms. "I've found something but it's completely farfetched and the omission of detail is crazy." She opened a large, leather-bound book in front of her and her finger marked an extensive passage.

Ebony stared at the feathery etchings of the spine. "That's from the mythical section," she commented.

"I know." Caleb swung his legs over the shelf like an eager boy, excited to not have to ruffle through any more pages. Stella cleared her throat and pushed her glasses as close to her eyes as she could until the emerald, green hue of her iris's filled the lens.

"There's a myth, about a necromancer called Atlas who lived when the universe was first created. He was a feared sorcerer who came from hell amongst other demons and wreaked havoc on our reality, before disappearing, never to be seen again." Stella closed the book. "That's it."

"That's it?"

"He's a fairy tale," she said, throwing her hands in the air in defeat.

Caleb pulled a face as though he'd caught a whiff of an unpleasant odour. "So, Atlas is an alias?"

"In which case, his name doesn't help us in the slightest," Ebony frowned.

"What about the letter? Does it have anything else for us to go on?" Oscar asked. Ebony pulled it from her pocket.

"Go nuts," she said, handing it to him. Spinning on the chair until the paintings on the ceiling became a blur when she looked their way, Oscar reread the letter carefully and Stella continued to pour over the book.

Caleb was all but asleep when Oscar cried out. The librarian shot him a disappointed glare, but Oscar panicked no more quietly.

"Look!" He pointed in alarm to the tatty bone white envelope which until that moment held no significance compared to its contents. "The date of when the letter was to be delivered is on the inside back of the envelope," he said. "Faintly written but clear enough, it says 08/07/2592. Yesterday's date."

Ebony leapt to her feet, her suddenness startling the tired Caleb. "We've lost a day without knowing it." She dreaded to think who was coming for her and her brain flung itself into overdrive. "We've got to leave, get to the edge of the city. Somewhere sparsely populated." She yanked Caleb's ankle and he leapt off the shelf. Stella sprang from her seat but disagreed.

"There's safety in numbers," she said. "How about back at your apartment?"

"You mean halfway up a full capacity three hundred story high rise? No. There's no safety in numbers. Not where Atlas is involved." Ebony wrung her hands. "He has no problem hurting people who get in the way."

"What about Chane park?" Oscar suggested. "It's closed for rejuvenation season." Ebony searched for other options. They could go to the authorities, but she had withheld too much evidence from them already to not be seen as guilty.

Ebony agreed. "I'll go to the park," she said. "Go home." Her suggestion was met with protest.

"We're coming with you," Oscar dissented as he grabbed his coat.

"If something goes wrong, we'll be there to help you out," Stella further reasoned.

"No," Ebony argued. "Whatever the hell this guy wants, I'm not putting you in danger. Go home," she demanded.

"Ebony..." Caleb trailed off as she turned to him angrily. She didn't blink as they locked eyes and eventually Caleb was forced to look away. He raised his hands in defeat.

"Go. Home."

"You're sure?" Stella asked. Ebony hesitated. Her conscience was torn between keeping them out of harm's way or asking them to stay so she didn't feel so alone. But her problems were for no one to mitigate except herself.

"Of course," she lied selflessly. "Don't talk to anyone. Go straight home. Be careful. Be safe."

"You too darling," Stella said, and she pulled Oscar and Caleb away, despite the objections. Ebony watched as they left, and the moment the door closed behind them and she was sure they wouldn't try to follow, she left too. The jump from the balcony to the stage wasn't high and being on a countdown where the zero hour was unknown, it saved her from taking the time-consuming stairs. A running jump vaulted her over the banister and into the bookshelves, rolling like a bowling ball as she came to a stop.

"Oi." The librarian waved his walking stick and Ebony cringed guiltily as the shelves fell like dominos, unsalvageable history crashing to the ground. He watched them fall in despair.

"I'm so sorry," she called, weaving her way through the backstage area. Emergency exit signs were plastered helpfully across every wall and since Ebony needed a swift exit, she followed them out the stage door and appeared in one of the colourful flea markets of the diesel underbelly of the city.

At this level, where pavements bordered the earth, the poverty ridden flea markets hid darkened side alleys and dodgy doorways. It contradicted the technological exterior of Chane, dark and musty with discarded industrial machinery which people fixed in hope of making their coin. There were plenty of places for Ebony to hide and equally plenty of places for people to take her by surprise. Intuition kicked in; the hairs on Ebony's arm rose into peaks, goosebumps rattled her skin and unwanted attention clung to her like sweat, as a stiff wind swept her hair around her face.

As she rounded the corner of the flea market, a man blocked the way. Dressed wholly in black with a matching motorcycle helmet to obscure his identity, the pin on his leather jacket was a pseudo of Ebony's necklace. Without question, he was there for her.

She glanced into a mirror, hung to be sold, on her left; it revealed a man dressed similarly approaching from behind. Walking calmly to blend in with the crowd, she headed away from her stalkers. In one smooth motion, she grabbed a long jacket as she edged through a cluster of clothes stalls and slipped it on as she rounded the corner, instantly changing her appearance. It confused one of the men who hurried in the other direction but did little to stop Helmet Face who didn't falter. Her pace quickened and soon she was joined by others, one of Atlas' men on her left and one on her right as well as the one behind.

In front of her, stairs to the roads above urged her onwards but she had no chance of making it if the helmeted man continued at his pace. Acting quickly, Ebony barrelled into a table holding precariously stacked crates of food. Fruit and veg toppled to the floor and behind her, one of the men slipped and stumbled into the owner of the stall. The owner, on seeing the mess, assumed it was made by the man and a small fight ensued between himself and Atlas' men, who were momentarily halted by the blockage of food, upended tables, and angry sellers waving their fists. Ebony stole her chance and took the steps three at a time until she was no longer in the dark, but illuminated by a flurry of streetlamps, cars, and ships.

Hurling herself onto a marbled pavement that fringed the busy highway, she vaulted over artificial bushes and past robot venders who attempted to stop her and sell their wares as their programming commanded. Up here, the crowd had thinned; the mottled streets were dedicated to the elite who abandoned the science sector of Chane at night to dine and party elsewhere, whilst the poor continued to try and make a living below. Ebony glanced to the building on her left, built with mirrored windows so onlookers couldn't see the scams and laundering going on behind the scenes of the city. It reflected herself back at her but also revealed Helmet Face sprinting behind her. Her own running was heavy-footed and unprofessional. The men behind barely made a sound, like a tiger stalking a clumsy, baby animal barely from the womb.

"Esso, can you hear me?" she yelled into her band as the traffic dulled out any other noise. It beeped and his face appeared, bobbing along beside her cheerily with no sense of the danger Ebony was in.

"Hello, Ebony. How may I assist you?" he asked.

"Can you get my ship to me?"

"Your ship is a class two ship, it cannot fit in the lower levels of Chane," Esso said.

"Direct me to the nearest police station then."

"Chane police depo is four miles from you."

"I can't run four miles!"

"I know."

"Dammit Esso." Ebony stumbled as her hair stuck to her face and cars honked as she swerved dangerously towards the thundering traffic. The man behind her was gaining ground. Desperate times called for desperate measures. "Esso, send motorbike materialisation codes to my band. Now," she demanded.

"Ebony. You have a Segway. You don't have a motorbike."

"Buy one."

"But the Segway—"

"--is slower than a dead person which I will be if you don't buy one!" she shouted.

"Which make?"

"Don't care."

"Price range?"

"Esso buy the first damn motorbike you see and send the codes to me now!" Ebony screamed.

"Okay," Esso said. "Purchasing now. Codes will be with you shortly. I shall delay next month's rent."

"Thank you," said Ebony. One issue solved, one left to figure out. She was running on the path against the traffic of the six-lane motorway but taking the time to stop and turn around with the motorbike put her at a higher risk of Atlas' men catching her. She considered driving the motorbike along the pavement, but the obstacles were unavoidable, and she'd likely crash. It left her with one choice.

"Esso?"

"Yes Ebony?"

"What's the survival rate of someone running into oncoming traffic on a six-lane motorway?"

"Um..." Esso was momentarily stunted as he did the math. "Four precent."

"So, there is a chance?"

"Yes. However, I would suggest not doing that. You're risking a whole manner of issues. Broken bones, punctured lungs, brain haemorrhage..." Esso continued to list the flaws as Ebony ran alongside the traffic, a piece of gum splitting itself in two as it couldn't decide whether to stay on the floor or find a new home on her shoe. It hurled by her at speeds that made it seem as though the cars were competing in a never-ending race. But she ignored Esso's warnings and attempted to jump out. To a symphony of horns, she scurried back onto the path and kept sprinting.

"Come on, it's easy. Like taking a walk in the park," she mumbled, except the walk in the park involved a significant lack of walking in a park and an unusual amount of running into oncoming traffic. She found trouble in convincing herself, but the men were dangerously close. "Come on!" she yelled frustratedly. The endlessly multiplying vehicles seemed to speed exponentially as she watched. Each time her feet found themselves running on the tarmac, another car would appear as if from thin air.

But it was a choice of being scared of being hit by a car, or what would happen to her should the men catch up. Seeing a small break in the traffic, Ebony lunged forward and sprinted across the road.

To the screech of brakes, she rolled into the grass marking the central reservation. The landing wasn't comfortable, prongs of plastic shrubbery stabbed her skin, but Ebony would have happily suffered more if it led to her escape.

The men chasing her stopped and stared but it didn't stop them from trying to cross the road too. Ebony had miraculously not caused a pile up and the motorists were no less forgiving with their speed. Helmet Face pointed to her with claw-like yellow fingernails and charcoaled fingertips, barking at the other men who gave chase. But they weren't as lucky, and Ebony whipped her head away as she heard an almighty squelch and the vehicles found something they would slow for.

"Ebony!" She heard Helmet Face speak for the first time, his voice threatening. He faced her and she gawked as with extreme skill, he began to dodge and weave through the cars.

Ebony panicked and ran again, leaping over hedges and swinging through tree branches as the unidentifiable man joined her on the central reservation. Through the trees she had the upper hand, Helmet Face was athletic but disinclined to parkour, whereas Ebony found it easy. But suddenly she felt a heat on her back, and when she turned to look, the plastic trees in front of Helmet Face were melting and he stormed through them effortlessly. How, Ebony didn't know. She drew focus back to Esso.

"Esso, how long for the codes?"

"…paralysis, paraplegia, diarrhoea…"

"Esso!"

"Twenty seconds, Ebony."

"Twenty seconds. I can last twenty seconds," Ebony affirmed but the man was hot on her tail. Her lungs screamed as they passed the point of bearable exercise and she sprinted for her life. But raw survival instincts kicked in and whilst a jarring pain shot through her leg as her ankle rolled on loose gravel, she continued to sprint like she never had before.

"Motorbike codes ready." Esso's voice was like music to her ears.

"Activate motorbike materialisation codes," Ebony yelled, holding out her wrist as she rushed onto the edge of the traffic she was running with. Without delay a motorbike materialised in front of her, and it couldn't have come soon enough. A sleek model with fiery orange wheels and jet-black body, yet Ebony didn't care for the look and make. She hauled a leg over the chassis, thumbing the pad to fire the ignition before she'd even touched the seat. Then with a howl from her assailant she was off, driving at the same speed as the rest of the traffic. She didn't know where this specific road would take her, but she drove it none the less. As long as it got her far away from Helmet Face she didn't care.

…As far away from Helmet Face.

As far away from the man in the helmet.

The man in the helmet…

Her ignorance hit her like a car.

"The man in the helmet," she repeated to herself. "The man in the motorbike helmet." Ebony checked over her shoulder and sure enough, Helmet Face was weaving in and out of traffic on a motorbike too, revving his engine angrily as he began to catch up with her again.

She groaned. "Esso, give me directions to Chane park."

"The quickest way is to follow the motorway and pull off at junction…"

"As the crow flies," she demanded.

"Pardon?"

"Ignore the roads, get me there quickly."

"Okay." Ebony could hear Esso's cogs whirring, "Turn left."

"When?"

"Now." A bullet train thundered on the railway line suspended above the motorway, its massive, magnetised pillars curving around the side of the road in short increments to keep the train up and the cars in. The gap to get off the motorway was small, and the speed of the motorcycle would have to be enough to get through the magnets. Ebony yanked the bike handles and pulling back, wheelied over the side of the motorway, narrowly avoiding the pillars as the magnet yanked her upward and gave her a boost onto a secondary road, one storey below. Her assailant followed fearlessly, trapped momentarily by the pillars but pulling off shortly after. Ebony's chest tightened as she panicked.

"Now where?"

"Take a right as soon as you can," Esso instructed. Ebony watched out for a road but couldn't see one. She revved the engine and praying the motorbike wasn't as heavy as it looked, swerved over the border of the designated vehicular area and onto the rooftops of some of the few buildings that hadn't been stacked like Jenga blocks.

Tiles skidded in all directions and Ebony's teeth rattled as she travelled along the uneven surface. Screams rang from those trying to enjoy a pleasant evening on the rooftops. Ebony ducked as a washing line hung across her path. She swerved hazardously to avoid a family barbecue. But a huge thud from behind caused the buildings to shake and Ebony accelerated as the combined weight of her, and the assailants' motorbike was too much for the older roofs and they cracked. He yelled as the washing wrapped around him but persisted and dust whipped upwards, causing Ebony to drive semi blindly as she went as fast as she dared. But she was quickly running out of a platform on which to drive.

"Esso? Where now?" she cried.

"Another left," he ordered but there wasn't one.

"Dammit," Ebony swore as a sturdy wall loomed, blocking her way. The jump to the next roof wasn't too high and although the motorbike wouldn't make it, Ebony could. Risking everything as the tenebrous bottom of the city taunted her from the precipice of the roof, she went from a seated position to crouching on the bike.

"Ebony, need I remind you of the health and safety hazards associated with riding motorbikes whilst standing up?" Esso frowned.

"Not now Esso," she muttered. "Not now." She had a hand firmly on the bike and with a 'here goes nothing' attitude, drifted it on its side and crashed it straight into the wall, using the force of the explosion to propel herself skyward.

"That was a horrendous waste of money," Esso said as she flew up.

The landing was as comfortable as landing on solid concrete from a height could be and Ebony rolled to a clumsy stop, but she'd made it onto the upper roof. She swore as she patted out the fire eating at her trousers and clutched her wrist which she was sure was broken.

"I'm fine by the way Esso, thanks for asking." Ebony said. She startled as police ships flew towards the explosion and ducked into the shadows before they could procure another reason to lock her up for life.

Before she fled, she glimpsed over the side of the building. Helmet Face had leapt from his motorbike which had too crashed into the wall, and he was standing on the roof below, staring at Ebony with no way to get to her. Police spotlights fell on him, and he raised his hands in surrender as they barked instructions. The assailant dropped to his knees and folded his hands behind his back. His rigid body and raised head suggested he was glaring at her through the helmet. Armed police hovered towards him on hover pads and Ebony looked at them jealously. A hover pad would have saved her a deluge of trouble had they not been reserved for the authorities. But she focused on the fact that she'd escaped.

"You deserve that, asshole." Ebony gave Helmet Face a middle finger and ran off along the rooftops, following Esso's final directions to Chane park.

Chapter 5

Ebony opted to run down the white studs of the road instead of the pavement. The streets were quiet in sector five, the law district, so she put as much distance as she could between her and the nearby buildings. They housed people who could be potentially endangered, and enough blood was already on her hands. The few passing pedestrians carried a cheerfulness that Ebony felt didn't quite match the atmosphere and with a glare they lost their sparky demeanour.

Chane park was the city's only woodland. The only way in and out were eight feet high, steel gates placed periodically around the perimeter; the gaps of the bars too thin for Ebony to squeeze through. You had to pay for the luxury of seeing a real tree up close.

Ebony took a step back and assessed herself. Of what she could see beneath the unwholesome moonlight, her face was caked in ash, skin raw and wrist swelling, but with stubbornness and a degree of disregard for her wellbeing, she decided to try and climb the gate. A foot firmly wedged across the horizontal bars that intersected the top and bottom of the gate, she hauled herself up, clinging to the bars tightly, but she couldn't pull herself further with one hand.

"There are easier ways to break and enter." Oscar's voice disconcerted Ebony and he caught her as she slipped off the gate.

"Oscar?" He gently placed Ebony on her feet, and she thanked him by pushing his chest roughly and instantly regretting it as her tender wrist crunched. "What are you doing here?"

"I was worried. I thought Atlas caught you." Oscar's eyes flickered up and down her body and he gasped at the mass of injuries accumulated in such a short time. "What happened?"

Ebony buried her arm in her jacket, biting her lip as it throbbed. "Some guys came for me, but I lost them. For now." Oscar glanced to the rising pillars of smoke and police ships marking from whence she came and put two and two together, but she brushed off his concern. "You need to leave; I don't know if we're out of the woods yet."

"We're not even in them."

"I'm serious," Ebony whined as she rattled the gates.

"So am I. I'm not leaving you to fight this alone," he said. "Look what happens when I do." Ebony was frustrated but she had to admit the company was welcome and as Oscar pulled an electric lock picker from his pocket, he compensated for her lack of wisdom which she welcomed too.

"Fine," she said. Ebony hadn't noticed but her hairs were standing on end. As they left the last of the population behind and squeezed through the open gates, the temperature plummeted, and wind howled intimidatingly. With breath that would have fogged her glasses should Ebony have been wearing them, she shivered. The trees darkened the sky and branches were casting sinister shadows as though they'd walked into the heart of a horror film. Ebony had the unshakable feeling they were being watched.

It was random impulse that caused Oscar to spin around whilst walking along the main path. A solitary man was sitting cross legged amongst the trees. With less than half a set of rotting teeth, he gave Oscar a fidgety grin and what Oscar couldn't tell was either a wink or just a twitchy eye. He braced himself fearfully, but the man made no attempt to move. He made the assumption it was a member of the homeless population finding a place to sleep.

Not watching where he stepped, Oscar strode into the back of Ebony, who had stopped dead in her tracks. On the narrow path before them stood two men, blocking the way.

"Ebony Echnovarria," one of the men announced, wearing the black uniform and shiny badge which identified them as nothing short of evil. Ebony grabbed Oscar's clammy hand as her body went rigid. He stiffened next to her.

They'd been surrounded in a matter of seconds.

Another voice caught their attention, wispy in the wind.

"Ebony, you do give a superb chase. Bravo." A man stepped out from behind a tree with unnecessary flare, clapping slowly. The man Ebony had tried so arduously to escape from. He was still wearing his helmet.

"How did you evade the police?" She was dumbfounded. Helmet Face laughed and twirled theatrically so his back was facing her. Slowly, for dramatic effect, he removed the helmet, revealing a nest of black hair and singular ear. Ebony couldn't place his figure until he pivoted around.

"Easily," he boasted. Ebony's blood ran cold.

"I... I..." words failed her. She stumbled back and Oscar held her as she tried to speak but she could only manage an incoherent stutter.

"Aww, she's shy. Don't be shy, Ebony." The man blew her a kiss. "You know me," he taunted.

"Ebony-" Oscar held her arm for support, "-who is he?"

"His name is Daegel." Ebony's eyes filled with fear as he hopped psychotically from foot to foot like a child. "But he died... you died?"

"You remember?" He rubbed his grubby hands together gleefully. "I was worried for a moment when I blew you up that I'd given you memory loss," he giggled. Oscar glowered at the man as realisation hit like a brick.

"You're the one who blew up the Transtar ships? You tried to kill Ebony?" The man shook his head innocently, placing his hand over his heart.

"Try to kill Ebony? I would never," he said angelically. "My orders were simply to find her and collect the key." With a click of his fingers the forest stirred, and Oscar yelped as from behind he was grabbed by a man and thrown into a tree. There was a crunch similar to the sound of Ebony's wrist but several times louder as several more bones were broken. Oscar groaned and doubled over, clutching his ribs but was yanked brutally into a standing position and pinned against the tree with a knife through his shirt collar. His body was flooded with the cold thrill of fear as the hands of the man who threw him reached around his neck. Ebony was left isolated and exposed in the centre of an occult circle of manservants. She winced as Daegel skipped towards her, but Oscar protested first.

"You leave her alone!" he spat, face red with anger. Daegel produced a knife and aimed it like a bayonet at Oscar's temple.

"Do you like it? It's new." The knife gleamed menacingly in the evening light; jewel encrusted hilt throwing sparks of random colours across the trees. Oscar went from confrontational to silent. Daegel turned to Ebony, casually wielding his knife.

"So, Ebony." He waggled his eyebrows. "You have a key for me?"

he asked sweetly. But his tone became serious as Ebony faltered. "Hand it over."

"No." Ebony shook her head. He smirked.

"You're trying to be brave?" Daegel's eyes widened and he squidged his cheeks together. He acted as though her fear was cute. But a new personality suddenly conquered his mind. It took her bravery as insolence. Daegel's henchmen laughed uncontrollably as he slapped Ebony across the face, leaving a burning handprint in his wake.

"Give it to me." Ebony flinched and Oscar spoke out.

"Stop threatening her," he growled. Daegel's inhuman laugh grated their ears. He clicked his fingers and one of his men raised a knife to Oscar's throat.

"Leave him alone," Ebony warned but her words provoked the man to push the knife and Oscar grimaced as blood dripped from his neck.

"Give me the key, Ebony," Daegel advised but Ebony stalled for time. She didn't want to know what would happen when Daegel discovered she didn't have it.

"What do you want with it?" she asked.

"Our great and wonderful Atlas requires it, silly," Daegel said unctuously, and Ebony shivered at his childlike speech. If he wasn't a psychopath, one of his multiple personalities was. She tried to find one that had some semblance of reason.

"To do what?" she pressed.

"He needs the original of our replicas to birth a weapon so powerful, it will be able to destroy galaxies."

"The original of your replicas?" Ebony repeated. Daegel stomped his feet like a child having a tantrum. He ripped the badge from his shirt and shoved it in her face. He pressed it against her forehead, wedging it between her eyes and she refrained from crying out as he pulled it away, leaving a red mark.

"This, you idiot," he scoffed as Ebony puzzled the pieces together. How was she supposed to know that was the key? Keys had certain structures. The badge resembled more the shape of an emblem. Ebony felt her necklace resting against her chest, hidden under her shirt.

"Enough of this," Daegel warned but as he watched a tear fall down Ebony's cheek, his personality yet again changed. "Oh Ebony, Ebony.

My dear sweet Ebony." He put a hand on either side of her face in concern and she gulped, trying to stay rooted to the ground as he forced her to look at him. "I'm sorry. Did I scare you? Did I make you cry?" he said rhythmically. He twisted his head from side to side. "Are you afraid?" Oscar fought against the man pinning him to the tree as Daegel hugged Ebony tightly. He inhaled deeply into her hair, and grabbed her arms, holding her back as he studied her. Oscar was repulsed. "Are you afraid?" Daegel asked again. Ebony didn't satisfy his cruel teasing. "I said, are you afraid?!" He screamed so loudly, birds in the distance fled as his patience failed him. Ebony looked at him.

"Yes," she admitted, her lower lip quivering and wrist bent awkwardly as Daegel let go. His frown evolved into a grin.

"You should be. Give me the key." He held out his hand impatiently and bravely, Ebony took a stand.

"Let Oscar go, and you can have it," she bargained.

"No," Oscar cried. Daegel shook his head roughly and grabbed her round the throat, holding his knife to her cheek. He hissed, his tongue flicking from his mouth like a snake and Ebony found herself being lifted from the ground; she was barely standing on her tiptoes.

"I'll give it to you, I swear," she choked, clawing at his hands. Then a burning sensation in her hands grew. Apparently feeling it too, Daegel dropped her and suddenly appeared more willing to bargain. A hint of worry arose in his eyes and the surrounding crowd shuffled unsurely, but all signs of fear left before Ebony could spot it.

"Ebony, I can't leave you here," Oscar argued, voice trembling as Daegel's hard gaze swept from Ebony and landed on Oscar to contemplate.

"The boy is annoying me," Daegel said. "Let him leave," he commanded his men who stood to the side, unpinning Oscar. "But-" he looked at Oscar, a hybrid stare of loathing and malice, "-if you come back, no one will leave these woods alive," he cautioned, before laughing hysterically.

"I'll be fine," Ebony said, convincing him to leave. Afterall, there was nothing Oscar could do. Whilst he possessed some muscle, he could punch someone once before inevitably being stabbed to death, and Ebony would rather not watch her best friend die.

"I'll wait for you outside the park," he said finally, slowly backing away until his slender frame merged with the trees and she could no longer distinguish his figure from the pale wood under the waning moon. Guilt crowded his mind as he left.

"Well. I've honoured my side of the agreement." Daegel faced Ebony. She pulled the key from her neck and Daegel's eyes lit up as she clenched it tightly in a fist. He was salivating. "I'll be taking that back to Ignis."

"We," a new voice corrected and Daegel turned to one of his recruits who had stepped forward a little.

"What?" Daegel snarled.

"*We*, sir. *We're* taking it back. You said we would all be favoured by our lord Atlas if we brought it back," he said boldly. Daegel stared at him, the whites of his eyes turning a veiny blood red.

"Oh yes. *We*," Daegel sang, batting his eyelashes. "Thank you for reminding me." He danced over to the man.

"You're welcome, sir," the man replied. Ebony shrieked as Daegel patted his soldiers' shoulder, pulling him into him. He impaled the man as he dragged him forward. There was a gut-wrenching squelch as the man gagged, blood spewing from his stomach and consequently his mouth. Daegel wiggled his knife as if digging around for something, before letting go. A gentle push with a single finger was all it took as the man crumpled down the hill and whether he was dead already didn't matter, because his neck snapped against a log as he rolled into the park lake, floating lifelessly on the shore. Daegel turned to Ebony, wiping his blade on his sleeve. She tried not to gag.

The key," he requested, acting like nothing had happened. Ebony nodded. Her skin was sweaty, and throat dry from what she'd seen. She tried not to view the riverbank, but she couldn't help but watch the body as it stained the crystal water. Daegel followed her line of sight, eyes gleaming with a sadistic pleasure morphing to savage greed as he looked back to the necklace.

However, what Daegel had failed to realise was during his confrontation with the now dead man, Ebony had switched the key for a second necklace she was wearing.

"Take your filthy key," Ebony said. Daegel smirked and Ebony stole her chance. Drawing her arm back, she lobbed the necklace into the trees, as far as she could throw. When Daegel turned to see where it landed, she threw her shoulder with full force against his spine, sending him crashing to the ground. With Daegel face down in the mud and his henchmen distracted by the key, she raced away as fast as her legs would carry her. Daegel howled.

"You little brat!" he screeched, wiping mud from his face. "Atlas will have your head!" Ebony continued her sprint although no one gave chase. The key was their prize and it had to be found. Her heart was pounding, head spinning, and she didn't notice until she left but she was drenched with the stench of death, her body so perturbed it was as though rigor mortis had taken hold.

"Ebony!" Across the bridge she spotted Oscar. He hadn't gone far but had called for assistance. Framed in silver from the circular floor lights that lit the mossy bridge, Stella and Caleb stood with a slightly more confident posture, their bravery not yet marred by a confrontation with Daegel. Ebony ran to them but stopped short, doubling over.

"Ebony?" Oscar called out to her. "They didn't hurt you, did they?" he panicked. She didn't reply. A sickly shade of green rose up from her neck to her temple as though she was transforming into the hulk. The bridge creaked as she gripped the railing and hanging the top of her body over, she was violently sick into the water below.

"Never go swimming in that lake," she said, coughing up the contents of her lunch. "I'm fine."

"Darling, you're not fine," Stella Sherlocked, not so fine herself. Her knees were knocking together, and she pulled at her jumper sleeve. Her appearance was of a striking tigress, but she was a feeble mouse at heart, heart skipping a beat with each unknown noise resonating from the tree line.

Ebony wiped her mouth with her sleeve. "Come on, we need to leave. Before they come after us."

"They?" Caleb asked, but Ebony had already taken off at a jogging pace and his comment was lost to the wind.

"Daegel," Oscar said, following Ebony with long, purposeful strides. Stella and Caleb exchanged a concerned look and swiftly drew up the end of the group with short, skittish steps. Barely a minute had passed before a shout behind them converted their walk into a sprint.

"Ebony!" They fled in terror as Daegel rampaged through the woods. A stream of vile curse words streamed off his forked tongue as his boots shook the ground. He was running furiously behind them, face covered in muck, hurling himself through the undergrowth in an attempt to catch up. He held a high-tech weapon of some sort. Ebony couldn't tell what it was exactly, the deep red glow it emitted was blindingly powerful and she couldn't visibly see the object.

Suddenly, as though an invisible forcefield had been raised, the men ground to a halt, devilish eyes glowing amongst the trees as they kept themselves concealed from the police ships flying above. It was only when they reached the gates and Oscar had to pause and pick the lock that Ebony looked over her shoulder to realise that the hunt was over.

Daegel curtseyed before backing away.

But when Oscar threw wide the gates of Chane park they all kept running and Ebony became hyperaware of everything in front of her, scared they were running into a trap.

The path ahead was empty, save a docile cat which meowed at the intrusion of its privacy. To avoid the prying spotlight of the police was easy enough, but the curiosity of civilians who wanted to know why four people had just illegally appeared from Chane park was harder, and Ebony directed the four of them to a more private area of sector five, Arts.

"I think we're safe here." She slowed to a stop in the alcove of a nearby alleyway of the city where the only interest in them came from rats. She rested against the wall. Her heart was pounding through her chest and the painfully clear image in her head of the dead man made her feel queasy. She was shaking roughly, her fingers curled as much as her wrist would allow around her jacket like it would protect her. Bruises were already forming around her neck. She rolled up her collar to disguise the discolouration.

The shadows of the night protected them as they caught their breaths.

"It's over now," Oscar said bravely, trying not to show the pain that cased his torso.

"Why did they stop?" Caleb asked, brushing his knuckles together nervously as he angled his body to hide Ebony's face from a policeman who strolled by.

Ebony was perplexed. "I don't know," she told him. A heavy silence settled over them as it dawned on them as to how much worse Daegel could have been, especially in light of Atlas' threats.

"How did you escape?" Oscar was still baffled that Daegel had let Ebony go.

"I gave him the 'key'," Ebony air quoted. "It was my necklace. But I gave him a fake and ran for it."
She reached inside her pocket and her heart stopped.

It was empty.

Her eyes widened and she gulped.

"It's gone."

"What?"

"It's gone," she whimpered, furiously checking her pockets until gentle pats of her clothing turned to an abusive rage of slaps against herself. "It can't have fallen out, the pocket's too deep." Stella allowed a precariously balanced tear to fall from her lashes and Oscar gritted his teeth, looking as though he would burst as his complexion reddened, and cheeks puffed outward. They had discovered the reason for the abrupt end of the chase. Oscar swore discreetly, trying to control the anxiety that wormed its way into his mind, but he couldn't. In a display of frustrated despair, he punched the wall behind him, screaming in defeat.

Ebony grabbed his arm to stop him, but his anger refused.

"Oscar, stop!" she yelled, pulling at his arm again. He turned round; fist raised. Although he would never dream of hurting Ebony she stepped back in fear as he stared with glazed eyes. She'd never seen him so furious. Caleb flung himself in front of Ebony and Stella instinctively, grabbing Oscar's wrists as he grunted, air swirling from his nostrils in the cold that had settled over them.

Caleb was normally the weaker of the two; countless arm wrestles had proved it over countless years, but Oscar's inflamed ribs disabled him, and Caleb yanked his hands down to his side. Oscar's eyes were bloodshot, nostrils flaring like a raging bull and hands clenched. The two of them stood shaking in an intense stare off and Stella and Ebony held on to each other. Caleb was acutely aware of the officer who seemed to have passed the same alleyway several times, and had now stopped, perched just out of sight on the pavement edge to eavesdrop on the commotion. His bloated figure was obvious to Caleb whose eye saw through the building.

"Calm down," Caleb quieted, his voice barely a whisper. "I'm as pissed as you are, but violence won't fix this." Oscar's face softened; he shook his head shamefully at himself as Caleb's fingers unfurled from his arm, white fingerprints left behind. Their ordeal merited anger, but it wasn't right.

"I'm sorry," he said, backing away. He ran his hands through his dishwater blond hair, but it stuck scruffily to his sweaty forehead, regardless of his best attempts to tame it. It was always a mess but only bothered him now. His mind swirled with concern and incredulity. In a lab, the answers to his questions could be found with a simple test or data calculation. Never before had he been in this situation and the lack of control truthfully scared him.

"What do we do?"

"We can go to the Roamers?" Ebony's words hitched in her throat from her shallow breathing. "If I told them I had the key, I'd be charged with withholding evidence and potentially aiding and abetting if what Daegel said is true, but it might get him caught."

"We're not giving you up," Oscar said.

"What did Daegel say?" Stella asked.

"Atlas has a weapon that can destroy galaxies," Ebony said. Caleb watched the officer move along; a galaxy destroying weapon sounded like a fairy-tale concocted by a group of drunk and disorderly friends and not a matter to be handled by him unless it came with a raise.

"Right." Stella looked heavenward. She struggled to maintain her calm composure.

"So, what do we do?" Caleb asked, running his hand across his lower lip.

Ebony fumbled with her zipper as rain began to fall. "Well, we have a starting point."

"Which is?"

"Daegel said he was taking the key back to Ignis," Ebony said. "So, we find out where that is and work out how to put an end to this."

Chapter 6

Ebony let the conversation between Stella and Oscar ensue without taking part other than to nod and agree where there was a pause, whether the conversation needed agreement or not. Her mind was anywhere else other than the thought of the mysterious Atlas. She needed a break. Not the type of break, however, that was plaguing her heavily bandaged wrist. At this rate, her whole arm would be a collection of scars.

A blank wall was wildly amusing when Ebony didn't realise she was staring at it. Sometimes her eyes would flicker to something else; a clock; a piece of laundry; but they always found their way back to the wall. That was until, the door that led through it opened.

"So, I phoned the Roamers and said to them, 'Hey, we found Daegel,' to which they said, 'Don't be stupid, he was a suicide bomber,' to which I said, 'There's a man called Atlas in a place called Ignis who has the ability to destroy galaxies,' to which they said, 'That's not possible, stop wasting our time,' and then they threatened to charge me if I rung again and hung up on me," Caleb said disappointedly. His forehead was wrinkled in concentration as he nudged the door open with his foot. Chocolate and junk food wobbled precariously on the piled-high plate he was carrying.

"Thanks for trying," Oscar thanked from the bed. He was lying outstretched, lethargic as the numerous medications he swallowed worked tirelessly on his ribs. Hospital would have been smart, but he insisted he was fit to help. Besides, hospital meant paperwork, and he did too much of that every day.

"No problem," Caleb winked. He slumped into the overstuffed armchair placed next to Ebony's bed. After the traumatising confrontation with Daegel, Ebony had decided they should continue their research in the comfort of her apartment, under the assumption he wouldn't be back for a while. Oscar threw a pillow from the bed; Caleb rested his back against it. He slung a leg over the chair arm sloppily and opened a packet of crisps, cramming them in as though they were about to be stolen. People were the rawest version of themselves when they believed no one to be watching. Except Caleb. For better or worse, Caleb was always himself. "Found anything?"

"Nope," Oscar said. "Ebony, you got anything?" She didn't respond. He cleared his throat trying to get her attention, which often worked, yet this time didn't. She was wrapped in a dressing gown, with fluffy socks warming her feet. The mug of hot chocolate she held substituted a hot water bottle, the boiling liquid burnt her tongue liberally. She sipped despite the blistering. Oscar touched her arm lightly and Ebony jerked out of her trance.

She blinked in quick succession. "What was the question?"

"Ignis is an island," Stella announced, peering over the laptop she had propped on her knees.

"Where?"

"An abandoned exoplanet called Ireos in Andromeda's Beta quadrant."

"Anything else?" Ebony asked.

"I can't find much," Oscar admitted, as he typed Ireos into the hologram workspace provided by his band. "There's a whole lot of superstitious crap." He read, "avoid the island at all cost... houses an active volcano... full of dark magic... evil sorcerer..." Oscar trailed off. A pink plaster stuck over his neck, courtesy of Esso who had an installed maternal instinct. It moved as he swallowed. "Matches what we found in the library."

"Do we know what's on the island?" Caleb asked.

"Definitely Atlas. Allegedly the weapon."

"I think I should go to Ignis," Ebony said abruptly. Three troubled looks pointed her way.

"Are you insane?" Caleb coughed up a crisp. "You barely escaped Daegel and now you wanna go make a house call?"

Oscar shared the same view as Caleb. "What exactly would you do? Waltz in on this genocidal maniac and ask him politely to stop being a dick?" Ebony glared at him.

"It sounds pathetic when you say it like that," she protested, setting aside her drink.

Stella took a kinder approach as Oscar and Caleb harshly battered her. "Darling you may feel braver now than when Daegel attacked but your courage doesn't mitigate the danger."

"Well..." everyone in the room was looking at Ebony but she refused to make eye contact, as she studied the unexpectedly interesting bed sheets. Stella made a fair point.

"I wouldn't have suggested it in the park," Ebony admitted, "but what if there actually is a galaxy-destroying weapon? Who else is there to stop them?" Ebony asked. "Caleb, you said it yourself, the Roamers wouldn't listen."

"That's a valid point," Caleb said.

"I wouldn't have to do much." Ebony continued to convince them as much as she was convincing herself. "Fly in, take a couple of evidential pictures as testimony and leave. Then the Roamers can handle it. I would never even get close to Daegel or Atlas."

The room fell quiet. It was obvious to all of them something had to be done about this supposed weapon and since the four of them were the only ones who believed it existed, it had to be them who did something. Ebony's idea sounded safe in theory and as long as they weren't seen, there was no danger.

Oscar raised his hands in defeat. "I'm here to help, whatever you need."

"As long as you're sure," Stella agreed. Caleb wiped his face with his hands and had a sudden urge to clap, once as he sat upright.

"Yeah, why not," he said. "Let's take down the bad guys."

"But how would you get there?" Oscar's mind wandered to the practical questions. "Public transport will take you a couple of days at least."

"You have a ship," Ebony said.

"We all have ships."

"But your one's bigger."

Oscar looked uneasy. "It's still only for interplanetary use. I doubt it would survive a trip to another galaxy."

"But theoretically it could," Ebony pushed. Oscar's nose scrunched as he did the math and let his head fall exhaustedly into his hands.

"Theoretically, yes," he said slowly, "but it's ill advised."

"So, I can use it?" Ebony pleaded. Oscar's brow furrowed but

Ebony's enticing puppy dog eyes and exaggerated quivering lip persuaded him conditionally.

"Only if I can come with you. It's my ship, you'll need a driver," he said firmly. Ebony didn't try to dissuade him. She was grateful for his company and support.

"I'll help," Caleb offered. "The Transtar subdivision I work for; they've been focusing on weapons recently. If you're going, you're going with protection."

Stella twiddled her thumbs uncomfortably. "Ebony, you know I'll always stick by you, and I'll help you in any way I can," she assured her, "but I'm staying here." Ebony dipped her head.

"Thank you." She reached over to the windowsill Stella was perched on, squeezing her shoulder supportively. "You'd be useful here. Keep pestering the Roamers and maybe they'll finally listen," she suggested.

"I will," Stella pledged, tracing an X over her heart with her finger.

"Esso," Oscar called, and the robot opened the door promptly, a frilly apron tied around his waist and the scent of freshly baked baklava sweeping in with him. It didn't blend well with the lavender musk of Ebony's room but made the four of them mouth-wateringly hungry.

"Nice apron," Caleb mocked.

"A human with taste," Esso appreciated. Caleb grinned, knowing that understanding sarcasm wasn't Esso's strong suit, despite his own skilled use of it.

"Esso, call my ship, serial code N.I.R.1076401?" Esso's eyes flashed as he processed the request.

"Operation complete. Expected arrival time, fifteen minutes," he said. "Ebony, are you leaving?"

"I am." Esso left with an accidental door slam that rattled the building and could be heard instantly busying himself in the kitchen, crockery clattering around. Caleb's fingers were jabbing at his arm as though he were drumming on a miniature kit.

"Right, I've got you a gun," he said. Unlike the others who had a band on their wrists, Caleb had gone a step further with an electromagnetic implant which lined his forearm. It was covered by a steampunk machine inspired tattoo and matched his character to a T. As a hologram collapsed back into his arm, he grinned.

"What gun?"

"A prototype that has yet to be named but I'm going to call it… the Stinger." Caleb seemed so proud of himself and the other three couldn't help but laugh.

"What does it do?" Ebony asked. Caleb cocked his head to the side. "Stabs people."

"That's not what I meant." Ebony lunged at him playfully.

"Roots, toots, points n' shoots," he said, with no further clarification. "It'll be delivered with the ship."

"And you're allowed to steal weapons from work?" Stella frowned.

"More like permanently borrow. Besides," Caleb shrugged, "security owed me a favour."

"Why?"

"Oh, it's a long story about a runaway camel, cherry Bakewell and a ship that atomised inside of the king of Foro's toilet." Caleb rubbed the back of his neck. The story sounded fabricated, yet no one doubted it had happened.

"Ebony," Esso interrupted, "I have packed your food." He held a salmon pink lunch box. Esso had practically raised Ebony and whilst he was a smart robot, he still occasionally treated her like a child.

"Thanks Esso." Ebony took the box although she didn't need it. Esso didn't have feelings, but she treated him like a human and didn't want to offend him.

"Ready?" Oscar asked confidently.

"Ready," Ebony said.

"Stay safe my darlings," Stella told them.

"And let me know how The Stinger works," Caleb reminded them. Stella gave him a dirty expression. "And of course, stay safe," he added, glancing at Stella with his hands outstretched in surrender. "I was going to tell them to stay safe too," he told her.

Each floor of the high-rise had an entrance at the end of the corridor leading outside to a small platform jutting from the building. It allowed the inhabitants to get on their ships with ease. Oscar's ship was parked next to Ebony's; bigger than hers but still a class two ship. Ebony hesitated as she climbed in. She was unsure it would get them out of the galaxy. But Oscar placed his confidence in the ship.

"It will get us there," he assured her. Inside, the ship was laid out similarly to Ebony's, but her and Oscar had made drastically different uses of the space. Her ship was tidy and sparse, a minimalist approach she took to both her ship and home.

Oscars on the other hand, was packed with science memorabilia, limited-edition old-world items and replicas of the rarest collectables dating back to the 2000s, and as the ship ascended Ebony worried that the weight of it all might plunge them back into Chane. But Oscar's confidence withstood Ebony's doubt and she waved goodbye to Stella and Caleb who eventually resembled ants as the ship shuddered out of the oxygen bank around the planet and towards Ireos.

The galaxy jump Oscar aimed for was an hour from Drognir. They joined a queue of ships leading into what bore resemblance to a huge rip in the fabric of the universe. Milky Way and Andromeda had four galaxy jumps, one for each quadrant, that conjoined and allowed regular travel between the two. Ebony still struggled to get her head around the science of teleports, but were thankful for their existence, otherwise the arduous journey would be ten times longer. The jumps were reserved for much bigger ships, but Oscar had weaved his way through the queue of vessels that choked the neck of the jump, avoiding the jump guards who would sternly suggest they turn around.

"How you feeling?" Oscar asked nonchalantly as he rested his feet against the dashboard, tucking his arms behind his head. He looked like he'd just got out of bed, which he technically had; messy hair falling into the lazy eyes he viewed Ebony with.

"Nervous," answered Ebony, "but we aren't going to be seen so there's no reason to worry." She tried to match his calm attitude but couldn't help but absentmindedly fiddle with Caleb's Stinger to ease her mind. The closer they got to the jump, the more ferociously it seemed to glow, and their small ship trembled as it entered. With an intergalactic Homestead ship positioned on one side and a planetary explorer on the other, Ebony felt like a fly amongst giants, gulping as she watched how indifferently close they were getting. But after a brief shaking, Oscar's ship made it through, the only detriment being that the shelves were now emptied of their memorabilia, the floor their new home.

Ebony and Oscar were now in a new galaxy.

"Custom warp portal, ahead," Ebony read on the signs. More frequent due to its cheap cost and tiny size compared to galaxy jumps, the warp portals allowed anyone to travel to nearly any customisable location within that specific quadrant. Oscar pulled up at the control booth, a steely yellow building cocooned within its own oxygen bubble.

"Where you two headed?" They were stopped by a warp patroller.

"Ireos please," Ebony asked. The guard, who's features were hardened by years on the boring job, was visibly taken aback.

"There's no admission without probable cause at this time," he said.

"Why not? Ireos is an open planet," Oscar queried.

"It's been closed recently due to storms covering extensive areas of the atmosphere," he explained. Something told Ebony he was holding back information. His eyes flitted between them and the warp portal, as though he was scared of what could come through, and his finger was happier resting on the trigger of the gun he was holding than in his pocket.

"A class 2 ship can handle a storm," Oscar pushed.

"I can't let you through."

"Please," Ebony pouted, and then she draped her arm around Oscar's shoulder and tucked her chair closer to him. "We're looking for a quiet getaway and we would appreciate it if you could let us through. Do us a solid?" She batted her eyelashes.

"No." The patroller stood his ground. Ebony groaned. She reluctantly reached over to her band, tapped it, and quickly scanned the man in front of them.

"One hundred coin in your account right now to let us in," she bargained. The man stared harshly and so did Oscar. He raised an eyebrow.

"Two hundred."

"One fifty."

"Done.

"Done," Ebony negotiated.

"Seriously Ebony?" Oscar sighed.

"We want to get in, don't we?" Oscar's response was an unenthusiastic face. He didn't really want to.

Ebony's account was low following the motorbike. She sighed as the money left.

"Destination Ireos," he said and as easy as the press of a button, the portal before them changed its terminus.

"Cheers," Oscar said and revving the engine, he flew through before the irritated patroller could change his mind. "Lovely fellow," he said sarcastically.

A low and unexpected grumbling caused the first panic and for a moment, neither Oscar nor Ebony had realised they'd gone through the portal because of the heavy cloud bank that donned the skies around them. Blackening the horizon and whipping waves into whirlpools, wind pushed against the ship unforgivingly.

"I see what he meant about a storm," said Oscar, the steering wheel trembling in his hands.

"Fly up Oscar," Ebony advised, "you'll avoid the worst of it."

"I can't."

"What?"

"I can't." He was pulling the controls with all his might, veins in his hands popping as he strained. "The wind is pushing us down." His composure was still mildly calm, but Ebony could tell by the hitch in his voice that he was unnerved.

Hail the size of basketballs broke dents into the ship's roof and a lightning bolt hit the wing, causing it to groan. The non-essential lighting powered down. Ebony's mouth went dry and as the lights went red, she tried to disappear into her seat. PTSD ensnared her mind and she felt as though she was drowning in the dark whirlpools below the ship as she remembered back to her ordeal on Transtar.

"Ebony-" Oscar watched as she dropped from the chair and to the floor, staring at the cold tiles trying to concentrate as the ship rocked. "-we're going to be okay," he promised.

"System failure alert. Secondary ventilation offline."

The ship said otherwise.

For a moment, Oscar left the controls and crouched in front of Ebony as she quivered violently, feeling disassociated with reality as images of Jonah haunted her mind.

"Hey." Oscar firmly drummed on her knees to get her attention. Ebony tried to focus on his voice. "We're going to be fine." He rubbed her hands soothingly.

She nodded. He grabbed the controls. Another spear of lightning cracked the sky like a whip before them, briefly lighting their surroundings and Ebony noticed a darker patch of clouds where the lightning seemed to disappear into a solid mass.

"What's that?" she pointed. The radar wasn't working so neither of them could tell, but in the middle of the ocean it was bound to be nothing more than the eye of the storm.

"Darker clouds?" was Oscar's guess. He was incorrect. With a yell from the two of them, Oscar yanked the steering wheel.

But too late was the attempt to save the ship.

It collided with what could only be described as a mountainous dagger; a curved, knife-shaped rock protruding from the ocean as one of many in a circle of jagged rocks.

The ship was smashed into pieces.

Their screams were heard, discarded and lost to the wind.

Ebony and Oscar were flung from their seats and into the freezing ocean below.

Ireos was appreciatively an oxygen rich planet, but its oceanic temperature was in near constant minus figures. As the two of them plunged into the water, an iceberg sailed over their heads. Ebony opened her eyes and they stung at the intense salt water. She could see tendrils of seaweed tugging at Oscar, who was struggling to swim to the surface. She swum to him and tore unrelentingly at the seaweed and as though it was a sentient creature aware of Ebony's attack, it let go. They swam frantically to the surface, bashing on the ice as it lingered over their heads, as if to try and drown them. But just as it felt as though their lungs could take no more, the ice sheet passed. They burst through the water's surface.

"Ebony!" Oscar yelled, choking as water forced its way down his throat.

"I'm here," she cried, swimming to him, but a huge wave swept over her and when she resurfaced, he seemed further away. "Oscar!" The roaring waves drowned her voice.

"I'm coming!" He swum powerfully against the waves trying to rip him away from her.

Icebergs were closing in like a pack of wolves. When Oscar finally reached Ebony, they were enclosed in a dangerous sheet of ice. Debris was raining upon them, and Ebony struggled to stay above the surface. Oscar grabbed the remnants of the ship's wing elevator that had lodged itself into the ice sheet and as Ebony was dragged beneath a wave, he stuck his hand blindly into the water and pulled her into him. He clung to her waist, grimacing at the cold metal against his other hand. But they couldn't stay above the water.

"We have to swim down," Ebony exclaimed as she clung to Oscar. Her fear was that they would be crushed.

Waiting until the last moment so they could savour every breath, they ducked as ice collided with ice. Below the surface, they prayed for it to pass. Ebony made eye contact with Oscar, and he shook his head; he was a strong swimmer but struggled to hold his breath for as long as Ebony. He pointed upwards frantically, and Ebony felt helpless as he bashed against the ice again as bubbles streamed from his nose and mouth. She grabbed his hands and shook her head, trying to urge him to conserve his energy but his body was screaming for air. Lungs burning as he writhed in agony, he bashed the ice one more time before, with a sorry look in his eyes, they rolled back in his head.

Ebony screamed out as his body convulsed and stopped struggling. She pulled his body into her, wrapping her arm around him as she clung on for dear life. She searched for a gap in the ice. A small one presented itself. It was a risk to go up but if Oscar had any chance, she had to.

Swimming to the surface, she took a deep breath of fresh air and was about to pull Oscar through when more debris from the ship plummeted into the iceberg. It scattered and bounced wildly. Ebony submerged herself but it was a futile attempt to avoid the danger. A chunk of wreckage slammed into the side of her, and she was thrown into unconsciousness.

They were both now at the mercy of the sea.

Chapter 7

"They'll be fine, won't they?"

"I don't know. They were in the water for a while. Seaweed had trouble getting a hold of them."

The funny thing about being knocked unconscious is that you don't tend to realise it's happened until you wake up, which was mighty confusing to Ebony, considering that she shouldn't have woken up. Why wasn't she drowning? She was under the sea.

Under the sea.

Breathing.

In an unfamiliar setting, questioning her survival, what she had perceived as some nightmare were actually the entrails of the reality she had narrowly survived. Beneath her fingertips, she felt the soft grainy texture of sand and the water that seeped into the soggy bandage around her wrist, rendering it useless. She rubbed the material between her thumb and forefinger, only vaguely aware that she was even doing it. Then water poured from her mouth, and she choked herself into consciousness with a start, as though in the middle of an emergency. It caused a reaction from the two people crowding her.

"She's alive! She's alive!"

"Shh Cordy, you're smothering her. Breathe, okay, just breathe. You okay?"

Ebony's eyes fluttered open, and she looked into the eyes of two identical girls, faces staring anxiously at her. The only difference between them was their hair, one a white afro and the other a braided, orange ombre. Otherwise, their brilliant blue eyes, cast with an expression of concern, and amiable smiles made Ebony think for a moment that she was seeing double.

"I think so," Ebony mumbled. They shuffled back as she sat up, tentatively touching her head. It was swollen and her hair was crusted with dried blood, the taste of which was lingering in her mouth. She blinked harshly, rubbing the remnants of sleep from her eyes and sand from her lashes as she tried to focus, despite the throbbing in her head.

The white-haired girl spoke on behalf of the two of them. "I'm Coraline and this is my twin Cordelia," she introduced.

"Hi." Cordelia held out her hand and Ebony shook it, noting the roughness of her hands and unkempt nails.

"Hi. I'm Ebony and -" her hands gripped the floor as she frantically looked to the side. Oscar was lying peacefully, breathing steadily. "Oscar," she exhaled, thanking her lucky stars he was alive. Ebony looked fondly upon his face which glimmered from the water droplets clinging to his skin. Then her eyes flickered upwards, and she finally noticed the environment she had neglected to look at. Her jaw hung open and a droplet of water landed on her tongue from high above them.

"Where are we?"

"We're on the ocean floor." Cordelia didn't sugar-coat it.

Seated on a dirt track in an abandoned town, wild west style buildings lined the sandy street around them. Stereotypical saloon doors led to a cobwebbed bar that housed a piano. It cased less than half of its keys, the remaining singing an out of tune song. A rickety sheriff's office with a rocking chair swinging on the wooden porch flaunted an iron prison. A once flourishing bank, with bullet holes cascading the wall, marked the end of the road and summarised the whole look of the town; forgotten and decrepit. The hangman's noose that rose from the ground on the path sat unfilled. It served as a warning to all who found themselves in the town and summarised the feel of the town; unwelcoming and dangerous.

Years ago, before water rampaged across the planet and the continents subducted below the ocean, Ireos would have been made to replicate parts of life on the original earth, to teach people how their ancestors lived before space travel became the norm. But now it sat, unused but somehow preserved in the unnatural bubble that surrounded it.

The weather and noise or lack thereof, were incredibly eerie. The air was stagnant, nothing moved. Nothing was alive here. But despite this, if it weren't for the sky, Ebony wouldn't have believed they were underwater. Roughly a kilometre above them the ocean swirled in deadly currents around an invisible dome, gushing down to create a thick wall of water and a circle of air which kept the town dry and breathable.

Sunlight streaking through the water gave the illusion of shadows through trees. It was dim yet impressive that any sunlight was able to pass the storm. The whole area was lit with an ultramarine hue, a cold and unsettling atmosphere created as a result. Maybe Ebony had experienced brain damage, or maybe she was used to expecting the unexpected, but she kept an impressively calm composure. A few gulps of air allowed the feeling of claustrophobia and nausea to wash over her, and she could comprehend the situation, with only slight confusion.

"How?" Ebony asked. Cordelia went to speak but Oscar stirred suddenly and she trailed off, knowing Ebony wouldn't be listening. Shivering in his saturated clothes, Oscar woke with less grace than Ebony, coughing inelegantly as water spewed from his mouth with the guest appearance of the lunch Esso had packed.

"Hey, hey." She held his shoulder as he keeled forwards and pressed his head against the dust, waiting for his head to stop spinning and ribs to stop burning. Unlike Ebony, the second he lifted his head, his eyes darted back and forth expeditiously as he comprehended the environment. It was not where he expected to be. His reaction was blunt and one of incredulity.

"Piss off?" He paused and Ebony gave him a moment to take in his surroundings. "We're under the sea?" Ebony looked at him apologetically as he dropped his head back into his hands. She'd brought him on this 'adventure' and felt responsible for the predicament they were in.

"We are," Coraline told him. He raised his head to see who the voice of the stained shoes he was staring at belonged to.

"And you..." he trailed off.

"Cordelia, Coraline." Coraline pointed to her and her sister again and fell silent, not wanting to tilt his precarious emotions in the wrong direction. His face contorted in a mixture of confusion, shock, upset and yet more confusion. Then, Oscar spoke.

"I'm good," he said, trying to calm himself although his shoulders were tense, and his tremulous voice was considerably higher than normal. "I'm good, I'm fine. Continue." He waved his hands for them to go on.

"How did we get here?" Ebony asked.

"Same way everyone does," Coraline answered, pointing into the dark ocean behind them where thick vines of seaweed danced amongst the fish. "Seaweed."

"Right, uh huh." Ebony tightly pinched the bridge of her nose. She had so many questions; wanted – no – needed answers. "Are we close to Ignis Island?"

"We figure about two miles away behind the cloud blanket," Coraline confirmed. "Were you headed there?"

Ebony nodded. "Were you?"

"Yeah. What for?"

"We're looking for someone. Atlas Sinclair."

Cordelia's face fell, a permanent worry line etched across her forehead. She and her sister had the same mannerisms as they pulled at the hems of their shirts. "Us to. But we ended up here, with no way of escape." The gloom of the situation sparked a melancholic atmosphere.

"Can't we just, you know, swim up?"

"Swim up?" Coraline almost laughed.

"Coral, be kind. They don't know what's going on." Cordelia nudged her sister's arm and she bowed her head.

"Stick your hand through the water," Coraline encouraged. They were sitting close enough to the boundary that Ebony didn't have to stand. She twisted around with an outstretched hand and her fingertips sailed into the water. The instant pressure of the ocean made her pull away and her hand ached from the second long encounter.

"See," Cordelia said, "if the water pressure doesn't crush you, you'll run out of breath halfway up. Atlas doesn't let trespassers off lightly." Ebony swung back round, flexing her hand.

"What do you know about Atlas?" She asked. "He's a bastard of a human being, but that's as far as we've got." Cordelia and Coraline shook their heads in sync.

"He's not a human being," Cordelia corrected. Oscar scoffed sceptically, pushing himself to his feet and wringing out his shirt as he spoke.

"Not a human being," he repeated, an aura of irritation behind his words. "What is he then, a wizard?"

"No," Coraline answered seriously, "he's not a wizard either."

Cordelia rocked herself back and forth on the road, fumbling with the stray pebbles beneath her fingers. "You're going to need an open mind to hear this story." Both Oscar and Ebony were eager for information despite the absurdity of it, and considering that they were going nowhere fast, now was the time for tall tales.

"We're listening."

Coraline and Cordelia stood, and Ebony noticed their ripped clothes. It was becoming evident that they had stumbled upon the strange town in the same way, but more disturbingly hadn't yet left it.

"Come with us," Coraline offered. "We managed to get a fire started a little way off. You're soaking." She gestured to Ebony's soggy clothes. Ebony hadn't noticed her teeth chattering, so her and Oscar gratefully took the suggestion, following the girls to an old saloon building that was lit with the comforting golden glow of a fire on the ocean floor.

"Ebony, did we die up there?" Oscar whispered as Cordelia stoked the fire.

"Don't be silly," Ebony answered. "Why would you think that?"

"Because this place is literally Davy Jones' locker. What if that's all we are now? Spirit's consigned to the ocean floor for eternity?"

"You're not dead," Coraline interrupted. She took her place in front of the blaze and gestured for her new companions to seat themselves. Ebony crossed her legs and sat on a blanket rolled out by the fire, and Oscar followed suit. Cordelia was sitting on the varnished wood of a broken window frame, staring out into the ocean where fish swam by their normal routes interrupted by the town. Clearing her throat, Coraline made her home on an upturned box and readied herself for an overwhelmingly whimsical yet truthful explanation as to what was going on.

"Our involvement with Atlas started with a box we bought at an antiques fair on Altuse. When we opened it, we found a book."

"A book?"

"A five-hundred-page handwritten biography about Atlas; the origin of him and others like him, his manifesto, his life." She paused to assure Ebony and Oscar. "We're not crazy."

"That's what a crazy person would say," Oscar whispered, and

Ebony nudged his ribs which hadn't yet healed. He wheezed.

"This story is just as weird to us," Coraline insisted. "Thousands of years ago, beings called Ancients escaped hell and fled to our universe. They ruled malevolently and without control, driven by greed to destroy galaxies in their bid to be the autocratic ruler. The Ancient who won and ruled supreme was Sonneillon, who, by all accounts, was more wicked than the devil. To help him remould the universe to his envisioned Edenic kingdom, he had three henchmen. Brothers Adremelech, Belphegor and Atlas.

There were only two rules Sonneillon commanded the brothers follow: acknowledge Sonneillon as their God and never associate with mortals beyond genocide. However, there were too few female Ancients and the lust the brothers felt overcame them. They disobeyed Sonneillon and all three had affairs with humans. Their magic created a new breed of person, the proto-Enchanteds, or original Enchanteds as they're referred to, who had the magic of the Ancients but the wisdom and compassion of humans. Their descendants, known as the Enchanteds, only had the lifespan of humans, but remained otherwise magically inclined.

Whilst the daughters of Belphegor and Adremelech remained neutral to their fathers' control, the daughter of Atlas, Vesper, tried to overthrow Sonneillon and almost succeeded, mortally wounding him. Atlas, fearful of the consequences, ratted out Belphegor and Adremelech to Sonneillon, lying and telling him their verboten children had tried to kill him. In a fit of rage, Sonneillon killed Adremelech and Belphegor, displaying their bodies as a warning to all who tried to betray him.

Sonneillon's actions maddened the other two Enchanteds, Orabella and Lorelei, who, together with Vesper, managed to kill him. They never discovered how Atlas betrayed their parents so rather than kill him, they banished him to Ignis island where he was trapped and unable to rule." Coraline sighed, throwing her hands in the air in exasperation. "That's where the book ends. Atlas was presumed to have died on the island and following his death, the Enchanteds died out too and we were left with no evidence magic ever existed."

"But apparently it isn't true." Cordelia recognised their surroundings. "Atlas is alive." She pressed her palms together and looked around. "Any questions?" Ebony and Oscar both raised their hands.

Ebony took the tale with a pinch of salt. "Why did you come after Atlas?"

"The box the book was in," Cordelia said. "Atlas sent this… sycophantic, psychotic nutjob with several screws loose to take it from us, claiming it was part of a lethal weapon."

"Daegel?" Oscar asked and they nodded, the name sending a shiver of fear through them. "The same thing happened to us," he said. "Ebony owned a necklace which he said was a key to a weapon." Oscar stuck his thumbs through his belt loops. "She gave a good fight, but they took it anyway."

"More than we ever did," Cordelia said, head hung in shame. "We were so frightened that we gave it to him and ran. But once we read the book and realised what Atlas was, we knew we had to stop him."

"But we were a laughing-stock to the Roamers, understandably, so we came alone, and the rest is history," Coraline finished. Oscar and Ebony were equally dumfounded, sitting, mouths agape as they tried to make some sense of everything.

"None of this makes sense," Ebony said. "I mean, come on, magic? That's the stuff of legends and fairy tales, not real life." Oscar, too, was sceptical, but he brooded over the flaws of science and fact in their current climate.

"How did Daegel survive the bombing of all those Transtar ships?" he questioned Ebony. "You said yourself in the footage he was clearly a suicide bomber; that he'd destroyed three previous ships. How could he have survived?" Ebony looked at him. She didn't have an answer but the lack of one didn't prove the implication that magic was involved.

"You're not seriously believing this?" she said.

"I'm just exploring all possibilities," he reasoned. "I don't know what to think right now."

"Well, one thing's for certain." Ebony clapped her hands to her thighs. "I'm not sticking about. Where's the way out?"

"Oh, there is a way out, we think." Oscar and Ebony stared at the girls who failed to share this information earlier. Ebony jumped up, the blanket nearly skidding out from beneath her across the smooth stone.

"Well, let's go then," she said enthusiastically but Cordelia and

Coraline firmly remained seated.

"If getting out was that easy, we would have done it a month ago."

"A month?" Ebony turned red as her anxiety to leave increased.

"Why haven't you left?" Oscar asked the two of them.

"Ignis is protected by a raging storm, impassable for uninvited ships as we've discovered," Coraline explained. "There is an exit. It opens whenever Atlas' men come through to check out a disturbance i.e: us, but only remains open for a short amount of time afterwards. I heard them talking about it," she clarified.

"He can't have guarded the island this heavily for no reason," Oscar said to Ebony.

"I know." In her and every other sensible person's experience, she kept her most valuable belongings under heavy security. She didn't bother locking her sock drawer for her socks didn't mean much to her. It worried her then, that Atlas' security was as intense as an entire planet of traps.

"So, you know where the exit is, and you know when it opens, but you haven't left?" Oscar was puzzled.

"It's better if we show you why." Cordelia threw a piece of wood on the fire to keep it fuelled before opening the saloon doors. On any other planet, burning wood would have been an offence punishable with a month's wages, but no one gave it a second thought.

Filing through the splintered doors and back into the sandy town, the twins led them through another street and around a hill of dead vegetation as though taking them on a tour. They emerged on the other side of the town where a pristine hotel stood in front of them.

Juxtaposing its surroundings, the hotel was raised on a bed of chiselled marble stone where the dust couldn't upset its appearance. Its albino exterior glowed in the shards of light let through, giving off an angelic ambiance astonishing of such a dreary place. Verdurous hedges decorated the golden gates and the paved footpath invited onlookers to walk upon it. The sophisticated architecture was trimmed with gold leaf, fake gold of course but from a distance it served its purpose and made the hotel look regal.

Despite the hotel having no guests, lanterns ornamented the hotel rooms, the cosy glow seeping through the windows and inviting in anyone who cast their eyes upon it. Time and effort had been invested into the hotel and it worked in alluring those who found themselves unwittingly under the sea, including Ebony and Oscar, who took a few steps towards it.

"The exit is somewhere in there," Coraline said, "but we couldn't find it."

"And you didn't stay and search because…?"

"There's a monster lurking within those walls. Its footsteps haunt the building, its eyes glow as it guards the windows, and it leaves a trail of butchery and evil wherever it goes." Cordelia's voice shuddered with her body but both Ebony nor Oscar bought into the dramatically mysterious answer.

Coraline clarified. "There are human bones littered across the hotel."

"Oh." Oscar shivered.

"So, how about we wait here until someone appears and follow them in?" Ebony suggested.

"The guards that come through are loaded with weapons," Coraline said. "We wouldn't stand a chance."

"Then we'll search for another way out."

"There isn't one."

"Are you sure?"

"… No."

"So, we look for another way out," Ebony finalised. "I'd rather die trying to escape than spend the rest of my life down here."

"I agree," Oscar said and with a determined look, he searched around for a direction to head in.

"Come with us?" Ebony asked. The twins looked at each other unsurely but with courage, they opted to follow Ebony.

Whilst their expressions implied unsureness, Ebony expected their half-heartedness and took it in her stride, leading the group away from the hotel and blindly into the town.

The wall of air dividing the ocean and city was easily passible as soon discovered; however, if the swim to the ocean surface didn't kill them, the ice and storm raging above would. The future was looking bleak in terms of escape and a nauseating fear built in the pit of Ebony's stomach that this could possibly be her final resting place.

They soon came across an underwater mountain pass, the summit of which passed the crown of the bubble and continued out of the water. A trench dug between the mountain elongated through the valley and into darkness. "I'd rather not," Coraline said, taking a step back as Oscar placed a firm foot forward.

"It's worth a look Coral," Cordelia overruled.

"Can't hurt to look," Ebony seconded. As she spoke, faint voices could be heard. At first, Ebony thought it could be a trick of the mind that she was hearing people in an abandoned underwater town, but the voices, a cohort of Atlas' supporters, were growing closer.

"Everyone into the trench," Cordelia ushered, "and they won't see us. They don't stray from the path." The advice was followed and they all rushed in blindly, watching as the guards sauntered by. The tenebrous trench was unnaturally windy compared to the rest of the bubble; a temperate wind which Ebony welcomed as it dried the water from her back.

The guards looked relatively unarmed compared to Daegel's decked out garments, and Ebony was about to suggest they follow them in, when in a random act of malice, one of them whipped a gun from their pocket, aimed it at the water and shot a Basa fish swimming too close to the old saloon. Four bullets fired from the gun when one would have been sufficient. He cackled maniacally as the fish floated to the top of the bubble before dropping from the apex and landing with a squelchy thud on the dirt track. Ebony watched, aghast and turned to Oscar, who's jaw had dropped, shoulders sagged in disbelief at the violent act.

"And that's why we don't follow them in." Cordelia's point was proved. The fish's body jerked one more time before lying still.

"Point taken," Ebony said. "Let's keep looking."

"Nope," Coraline said. They turned to her. Her complexion was that of someone seriously ill and her hands had developed a shake that would not stop, instead transferring to Cordelia when she touched her sister's hands. She pointed downwards and into the gloom. It was hard to differentiate what she was looking at from the rocky backdrop, but slight movement made it obvious that whatever she was looking at, wasn't inanimate. A long appendage of flesh was curled up on the floor.

"That's a tentacle?" Oscar's alarm made the affirmation mundane as the shock disallowed a stronger reaction.

"It's huge." Ebony was stunned.

"Like an octopus tentacle," Cordelia said but Coraline's words added more severity to the situation, or stupidity depending on the belief of the person.

"More like a kraken tentacle," she said. Cordelia panicked but it soothed Oscar who laughed.

"Krakens don't exist," he said, in a 'don't be silly' tone.

"And neither do abandoned underwater towns with random magical forcefields yet here we are," Cordelia whispered harshly.

"Maybe it's a Space Thing," Coraline said, "finally finding somewhere to settle."

Space Things were famous across the universe. Wherever humans went, stories of giant deformed entities that couldn't be classified as anything but monsters followed. The universe was a big place, and when humanity delved into its most formidable corners, horrors spawned to defend it. When planets couldn't be inhabited, it was blamed on Space Things that apparently wandered the world. When ships broke in the middle of deep space, it was blamed on Space Things. To most, they were nothing but stories that parents told their children to scare them, but to a few, Space Things were all too real.

They all shuddered as the wind blew again and an important distinction was to be made regarding it.

"Is that wind, or breath?" Coraline asked.

Oscar shook his head at the comment. "Wind," he decided. "There's no such thing as the kraken." However, his defiance of its existence didn't suddenly make the tentacle go away.

"There's no such thing as the kraken." Ebony joined him in trying to cling to rationality until their eyes became accustomed to the darkness and the overwhelming fact remained.

It was real.

What they first considered to be mountains were, in fact, the huge legs of the beast, who must have been centuries old to accumulate the molluscs and coral that alluded to its legs being rock. More critically, and Ebony was thankful that Atlas' men had distracted them, had they walked further, they probably would have found themselves in its inescapable mouth. Ebony struggled to speak. When she did, her voice was hoarse.

"It's asleep." Her heart pounded in her chest so loudly she was convinced the kraken would hear it. "Let's go before it wakes up."

No one needed telling twice. They crept away like mice, holding their breaths as though the water had submerged them as it should have done.

"Hey!" A yell startled them, and they winced at the loudness of the sound. Towards the hotel, one of the guards had momentarily stopped to relieve himself without the group noticing and was now brandishing his gun angrily. He loaded a new magazine and Ebony gulped.

"Don't shoot," she called, as loudly as she dared. "Don't shoot!" But the guard sniggered.

"Sorry." He shrugged and fired the gun. His aim from a distance was lousy and missed the four of them but what it didn't miss was the monster behind. The wind stopped half breath, and everyone turned as the air turned static and the bubble was silenced.

Eyes opened.

Orange eyes.

Four of them.

Glaring at them like intense car headlights.

At first, the eyes seemed tired and unbothered, but then they focused like a spotlight upon Ebony, Oscar, Cordelia and Coraline.

"Shit." Ebony felt like she'd taken an adrenaline shot to the heart as it pumped faster than what could possibly be safe. She took several steps back, dragging Oscar with her.

"Run," she said, rattling Cordelia and Coraline from a comatose stare. "Run!" The sea monster began to move. Even the guard yelped in fear. He dropped his gun and trousers around his ankles, sprinted away into the safety of the hotel. Oscar swiped the gun from the ground as they careened past.

The ground trembled and shook, and the kraken stood up.

Chapter 8

The odds certainly weren't in favour of Ebony, Oscar and their identical friends and it was worth betting that the kraken was going to have a wonderful lunch. Kraken was a term they used, simply because it was the only word in their vocabulary to describe the Eldritch abomination.

The doors of the hotel had mocked them sardonically by locking seconds before they could get in and they now had no choice but to sprint back through the ruined town, with hopes the kraken would get bored.

It didn't.

Slimy reptilian tentacles rained down with fury upon them. The kraken clearly wasn't a fan of being woken up and was in an incurably hangry mood. Immensely strong suckers ripped the unstable buildings from their foundations before hurling them at its lunch. It was agile in water so floated above the town, never losing sight of its prey. Its mouth had several rings of serrated, daggered denticles; saliva dripped from the top of the bubble as its appetite increased, creating puddles of gunk below that smelled like the dregs of a nuclear waste plant.

"How do we stop this thing?" Ebony cried, throwing her body sideways and away from the kraken's foot as it levelled a house and cratered the ground. She hadn't rolled to a stop before she was on her feet and running again.

"I don't know. Funnily enough, never fought a Kraken before." Cordelia's fear excelled through her sarcasm.

"I have a gun," Oscar said.

"Scales are impenetrable. What else?" Ebony asked in exasperation.

"Can't you materialise another weapon? You guys have bands," Cordelia pointed out.

"Nope. In our galaxy, President Waltare stopped the materialisation of weapons off our home planets to avoid interplanetary terrorism."

"What a dumb idea."

"Apparently so."

"I have an idea. Sounds stupid and crazy and absolutely

ridiculous…" Coraline listed.

"What?" Ebony yelled, with no time to dawdle.

"We have magic."

"Bullshit," Ebony and Oscar said in unison.

"I know it's silly but this whole place is magic," Coraline said. "You heard the story."

"It's got to be science," Ebony argued. "Same as airlocks on ships, air is pumped around a confined area to make it breathable."

"Says the girl who's running from the kraken." Ebony frowned.

"Point taken. Again."

"Maybe we can use it to help." Coraline was hoping for a plan to evolve but nothing came from it. They continued to run but it was ultimately pointless. The kraken, getting increasingly frustrated over not catching its food, thrashed at the buildings in front of them to block their paths until a cascading pile of rubble cornered them.

"We're screwed," Oscar said. He stared up at the beast who's eyes he couldn't even see; it was of such a monumental height.

"Not if I can help it," Ebony said. "Give me the gun." Oscar handed it to her, and she cocked the barrel, deciding to give an impromptu and brief science lesson as she did. "Now, science *not* magic dictates that the softest part of a reptile is its eyes. So, fire enough of these into the pupil, expose the brain and kill it."

"Seriously?" Cordelia was bewildered. "No one has that good an aim, you'd have to be right up close." Ebony caught her eye and winked, and Oscar instantly grabbed her arm.

"No. No, Ebony Echnovarria, I know you and I know what you're thinking, so no. There's no way." He spoke firmly but just instilled more stubbornness within Ebony. She set her jaw firmly and stared at him.

"What other choice do we have? If we're not careful that thing will trample the hotel and we'll never escape. This way at least we have a chance." She shook her arm free of Oscar's grip and he was forced backwards as a park bench was launched between the two of them. She stole her chance; her hands quivered, and her inner monologue screamed at her to not do it but with the gun clasped tightly in both hands, she sprinted for the leg of the beast as it landed and began to climb.

"She's crazy." Cordelia held her braids over her eyes, scared to watch.

"She's gonna die up there," Coraline said, and Oscar gave her a nasty look. But then the look in his eyes changed as if a lightbulb lit above his head.

"Not if I can help it," he decided, clambering over the bench awkwardly. "You two, stay hidden." He stood with a new sense of courage.

"What about you?"

Oscar's sanity was questionable. "I'm going to kill a sea monster."

From her precarious perch atop what Ebony could only assume was the kraken's knee, using dead tube coral to cling on, she caught glimpses of Oscar as he parkoured through the ruins. She had no idea what he was doing and hoped he was headed for safety. But, rounding the side of a building he changed direction and headed for the underbelly of the kraken.

Ebony shouted for him to stop but as she did, the kraken lifted its knee to demolish the remains of the town and she was thrown into the air. She braced herself to fall, body curled up tightly, but the force of the movement was so strong that she was thrown through the top of the bubble and into the rough waters.

A tentacle lashed out with remarkable precision, whipping itself around the bottom half of Ebony's body. She yelped, suckers tugging at her skin as the tentacle recoiled towards the mouth. Even the seaweed receded in the presence of the beast and the surrounding ocean emptied of sea life. The kraken was watching her with beady eyes and paused all other movement as it focused on bringing Ebony to its tooth-lined cavern of a mouth. The breath was ferociously strong, even through the water, but Ebony remained focused, sealing her nostrils.

"Please work, please." She aimed the gun through the water; she'd never fired one but was willing to learn, and fired. The kraken recoiled in pain, letting out a screech so loud the force of the sound sent Ebony spinning through the water as it let her go. The top left eye of the beast was no longer glowing, instead it was a gaping hole. Ebony realised she could easily blind it but without the light of its eyes guiding her to its most vulnerable points, she had no way of seeing properly to kill it.

Partially blind, but still hungry and remarkably pissed off, the kraken caught her in her tentacled grasp again. She cried out as it dragged her through the water and to the top of the bubble. She could breathe but dangling above nothing with a threatening bed of solid earth below was, funnily enough, rather dangerous.

"Hold on tight Ebony." Oscar's voice trembled in anticipation. He had no way of knowing if his plan would work and with every shake of the ground, the kraken's feet were one step closer to turning him into mush. He was standing below the Kraken's neck, his arm held out as high as he could reach. He looked like Thor beckoning Mjolnir, muscles taut and head raised to the sky. The glare he gave could have been mistaken on someone else's face for anger, but as Oscar gave an enraged Kubrick stare all he could think of was revenge. The kraken had attacked his best friend, and he was having none of it.

Something entered the ocean like a meteor and the kraken shrieked. Ebony felt a sticky liquid drench her with a vomit inducing smell, as the kraken slowly fell to the ground. She clutched the tentacles that loosened around her. The fall was worse than the landing because of the anticipation of a pain that never came. The landing was softened by the convulsively twitching tentacles that thrashed at the watery walls as the kraken breathed its last. Oscar, who was one giant footstep away from being a pulpy, trifle looking mess on the floor, sprinted out the way of a deluge of blood and fish carcasses, and when the beating of his heart could no longer be heard, neither could anything else.

Pure silence. The kraken made no more movement. No more noise.

"Ebony?" Oscar pulled at the cumbersome tentacles until a hand reached through and grappled at the air.

"Oscar?" Ebony was buried under mounds of flesh and squealed in abhorrence, as she wiped off what she presumed to be blood despite the slimy nature of it.

"You okay?" he asked as Ebony ogled at the monster in front of her. It was well and truly dead, and she quickly noticed the huge chunk taken from its neck and a huge hunk of metal crashed into the floor.

"I'm fine." She totted up a quick count of her limbs to make sure, and then met Oscar's gaze with a mind blown look. "What did you do?"

"Took a chance on the ship," Oscar said. "It may be in several pieces, but I can still summon it from my band. Requested full speed on the

92

delivery, and since its object sensors are ruined, it didn't see the kraken." The remains of the ship flashed with a red warning light.

"Hull integrity breached," the warning alarm said, before the whole ship died for good.

"You're a bloody genius," Ebony praised. From what was the only remaining building save the hotel, Cordelia and Coraline peered out, queasy at the overwhelming stench of rotting fish.

"Is it dead?" Coraline asked. "Properly dead?"

"It is," Oscar said.

"You're both mad," Cordelia said. "Absolutely insane. But thank you."

Oscar blushed a little, the success going to his head. "All in a day's work," he said modestly, clapping his hands together to rid them of sand.

"Anyway -" Ebony could see Coraline begin to swoon and stepped in, "-following that rather extreme detour…" She spun on her heels, insinuating her intent to get to the hotel without any further interruptions, but Cordelia grabbed her sleeve, yanking her back harshly.

"Are you crazy? We're dead if we go in there," she exclaimed but Ebony pulled her arm away.

"And a minute ago we were nearly dead staying out here," she argued. "Stay if you want but you won't get out without going through the hotel." She shot Oscar a 'you're coming with me and that's the end of it' look with narrowing eyes.

Oscar gave them a parting piece of advice. "She's right you know. I'd come with us if I were you." He headed after Ebony with a skip in his step, high from his victory. Not many people could say that they fought the kraken and won, and it would most definitely be a story Oscar told for the rest of his life.

They walked briskly to the hotel and the door opened automatically with a foreboding creak. Ebony was convinced people were at the windows watching them but every time she looked, no one was there. Eery shadows plagued her peripheral but never dared go further.

A little time had passed, the dark water suggesting it could be night-time above them, and Cordelia and Coraline crept over after discussing harshly amongst themselves what was to be done. Ebony smiled gratefully; she was glad the four of them could escape.

A bell, which they previously hadn't heard, rung from a grandfather clock indoors.

"Ready?" Ebony asked.

"As we'll ever be." Cordelia and Coraline locked hands and followed Ebony through. Oscar brought up the rear, watching their surroundings. If four random strangers in the hotel didn't set off alarm bells, the town's new Kraken carcass centrepiece certainly would.

The hotel's beguiling frontage was a first-rate façade. Shaded glass windows in the lobby prevented the sunlight that had fought so hard to reach the ocean floor from shining through. Cobweb covered bones, ghostly swinging chandeliers and the stagnant reek of death made Oscar and Ebony both agree, it felt like they'd walked into an over glorified graveyard.

A song was playing which took Ebony a moment to identify. The familiarly haunting tune titled 'Even the Devil Ran' made her increasingly nervous as to what awaited. As the piano played, they remained quiet, not in appreciation of the music but in case their presence provoked uninvited company.

"Where do we go?" Oscar asked. Four possible exits to the lobby surrounded them, two hallways and two stairways. All guarded by decaying areca palms and flickering lights. None looked particularly pleasant.

Coraline pressed her shoe into an indistinct footprint in the cardinal carpet of the first step of the leftmost stairway. "Upstairs?" she suggested, twisting her toes into the flattened yarn.

"Sure." Oscar shrugged.

Coraline led them through the hotel with no better clue as to where the door was but with determination to find it as soon as possible. They searched relentlessly, from kitchen to bedroom, games room to janitor cupboard, but to no avail.

Eventually Cordelia stopped them as she harshly shut the bedroom door of the presidential suite. She locked it, protecting them from something they weren't even sure was there.

"Look, we haven't got long until we're stuck in here. If we can't find it now, we need to leave and try again when the door next opens." Cordelia urged them to go back to the entrance. Ebony sucked on her teeth.

She didn't want to.

It would mean hours of endless traipsing around the ruined town, whilst Cordelia and Coraline inevitably tried to convince them not to go back. It was time she wasn't sure they could afford. But both Cordelia and Coraline were so afraid of whatever was inside the hotel, that with a defeated sigh Ebony agreed.

They retraced their steps to the entrance hall but slowed abruptly in unified confusion. The door was gone.

"That's not possible." Cordelia acted first, rushing to the thickly wallpapered wall where the door should be. "It's got to be a trick, right? Maybe it slides? Or we push something? Or we're in the wrong place?" She pushed at the wall desperately, and then took a step back to see the bigger picture. Her mud daubed hands left a singular handprint next to hundreds of handprints from victims that had all tried the same thing prior. The handprints of the bones that now piled on the floor.

Oscar walked to the window. He tugged on it, but it wouldn't open. Decades of fingerprints were etched into the dust where his fingers rested.

"We're in the right place. The view is the same," he said. pulling his hand away from the window, he noticed it was wet from condensation. The glass had steamed up.

"Is it me or is it getting hot in here?" Ebony asked. She fanned her hands around her face.

"Are they cooking us alive?" Cordelia cried. Instantly, thoughts went to the worst-case scenario. It had occurred to everyone and as the temperature rose, it became a more likely denouement than they would have hoped.

Oscar suddenly crouched to the floor. He squinted at a singed circle, what he had once believed to be part of the quatrefoil pattern of the carpet.

"Why are there burnt holes everywhere?" he questioned. The other three squatted in unison. Dotted around the lobby were several holes, roughly as wide as a football and so deep the bottom couldn't be seen. In the gloom they'd gone undetected and thankfully avoided. Ebony wiped her finger along the edge of one and drew it away, now caked in soot.

"It's where the heat's coming from," she said. She waved her hands over the hole, and they caught a warm updraft. Then, an aureate firelight appeared at the bottom of the hole they'd squashed themselves around and then at the foundation of all the others.

"It's getting brighter," Cordelia said, her cuffed earring reflecting the light into Ebony's eyes.

"No," Ebony corrected. "It's getting closer." They watched, too stunned to look away as the pulsating glow slowly climbed the hole.

"I think we should go." Oscar backed away, flapping his shirt collar as it stuck with humidity to his body.

"It looks like lava," Coraline whimpered. "Does this place fill with lava?" The four of them clambered onto the first step of the stairs, where the indent seemed to be less of a leading footprint and more of a victim's retreat, watching to see if her suspicions were true.

She was correct. Magma was rising from the ground. But it had gained some misinterpreted, half wired sentience and as it spread from the cavities, it built upon itself until an animalistic body with pulsating tentacle-like limbs had formed. It didn't have eyes as such; sunken areas of rock replaced the sockets and balls of lava created pupils if you could call them that. Gunky orange drool was spilling from a fang laced mouth embedded in what could only be called a head because the it's where the eyes were, and not because it resembled one. Others continued to form, until the humans were outnumbered three to one.

Oscar's clammy hand gripped Ebony's. "What do we do?"

Ebony looked at Oscar. "Flee for our lives," she recommended.

They fled.

Skidding into the nearest room, a dining room, Oscar slammed the door and nearly broke the lock as he twisted the ancient key. As Coraline and Cordelia tried their best to prise open a window with rusted silverware, Oscar rushed to the end of the table and shoved it into the door as a barricade. Still, there were thuds from the other side as the Magma men charged the door relentlessly.

"We'll be okay. We've just got to figure out what we're gonna do…" Oscar's breathing quickened as he looked to Ebony for an answer. "What are we gonna do?" He was hyperventilating, body twisting back and forth as he looked for a way out.

"For a start, how about not barricading ourselves into a room when the things chasing us can burn through walls?" Ebony said with a quavering voice as heat waves made the door seem to wiggle. The handle dripped boiling brass as the Magma men melted the lock.

"Didn't think of that," Oscar admitted. Cordelia hopped nervously from one foot to the other, pulling at her arm hair. Her ear-piercing scream suddenly shattered a wine glass across the floor. A cleft had ripped beneath her feet and magma had spilled through, latching on to her shoe.

"Cordelia!" Coraline shrieked, dragging her away from the clutches of the magma man. It conceded the foot and shrunk back into the hole. Gone, but not for good.

"Get her up," Ebony commanded. She flung a chair in their direction and her and Oscar scrabbled to the table, clinging to each other in a sweaty and matted clump of terror. Coraline hoisted Cordelia onto the chair, and they balanced precariously as Cordelia screamed in pain.

Ebony gagged at the sound of sizzling flesh. Cordelia's canvas shoe proffered no protection and her heel had been incinerated. Flesh was seeping from her foot, like ice cream on a summer's day.

"Oscar." Ebony shook his shoulder as his eyes bulged at the injury and he couldn't take his eyes away. She forcefully turned him towards the door as he retched. "Coral, use your jumper," Ebony said, "and wrap her foot. Quickly."

"Coral," Cordelia sobbed as Coraline quickly shook off her jumper.

"It's okay Cordy. It's okay," Coraline soothed as she tentatively put a foot on the floor. Her hands trembled uncontrollably as she wrapped her clothing around Cordelia's foot, blenching at her cries.

An unscalded lamp sat in the corner. It was useless without a bulb, so Ebony put it to good use, snapping the pole into a daggered point.

"We have seconds before they're in," Oscar warned, leaping from the table and to Cordelia's side.

"We can't move her," Coraline cried.

"We have no choice," Ebony answered. "I'm sorry I forced you in here, I should have listened. But now we're here, and we have to go." The two of them were in a silent war as they stared at each other. Oscar intervened.

"Let's go," he said firmly. Although Cordelia's agonising screams begged them to not move her, Coraline and Oscar each snaked a hand around her waist and lifted. Ebony covered her hand with her sleeve and pushed the door handle outwards. Pole brandished, she held the Magma men at bay as the others escaped behind her.

"We can't do this for forever," Oscar said, shoulder uncomfortably weighted down as Coraline struggled to hold both her sister and herself together. "Cordelia needs medical attention immediately otherwise that foot's as good as gone." Cordelia gasped loudly as she tried to catch her breath and Coraline glared. "Sorry." Oscar held up his hands at the insensitivity.

"No, you're right," Ebony said, glancing at Cordelia's blueing toes. They had traversed a maze of straight corridors; each looked so similar it was impossible to tell where they had been and where they had yet to go. However, a distinguishable fork in the path ahead looked promising. One route was murkier than its associates and Ebony was dissuaded from going down it but rationally, if the forbidden exit was to be anywhere, it would be where people wouldn't want to go.

Magma men were slowly following behind. They never moved faster than a walking pace but were constantly, equidistantly, behind. Always following.

"You'll be fine Cordy, I promise you," Coraline said. She looked between the corridors and then to Ebony. "Left, or right?" She asked, waiting for a decision.

"Right?" Ebony made an educated guess.

"The one that looks like a trap, you mean?" Avoiding anything that reminded him of death was clearly Oscar's top priority as he disagreed with Ebony. But the Magma men decided that there was no time for indecisive arguments and a barrier of living lava rose between Ebony and Oscar, Cordelia and Coraline. Ebony was in another interchangeable hall of mustard walls whilst Oscar carried Cordelia into the darkness.

"Ebony?" he yelled as he lost sight of her.

"Listen to me," she called bravely, "if I don't find you in five minutes…"

"…No Ebony, we're not going to leave you!" Oscar fought.

"…I was going to say 'wait longer' but… thanks Oscar." She brandished her lamp pole bravely. "I'll find you eventually," she called, heading into an all too familiar setting.

Several locked rooms and a steeply rising maids' staircase later and Ebony came to the realisation she had been forced down the wrong corridor; her only consolation being Oscar may have followed the correct one. She kept a firm grasp on her trusty lamp pole, stabbing the Magma men at a distance as she slammed a door between them and her. It was a dead end, nothing but a laundry cupboard. Ebony yanked the shelving units from the wall in hoping it would reveal a secret passage. But of course, it didn't.

Bang.

The hairs on the back of her neck stood on end. The door was lying splintered on the carpet and the Magma men were slowly traipsing over it. They swarmed into the laundry room around her.

"Evening gents," Ebony said. "Nine's a crowd don't you think?" she joked, trying to cope with the thought of her inevitable death.

The Magma men didn't seem to care for the lamp pole, or for light banter. Ebony felt the wall against her back. The Magma men were taking their time. They had trapped their prey; now they could savour the thrill of the kill.

She had no choice but to go through them. Springing on her heels as she waited for an opportunity that didn't seem to be presenting itself, Ebony prodded her pole forward, but a magma man slid on top of it, relieving her of her weapon.

Ebony was having none of it. "Oh no you don't," she said. She yanked the end of the pole upwards and the living lava flipped. It couldn't rescue itself from melting face first through the floor and Ebony realised something. The creatures had something underneath their sluglike soles, a lustrous grey metal; Ebony guessed tungsten. When they rose from the floor, they weren't sunk by their cursed abilities as the tungsten kept them afloat. But they didn't have the same protection on their scalps.

"Now that is a major character design flaw," Ebony commented and with a newfound courage, jumped down the hole the magma man had made. She landed in a similar looking room, but it was hemmed with a blue glow from beneath the carpet. She yanked the fringe, and it came away from the wooden floor and through the decaying slats the blue glow guided her with a renewed optimism. It had to be the exit below her.

Another magma man who hadn't learnt from his predecessor jumped down and tried to grapple the pole from Ebony, but she flipped him too. Then came a yell from below.

Ebony looked through the hole.

A swirling blue portal of eccentric design was covered by an impenetrable energy field. Battering it with her fists was Coraline who had given up punching random combinations into the keypad to her right. Oscar bravely fended off the Magma men with a not so impressive candlestick as he held Cordelia up. She was nearly limp in his arms; the jumper around her foot was saturated with blood and Ebony feared the worst.

"Need some help down there?" she called. Oscar's head snapped upwards.

"Ebony, behind you!" he screamed and Ebony agilely sidestepped a prowling magma man and capsized it. Oscar ducked as the ceiling caved inwards, plaster falling like snow and the magma man sinking past his feet.

Ebony dropped into the room, still brandishing her precious lamp pole.

"Thank you," she said brightly. Oscar furrowed his brows at the sudden cheerfulness that had overcome Ebony.

"What was that?" he gawked, pointing to the magma man that was still sinking.

"Our way out," Ebony replied. Oscar shook the plaster from his hair and lifted Cordelia into his arms. The Magma men at the door, who had halted their progress at Ebony's guest appearance, suddenly lurched forward. But Ebony's lease of confidence gave Oscar a jumpstart and he flung himself and Cordelia out of harm's way. Ebony contended with the Magma men, who, if they were capable of such emotion, were fuelled with rage over their fallen friend. But Ebony, unphased, created a human shield between them and her friends.

"Coraline, away from the portal," Ebony ordered. crouching to the ground, she allowed a magma man to slide atop her pole. It did with assumed victory but with a grunt, Ebony yanked it upwards and the magma man, too cocky to balance, toppled. Before it could sink through the floor, Ebony leapt behind and rammed it into the energy field with a satisfied yell, a trail of burnt floorboards in her wake. The field sputtered, sparked, and then the blue light surrounding it vaporised. She looked at Oscar with a toothy grin and chucked him the pole.

"Let's get out of here," she said. Oscar threatened the last of the Magma men as Ebony stood in the portal, beckoning for Coral and Cordelia. She was abruptly sucked through and a horrendous sensation of falling from a height overwhelmed her stomach, but it was over in a moment, and she landed on the beach of Ignis Island. A gorgeous beach of white sand covered shores resting against a glassy, turquoise water. A beach overflowing with fresh air.

There was a whipping noise behind Ebony, and she turned.

"We're out?" Coraline gasped, stress alleviated as seagulls cawed above them. The sun scorched the earth, but shade was plentiful from the dense, tropical forest growing behind, and then the volcano behind that, and Coraline gently set Cordelia down amongst the dunes.

In the natural light, Cordelia's face looked washed of colour, and she seemed about to faint, but still mustered a smile as she looked out to sea, relief washing over her like the waves stroking the shore. The breeze blew the sound of crashing waves their way as finally, Oscar fell onto the beach. On feeling the air against his face, he burst out laughing.

"We did it," he said, grabbing Ebony's hands. She gasped as he pulled her up and spun her around the beach.

"We're alive!"

Chapter 9

Ebony and Oscar were hidden behind an overhanging tree, its branches laden with temptingly fresh but poisonous fruit. In the heat of the midday sun, they had started travelling along Ignis' beach. Unsure of what their intentions were, walking made them more productive than sitting around. The smell of driftwood and salt gladdened Ebony, and she had stopped to retrieve a conch shell buried partially in the sand as they wandered.

Cordelia and Coraline had since departed. During their aimless ambling, they had found a prodigious aircraft hangar carved into the base of the volcano and there were ships inside. The four of them had theorised that Atlas' ships were somehow protected from the storm. They didn't know how but they had no other explanation. Cordelia couldn't walk, let alone climb and Ebony forced them to leave, in spite of their protests. But they had offered supplies from the ship they commandeered first to help Ebony and Oscar on their way, especially as along the beach, Atlas' men scoured the area.

"Have we got a plan?" Oscar, with a sandwich in his mouth, pulled a clean shirt over his head and frowned as peanut butter smeared on the inside of it. Ebony cocked the barrel of the gun she held.

"Maybe?" She crinkled her nose, the thinly spread parts of a plan assembling in her mind. "Climb the volcano, take some pictures of the weapon, then steal a ship and fly home."

"So basically, you have a sequence of events planned out in your head that are highly unlikely to happen and that will most likely go very, very wrong."

"Yeah," Ebony answered cautiously. Oscar raised an eyebrow. He preferred having a plan to follow. A month prior, back on Chane, when someone had chaotically suggested a meeting which threw his plans off track, his face was folded in a stern wrinkle for the rest of the day. But to Ebony's surprise, Oscar smirked and laughed a little.

"Better get going then." He grabbed a backpack of medicine and food and flung it around his shoulders.

"You're in a questionably good mood," Ebony said suspiciously.

"I mean, as long as we don't get spotted, this is basically just a recreational trek," Oscar said, shrugging on a backpack. Ebony enjoyed his new outlook, stemming from the relief of their survival. He felt invincible as they started their long ascent.

The humidity became apparent as they trekked through the overgrown jungle, cutting through vines, and climbing over thick vegetation until the greenery became sparse and the soil under foot became loose rocks, sloping harshly upwards. The volcano loomed over them intimidatingly; tumbling black rock imperilled a fatal fall back to the beach and although the top was shrouded in cloud, it still burnt brightly, adding to the danger of it being an active volcano.

"There's got to be a better way," Ebony said, already struggling with her wrist as they climbed. Oscar glanced at her and quickly nodded in agreement.

"There probably is, but I guarantee it's crawling with Daegel wannabes," he reasoned. Ebony willed herself to keep going, following Oscar's lead as he climbed. He was a boy of medium but toned build and Ebony struggled to match his pace as he effortlessly hauled himself up the near sheer cliff face. Despite her fear, Ebony wore a brave face and at every opportunity Oscar offered her to turn back, she adamantly claimed she wanted to keep going.

According to Oscar, who had also decided to give Ebony a geography lesson on the way up, the volcano was a shield volcano, small and relatively gently sloped compared to most, so they were lucky. But Ebony didn't like exercise and she certainly didn't like a lot of it, so by the time they got to the top, roughly four hours after they'd started to climb, Ebony didn't care what type of volcano it was.

"That. Was. Awful." She flopped over the slide of the cliff onto the top ledge, her chest rising and falling heavily.

"But we made it." Oscar used his backpack as a chair, taking a gulp of water as he scouted their location. With a gust of wind, the accompanying fog rolled away and with more visibility, Oscar noticed a fortress of a building. He strained his neck to even see the top.

"Ebony, look." He nudged her and she rolled over from her enervated foetal position. The building, black obsidian and fortified cheval de frise, towered over the island and shaded them in a frightful shadow.

"Well, if I was an evil dick, I know where I'd be hiding," Ebony observed. "Let's find a window."

Oscar was equally happy that she didn't want to attempt to get inside. However, finding a window was harder than first anticipated; the building was so heavily embattled they found only one. Balancing on the sharp rocks decorating the side of the building, the high standing window was their only view into the murk.

"Camera ready." Ebony's band, amongst many things, could take pictures and she held it to the window. She peeked in and as her eyes adjusted to the darkness, she descried a figure on a throne in the middle of the room.

Ebony gasped as Oscar rammed his head into the gap. "Is that him?" she sputtered. "Atlas?"

"I don't think it's going to be anyone else." Oscar was trembling slightly, and Ebony took his hand supportively. They both spied back through the window.

Atlas was gone.

"Where did he go?" Ebony feared the worst, grazing her cheek against the rock as she pulled away.

"He can't have moved, we looked away for less than a second." Oscar sounded panicked and Ebony felt a lump rise in her throat as she had the inescapable feeling she had only experienced once, in the park back on Drognir. That they weren't alone.

"Oscar." She wrapped her arms around his and clung on tightly. "I think we should go."

"Yeah, I agree," Oscar said but he was unable to turn around before someone behind them stifled a snorty laugh.

"We never have visitors." Said person clapped in excitement. "It's so good of you to pop in and see us, Ebony." Ebony felt her knees buckle. She looked left and right. They were surrounded by a retinue of overly armoured guards, with one standing prominently in the middle, smiling in his normal sadistic triumph.

"You piece of shit." Ebony pointed her gun but, with a click of his fingers, the gun swelled to a lump of heated metal, and she had to drop it, leaving red blisters across her hands.

"Hello again," Daegel said, pulling out his beloved knife. "I think you'll be coming with me."

Ebony grimaced as Daegel twisted her arm behind her back, shoving her through corridor after corridor of never-ending stygian walls.

"Oscar," she called but Daegel rolled her hand further until she felt the same wrist crack. She yelped. When Daegel had surrounded them, they hadn't touched Ebony on Atlas' orders, but Atlas cared nothing for Oscar's wellbeing. They'd beaten him black and blue with clubbed weapons and he was being dragged roughly along the floor. She wondered how the man who was dragging him, a man of half his height and probably half his weight, was doing it.

"Please. I'll do whatever you want if you leave him alone," she pleaded, unsure if Oscar was conscious, or even alive. Daegel snorted.

"I've heard that one before and remember what you did?" Daegel grabbed her hair and she gritted her teeth, not giving him the satisfaction of yelling. With misplaced confidence he kicked open a door and walked into the huge chamber Ebony and Oscar had been staring into. He was unbearably smug at his success, but his attitude quickly changed as there was a horrendous yell.

"Daegel." Ebony froze, clapping her free hand to her head as she ascertained what had happened. Atlas hadn't disappeared from his seat but her and Oscar had been moronic enough to look through the only window supplying light to the room. Sticking their heads in had simultaneously blocked the light. It had obstructed their own view of Atlas and got themselves caught.

Daegel dropped to his knees respectfully in a deep bow, taking Ebony with her and forcing her head down but this made Atlas angrier.

"Let her go!" he shrieked. "Don't you dare treat her like that. You know who she is."

"I'm sorry, Sire." Daegel let Ebony go without hurting her further, even going as far as to wipe the blood from her cheek with her collar. Ebony stood but kept her shoulders hunched in submission, waiting for someone to break the silence. But Atlas remained quiet and Daegel didn't dare move from his bow, so Ebony stooped by Oscar who was groaning on the floor, cradling his face. She leant over him protectively.

"I'm not going to let anything else happen to you, I promise," she whispered, although so much damage had already been done. His cheek was split from eye to jaw, and so swollen he could have been growing a new face. Atlas, watching with a cocked head at the love Ebony was showing Oscar, held out a crooked, ashen finger.

"Come here, Ebony," He beckoned. As much as Ebony wished to stay by Oscar's side, she didn't want to see what happened if she made Atlas ask twice, so she stood and delicately walked forward, her neck receding into her shoulders. Dim lights flickered on, and Ebony took a sharp intake of breath as she beheld Atlas in all his grandeur. He was epitome of terror; sharp, fanged teeth sat beneath his twisted lip, black, hooded eyes that showed not an inkling of emotion, and an overt throne of human bone.

"You're Atlas?" She made sure.

"You're correct," he confirmed, sitting back. "And you're Ebony. Good to put a name to a face. I apologise for Daegel's rough treatment of you. Tea?" he offered, not forgoing the pleasantries.

Tea?

Ebony was in the lair of a murderer being offered tea. A lair, it might be added, that had bodies littering the floor behind the throne, which hadn't gone unnoticed by Ebony nor Oscar. Yet, a small table of dainty China cups sat by Atlas' side, unnoticed due to the freshly polished skull that overlooked them. Ebony's confusion kept her silent, so Atlas continued.

"I'm glad you're here," he said, pouring himself a cup with liberal helpings of sugar. "I must admit, I was going to send Daegel to collect you at a later date but since you're here now, we may proceed."

"Proceed?" Ebony repeated. "With what? Your weapon?"

Atlas' eyes gleamed with menace. He clicked his fingers and the sound heavy machinery whirred in the ceiling, and lava began to pour from it.

"Lava on tap?" Oscar scoffed quietly. Ebony shielded her eyes, beginning to sweat. Atlas was unphased by both the heat and the light and instead chose a contradictory cold smile.

"What's this for?" Ebony asked. He looked at her and his eyes pierced straight through her soul. She felt indecently exposed, standing before him.

"For added flare." She wasn't impressed.

"You have lights." She nodded towards the ceiling. He scowled.

"I have waited thousands of years for this," he said, "lights don't cut it."

"You'd think he could have at least polished his crown," Oscar mumbled, looking at the rust bucket that sat on his head. But Atlas was least concerned about Oscar's opinion of him and was more taken by Ebony's bland reaction to his comment.

"Thousands of years," Atlas boasted, waiting for Ebony to react. She let out a small yawn. "Thousands of years," he repeated. "Does that not shock you?" Ebony shook her head. She had, until this point, been scared but as she heard Oscar cry out behind her and watched Daegel carelessly kick him as he bowed and walked out, she lost her cool.

"No, it doesn't shock me, not at all," she spat. "I know what happened. You betrayed and lied to Sonneillon, Belphegor and Adremelech and was banished to this island for being a traitor." Ebony hoped she'd remembered the names correctly. Atlas sat a little straighter in his chair and she expected him to yell but he didn't. Yet, his silence was chilling.

"You've done your research," he applauded, teeth gritted. "No matter now. They'll be back soon, now you're here." Ebony's heart began to race.

"What do you mean?" she asked. She wanted to cry. The question had no humorous connotations, but Atlas threw himself forward with a howling laughter like it was the funniest thing he'd ever heard. Then he snapped back to his semblance of sanity like the laughter had never been real.

"For someone who knows about me and my brethren, you certainly don't know much about yourself," he insulted. "You, Ebony, are special. You're like me. You have magic coursing through your veins." Ebony froze. Even the notion of being like Atlas repulsed her. And magic? She didn't know where to begin with that comment.

"You're lying," Oscar grunted. He had climbed to his feet and wheezing with every step that pressed his ribs into his lungs, hobbled to

Ebony. She grabbed his waist for support, and he rested his chin against her shoulder. "Don't let him scare you," Oscar whispered to her.

"Your friend is insignificant, so is his opinion," Atlas contributed to the conversation.

"Not to me." Ebony spoke with defiance. "What are you even doing here? Why do you need me?" she asked but they were interrupted as the doors behind opened and Daegel let them collide with the walls. He had arrived and wanted all to know it. He was the first in a brigade of seven, delicately carrying the key in an open box. Ebony glared at him as he went past. He was followed by others; the first carried another open box but it was empty, and Ebony took it to be the box stolen from Cordelia and Coraline. It was raggedy and threadbare from the very same years that ate away at Atlas' powers.

The second man carried another box which was sealed tightly. It was as black as night and Atlas doted upon it with hungry eyes. But what scared Ebony most was what the next men brought in. They were carrying two coffins. Ebony's face drained of colour in utter mortification and Atlas obviously noticed because he laughed at her again.

"They're not for you," he assured, which made Ebony feel marginally better. "They're already full."

She felt worse again.

Atlas, who was gathering an appalling amount of enjoyment from Ebony's upset, took a sip of tea and drummed his fingers against a vaguely new looking skull on his chair, directing Oscar's attention to the fact that his could very well soon be up there too.

"What is all of this? And why do you need me?" Ebony dreaded the answer but asked anyway. As though a switch had flicked in his brain, Atlas' amusement dulled, and he tired of her questions. He waved his hands and she felt herself sink to her knees, Oscar beside her. They both tried to stand but to no avail, as if placed in a cramped invisible box. Ebony was properly frightened.

"You see Ebony. When the universe expanded, humanity endeavoured to proliferate alongside it. Scientific invention and explainable facts overhauled mystery and forgotten were the magical myths of the old world. I was forgotten," he said spitefully. "Me, an

Ancient so powerful I could once topple an empire with a single thought, ruin cities with—"

"—I get it. You're an attention seeker," Ebony said rudely. If she was going to die, she certainly wasn't going to go quietly.

"Excuse me. I was monologing," Atlas growled. Daegel knelt by his side, shuffling about in anticipation.

"Atlas." He handed him the key. Atlas held it, staring with an insatiable desperation for power. His zeal infatuated him; he studied every inch of the key rapaciously.

"Incredible," he said, marvelling at it, "how one small key can be the answer to so much power."

"How did you get that?" Ebony asked, recalling how it had magically disappeared earlier.

"I hire men of particular skills. One of which is telekinetic. It wasn't hard," he said. Ebony didn't believe him simply because he sounded ridiculous. But then he waved his hand again and the open chest flew to him. Oscar squeezed his eyes shut and opened them again, but the box was still floating. He searched for translucent wires but could see none.

"Why do you need a key for an open chest?" Ebony spoke up. "What's in it?"

"The real question is, what isn't in it that should be?" Atlas stared at her, but she didn't play his guessing game.

"What?" she asked bluntly.

"Death."

"Death is the weapon?" Ebony's eyes nearly popped out of their sockets. The man was insane. But Atlas licked his lips, serious in every word, and she shuddered.

"You see, Ebony, if I can trap death, I control it, and you know what that means?" Ebony shook her head. "It means I can revive the bodies of my brothers," he smiled. Ebony tried to stay calm.

"So that's what this was for," she said. "You betrayed them, and now you want to revive them, for what? Your precious ego?"

For the first time since their meeting, Atlas stood up. At close to 7ft, the broad shouldered giant towered over Ebony and Oscar. His mind was torn between explaining himself and killing them both. He had been on Ignis for a long time. Recycled conversations bored him, but he rarely had new company.

"I want to rule again. These pathetic mortals have been in charge of my universe for too long, destroying it with their science whilst claiming it's all in the name of progress." Atlas looked carelessly at Oscar and ignored Ebony's accusation. Nonetheless, he clenched his fist and Ebony could tell she was right about his underlying reasons for doing it. He yearned to look good in their eyes. "I will bring Belphegor and Adremelech back to life-" he acknowledged the coffins, "-and we will bring to life our lord Sonneillon. His magic and soul couldn't be destroyed; it was too strong. So, it was locked away a box and thrown into the deepest corners of the universe until I found it again." Ebony was confused. The entire plan was inconceivable at best, and she didn't see how and where she came into play as part of his delusional plot. She didn't even believe in the magic he was speaking of, and the key had been given to her as a baby; she didn't take it.

"But if you don't have Sonneillon's body-" Ebony pointed out, counting the coffins, "-how's your plan going to work?"

"That, dear Ebony, is where you come in," Atlas said. "Ancients don't die unless killed by special means, their vessel is simply destroyed, and their soul trapped in limbo until another vessel is found." Ebony subconsciously pieced the puzzle together, realising why she was needed.

Oscar was slow on the uptake. "So why do you need Ebony?"

"I need a vessel, a vessel with magic strong enough to keep Sonneillon's soul in. You, Ebony." Ebony shook her head.

"No," her and Oscar said in unison.

"I don't have magic. I'm not some magical being!" Ebony yelled. Atlas, who was in a good mood and found the whole thing humorous, cackled again in sinister amusement, his face contorting into a maniacal grin.

"Why do you think I didn't let you get hurt?" Atlas said. "I need your body in prime condition."

"You literally tried to blow me up."

"Well, I had to find you somehow, didn't I?"

"Have you heard of the internet?" Atlas sat back in his chair.

"I knew you were powerful enough to survive it. Your dormant power saved you, whether you were aware of it or not. It proved your power." Atlas scowled and punched his hand to his fist. "Enough of this small talk. I've not brought you here to bond." Ebony looked at Oscar who, through a bloodied face she could tell was scared. He had one of those nervous quirks identifiable only in the most serious of situations; when Oscar bit his nails, something was terribly wrong. She gently moved his head from leaning against her and pulled his hands apart in one last caring act.

"Goodbye Oscar," she whispered. He looked at her with a peculiar expression, clearly drained. Ebony stood and glanced around the room. The lava had fallen into specially designed pools which had flooded around the chamber, meaning they were standing on more of an obsidian bridge. Ebony made a rash decision; it was a hundred billion people or her. So, fighting every instinct telling her not to become like the bodies in the room, she ran forward, her stomach knotting as she dived into the lava-filled pools. Oscar and Atlas both screamed and lunged forward.

It was Atlas who caught her. He was holding his hand out, a strong transparent force that rippled the air coming out of it, and it kept Ebony floating in mid-air, suspended barely centimetres from the lava. Sweat was running down her face and as it dripped into the lava, it sizzled and burnt. Ebony was simultaneously thankful and terrified that Atlas had stopped her, and she braced herself for what would happen next. He threw her roughly back like a bowling ball into a pin: Oscar, and sat back in his chair, studying her. The world swayed below him, but he composed himself, not wanting to let on to such a potentially powerful enemy how years on the island had weakened him.

"You're brave," he observed. "Stupid. Insolent. But brave." He focused his attention back on the key as Oscar, who had softened Ebony's landing at the expense of his breathing, pulled her into him with worryingly shallow breaths.

"Don't do that," he cried, pressing his fingers aggressively into her arms, without intending to hurt her but certainly with the intention to never let go. "Don't you dare leave me." He was extremely shaken, and Ebony felt a wave of guilt hit her like a boxer's punch to the jaw.

"I'm sorry," she murmured. "It's me or the universe. That's a small sacrifice."

"The universe isn't worth you," Oscar replied. She couldn't prevent the corners of her mouth curving into a faint smile.

A huge bang erupted from Atlas' direction and Ebony and Oscar whipped their heads up; Atlas had the key in one hand and the open chest in the other. He looked to be having a fit; fiery black and blood red tendrils of smoke billowed around his torso, and he grimaced, eyes bulging as he bent and squirmed as the smoke desired.

"My lord..." Daegel had stepped forward, but Atlas wasn't accepting help.

"Leave me," he demanded. "My necromancy is unmatched. I nearly have him." Daegel bowed deeply again, a florid display of gesticulation to show his admiration before he spat on the floor at Ebony and Oscar's feet and paraded to the door. His other servants snaked out behind, leaving Ebony and Oscar to watch.

Atlas was trying to trap Death.

None of his slaves seemed to be phased by the term necromancy or the fact Atlas was attempting it. Ebony's mouth hung agape.

"We've got to do something," Oscar said, wiping his face of blood. "What?"

"He's distracted; we could make a break for it? If he needs you the best thing to do is get you out of here."

"But if we leave, he'll still have Death. We need to stop him." Ebony shifted her weight from side to side, unable to take her eyes off Atlas as she panicked.

"You still believe this is real?" Oscar cried.

"Are you seeing what I'm seeing?" She thrust her hands in Atlas' direction as he fought smoke that had a conscience. "We steal the key. That's the easiest thing to get," she said, "then we destroy it, throw it in the lava and bolt?" She was asking Oscar if it was an okay plan. It clearly wasn't but in weighing the options, it was fight or sit and watch Atlas take over.

"Fine," Oscar settled. Ebony, who had taken several steps away from Atlas, now forced herself to move forward, having to physically stop herself from running in the opposite direction.

"Come on." She coaxed her brain into action with a simple task. "One step and then the others follow." She began to move. Oscar, doubled over in pain, trailed the side of the bridge going to Atlas' right. It was an unspoken idea but theoretically, whoever Atlas tried to get rid of first, the other one would go for the key.

Ebony prepared to pounce. Atlas was still struggling to control the smoke enveloping him and she assumed correctly that the smoke wasn't actually smoke but the unhuman manifestation of Death itself.

As she got closer, she could hear it screaming. It wasn't loud but tore into everyone's minds like a telepathic line of defence. Oscar had one hand pressed to his ear to stop the scream penetrating his mind as he got closer.

Atlas abruptly stopped moving and had one fist victoriously in the air, with coils of Death trapped inside it. It was writhing as though in agony and despite what it was, Ebony felt bad. But she didn't have time for emotions; Atlas looked to his left and saw Ebony in a wide stance and immediately lashed out. She rolled back neatly, and Atlas tried to stuff Death into the box as it fought him with the power it had left.

However, what Atlas failed to notice was Oscar whom he drastically underestimated. He flung himself at the throne and Atlas swung a punch which sent Oscar soaring but not before the palm of his hand found the key, which was floating in mid-air. He swatted it out of orbit, and it rolled onto the obsidian, bouncing across the room.

"Give it back," Atlas roared. The box of death had three locks and he had only closed two, so whilst Death was practically trapped, it was still present in the room and was rather disgruntled over its situation. Ebony wasn't sure how much autocracy Atlas now had but as she slipped down the stairs and crashed to the floor, grabbing the key, a pair of anaemic, bony feet appeared in front of her. She looked up. Oscar boldly stooped in front of her, and they crouched back to back as they were surrounded.

Reapers lined the walls.

Atlas had control of Death.

Chapter 10

It hadn't been the best day. Ebony ranked it as the worst day of her life. The tea was spilt. The China cups broken on the floor. It was a disaster.

"Give me the key," Atlas thundered. Ebony didn't. She waited for him to take it by force, but he looked utterly drained. Ebony didn't think he could.

"Not unless you release Death," she bargained, holding it tightly to her chest.

"You. Making demands?" Atlas looked as though he was going to try and stand but he didn't make an effort to get up. "Look around you." He flung his arms wide. "You're trapped. The only way to get out of this alive is to hand me the key." Ebony was surrounded by translucently white reapers whose cold metal scythes begged to be used; held in an attack ready stance. But she stood her ground amongst the sea of grey veiled bodies.

"No." She was in a recklessly mutinous mood. "I don't answer to you."

"Your choice," Atlas said. "It's a shame it has to end this way for you. Such a waste of a vessel but I can find another." He looked around. "Reapers? Kill them." Oscar's heart lurched to his throat as he looked to Ebony who cowered from the scythes. But the reapers didn't move.

"Kill them," Atlas repeated. "I control your master, so I control you."

"Weeeelllllllllllllll," a high-pitched voice said, "there is currently a teeny tiny flaw in your plan. Two locks are sealed, one remains open. So technically you don't control me." The smoke pluming from the box shot upwards and manifested into a shadowy figure. As it did, the lights which until then had been turned off, flickered ominously in the room. "Ebony Echnovarria, Oscar Riverthorne, hi. It's good to meet you. I'm Death," he said cheerfully, and Ebony's mouth dropped. She expected an evil entity not a friendly shadow.

"Hi?" Oscar managed to say. Ebony blinked rapidly. She couldn't muster a single word.

"Sorry about all the tendrily bits." Death gestured to his form and apologised. "I'm not exactly a being on my own, rather a creature comprised of the souls of the dead," he explained. "Sounds morbid I know but it's not too bad. Dave!" he yelled, slapping a tendril that weaved its way around the light, "I know you're from the 1600s but stop playing with the lights. They're not that exciting." Ebony stared as the lights settled. Atlas' face went red, and he looked like he was about to explode with fury.

"I–" Ebony started, but Death noticed the dead bodies in the room and clicked his fingers at his reapers.

"What are these dead bodies doing here?"

Oscar couldn't help himself. "Not much." Death finger-gunned Oscar's jest and Atlas flew off the rails as the reapers moved to clean the mess.

"Death. I am Atlas Sinclair. I control you now and I command you to kill these insolent mortals and restore the lives of Belphegor and Adremelech," he ordered. Death practically spat in his face laughing, and it smacked such a look of shock across Atlas' face that Ebony instantly warmed to Death, something she didn't think she'd ever do. But the day was a day of firsts, and liking Death was the next first to be crossed off her list.

"Atlas! My man, long-time no see. You used to give me a hell of a hard job with the daily planetary massacres. The number of souls I had to process; I tell you…" He looked to Ebony and Oscar and sighed with deep disappointment. "And where did the fancy surname come from? Demons don't have surnames."

Atlas huffed. "I needed one to sign up for Congo delivery."

"Well, Atlas *Sinclair*, get back in your bone throne and calm down." Death rolled his eyes. "Let's all take a deep breath. I feel some tension in the room that needs to be worked through." A chaise lounge manifested beneath him, built from the souls that crowded his form, and he draped himself across it. "Ebony. Begin by expressing your feelings. How do you feel towards Atlas?" Both Ebony and Atlas stared at him.

"Therapy? Really?"

"Hush hush. It only works if you immerse yourself." Death gestured for her to speak.

"I think you need to dislodge your head from your ass and stop wearing it as a hat."

Atlas cried out. "Death, she's disrespecting me."

"Tell her that."

"But—"

"--Uh, uh." Death waved a hand. "You need to learn to communicate with each other."

Atlas, who wasn't used to being told what to do, scowled at Ebony. "I feel like you're disrespecting me."

"I'll stop disrespecting you once you stop disrespecting every human in existence."

"Death, how is this fair? She's asking too much."

"Too much?"

Death leant forward. "Keep going. This is good. It's going well...Maybe... Is this good?" he looked to one of his reapers who shrugged. Oscar avoided eye contact.

"You cannot touch my body without my consent, and I don't give consent for you to shove a demon inside me," Ebony said.

"Oooh, that's a good point," Death said.

"Nothing would physically touch you," Atlas sassed, "he would just take over your mind and soul."

"Another good point. The scoreboard's looking even," Death commentated.

"Scoreboard?" Ebony scowled. "Seriously Death?" She had run out of patience. "If I destroy this key, can you get out of the box?" Death straightened up. He glided to her.

"Alright Ebony-zer Scrooge. You're no fun."

"Death."

"I could theoretically," he said, "but then Atlas wouldn't have it."

"I don't want him to have it."

"I know." Death's form shimmered. "I don't need the key to escape but—" Ebony interrupted him.

"--Then it's settled," she said and raising her arm, she threw the key as hard as she could and it shot like a bullet into the lava, melting within seconds. Atlas acted as though she'd destroyed a part of him. He grabbed his chest and he shrieked. It was an unbearably painful noise and Ebony was forced to her knees, burying her head in her lap. Oscar's actions were similar, but Death didn't falter. He sighed and shook his head. As everyone panicked, he floated over the lava and absorbed the magical entrails left behind by the key. Then he clicked his fingers and Atlas' scream was cut off as Death squeezed his voice box.

"Atlas, you're a grown man and you're having a tantrum. Give it a rest." Atlas, without turning, returned to his seat, the eery soundlessness of his glide scaring Ebony as his eyes never left hers. Death turned to Ebony. He sounded disappointed. "Perhaps this makes things easier. Reapers, take them away somewhere they can't interrupt us."

"Atlas has a dungeon," a reaper said.

"You have a dungeon?" Death cocked his head. "What kind of kinky shi...? Never mind. Take them to the dungeon. I'm going to have an adult conversation with Atlas." Ebony and Oscar protested, as this time the reapers listened to their orders. They didn't have to touch Ebony and Oscar to remove them from the chamber; the both of them were forced to walk as the scythes created a sharp cage around them, threatening to spill blood at every turn. Ebony looked over her shoulder.

"Please Death, don't help him," she tried one final time. Atlas grinned at her and waved goodbye through his wiggling fingers. Death looked away. The reapers kept walking and they were escorted from the room, leaving Death and Atlas alone to speak.

"Well, this is a nice change in scenery," Oscar said. As far as dungeons went, this one was clearly one of the worst. The grungy walls of the cell ran with muck and the floor teemed with Ireos' version of rats; mutated six legged rodents, scurrying alongside excrement and bones.

"We're in a prison cell."

"Sarcasm, Ebony. Sarcasm." Oscar folded his arms. "I can hardly see it." His eye was a messy artwork of deep purple and black bruising. He rested his back against the cobbled wall and Ebony clung to the iron bars, rattling them. They wouldn't budge.

"We're doomed," Ebony said pessimistically, "we are actually doomed. Death's going to let Atlas do what he wants because he's Death. The actual Death. More dead people the better, right?" She wiped her face, smearing the little makeup she had retained down her cheeks. Mascara ran like claw marks from her eyes, and she could have sworn she'd grown wrinkles in less than a day from the amount of frowning she'd done. Oscar was in a similar state; bent over awkwardly where Daegel's boot had smashed into his ribs no less than twenty times. Ebony was just glad to see none poking from his body.

"We'll get out of here," he said confidently. Although they were stuck in a dungeon, they had done more than they'd set out to do. They'd destroyed the key Atlas needed and stopped his plan. Whilst they weren't out of the woods yet, Oscar was proud of the little they'd achieved.

From the end of the corridor there was a clanging rattle of keys and a woman appeared, carrying the box Death was in. When she saw Ebony she stopped and stared in shock, until Ebony felt remarkably discomfited. The woman didn't speak for a moment but even from a distance, Ebony could have sworn she wiped away a tear before she approached them.

"Ebony? How are you?" she asked. Oscar took offence at not being asked and Ebony didn't reply, staring in disdain. The woman sighed inwardly. "My name is Joplin. I've come to tell you that you're free to go." Oscar stood as Ebony erred on the side of caution.

"Why?" she asked, glaring suspiciously at Joplin. She was convinced she'd seen her somewhere before.

"Death has negotiated a deal with my husband, you are free." Ebony gasped.

"You're married to that monster?"

"I am."

"I'm sorry," Oscar said inaudibly. She stared at him scornfully but continued to open the cell.

Joplin was elegant, wearing an old-fashioned dress which made her look stately, nearly royal. But she looked afflicted, with sunken eyes that gave her a permanent morose look and Ebony was convinced the marriage couldn't be a happy one.

"What's the deal?" they asked, as she led them through a maze of corridors until light finally broke into the fortress and they weren't walking in toxic squalor. "Atlas didn't just agree to let us go."

"An unbreakable deal," Joplin said, ensuring they understood that it wouldn't be changed. Ebony scowled but Oscar patted her shoulder. "Here." Joplin cracked open the box and Death slithered out.

"Hello again," he said.

Ebony and Oscar said, "hi," but acting as though it was ordinary for them to be talking to Death felt peculiar.

Death continued from where Joplin left off. "Lava can't destroy magic, it can only destroy what it's held in," he said, and Ebony cut him off.

"What's with all these rules?" she complained. "Ancients can only be killed by special means; magic can't be destroyed in lava."

"I don't know, I don't make them," he said, although he probably could if he wanted to. "I salvaged the magic from the key, and I've given it to Atlas who now has to go through the trouble of trying to make a new identical one for Sonneillon's box. I have also agreed to revive the bodies of Belphegor and Adremelech as and when he needs, in return for your immediate freedom. However, how Atlas plans on reviving Sonneillon is up to him, whether it involves you or not. I also told him to explore all possible avenues of therapy and counselling because I think he needs help."

"Great," Oscar said sarcastically, as his confidence in the success of his and Ebony's mission plummeted. "So, all we get from this is a little freedom before Atlas inevitably captures Ebony and brings her back here?" They had now reached the entrance of the fortress and stood looking over the beach.

"Those were my terms," Death said.

"But why?" Ebony asked. "You can see Atlas' evil intent. Can't you just, you know…" Ebony ran her finger along her throat. Joplin didn't look too displeased.

"My dear-" Death floated to her level, "-I don't choose when to take people from this existence. Everyone dies eventually, so why take them before time has run its course? That on my part would upset the natural balance of the universe, as would interfering for the sake of good versus evil. I'm not the insidious creature myth and legend make me out to be. I simply maintain balance, guide you from one state of being to another and do couples therapy as a hobby."

"So, your helping Atlas is 'maintaining balance?'" Ebony air quoted. "Don't you care that he could destroy the universe?"

Death sighed. "It is not my place to do more than I have already done. I'll see you again Ebony. Oscar." Death bowed his head and floated back into the box, which Joplin shut behind him. She then released the two sealed locks which didn't need a key to be reopened, and a surge of energy burst into the sky, disappearing in a flamboyant flare of fireworks. Death had style, but Ebony didn't know how well meant his goodbye was. She was left infuriated, and Oscar looked like a deer in headlights in his state of bewilderment.

Joplin kept them for a moment longer. "You have time," she said. "Time to work out how to stop him if it's what you want to do. Death may not be able to intervene, but you can." Ebony was confused about the change of heart. Joplin leant in close as if not wanting to be heard. "You know how Atlas fell from power? He was banished by an Enchanted. Their magic is strong enough to subdue him. Learn how to use yours and you can do the same," she advised.

"My magic?" Ebony scoffed. "I'll do the jokes."

"Why do you care what happens to her?" Oscar asked. He could see in Joplin parts of Ebony, similar eyes and the same forlorn smile and it spooked him. Joplin neglected to answer.

"Be careful with Atlas," She instead said. Ebony at this point, was not convinced of anyone on the island's sanity.

"Well——" Ebony didn't have much she could say, "-thank you?"

"You're most welcome. Ships are stored in the bottom of the volcano; take which ever one you want," Joplin offered. "Goodbye Oscar. Goodbye Ebony." She bid them farewell and rushed away without looking back, heels making an irritating high-pitched click against the stone until she was out of ear shot.

Oscar's arms were outstretched as he pursed his lips in confusion and Ebony's mind was scattered. Leaving Atlas, Daegel, Death and Joplin behind, they descended the volcano, taking the floating gondola ski lift used by the guards. One of them climbed in behind and Ebony and Oscar were convinced they were done for. But the guard peered at them with distain, muttering under his breath, and under Death and Atlas' direct order, was forced to leave them alone.

Even as they reached the bottom of the volcano and climbed into a ship, Ebony and Oscar still didn't feel free. Atlas was expected to appear at any moment to seize Ebony and it was only as the ship took off and Atlas' guards scowled as they could do nothing but watch, did they understand. For the time being at least, they were truly free to leave Ireos.

Words couldn't describe the look Oscar gave the warp patrol officer as they drove through the portal. He looked surprised that they'd survived and hoped a compliment on the avant-garde ship design would get him off the hook. Ebony barely noticed as Oscar socked him around the face and demanded back Ebony's bribe and a hundred coin on top of it. Then, he thanked the man on the compliment. It was a smart ship, even nicer than his original, he thought, although his memorabilia would be sorely missed.

"I didn't think we were getting out alive." Ebony spoke aloud the thought running through her head. She let her body slack in a deluxe and opulent leather passenger seat, watching cautiously for any spacecrafts following them. There were none, although Ebony had taken fright at a cargo ship flying above them.

Oscar drove. His face was fresh and clean although enflamed and by the way he was hunched, both him and Ebony predicted he had at best two broken ribs.

"Me neither," Oscar agreed. Ebony's eyes filled with guilt. She never wanted him to feel so unsafe.

"I'm sorry Oscar-" her lip quivered, "-for everything that happened to you. I shouldn't have made you come with me." Oscar stared at her with his one good eye and surprised her with a surely chuckle.

"In my recollection I chose to come with you," he said. "Don't apologise." The furrowed brow and uneasy fidgeting didn't subside, despite Oscar's forgiveness. "You still look worried," he commented. "Penny for your thoughts?" He held up his band. Ebony tapped hers against his and he transferred her back the lost money.

"This is a world of science," she said as they locked wrists. "Look how far we've come. We can create almost anything, we've discovered nearly everything, there's basically nothing we don't know." She paused for a deep and calming breath. "The one thing that has never been discovered is magic-" she crossed her arms over her knees and rested her head on her hands, "-and suddenly it's existed since the dawn of time? Death's an actual being, and we're facing a demon who's trying to revive an even worse demon who is going to rebuild the universe with two other demons and thrust humanity into the realms of extinction…"

"…And we have no way to stop it."

"Exactly," she said. "Being told by a psychopath that I'm magical when I can barely function as a normal human being these days -" Ebony laughed joylessly, "-that's a lot to take in."

"So, you don't believe him? You don't believe in magic?"

"I don't know. Do you?"

Oscar shrugged and winced at the effect the movement had on his body. "I can't explain anything we've been through with science. So, I think I might." He drummed on his knees unsurely as he mused.

Ebony tried to rationalise what she'd seen but couldn't explain what had happened either. "I think I do," she realised, and then shook her head as though trying to prevent herself from succumbing to some deluded propaganda. But deep down, she believed it.

"Atlas said you had dormant power," Oscar reminded her. "It's what saved you."

"Which is a step too far," Ebony said firmly. "Magic I can try to believe in. I like the idea of magic existing, despite its lack of cohesion to science. But being magical myself? It's crazy." Ebony despised the idea. To think she was accursed with some cryptic powers was detested.

"If I've learnt anything from this mental little escapade of ours, it's that you can handle it," Oscar praised. Tears suddenly brimmed Ebony's eyes as she hugged her shoulders.

"I don't think I can," she said numbly. Oscar's heart smashed into pieces looking at the broken shell of her former self that Ebony had become. He had never been good at consolation. He relied heavily on Stella, but she was lightyears away. Locking eyes with Ebony, he reassured her to the best of his abilities.

"You might not be able to deal with it," he said, "but you'll never have to deal with it alone."

Chapter 11

Twenty-one Drognir days had passed since Ebony and Oscar returned from Ignis. They hadn't seen Cordelia or Coraline but were receiving constant updates in regard to Cordelia's foot. By all accounts it was in a better condition, although she'd paid the price with a noticeable limp and significant lack of toes and heel. But it was nothing that couldn't be fixed with a sprinkling of anthro-scientific machinery, and within five days of the incident she had received a brand-new set of high-quality neuro-stimulated prosthetic toes and a skin graft that made the heel look untouched.

When Oscar and Ebony had first arrived home, Caleb and Stella were the first to greet them in a flurry of weeping and worry. The ship's destruction had prevented all contact and the worst was feared from both of them. The two of them had been unsuccessful in getting the Roamers to listen and although he tried to hide it, it was obvious Caleb was most upset about losing Stinger, which had never even got to be tested.

Ebony was devoid of sleep and in a constant trance-like state from extreme mental exertion. Over the three weeks, she tried to solve the questions that desperately demanded answers. In frantic attempts to either prove everything on Ignis had a logical scientific explanation, or to expose the magic she supposedly had, she had overdosed on coffee more than once. But with every dramatic flourish of her hand, or yell at an inanimate object to move, she felt progressively stupider and eventually stopped. No progress was made except for the degradation of the function of her own brain.

To help Ebony focus, there was a bench that she liked to sit on halfway through her morning run where she would clear her mind. Esso was under the impression she ran for an hour every day. He was proud of her for that.

She didn't.

She ran for thirty minutes.

The other thirty were spent on that bench, where the sun rose directly between two skyscrapers and cast its glow in a thin line as Chane woke up. The bench's memory bank held a mould of everyone who had sat on it recently and Ebony sunk deeply into the comfort of her own. But today, as the sunlight rose past her knees, her productive sitting was cut short by a call from Esso.

"Ebony." She groaned as the familiar aches of her body stimulated themselves when she stood. When her daydreams were better than reality, she hated to leave them behind, and clasped her water bottle as though clinging on to the memories. Her reluctance to move was immovable.

"What?" she burbled.

"I have told Transtar that you are going in to work today."

"Essoooooooo." Ebony's groggy eyes stared at his hologram accusingly. "I swear, I'll deactivate you."

"Ebony. With respect, you wouldn't know how," he said. "Transtar has requested you study the biological implications of plants on Egoran, and you've put it off five times already."

"But I'm ill." Ebony faked a cough.

"That was excuse one and four. Excuse two was a distant cousin's wedding, three was your car was stolen and five was that family came to visit," Esso listed. "Now, considering Transtar knows you're an orphan and you have a ship, not a car, their patience is wearing thin." Ebony felt a familiar sense of dread rise in her stomach.

"I don't want to," she cried. "I want to sit on Drognir and live a normal, boring life." She stretched until she heard a satisfying click in her back. If Esso could show it, he would be repulsed.

"I understand, Ebony. Fear is a strong emotion, but you cannot afford to remain here because of an accident," he explained. Ebony shuddered, if only she could tell him that the storm on Ireos wasn't an accident.

"You're sending me to my death."

Esso thought she was being sarcastic. "Then die," he replied. She groaned loudly and bystanders stared.

Ebony reluctantly hurried home and collected her things when she received what was the first and only good news of the day. Transtar had assigned Oscar, Caleb, and Stella as her colleagues for the trip which Esso adamantly denied any involvement in, and she met them with a wide smile by the interstellar terminal station. Watching as rockets shot into the sky in rapid succession, they headed on to the not-so exciting workers' flight depot, where the less luxurious ships awaited them.

"You excited for today?" Stella asked. Ebony's glum frown spoke volumes.

"It'll be great," Oscar said, in a lively spirit considering his bandaged body. "Egoran has some of the most diverse biological life in the Alpha quadrant. Not to mention the pyramids."

"Are you even going to be able to see it?" Caleb prodded fun at Oscars bruised eye.

"Are you?" He tapped Caleb's arm and his cyber eye powered down. Caleb muttered something about mocking the disabled and Oscar laughed.

On the overhead speakers, the universally used female robot voice made an announcement. "Last call for the 10.15a.m flight to Egoran."

They rushed for the flight, jumping on board as the doors slammed with a tight oxygen seal. The working-class transport for short interplanetary commutes were ships modelled on retro trains; carriage after carriage of seating, with fluorescent lights lining the floor and a ceiling made completely from glass, so passengers could enjoy the view. Egoran was a mere hour away.

"Ebony," Caleb whispered to her as they flew. "How are things going with the whole magical situation?" Ebony held up a solitary finger.

"We're not talking about it," she said firmly.

"Okay. But if you want to talk, I'm here to listen, or give advice, or whatever you need."

Ebony smiled but repeated herself. "We're not talking about it. I need a day off." Caleb nodded and settled back into his seat. He would ask again tomorrow.

"Ladies, gentlemen, robots and all, we have reached our destination of Egoran, please disembark in an orderly fashion and enjoy your stay," the scratchy female voice announced.

The group left the ship. Caleb hotfooted it through the station and kicked his sandals off, wiggling his toes in the warm sand as the others caught up. It was baking hot and even walking ten minutes to the pyramid itself was set to be tiring.

"This place is stunning," Ebony admitted. Directly before them sat two mountainous, trilateral pyramids and the remains of an ancient town, mostly eroded but with pillars and statues standing proudly. The town itself was never there and the remains were old when they were built to add to the longevous style of the area. Towards midday, the sun was positioned directly between the pyramid tops and tourists flocked to take pictures before they moved on to why most tourists came to the famous holiday destination.

The immediate land around the station was filled with an extensive and futuristic bazaar within the compound of an Arabian town, selling exotic and rare treasures which attracted many. But in the far distance was the main attraction. Oases of all shapes and sizes could be seen and where the oases sat, holiday resorts and tourism companies followed. After all, nature was much scarcer than it had been when the pyramids were first built. Trams chugged tirelessly back and forth from the oases, carrying both humans and their holographic counterparts and Ebony, Stella, Oscar, and Caleb were the only ones left from their flight as they walked through the market.

The locals were easily differentiated from the tourists. Egoran had a low oxygen count which after months of living with could cause damage to the human body. Thus, the locals adorned oxygen masks which were fashion statements amongst the community. Some had flowers blooming from the exhalation valve, others hung charms across the straps, and some were covered in a mess of stickers.

"See, aren't you glad you came now?" Stella said knowingly, as she admired a silk scarf with a fitted oxygen tube. It complimented her tanned skin but then again, Stella had an unrivalled attractiveness about her and could pull off anything. The scarf accentuated her sharp jawline and swanlike neck as she flaunted it to Ebony who nodded in approval.

"I am," Ebony admitted. Stella punched the air triumphantly.

"Knew you would be, darling."

"This place is huge," Caleb commented, peering through a pair of sunglasses which complimented his now platinum hair. He tossed a coin to the seller and set the glasses on his head, using them for more of an accessory than an aid to his eyesight. His cyber eye naturally shaded the sun for him. He squinted the other, giving him a woolly expression.

Ebony admired a stall of exotic birds that squawked in force fielded cages, and then let her nose lead her to a stall of Egoranian's speciality cuisine.

Birds.

Oscar was staring, mouth hanging loosely, and Ebony jokingly poked his chin as she wandered past. He shut his mouth and blushed.

"This is amazing." He couldn't hide his excitement. "Pyramids were known by the original humans as a wonder of the world, before being destroyed in the 2087 great climate disaster. But these are some of the most accurate replicas ever built." He gave them a history lesson as they walked. "Sucks that we can't see the originals though."

"But if the climate disaster hadn't happened, humans wouldn't have fled Earth and we'd all be trapped on one planet," Stella said, "and that would be boring."

"We would have left eventually," Caleb said. "Imagine living your whole life on one planet. I couldn't do it."

"Me neither," Oscar agreed. They took time to browse through the bazaar, awash with overwhelming colours, textures, and smells, before heading towards the closest pyramid, gaining access through a cramped, dark tunnel. It wasn't so admirable as the view outside but was much cooler, which was welcome.

"Why is it so dark in here?" Stella queried and received a rude reply from the receptionist sitting in the darkness behind a desk.

"Cuz they hadn't invented lights when the original pyramids were made," she answered curtly, mouth forming into a wry smile. Stella reddened and clenched her fist.

"We knew what you meant," Oscar muttered under his breath.

"Hi, we're here for a tour, we're from Transtar," Ebony introduced, trying to avoid a confrontation. The woman revealed several torches stacked in a drawer.

"Take one each, follow the signs, don't get lost, I have plenty of other customers to serve and don't have time to find you." The receptionist clearly wanted to be in the oasis like the other imaginary customers queuing out the door.

"Cheers love," Caleb said, and she gritted her teeth, displeased at the way he addressed her. Caleb curtseyed and wandered away.

"Thanks," Ebony said. She smiled at the girl, but she already had a hologram magazine floating in front of her and clearly didn't want to be disturbed further.

"Right then." Oscar rubbed his hands together eagerly as he handed out torches; light orbs that could be attached to the bands. "Let's go." He was earnest to get started.

Heading through tunnel after tunnel, they explored where old booby traps once caught anyone who dared enter and where mummified remains lay in grand sarcophagi. They weren't the remains of glorified pharaohs; however, they were the remains of the architects who created the pyramids. Oscar opened the backpack he was wearing and pulled out a collection of assorted test tubes and swabs, deciding to complete the task they were sent to do. Carnivorous weeds champed at his fingers as he yanked them, roots, and all, from the ground.

"They replicated all of the traps too," Stella read from the brochure, projected on the wall from her band. "I wonder how they disarmed them all. It must have taken forever." Working in dark, damp conditions, where the warm comfort of sunlight couldn't reach them for possibly days on end, Stella shivered at the idea. She couldn't do it. In a flash Oscar grabbed her and she shrieked, lashing out.

"What if they're still active? Ready to strike you down?" he joked, and she pushed him off, grumpily.

"They wouldn't let people in here if it was dangerous," she argued.

"Eh, historically speaking there could be upwards of a million traps in here, it's doubtful all have been deactivated," Caleb added.

"They're messing with you," Ebony said. "Ignore them. I do." Oscar grabbed his equipment and they continued but Stella paused a step behind the others.

"You all right?" Ebony asked, worried they'd said to much.

"Shoelace," Stella wiggled her foot. "I'll catch up." Ebony left her as she leant on one knee and quickly tied her laces. But, as she stood, she tripped on the uneven floor and reached out for the wall to steady herself. It made a huge groaning noise like she had set off some clockwork behind it, before the brick she'd touched collapsed under her hand. She shrieked, pulse racing but it was too late to stop the process in motion. The wall clicked and caused the ground to rumble, throwing the four to the ground as rocks bounced around.

"What's happening?" Ebony cried, protecting her head in case anything fell.

"I think it's caving in?" Caleb pulled his rucksack over his head.

"I touched something; I don't know what's going on," Stella cried as she held her glasses to her face. Suddenly, the wall she'd hit revealed another one which smoothly glided forward, as though its mechanics were brand new and the passageway was sealed off.

"No!" Stella exclaimed. She wanted to pound on the wall to see if it would give way, but she was too scared to in the event of another mechanism activating. Behind her was the exit, and she had trapped Ebony, Caleb, Oscar, and an unknown number of tourists on the other side.

"Guys, can you hear me? Are you okay?" Stella called frantically. It took a moment before she heard a muffled reply.

"We're fine," Ebony called, helping Caleb to his feet. Oscar wiped the dust from his shorts and did such a big eye-roll that Ebony was sure his pupils had gone to the back of his head.

"Wonderful," Oscar said. He was being sarcastic but wasn't unnerved. In fact, he was quite fascinated by the wall, stroking his fingers against it like it was some majestic creature. Caleb's chest was rapidly rising and falling; he was claustrophobic, and the darkness made the hallways so much smaller than they were. He pulled at his fingers anxiously.

"We'll be all right Caleb," Ebony reassured him. But she tapped at her chest where her necklace once lay, and her stomach knotted with the idea that Atlas could be behind the moving wall. She had been raised on the belief that everything happened for a reason and coincidences didn't exist. She was worried.

"Pyramids were always built with several exits, we've just got to follow the path," Oscar told them. "Don't worry about it." He was casually optimistic that they hadn't just been doomed to die, and Stella took a leaf out of his book.

"I'll notify... someone," Stella called, not wanting to talk to the woman they'd left behind, "and I'll meet you at the next exit." Ebony listened as her footsteps faded away and deciding it best to search for another exit rather than rely on the woman at reception, they headed deeper into the labyrinthine tunnels.

"Ebony, I think we are well and truly lost," decided Caleb, shining his torch across the floor. No wall was unique enough to serve as a landmark capable of guiding them in a definite direction. They had left the clearly marked areas and were following a sketchy map Oscar had drawn up. He wasn't too happy either.

"I'm hungry and tired and my feet hurt," he complained.

"You'll be a lot more than hungry if we don't get out of here," warned Ebony.

"Or maybe I'll have to eat you," Oscar laughed, grabbing her. She couldn't see him well in the dark but pulled away from him as she felt a sharp pain in her hand.

"Did you actually just bite me?" she asked in bewilderment.

"Of course not." Caleb shone the torch towards them. Ebony let out a disgusted noise as a yellow bellied spider scurried across her shoe.

"That was gross."

"Don't worry," Caleb said, "they aren't venomous." He walked over to where it sat, waving its front feet in the air threateningly and he stamped on it, squashing it under his sandal. But the tile sunk straight into the floor and opened a trapdoor right beneath Oscar. He yelped as he fell through the stone hatch, and something yelped as he fell on top of it.

"Did you not learn from Stella to not touch anything?" Ebony cried, close to tearing at her hair. Springing down to Oscar, Caleb followed shamefacedly.

"Sorry Oscar."

"No worries," Oscar said. "Someone broke my fall." He shone the torch around and jumped in shock as it outlined a silhouette.

"Hello?" Ebony asked and steam came from Caleb's ears.

"Hello? How about hell no. You do not yell 'hello' in a horror film," he scolded. Ebony rolled her eyes.

"We are not in a horror film. We're in a dark corridor," she said, "and I didn't yell, I asked. Civilly." Oscar raised the torch slightly to reveal polished black shoes and frilly socks.

"Not in a horror film huh?" Caleb raised an eyebrow. Oscar walked forward and the torch fully exposed a little girl standing a couple of metres away. Caleb tapped his cybernetic pupil, a gesture that always made Ebony and Oscar squirm. "Are you seeing her?"

"Of course," Ebony said. The girl had curly, golden locks and bright, blue eyes but they were eerily expressionless. There was a haunting uncanny valley about her. She smiled at them, but her eyes remained in the same chilling state. She wore a dress with a satin, Saxe bow tied round her waist comparable to a porcelain doll. Oscar bent down and slowly moved towards the little girl so as to not scare her.

"Hi sweetie," he said. "I'm so sorry I fell on you, are you all right?" She nodded her head eagerly and Oscar felt a weight lift from his chest.

"Are you here alone?" Caleb asked her. She didn't react.

"What's your name?" Ebony asked.

"043-2," she replied. Ebony cocked her head.

"Did she understand you?" Oscar asked. "That's not a name."

"Thanks captain obvious," she said. "I think she's concussed." Ebony knelt down and opened her backpack to look for a first aid kit. The sudden responsibility of looking after a child distracted her from the intrusive thoughts rattling at the back of her mind.

"Where are your parents?" Caleb asked, continuing the interrogation.

"I don't have parents," 043-2 replied.

"Ebony, I don't like this. We find a random girl walking around under a pyramid. This doesn't just happen," Caleb fretted. Back when Caleb had a summer off to recover from his cybernetic operations, he had watched many a horror film. Several, mainly ones where a little girl was present in an ominous hallway, were causing him to worry in the present moment.

"Relax, it's a lost little girl. The spider is more harm to us than her." Ebony brushed off his concern and Caleb turned for more questioning.

"Where are you from?" Caleb asked. "Maybe we can take you home?"

"I'm from Ignis, Ireos."

"So we're not taking you home then."

Ebony's back straightened as she unzipped the med kit in her bag. A small knife was inside for emergencies, and this was definitely one.

"I was made by Atlas." 043-2 smiled sweetly as Ebony nudged

Oscar's arm and tugged him with her. She swung the rucksack over her shoulder. The knife was in her hand. The three of them backed away.

"This is not great," captain obvious Caleb said.

"It's been less than a month," Ebony said. "Three weeks and he's already after us."

Oscar shared Ebony's concern. "Where is he now?" he questioned the girl. 043-2 took several steps forward and the three of them took several back to compensate, watching her in trepidation.

"He is waiting outside for Ebony."

"I thought he couldn't leave Ireos?" Ebony panicked.

"Deaths doing?" Oscar shrugged.

"Then why hasn't he come in here himself?" Ebony asked her, "and where's Daegel?"

"Atlas is saving his power to bring back Sonneillon and Daegel wants you dead. Atlas wants you alive."

"Well, that's good news at least," Caleb said.

"So, he sent me." 043-2 reached behind her back and pulled out a jagged knife.

"Where was she keeping that?"

"Caleb, shush," Ebony said. Caleb talked too much when he was nervous.

"I don't know about you guys, but I think we've overstayed our welcome here," Oscar said. He stared at them, arching his eyebrows and inclined his head down the corridor away from her.

"We can take on a little girl, can't we?" Caleb said. 043-2 haphazardly leapt forward, waving the knife threateningly at Caleb's face. He shot backwards. "Right. Got the message."

They ran.

043-2's footsteps pattered behind them, keeping up easily. Ebony turned to Caleb who matched her pace.

"On a scale of one to ten, how bad do you think—"

"--a hundred."

"You don't even know what I was going to say."

"I don't need to know. It's all a hundred. Everything's gone to shit."

"Stella went to the entrance to get help," Oscar suddenly said, "which means she's played right into Atlas' hands. Is he going to hurt her?" He flashed the torch at Ebony who had gone a shade of white and then to Caleb, and it wasn't unreasonable to say that, for the first time in his life, he was speechless.

"I don't know," Ebony admitted, although she presumed if Stella had run into Atlas, he wouldn't let her go free. They kept running blindly down corridors, unable to tell if they were going in circles, until the footsteps behind them subsided.

"Do you think she's gone?" Ebony asked, hands on her knees.

"I don't think she'd give up," Oscar cautioned.

"Why are you running away?" The dead voice of 043-2 echoed and Ebony reluctantly unbent, and they kept running. "I want to play a game."

"This *is* some horror movie shit." Caleb knew it. "Go away!" he yelled. "We don't want to play." He tried to deter her, but she was an obstinate child.

As they ran, they reached a widened passage. The walls were striated with holes and as they sprinted through it was as though their presence triggered a reaction from the pyramid.

"Watch out!" Ebony ducked as darts began firing from the wall, soaring in every direction, and lodging themselves in whatever they could find. All but one missed, and Oscar yelled as he was shot in the back of the neck, the dart lodging itself under his skin. 043-2 was being belaboured by the darts; she may have been fast, but she certainly wasn't agile, and it gave the others a chance to rush into a room and hide.

The room held a sarcophagus of nearly pure gold, with more jewels than imaginable piled high and grand tapestries strung from the ceiling. Mummified animals littered the room along with other Egoran sacrifices and as Ebony presumed, it was a pretty important person lying in the centre of the room. For the right price, anyone could be in the pyramid.

"Ow, ow, owwwww," whined Oscar as he tore the dart from his skin. Welts swelled up on his neck instantly, his peachy pores filling with a pussy shade of green.

"I think it's some ancient type of poison, maybe…" Ebony couldn't finish. Caleb put his finger to his lips, and they concealed themselves behind the tapestry as 043-2 scuttled past the doorway, trying to find them.

"You want to play hide and seek?" she called, her voice sending shivers up Ebony's spine. "I want to play hide and seek too." She clapped enthusiastically. Suddenly, her head appeared round the corner of the room, and she stood, occluding their exit with her hands splayed, ready to catch them if they tried to escape. The onslaught of darts had not been kind, but despite the swelling, 043-2 wasn't particularly bothered.

"You hide and I'll seek," she gleamed and in a high pitched, raspy voice, she began to count. "Six."

"Six? Nobody starts a countdown for hide and seek at six!"

"Five."

"Do you really want to argue with her?"

"Four."

"Not really."

"Three."

"By the way, if we die, our entire afterlives will be spent by me reminding you what an absolutely awful idea it was coming here."

"Two."

"That's fair."

"One."

"I don't want to know what happens when she reaches zero."

"Zero."

There was no sudden movement, no yell or war cry.

Oscar peered out from behind a pile of jewels. "I can't see, pass me a torch." His had been dropped and smashed whilst running and he was walking like a mummy, arms outstretched to find the two of them.

"Don't turn it on," Ebony quietly warned. They wrestled silently over her torch for a moment before it slipped from the clasp attaching it to her band and rolled across the stone floor.

"Well done," Caleb groaned in exasperation. He expected 043-2 to jump scare them; the best horror films waited until the unsuspecting protagonist felt safe, but it was still silent.

"I think she's gone," Ebony said. They slowly emerged from their hiding spaces, taking the greatest care not to make any unnecessary noise. "Where is the torch?" In a normal situation, Caleb's cyber eye would be able to see in the dark, it's how he saved hundreds in electricity bills, but he kept it closed in fear 043-2 would see its glow. He hurried over to Ebony and Oscar but as he did so, he slipped over the exact thing they were searching for.

"I've got it." Caleb grabbed the orb. "Shall I turn it on?"

"Yeah, I think she's gone," Ebony said. Caleb opened his eye cautiously. After bashing the torch against his hand for a moment, it flickered on like it was also worried to reveal their location.

"Got it," Caleb said victoriously. He shone it around the room and saw the figure of 043-2 crawling, like a tiger hunting its pray, towards Ebony.

"Ebony!" 043-2 pounced forward, hands out and aiming for Ebony's throat but Caleb got to her first, dragging her to the side and behind a sarcophagus.

"Whack her," Ebony cried as Caleb brandished the torch.

"It's a little girl."

"I don't care."

"Seriously?" As 043-2 prepared for another attack, Caleb sprung at her, using the sarcophagus to launch himself upwards into an air strike. With a battle yell he smashed 043-2's head with the torch and she barrelled face first into the corner of the room.

"You know, I thought that would do more," Ebony said. 043-2 wasn't crying like a normal child would. Instead, her eyes grew dark with anger, and she held her head as blood trickled through her fingers, staining the pretty white lace on her dress. Her blonde hair matted crimson with the blood, and she stared demonically at Caleb. He gulped.

"Let's go," Oscar suggested. Caleb flashed his torch to lead the way and they sprinted back through the passageway, but it was quickly evident something wasn't right. The hallway they were sure they'd come from was closed off.

"You've got to be joking," Ebony said. She didn't want to die under a pyramid as much as the next person.

"Great," Oscar said. "Now we're trapped with little miss 'let's kill everyone'. Brilliant." The pain he was in made him hugely agitated. His hand came away from the back of his neck with an unhealthy amount of puss stuck to it, which he quickly wiped away to avoid a fuss. The room span slightly, and spots dotted his peripheral as he was overcome with queasiness.

"Now what?" Caleb asked, keeping a slight distance from Oscar, who looked like he'd contracted all the symptoms of the plague at once.

"I found you." 043-2 advanced on them, swaying unsteadily at her head injury. "Atlas is going to be so proud of-"

Bang.

Ebony's toes curled and she looked away. Caleb nearly threw up then decided he was okay. But he wasn't and vomited liberally in the corner. Then the bilious sensation passed, and he sneaked a glance but was instantly sick again. Oscar screwed his eyes tightly shut, then covered them with his hands and faced the opposite direction to make triple sure he didn't see.

As Atlas' devil child prowled towards them, she had trodden on a loose brick, much like Caleb had. But this brick didn't open a trap door and instead had caused a wall to slam across the hallway again. And the enormous crunch signalled that 043-2 hadn't got out of the way in time. When any of them had the courage to look, all they saw was a heap of human mush on the floor.

"Eww."

"That was the most disgusting thing I think I've ever seen," Ebony said, thankful that 043-2 was gone, although she couldn't shake the guilt of their actions. After all, it was the life of a little girl that had been lost.

"That's rank," Caleb commented.

"So how do we get out of here? Do a little tap dance, hope the same thing doesn't happen?" Oscar asked.

"Yep," Ebony said. Caleb glanced quickly at the pile of remains. His cheeks bulged. He didn't want to end up like that but the prospect of being left to rot beneath a pyramid was less than thrilling.

They prodded at the walls, looking for a loose stone or crumbling block. Eventually they did find one and the walls moved. But it was not in the direction they wanted. The insufferable sound of scraping brick along brick set Ebony's teeth on edge as two parallel walls began to travel towards each other and the three of them fled to the centre of the room.

"We'll be crushed," wailed Caleb. His eye scouted for a way out, but it didn't pick up anything. He could see freedom on the other side of the wall, but not how to get to it. The cogs behind the walls were too complex for the short time he had to decipher them.

"You've experienced worse," Ebony told herself. She looked around. The walls travelled slowly and she still had time to think. "Think rationally."

Caleb and Oscar frantically stomped on the floor and whacked the walls. Ebony blinked harshly.

"Guys give me a boost up," she demanded. "It might be in the ceiling." She grasped their shoulders firmly as Oscar and Caleb put their hands out. She used each one as a foothold, climbing and banging on the ceiling as they held her firmly.

She quickly thanked her intuition.

She poked a brick and squinted as dust fell into her eyes but not a moment too soon.

To put it in perspective, Oscar and Caleb now had their hands touching, backs straight and heads pressed into Ebony's legs in an effort to make themselves as small as possible as the walls pressed into their backs. But the bricks groaned as if disappointed to not crush anyone, and effortlessly receded. Caleb, Ebony, and Oscar grimaced again as the wall grinded over the gooey remains of 043-2 and disappeared into the main wall. The trap was set for the next person.

Caleb shuddered. "Never thought I'd see a human trifle."

"Did you have to call her a trifle?" Ebony moaned.

"What's wrong with that?"

"I loved trifle; it's my favourite desert."

"Not anymore." Caleb collected himself and Ebony rolled her eyes.

"Guys, can we leave?" Oscar wasn't joining in on the celebratory banter. He looked incredibly sick, and Ebony tried not show her worry as she noticed blood staining his collar.

"Let me see your neck," Ebony asked. Oscar tucked his hair behind his ear.

"That looks…" Caleb was going to say repulsive, but Ebony gave him a deathly glare and he coughed, "… like it's getting better." Oscar sighed.

"Doesn't feel that way," he grumbled. The dart had been laced with some sort of paralysis poison. His veins, an inky black mess of spiderwebbed cracks across his neck and upper back was the first indication. The second was his increasingly slurred words.

"We'll get you out of here." Oscar's arm fell limply by his side and Ebony wrapped it around her shoulder. "And we'll find Stella," she said, although she wasn't sure they were going to like what they found, when they found her.

If they found her.

Chapter 12

As Oscar had predicted, there were several exits to the pyramid. Once they'd found the trap door and clambered back through, they relocated the guided route and followed the tour until they could feel a cool breeze sweeping around and no longer needed their torches.

Ebony leant Oscar against the pyramid's exterior wall. He was sick but now in the light she could see that Caleb was an even more sickly shade of pale.

"Caleb." Ebony rubbed his arms soothingly. "You all right?"

"Bit shocked," Caleb said. He furrowed his brow and Ebony could practically hear the cogs whirring in his head as he tried to work through everything.

She scrunched her eyes in the sunlight. "We've come out at the back of the pyramid," she said. "If we can get around to the front, we can get Stella."

"How do we even know if Stella is okay?" Caleb asked numbly. Ebony cracked her knuckles as though prepared to go a round in the ring with Atlas.

"We don't."

Behind them, Oscar slid to the floor. Shivering despite the heat of the desert sun wasn't a good sign and he clawed at his clothes, wrapping them tighter around himself to try and conserve warmth.

Ebony grabbed the strap of Caleb's vest and pulled him away, out of ear shot from Oscar. "He's not looking good."

Caleb agreed. "I've never seen anything like it. He looks like he's been attacked by a bunch of crayons." Ebony slapped his arm.

"This is serious," she said but he wasn't wrong. The two of them glanced at Oscar's neck, it was swelling rapidly in a conglomeration of every colour except the colour his skin should have been. Hair was stuck to the gunk around it; Ebony always told Oscar to cut his hair, but he used the abundance of it to hide is futile attempt at growing any facial hair. Consequently, he appeared much younger and although counterweighed his appearance with his height, still looked like a frightened child in this moment.

"We need to get him out of here, now. But we also need to get Stella," Caleb worried. "She could be injured." He didn't add 'or dead' to the end of his sentence but they both thought it.

"We can't use public transport to leave Egoran, Atlas would kill everyone on board." Caleb tapped his forearm and swiped upwards with two fingers to his wrist. The small capsule inserted inside suspended a holographic keyboard above his hand and a 3D map appeared in front of them. He searched eagerly for something useful.

"How about that?" he raised his eyebrows. "The interstellar flight facility for SpaceLink Enterprises is about a mile… that way. Behind the station," he pointed.

"What are you suggesting?" Ebony questioned. "Steal a cruise ship?" He nodded eagerly. "You can't be serious?"

He was.

"I won't take a big one. And we'll give it back."

"Oh, we'll take a small one, we'll give it back," Ebony mimicked, kicking the sand. She paced about for a moment before throwing her hands to the sky. "Do you even know how to drive one?"

"Same as a normal ship. Just a hundred times bigger," Caleb said. Oscar interrupted them with a pained groan and Ebony and Caleb rushed back to him as he fell to the side. Caleb caught him and stared at Ebony harshly. He didn't need her permission, but it would be nice to have her support.

"Fine," she decided. "Take Oscar with you."

"Run a mile with Oscar on my back?"

"He's paralysed, he can't run," Ebony pushed.

"All right bud." Caleb observed him quizzically for a moment, then slung Oscar's arm around his shoulders and winked at Ebony before he took off running, ploughing through the sand and away from the pyramids.

"Right." Ebony's mouth went dry again and the familiar fear built in the pit of her stomach as she edged round the side of the pyramid. A bench marked the entrance and she crawled underneath it, using it as feeble cover as she peeked in.

Atlas was in the pyramid.

So was Stella.

She was suspended from the air, dangled from her ankles by a smoke-like rope. Ebony couldn't see if she had been severely injured, but it didn't seem so. Perhaps Atlas was keeping Stella pristine to use as a bargaining chip.

Joplin briefly contemplated Stella's body but chose to walk away from it and settle in the corner, hands placed daintily over her crossed legs as she patiently waited. Atlas was stood, practically paralysed in the middle of the room, staring intently at the entrance way which he had managed to unblock. Ebony gulped and shimmied away from the smoke.

"Smoke." The word handed Ebony the solution. "Smoke." She clicked her fingers and quickly rushed away.

A hot and sweaty mile away, Caleb groaned as he tried to gently put Oscar down by the entrance to the flight facility. The quartz porch provided an uncomfortable seat and Oscar moaned as he sat.

"You'll be all right," Caleb said, gripping his shoulder. "Oscar?" He snapped his finger, but Oscar couldn't form a coherent reply and his eyes were glazing over. Caleb worried. He wrapped his hands under Oscar's armpits and glancing into the building, noticed a security guard sitting at the front desk. So, he hobbled around the side of the building, dragging Oscar with him until they reached a low-standing window.

Fingers covered with chunky rings, Caleb drew his hand into a fist and slammed it into the window. It cracked. He drew back and punched through the window again. Avoiding making more noise as glass embedded itself in his arm, he bit his lip, blood snaking through his fingers and staining the sand. Using his backpack to cover the sharp shards sticking out of the window frame, he pulled Oscar inside and jumped into the building.

"Not too shabby," he admired. He'd broken a window into the aircraft hangar, which from the outside didn't seem nearly tall enough to house ships. However, climbing onto a walkway, he looked down and the hangar continued a mile into the planet, housing a ship bigger than any Caleb had seen. There was no one around guarding it and Caleb took it as luck being on his side. But whilst he continued, blissfully unaware, the cameras that were attentive to the ship retrained their points of focus and were now watching him.

A small door into the ship opened with nothing but brute strength; it wasn't even locked. Caleb grabbed Oscar but before he could move him his forearm rang.

"Hey, Ebony, all going well?" Caleb whispered.

"Funnily enough, no. You close to getting a rocket?"

"Pfft," he puffed boastfully. "The security in here is as good as in a bus terminal," he said. "I've got my eyes on one." He heaved Oscar towards the ingress as they spoke.

"I need you to get here as soon as you can. I've found Stella and I think I can get her out."

"What are you going to do?"

Ebony pouted her lips, unsure about what she was going to do but she said it confidently anyway.

"I'm going to start a fire."

"You're kidding me," Caleb said. "I thought after the whole incident with the exploding ships and the creepy, lava monsters you'd been put off your pyromaniacal ambitions?"

"You just focus on the ship. I'll be waiting with Stella," she demanded, hanging up.

Ebony rushed to the exit she'd come from. Every exit had benches lining it and thankfully for her, they were old, faux wood slats, presumably to match the pyramid aesthetic; she didn't know. Making sure no one was around, she kicked violently, and her foot went through the bench, breaking the ignitable material. She ripped it from the frame and stuffing several strips under her arms, half ran, half tripped through the sand towards the front of the pyramid. Piling the wood, she silently made a bonfire outside the foyer, praying that no nosey tourists would take an interest in the new structure as they flocked from the shuttle that had just landed.

The faint sound of an engine rose in the distance. The horizon shimmered with the heat of the sun, but Ebony could clearly make out one of the ships rising upwards.

"Small ship my ass." She frowned at the jumbo interstellar cruise liner flying upwards. Pulling from her rucksack a lighter from the days where she socially smoked, she pressed the spark wheel and in a matter of seconds, the plank was ablaze.

Ebony held the wood in her hands and allowed the fire to blow for a moment. The breeze blew towards the pyramid; the conditions were perfect. She stuffed it into the rotting wood pile. As the flames enveloped the wood, Ebony reached into her trusty backpack again and whipped out a small vial of solution which until that very moment had only served the purpose of preserving any biological items that she thought may be of interest whilst they were transported back to Chane. She unstoppered the bottle, hand covering the label that said 'caution', and poured the solution over the fire. The smoke evolved from a cloudy white into a diesel black. As Caleb drove the ship closer the wind picked up and black smoke crowded Atlas and Joplin.

"Atlas, could you please control yourself," Joplin asked. Atlas, who was yet to notice the smoke, growled at her. "You're more powerful than you think," she added, and his snarl evolved into a conceited grin as he strode towards her.

"Magic is unpredictable," he said, "especially power of such calibre."

"Of course," said Joplin, holding back a cough as the smoke carried further into the room. When Atlas too began to hawk a wet, phlegmy noise, Ebony made her move. He scowled and his hands raised parallel with his shoulders. With fingers splayed, the air in the room was displaced as the smoke was sucked inwards.

Ebony covered her nose and mouth and squinting, crawled into the room. At this point, it was near impossible to see, and Atlas had done exactly what Ebony had hoped he would. He had assumed all the smoke in the room was originating from himself and so was dragging it back into his chest. Ebony recoiled as there was a thud and Stella crumpled to the ground in front of her.

"I was going to catch you," she apologised under her breath. Tucking her hands under Stella's arms, she tugged her from the room. She nearly screamed as Atlas' cloak slid over her leg as he spun round, trying to clear the smoke. However, by some miracle, he didn't see her. But Ebony was convinced Joplin did. The two of them made eye contact for less than a second but Joplin acted like she'd seen nothing.

"The smoke is particularly thick over here my love, do you mind?" She coaxed Atlas away from Ebony and Stella's hunched bodies, and with the unexpected help, Ebony managed to get Stella into the sun.

Ebony had been so preoccupied with rescuing Stella that she'd neglected to hear the droning engine until she got outside. The ship had nearly landed, Caleb had steered it above the sand dunes to unsuccessfully try and avoid blowing the bazaar away.

"Yes, Caleb, yes," Ebony grinned. She leant over Stella and lifting her up in a firefighter carry, rushed towards the ship.

There was an outcry from behind her.

Atlas had worked it out.

She glanced over her shoulder and watched as the smoke flew from the entrance, dissipating into the sky with a bassy bang Ebony felt in her heart. It didn't take long for Atlas to realise he'd been tricked, and he wasn't thrilled by the revelation.

"Ebony!" A small door of the cruise liner opened, and Ebony could see Caleb waving madly. She persevered. His face was a picture of fright, brow furrowed nearly to the tip of his nose as he saw Stella's limp body, and then for the first time, was witness to Atlas.

"She's alive." Ebony panted and Caleb took her from Ebony's arms, eyes still trained on Atlas as she hauled herself on board.

"That's good news," an attractively husky voice said. "Caleb, take Stella to the med bay, leave her with Oscar. I'll get us out of here." Ebony hadn't even registered someone else was on the ship with them. She looked up to see a young, golden-eyed man standing in a smart navy suit, watching the situation intently.

"I'm sorry-" Ebony was taken aback, "-who are you?" He smiled mysteriously and opened his mouth to respond but the ship jolted, and his words failed as the two of them were sent sliding across the floor. The ship adjusted itself but in doing so, inadvertently hovered over the bazaar. People fled as the stalls were destroyed; those who were physically present ran for the station whilst holograms disappeared into thin air.

But the ship was only partially to blame for the destruction. Ebony looked through the door and Atlas was marching towards them, throwing disks of dark matter which hit the ship like bullets. She could hear him screaming in fury, sandstorms rising around him as his emotions took their toll on the environment. Storm clouds descended like a thick blanket and gritty twisters rose to meet them, creating an arena of shingle and grit that trapped the ship within Atlas' sandy grasp.

Ebony was about to stand when the slim man stood over her, holding his hand out. She took it and he pulled her up.

"We need to leave," he said, pulling the door shut. He rushed out of the room and Ebony followed him hastily. She had so many questions but even more popped into her head as he answered the lot without her saying anything.

"The name's Emmanuel Rutherford," he introduced. "My Uncle owns SpaceLink, that's why I'm here. Yes, I know who Atlas is and what he wants from you and thank you." He inspected Ebony as they paused, waiting for a door to slide open. "I'm flattered you find me attractive." She blushed deeply. How did he know what she was thinking? He was above average in the looks department; bouncy, curly hair, chiselled face, permanent smile lines and the cologne he was wearing was one of those cloying aromas where too much would choke you whilst enough would make you swoon, and he was wearing the perfect amount. And Ebony considered Oscar tall, but his head barely reached Emmanuel's shoulders. Yet she'd dismissed his attractiveness for more important matters.

"Right Ebony." Emmanuel gestured to a chair as they appeared in the control room, and when she sunk into the plump cushioned chair, he curled her hand around a joystick. "The controls are pretty simple. Pull this backwards to go up and sideways to change direction and push this forward to go forwards," he said, "and whatever you do, don't stop."

"I... I..."

"Ready? Great." He whacked the ignition, and the ship began to shake. Ebony didn't know what she was doing so ip dip do-ing with a loosely flailing finger, she pulled on the joystick as hard as she could until the rocket lifted off the ground. Sand covered every window as it morphed into a giant hand, trying to stop Ebony from taking off. She faltered, but Emmanuel noticed.

"Keep going," he encouraged, shrugging his shoulders, and relieving his torso of the jacket he wore. "I'll get rid of the sand." He rolled up his shirt sleeves and stood at the window, staring at Atlas. He had a hand pressed to his temple and Ebony could see that not only were the giant hands falling away from the window, but whatever Emmanuel was doing, it was having a direct impact on Atlas' head. Atlas paused and covered his ears, distracted by a disturbing noise.

"What are you doing to him?"

"I'm singing in his head as loudly as I can, the worst songs I can think of. Although…" Emmanuel trailed off, "I think it's more like a banshee wail. I can't sing." The confusion in Ebony's mind was insurmountable, almost leaking from her ears. She focused on steering the rocket out of Egoran's atmosphere and into space, slowing when the blue sky turned black.

"Keep going," Emmanuel said again, "there isn't much traffic today." Ebony pushed at the joystick.

You're trembling. Ebony heard a voice, one awfully like Emmanuel's in her head as Emmanuel slipped his jacket over her shoulders. She hadn't noticed it herself, but the voice was correct. Her eyes swam with tears and the open freedom of space in front of them provoked a turbulent reaction of her emotions as her body shivered. She checked behind them to Egoran and could now only see patches of the many green oasis scattered across the planet and the white hexagonal roof of Space Link's station. She wasn't sure if Atlas could follow them into space, but she didn't want to stick around to find out.

"He's not following us," Emmanuel said, noting the lack of sand hand monsters. "Don't be scared, he won't follow us out here. He needs time to recover."

Ebony was sure she had spoken none of her thoughts aloud. "Are you reading my mind?" she asked curiously.

"I am. Do you not want me to?" he asked nonchalantly, as if mind reading was as casual as speaking.

"Not really," Ebony replied, her privacy unwantedly invaded. She was astounded he could but as with many things she'd witnessed recently, she was expecting something out of the ordinary.

"Then I won't," Emmanuel promised. He went to sit but changed his mind. "Come with me. I need to talk to you about Atlas." Ebony complied and followed him out of the room.

"Welcome to SpaceLink Enterprise's fifth and biggest ship. The

Hyperion," he said warmly. Ebony's eyes widened.

Classy couldn't begin to describe the bravura and sophistication of the ship. Hyperion was a stylish blend of retro and industrial environs, concealed within a chassis resembling two tightly-packed art deco skyscrapers; the top doubled as the front of the ship and coalesced into a single room, a glass topped botanical garden. The bottom was fitted with more engines than was countable; everything in between was designed for a faultless journey through deep space.

The interior of Hyperion offered its guests luxurious travel on an esteemed level. Where passengers were allowed to roam, period mahogany-panelled walls with a golden outline, faux leather sofas and polished quartz floors followed with a flawless finish. It had enough greenery to make it feel planet-ish and homely but sufficient glass walls to remind the passengers they were in space. Industrial zones where the employees busied themselves were built from durable metals and stainless steel with a more time-appropriate guise. Ebony had the privilege of viewing both sides of the immaculate Hyperion as Emmanuel took her on a brief tour.

"It's beautiful," she commended. Emmanuel straightened his back proudly.

"It is, isn't it?"

"Thank you for helping us and... I'm sorry we tried to steal it."

"Water under the bridge." They walked through the main lobby in the heart of Hyperion. It was several storeys and had a waterfall cascading into the middle into a coy pond. Behind this, a central lift carted them swiftly to the top floor.

"How's Oscar doing?"

"He'll be absolutely fine. His wound was poisoned but the medical bay on this ship is stocked with enough medication to deal with exactly forty thousand diseases, viruses, poisons, infections etc..." Emmanuel said. Ebony stifled a chuckle, clearly, he'd given this pitch many times to his long-haul lightyear customers.

"Good." The two of them paused inside the well-kept botanical garden and sat with the universe above them to talk. Panes of clear glass were replaced by stained glass and enchanting beams of light dotted the floor, illuminating the two of them as they spoke.

"You know about Atlas? About what he is?" Ebony asked. Emmanuel dipped his head slightly.

"I didn't know he was alive," he said. "Your friend Caleb was wrong about the security we have at our facility. It's state of the art. But his shoddy attempted break in told me he wasn't exactly the normal thief and all I could read in his mind was him trying to save his friends — you, from Atlas," he explained. "I wanted to see for myself if it was true."

"Unfortunately, so."

"I read your mind. Atlas told you that you were an Enchanted. Are you?" Emmanuel questioned, subconsciously leaning forward in his curiosity. Ebony took a deep breath.

"I don't know," she replied.

"Well, there are lots of us out there, with abilities," Emmanuel explained. "We're descendants from the original Enchanteds."

"Seriously? You have actual magic?" Ebony didn't know what to think and was worried that if she thought something offensive of Emmanuel that he would know.

"How else would I read your mind?" he asked. Technological advancements were plentiful, people could hardly keep up with the next miracle procedure but there was no technology Ebony had heard of that could accurately read minds, only ones that could destroy them.

"But, if there are lots of Enchanteds, why hasn't he gone after any of you. Why me?" she asked sadly. Emmanuel's shrug with such straight posture was dainty.

"I admit I was so intent on stopping Atlas from destroying the ship, I didn't read his mind," Emmanuel said. "I have to be within a certain radius, but he's already left the planet and clearly so have we." Ebony stayed silent, staring in a mixture of shock and disbelief. "Ebony." Emmanuel lightly brought her back to reality. "If Atlas is back and he's intent in bringing Belphegor and Adremelech to life, then we need to prepare for the worst."

"I know," Ebony said. "But if he doesn't have me, he can't bring them all to life, right?" Emmanuel's furrowed brow expressed worry. He tossed his hand in the air unsurely, staring at the plants surrounding them as he chose his words.

"I think we have to prepare for the worst," he repeated, suggesting he didn't know, "but myself and other Enchanteds, we'll help you through this. Atlas is a burden that all gifted people have to bear, so you won't be alone in trying to stop him," Emmanuel promised.

The way Emmanuel spoke, ensuring Ebony that other Enchanteds would help her, placed a burdening mantel of responsibility on her shoulders that she wasn't sure she wanted.

"Thank you," she said anyway. Emmanuel's eyes crinkled.

"You're most welcome," he responded. Ebony fell silent again and Emmanuel changed the topic. "It must be hard to take in considering your science background." Ebony glanced at him, and he put his hands up.

"Sorry," he apologised. "Last time."

"It's true," she admitted after a moment. "Trying to contemplate magic when I understand factual science is confusing to say the least."

"If it helps, magic is ubiquitous within science. A lot of things can be attributed to it, with more simple explanations too." Ebony tilted her head in a sceptical expression.

"I disagree. No, science is based on evidence, magic is… weird," she argued. Emmanuel smiled widely, glaring white teeth exposed and Ebony braced herself.

"People think science explains everything. Tinnitus, for example, isn't a medical condition," Emmanuel said. "It's the noise of people's minds when they're not focusing on what others are thinking. Many people who have Tinnitus are descended from Ancients. They lost the magical gene giving them the ability to perceive what others are thinking." He tried not to grin at Ebony's astounded face. She wasn't entirely convinced but wasn't outright denying it either.

"Is there anything else?" Emmanuel jogged his shoulders.

"Everything can be related to magic somehow. Heterochromia is in humans who have a hypnotism gene."

"That's a thing?" Ebony worried.

"Thankfully not any more. Only one Ancient could hypnotise people and the skill died out with her." Emmanuel continued, "different skills have varying levels of rarity. All Enchanteds have the basics, increased strength, heightened intelligence, better hearing and sight etc… but we then specialise in certain areas." Ebony had the thrilled astoundment of a child left to its own devices in a room full of sweets.

"That's incredible!" she exclaimed.

"Vitiligo in this science age is attributed to a lack of pigment." Emmanuel shook his head at the insolence of scientists.

"It's not?" Ebony rubbed her forehead and briskly rethought her life's work.

"Nope. Shapeshifter gene. Their body at some point has tried to change form and got stuck," he chuckled. "I could go on."

"I get the point."

"Well." Emmanuel admired the hibiscus next to him as its flowers scattered an offering of petals over his leg. "I'm glad we found you Ebony. You and your friends are welcome to stay until you see fit to leave," he offered, "and if you need me for anything, think of me. I'll hear you." With a smile that stretched beyond his eyes he stood up, buttoned his suit, and strolled off, hands slipping casually into his pockets. Ebony was thankful he'd promised not to read her mind.

Chapter 13

Room 317 wasn't special. Had the ship been full of passengers, it would have been reserved as sleeping quarters for one of the cleaners, who were given less than adequate lodgings for their service to the giant ship. But it had a view and Ebony chose it as an escape to solitude. Rare were the opportunities she had to sit quietly and normally it was anathema to her; she liked to busy herself. But she needed a moment to think without a sense of impending fear and the discovery of another Enchanted had somewhat eased her mind.

Her fingers mindlessly picked at the cool metal floor where she sat, leaning against the ovoid floor to ceiling window. A bed set in a raised recess on the opposite side of the metallic box invited her to sit in its warm sheets. She ignored its beckoning and chose to rest against the glass that vibrated with the ship, calming her nerves. Constellations she could recognise she traced with her fingertip as an infinitude of stars dazzled the sky and she pitted ships travelling past in an imaginary race against each other. It was almost childish but was the escape Ebony needed.

Ebony? The ship she betted would win was overtaken as Emmanuel called out, rousing her from her reverie.

"What?" she yelled but he didn't hear her. She left 317 and started down the corridor to find him.

Ebony? I need you upstairs in the control room! He was shouting telepathically, his voice filling her brain.

I'm coming. Punching the lift button, it shot upwards through the centre of Hyperion. When she reached the control room, Emmanuel was waiting for her with an incredulous look on his face.

He inhaled sharply. "You answered me telepathically." Ebony shook her head aggressively.

"No, I didn't."

"Yes, you did."

"No, I didn't," Ebony squabbled. Emmanuel didn't press further. He didn't want to agitate her more when the news he was going to give her was bad enough on its own.

"Something is happening on Drognir. Something bad."

"Drognir? That's my home," Ebony said but Emmanuel already knew that. She followed him to a secondary room with bleak white walls, undecorated save a huge hologram of Drognir on the middle of a table. On the hologram, a red blip showed a large part of Drognir being battered with something. Then, an alarm accompanied it and Emmanuel gulped.

"What does that mean?"

His eyes were clouded with pain. "People are starting to die."

"What's going on?" Ebony cried, clenching her fists. "That's Chane city. What's happening?"

"It could be a natural disaster, but if I had to guess…"

"Atlas," they said simultaneously. It was as though someone had called battle stations and they split, hurrying in opposite directions. Ebony knew when to ask questions and when to get on with the matter at hand.

Emmanuel grabbed the ship controls. "I've called the others," he said, "told them to get dressed. There's armour in the wardrobes." Ebony, who was going to tell them herself skidded to a halt and turned.

"If it's Atlas, we need to stop him," she said. She was certain Emmanuel hadn't read her mind this time, but he happened to be thinking the exact same thing.

Weaponry is past the gym, on your right. Ebony rushed off.

"Ebony, what's going on?" Caleb asked as he rounded the corner, armour spilling from his hands as he kept a firm grip on a half drunk bottle of Metaxa. He clearly found the signposts across the ship and followed them straight to the bar. The proof of magic was easier to take when tipsy.

"Atlas is attacking."

"Us?"

"Chane." Ebony yanked the bottle from Caleb's grasp and let it fall to the floor, pulled his sleeve and he twisted round, now following her obediently whether he liked it or not. "We need weapons, as many as possible."

"Stinger, version two," Caleb said. He complied and they rushed past Oscar as they went. The bandage around his neck he flaunted like a fashion accessory, and he was wearing a deep black suit with a material resembling scales. By the way he was tugging at it, he didn't like it. It chafed in all the wrong places. Marching urgently, he barged in to where Emmanuel was steering the ship, using a foot to open the door. Emmanuel had quickly slipped the armour on too and had no complaints to its slim fit.

"How long until we arrive?" Oscar asked.

"About fifteen minutes," Emmanuel guessed, forcing the engines into overdrive, "and those suits; made from metamaterials and used in the last galactic war, so they may not be fashionable, but they'll work." He read Oscar's mind and Oscar scowled.

Ebony had found Oscar in the infirmary and informed him of Emmanuel's abilities, which he had doubted until Emmanuel began recounting Oscar's own life story, neglecting to leave out any embarrassing childhood memories on the way. Considering that it was their first formal introduction as Oscar had been unconscious when they first met, he wasn't Emmanuel's greatest fan.

Not a minute later and the others assembled. Ebony's heart was pounding in her chest and her stomach was twisting in knots, but she wore a brave face for the sake of morale. She didn't have much but the few things she held dear to her, like Esso, was in Chane and she didn't want to see it destroyed, for the sake of her and the whole population.

"I've called for some back up," Emmanuel announced.

"People like you?" Stella piped up. She had remained intimidated and fearful of Emmanuel's powers, especially following Atlas' attack. Her one on one encounter was never to be forgotten.

"Enchanteds? Yes. Telepathic? No." Emmanuel spun in his chair, putting faith in the autopilot. "One of them has apportation, one shares the power of aerokinesis, hydrokenesis and pyrokenesis, one is a clairvoyant, and one is a shapeshifter."

"English please."

Emmanuel reiterated. "Teleporter, controls elements, sees the future and-" Emmanuel frowned, "-shapeshifter."

"Thanks."

"But you don't have to be afraid of any of our powers," Emmanuel added, "and you…" he eyed Ebony curiously. "You have magic too, we just have to figure out what." Ebony didn't argue. "Listen Ebony, when you yelled at me earlier, I could have sworn you spoke to me telepathically." Emmanuel's eyes widened into wholesome circles. He was hopeful. "Maybe you're like me?" Expecting Ebony to deny an ounce of magic in her body, it came as a surprise when she placed a step confidently towards him.

"How do I find out?"

He grinned. "Well, I learnt by-" his face dropped slightly at a recollection, "-I learnt by spending three months in a psychiatric ward on a Christian camp on B-Earth after being convinced by a goldfish that I was insane. Magic wasn't mentioned in the bible, so it was a sin, and I was punished for it. So-" Emmanuel scratched the nape of his neck, "-don't do that… Just think, but aim your thoughts at someone."

"I'll do it," Caleb offered enthusiastically. "Hit me." His chest puffed as he beat on it with his fists. Ebony smiled and sank into the chair. Emmanuel turned it as though he was aiming her like a gun towards Caleb.

"Just think," Emmanuel prompted. There wasn't much more he could say. He hadn't been taught how to use his powers, but as hard as it was for him it had moulded him into a good man. After escaping the psychiatric ward, he was stolen away by his uncle who too had rebelled against his religious upbringing and joined SpaceLink, using the ships to scour the universe for Enchanteds like him, who were taught to be afraid of their powers, and help them instead. Enchanteds, for example, like Ebony.

Ebony stared at Caleb who stood with his hands stretched, expecting a physical thought to hit him. She felt a little lightheaded from straining herself but kept pushing. Unsure of what she was doing but with a presentiment it would work she narrowed her eyes and continued to stare at him. Caleb suddenly pulled an offended but impressed face.

"Hey!" His eyes widened. "Hey, hey, your lips didn't move. I heard that!" He jumped around excitedly. Ebony leapt from her seat and Stella and Oscar closed in, eager to join in.

"What did I say?" Ebony checked.

"You said my hair was stupid," Caleb said but he didn't take offence.

"You heard me?" Ebony's draw dropped as Emmanuel clapped her on the back.

"I don't believe it," he exclaimed. "Another telepath! Keep going," he urged and Ebony dropped back into the seat, but his excitement plummeted as the ship's forward-facing thrusters launched and everyone staggered (Ebony glided) three paces to the right.

Out the window, rainclouds doused the glass in an opaque layer of streaming water, concealing the outside world.

"We're entering the atmosphere," Stella said. Suddenly, a hologram of a girl flickered on the screen.

"Emmanuel? Emmanuel, can you hear me?"

"Cascia?" Emmanuel whacked several buttons. The hologram spluttered as if coughing violently, then a brief portal appeared and suddenly she was standing in the room with them.

"Emmanuel." Cascia hugged him tightly. Her sylphlike figure was dressed in the same suits they were wearing, her black hair tied back in a messy bun and olive skin tainted with blood, a mixture of hers and others.

"What's happening?" he asked her.

"Atlas is attacking, that's what's happening, and he's raised the dead to do his dirty work." She shook her head in exasperation. She was carrying her weight awkwardly, obviously injured, but if she felt the pain they couldn't tell as she hid it behind a stoic face.

"Zombies?" Oscar folded his arms dubiously.

"His preferred power is necromancy. What were you expecting? Flowers?"

Oscar shook his head. "I thought Magma men were bad enough," he said, with a resented sigh.

"Oh, don't worry," Cascia said, mimicking sympathy at Oscar's apparent concern. "The whole families gathered for the occasion." She suddenly pointed at Oscar. "Have we met?"

"This is Oscar, Stella, Caleb and Ebony, she's another Enchanted," Emmanuel introduced, pointing to each of them in turn. A small chorus of hellos ensued. Cascia looked the four of them up and down briefly.

"Nice to meet you," she said, touching her tongue to the corner of her mouth as she grinned and winked. She had a wild temperament that flicked between flirtatious and hot-tempered like a light switch.

"Cascia, we don't have much time," Emmanuel reminded her.

"Right." She brushed her hair from her face. "I saw something."

"What?"

"You're aiming to land outside of the fighting zone, right?"

"Of course."

"Well, don't," Cascia advised. "I had a vision. Atlas has traps set up outside the line of fire. Magma men lining the sewer system. You won't be able to get through them, I've watched you die trying." She gripped the chair as the ship braked to land.

"You want me to land in the middle of it all?" Emmanuel spluttered.

"That doesn't sound like the greatest idea," Caleb said. Cascia folded her arms.

"You have a better plan mop head?" she asked. He shook his head roughly, disappearing into his shoulders in her presence.

"Then land us on top of everything."

"Yes ma'am," Emmanuel saluted before diving into the seat, pressing buttons so frantically his fingers were no more than a blur. Everyone took three stumbled steps back to the left as the ship began to descend over the dockland; at least Atlas had picked a fight in the less populated area of the city.

Suddenly, a huge roar attracted them all to the window. As they broke through the clouds, it was as though they were about to land in some fantasy film. A huge, scaly monster was attacking a building, on which stood a plume of smoke so black it could only be Atlas. Caleb pressed himself against the window in awe, fogging the glass.

"Is that Godzilla?" he marvelled.

"No, that's Jeff," Cascia introduced. The quizzical looks were telling her that they'd never met a Jeff before. "Shapeshifter," she clarified.

"Awesome!" Caleb approved. "Can he shapeshift into anything? Could he shapeshift into me?" He was getting childishly giddy with excitement, but it was easy to see why.

"No. He can only shapeshift into animals."

"Dang," Caleb said.

Noses pressed to the windows that flared with fog at every breath, they never took their eyes from the fight, and as Emmanuel steered them ever closer they could see a person shifting in and out of reality. Disappearing in one place and appearing in another, he too was attacking Atlas.

"Who's that?" Stella asked, squinting as she went to push her glasses up before remembering they'd been left far behind on Egoran.

"That's Noah," Emmanuel said. "Teleporter."

As the ever expanding shadow of their ship ascended over Atlas, his eyes met Ebony's. She gulped but clenched her fist and tried to put her newly discovered magic to good use. She stared at him, and he reeled his head back in shock. Emmanuel, despite the circumstances, laughed.

That was brilliant.

"What happened?" Oscar asked.

"Ebony's practising her magic on Atlas."

"What did you say?"

"I told him to go acquaint his head with a brick wall." Ebony smiled. She felt confident surrounded by the eclectic group of people who had all been brought together under unfavourable circumstances. However, her heart fell as she saw the devastation across the city. An ever-growing circumference of destruction was devouring infrastructure as Atlas pushed forward with his troops, who, as Cascia had described, were running sporadically, attacking mercilessly, and reminded Ebony exactly of zombies. The problem was simple; the city was defended thoroughly from science but not at all by magic, let alone necromancy, and it was now under siege with no hope of surviving.

"We're right overhead but we've got no chance until Atlas' hordes have been dealt with. Emmanuel, get Belize." Cascia barked orders as she herded everyone to the door. Emmanuel closed his eyes briefly.

We're dropping in ten. He opened them and inhaled deeply in anticipation.

Minutes?

Seconds.

Coming.

"She's coming, we can go." Sliding the door open, the noise of war hit them like a brick and Ebony's first instinct was to cover her ears, but she stood bravely in hope of inspiring her friends. She looked at them; Stella and Caleb were clinging to each other like sloths on a pole, slowly backing away from the door in fearful retreat. Oscar face blushed a shade of green contrary to Cascia's delight as she grabbed his arm.

"It's going to be fine. Stick with me," she offered.

"Uh huh," said Oscar unsurely.

"We're going to jump, on the count of three." There wasn't time for questions or toilet breaks.

"One."

Every bone in her body told Ebony not to.

"Two."

Oscar gripped the side of the ship, hoping he wouldn't have to let go. He'd jumped out of a plane before, but there was a parachute attached to him, and even then, he hated the experience.

"Three."

They all screamed, Cascia and Emmanuel in glee and everyone else in terror as they fell through the air. But they were caught abruptly by a huge gust of wind which carried them across Chane, instead of to their deaths. Out of the blue, a girl joined them, squealing in glee. She was barely an adult, a child too young for the likes of war. Wearing a dress fit for a princess, Ebony assumed she was from Siren, a planet in Andromeda where people lived and dressed like royalty. She caught her eye and Belize swum through the air towards her.

"You must be Ebony," her high-pitched voice sang out. She held a hand out for Ebony to shake, which she did whilst they were suspended in flight. "I'm Belize," she introduced, blonde hair perfectly framing her face with not a single strand displaced despite the howling wind.

"You're the elemental?" Ebony said.

"Yep," she grinned, before soaring into the sky as though to prove a point. Ebony stared in awe at the people around her until she had to remind herself to blink. Cascia, who had several guns strapped around her waist was shooting at the ground, whilst Emmanuel was distracting the zombies, presumably singing to them. He was like a haphazard siren who'd lost its voice but reached the same end goal in luring them in as they flocked to noise. He too shot at them with pinpoint accuracy.

Belize was having the time of her life. She had the coastline under her complete control and was dragging zombies out into the choppy ocean which on Drognir was too acidic to swim in without protection.

She was also in the process of creating a circle of fire around the zone in which they'd been fighting to contain it. Jeff was no longer Godzilla and Ebony grinned as she watched him transform into a not so big but equivalently as deadly dinosaur, as you do. Sprinting through the crowd he displaced several hundred zombies from their limbs at once.

Suddenly, Ebony felt something on her leg. She shrieked as someone dragged her into a portal and appeared alone with them in an alleyway sheltered by the overarching train tracks above. The stranger had scruffy, brown hair and the makings of a dashing smile if he wasn't currently frowning. He had a handsome, trustworthy face but it didn't put Ebony at ease.

She tried to scream in his head as she'd done with Atlas and turned to run but he stopped her, slinging a portal over her body which brought her right back to him.

"I'm sorry I grabbed you Ebony, I'm Noah," he introduced. Ebony felt her tight chest release.

"You scared the hell out of me," she scolded the teleporter.

"I couldn't risk Atlas getting to you before I did. You're very important," he informed her. "He's attacked because of you."

"Yeah, I figured."

"But you don't understand." Noah's brown eyes bore into hers as he tried to get his point across. "I asked Atlas why? Why you? Because no offence meant, you have no more magic than the rest of us."

"You were talking with Atlas?"

"I don't like a quiet fight," Noah said, almost proudly. "I got close enough to Atlas to start a conversation."

"Right." Ebony was aware her friends could be mid battle and she subconsciously tapped her foot in anticipation as they spoke.

"Listen, I found something out and I don't know if it's true, but—"

"--But what?" Noah tried to choose his words carefully but being sensitive wasn't his main concern at the present time, so he gave it to her straight.

"Atlas thinks you're his daughter i.e., a direct descendant from him and the Ancients. An original Enchanted." Ebony twitched. She tried to catch her breath. "Which explains why his plan about using your body to revive Sonneillon can't be done with any of us. We're not strong enough to harness that kind of power."

"My father?" said Ebony. "He's not my father." Her vision blurred and her breathing heaved, and she trembled as a familiar tightening pain rose in her chest.

"Ebony, it doesn't mean you're like him. It doesn't make you a worse person." Noah helped her to the wall where she clung onto it, struggling to find her voice.

"My, my father-" Ebony stammered, "-no, I... I can't be related... not to him." Her legs felt like jelly and Noah shared his concern as the two of them heard the growls of zombies growing louder.

"We should move to safer ground," he said, and she shook her head firmly. Noah checked behind them. The back door of an empty restaurant and a tall metal fence. They couldn't be surprised but they could be quickly cornered. He drew a portal to his hands just in case, sparks flying from his fingertips.

"Give me a sec." She waved her hand, but Noah was aware of the zombies getting closer. Ebony still couldn't believe it. "It's impossible," she stated plainly. "His daughter?" She felt as though she was going to faint, but Noah clutched her arms and held her up.

"That's what I said," he clarified. "I told him I thought he was a bit too old and a bit too ugly for a girlfriend but then he threw a bus at me." He rubbed the nape of his neck. "I'm sorry to burden you with this but if it's true, it means you are a lot more powerful than anticipated." Ebony focused on his eyes and she could see the truth in them.

"But what good is telepathy?" she asked. "What do I do? Shout at Atlas until he decides to rain on someone else's parade?"

"No, Ebony I don't think you're grasping the size of this revelation," Noah said. Without warning, a huge explosion went off behind them, blowing the foundation of the bullet train track they were beneath to smithereens. Noah was flung forwards and smashed into a wall, bouncing off and landing awkwardly on the floor as Ebony was blown into a group of wheelie bins which scattered as if fleeing the peril.

From around the corner whence the explosion came, grew an army of shadows, which collected until a mob of zombies rounded the corner. Ebony rushed over to Noah who groaned but didn't stand up.

Emmanuel. We need some help she shouted. The zombies advanced slowly enough that Ebony could grab a broken lamppost which had been thrown over. Brandishing it like a spear, she moved slowly towards the zombies, stomach churning as they advanced. They snarled, rotten fingernails clawing at the air to reach her. The smell of flesh that had previously rotted only to regrow and stitch back together was vomit inducing, and the look of their semi decomposed faces and lips curled back into a snarl was the stuff of nightmares.

She swiped at their feet, hoping perhaps they would be like Magma men. They toppled over but instead of melting through the floor, got up with a more pissed off vendetta and continued.

Ebony looked for a way out but couldn't see one. It was looking like the end of her, until a man jumped into the alley, clad in a laid-back Hawaiian shirt, and grabbed both her and Noah. Nothing really stood out about him until Ebony's eyes trailed to his torso and then to his hands. They were spotted with the remnants of dinosaur scales.

"Nice to meet you Ebony," he said, quickly brushing his hair up into a high ponytail with no thought for the zombies.

"Jeff, I presume."

"The one and only. Get on." He squatted in front of her. Ebony contemplated him questioningly. "Like a piggyback," he said, "and trust me, you're going to want to hold on tight." Ebony, who felt a huge burst of excitement as to what he would become, jumped on enthusiastically. Noah lay by Jeff's feet, making no attempt to stand and after a couple of seconds, it was no longer Jeff towering over him but a huge eagle. Ebony gripped the silky feathers of the golden bird, and the wind generated from its wings alone blew back the zombies leading the charge. He let out a screeching peal, and Ebony noticed on his beak what looked like a word, engrained in a smudge of ink. Jeff ruffled his feathers, then grabbing Noah in his razor talons, launched into the sky.

"This is incredible." Ebony dared to trail one arm behind her in the wind. Jeff squawked back; not being able to talk was one of the only downsides of shapeshifting. Noah held onto nothing, his body open like a starfish as he enjoyed the ride.

"Where are we going?" Ebony asked as they left behind the war raging below. She caught the end of his thoughts.

...on the rooftops. He hastily landed atop a skyscraper where the

zombies could only angrily growl at them from below and he shifted back into a human.

"Stay here Ebony. You're too important," Jeff said. He turned and ran towards the edge of the building and Ebony yelled out to try and stop him, but he was gone before she could utter a word.

"Come back. Please, I want to help," she cried. "Dammit." She kicked a stone and it bounced off the skyscraper and into the crowd below.

"Ebony, he's right," Noah said, watching as Jeff's swan dive turned into an actual swan and he flew across the battling figures, trying to find a place to land. When he was out of sight, Noah trained his thoughts back to Ebony whose hands were on her hips as she awaited an explanation. "Listen to me. The direct descendants of the Ancients, Orabella, Lorelei, and Vesper, they didn't specialise in a certain form of magic. Because their parents were Ancients and could master any magical ability, they could also do anything," Noah explained. "Don't you see? If what Atlas said is true, if you are actually his daughter, then you can do anything. You've got the innate ability to produce magic of any kind."

"I—" Their conversation was interrupted as the skyscraper began to rumble. "Can't we get through one conversation without being interrupted?" Ebony screamed out. Noah froze, staring past her figure and something told her it wasn't an earthquake that was causing the violent shaking.

Something was behind her. Something so tantalisingly close it could reach out and touch her.

Atlas, for the first time since the battle ensued, had left his podium, and was soaring towards them. Ebony scanned the ground below. The zombies were following his lead, abandoning their battles to join his, and it was safe to say there were thousands. However, some had stopped and as Ebony squinted, she saw her friends, surrounded and fighting valiantly. Most had never even fired a gun, but they were doing their best.

"We have to get down there," Ebony demanded. "Noah, get us down there." He didn't need telling twice and started to create a portal, but the building shook again and with an almighty groan, began to collapse. Magma men absorbed the steel foundations hungrily and without legs, it toppled like a block of Lego. Noah's concentration was knocked, and the portal simmered out.

"Climb," Noah commanded and yanking Ebony away as Atlas lashed at where they stood, they rushed to the edge of the building. As they stood on the roof, the roof became the walls, the walls became floors and Ebony felt her heart lurch to her throat as they began to run down the side of a collapsing skyscraper.

Falling was unavoidable as an explosion from within caused them both to tumble and they started to slide. Swearing as he tumbled over a loose beam and his leg was lacerated, Noah tried urgently to conjure another portal to teleport away, but it wasn't working. His powers weren't as refined as the others. In front of them, a gaping hole in the glass window absorbed them, and they were suddenly falling through the inside. With a thud, they landed on the interior glass of the underside of the skyscraper which cracked but didn't break. and an ear splitting screech deafened them as the skyscraper came to a stop, bowling into a neighbouring one which struggled to take the weight.

"Noah. Portal. Now." Ebony's knees were bent as she tried to evenly distribute her weight on the glass. Noah's hands shook like a leaf in a hurricane as he mustered a portal for the two of them.

"Here." He took a step towards it, weight solely on the leg that wasn't maimed, and Ebony yelled for him to stop but the glass beneath them shattered as he moved all of his weight onto one point.

They fell.

The glass hole loomed above them, almost mockingly as they fell. It felt like slow motion.

Ebony held out her hand to the skyscraper.

She begged it to catch them.

But someone else did.

"Hey guys, need a hand?" Belize glided by them.

"You think?" Noah shrieked. Belize beamed and with a quick flick of her hands, had both Noah and Ebony safely up in the air.

"Ebony!" She shuddered as she felt a cold shadow over her. Atlas was gaining on them, floating through the air with ease. He could do exactly what Belize could do, but better. Belize clenched her fists and earth rose from the ground, creating a barrier between them. It worked well momentarily but she couldn't see where his attacks were coming from and she dropped altitude as shadows flew into the wall of earth, devastating it with ease. She tried to build another but Atlas, reading her mind, knew her plan almost before she did and destroyed the earth as it was leaving the ground.

Pathetic offspring, he spat. With even less effort, he clicked his fingers and the shadows flung themselves into Belize. In her final moments, rather than save herself, she catapulted Ebony and Noah as far away from Atlas as she could. Dark energy shaped itself around Belize and began to slice into her, dissolving whatever it touched. As the shadows attacked, she writhed around in pain; pain which was projected in her power as the ocean raged and fire flared. Her body started to disappear.

"Belize no!" Noah screamed, trying to reach her. His fingers were sparking as useless portals formed and simmered out. He wasn't able to concentrate as Belize's tortured cries haunted the air around them. As her body wore away, so did the magic keeping them afloat and Noah and Ebony were helpless to do anything as they fell to the ground.

"I've got you," Cascia yelled, flying beneath them. She had stolen one of the smaller launch ships concealed within the intergalactic ship's helm and was flying it with remarkable agility, catching both Ebony and Noah mid-flight.

"Belize…" Noah had tears dripping off his jaws.

"We've got to keep going," Cascia said solidly as she lost Atlas in a crowd of buildings. "Ebony, I'm taking you to your friends, Noah, you're leaving." Noah turned to her in alarm.

"I'm not leaving," he said defiantly.

"You have to," Cascia said. "I had another vision. If you stay with Ebony, it will set off a chain of events leading to a horrendous accident. If you leave, we have a chance of survival." Noah brandished his hand, a small spark brimming on the end of it.

"I'm not leaving," he growled firmly.

"You are." With the rest of her body rigid, Cascia's leg kicked out behind her and into Noah's chest. He reached for something to hold onto in horror as for not the first time, he found himself falling through the air. But not for long; skilfully, he flipped himself over until he was shooting towards the ground headfirst. He summoned a portal and the world flipped for him as he popped through the floor and onto the city streets. The concrete took a beating as he crashed his fists against it.

Cascia bulldozed the ship through zombies, and they came to a bumpy stop.

"Get out," she said. "Belize is dead because of you. If you're gonna get anyone else killed, it should be yourself."

She left.

Ebony's body felt cold as those words drifted through the air.

"Ebony!" She spun and ducked in the space of a second as Oscar threw a pole like a javelin at her, and it hit the zombie lurking behind. Its intestines spilled into the road as it was pinned down, but it continued to try and fight, with no other meaning in its life other than to devour flesh.

"Thank you." She stumbled as he pulled her into a small circle which had been created by himself, Caleb, Emmanuel, and Stella. Ebony watched them fighting, it was a huge effort for little to no effect, but she picked up a gun, nonetheless.

"Here darling," Stella chucked a gun at her. "Watch the recoil."

"Where did you get these?" Ebony gripped the gun as she aimed at one zombie. She shot and the bullet hit the zombie square in the chest. It stumbled and took a moment, before adjusting its posture and continuing forward.

"Dad. I called him," Stella said. Her adopted father, Simon Braxton, was the general of the Milky Way Alpha quadrant army. "They've made a blockade around this area so the zombies can't go any further but won't drop bombs in fear of hurting civilians until Chane can't be saved."

Under normal circumstances the comment would have been of some comfort to Ebony, but Chane smelt like a bonfire and looked more like a warzone than a normal warzone would. The sound of bodies dropping to the floor played in her ears. But she bit her lip and persisted.

The zombies were another level of threat compared to the Magma men. With a ferocious mob mentality, they climbed and trampled each other to reach their prize. Their cannibalistic tendencies towards anything that moved would have been scary enough but their desperate and insatiable hunger that caused them to chew on each other was worse.

Caleb groaned as a zombie took his bullets to the chest in its stride. "These guns aren't going to hack it."

"And no offence to these Enchanteds but magic isn't working effectively either; except for Jeff," Stella said.

"None taken. I agree," said Emmanuel tiredly. What could he do? Scream into the minds of mindless beings?

"So we go back to good old fashioned science," Ebony decided, scanning over the top of the zombie's heads. In the not too far distance, a store decorated with a neon orange light edged the port. "To the hardware store," Ebony urged.

Why? Emmanuel asked.

Trust me. They lumbered towards it, ploughing through as many zombies as they could, until Ebony kicked the door open and they shuffled in. The slam of the door rattled the shelves.

"Hold it shut," Stella ordered. Emmanuel and Oscar each held a glass pane, arms shaking as they fought against the force of the zombies unremittingly pummelling the door.

"Ebony, what are we doing?" Caleb asked as they rushed through the aisles where an employee had unhelpfully arranged everything by colour instead of alphabetically.

"Here." She chucked a huge cannister of bleach into his arms and his eyes widened as she uncapped a bottle of rubbing alcohol.

"Bombs?"

"I like it," Stella said and zigzagging through the other aisles she collected more ingredients. Caleb galloped between the shelves, fingers tracing the assortment of cannisters.

"I shall make my favourite," he announced, grabbing a tank of gasoline from the shelves, "Molotov's." His lips split into a wide grin. If Ebony didn't know Caleb well, he would worry her.

"Emmanuel. Tell Jeff he has a package to collect at the hardware store," Ebony demanded.

"Already done," Emmanuel said as they poured their concoctions into barrels which fizzled and hissed explosively. They rolled the barrels towards the door where clueless zombies lined up for their death.

"On my count," Ebony said. Emmanuel and Oscar gripped the handles tightly, ready to swing the door open. Ebony watched as Jeff soared over the crowd of zombies, his dragon form burning the ones closest to the door.

"Now!" Oscar and Emmanuel pulled the doors, and the barrels went rolling out, pushed by Emmanuel's telekinesis. Jeff, lying in wait, pinched them in his powerful talons.

X marks the spot he thought and with pinpoint accuracy, dropped them in a row, saving Caleb's specially concocted Molotov for Atlas. Atlas roared as he was engulfed in the explosion.

Spurred on by his brutal blow, they continued to shoot the zombie hordes which had significantly lessened in numbers. Many fled from the scene, burnt by the flames. Others lay on the floor, an unalive kind of dead. Their tactic had worked, and they tried to get back in to the hardware store for another round of bombs, when Atlas threw a screw in the works.

"Ebony!" he screamed. It was a struggle on his part as his body shook, but he ripped a cruise ship from the water. As though it was as light as a ball, he launched it at her.

"Everyone, look out!" she yelled. Grabbing Stella, she forced them both to the floor, but the trajectory of the boat meant that unless something knocked it off course, it would flatten them all.

A screech of brakes came all too late and wasn't enough to save the bullet train speeding around the track. Where the earlier explosion had ruptured the foundation for part of it, the weight of the train caused it to splinter and topple.

As the train flew from the bent rails and gained air, it crashed into the side of the ship. An eruption of metal and fuel burned the sky and plummeted onto the docks. Debris narrowly missed their heads as it flew into the ground, but instead landed on the hardware store, the ships propeller blockading the door. There was a mighty explosion and the potential for more bombs was lost.

But it was far from the end of their problems. Ebony cried out as a train carriage speared the ground and it began to tremor. The blunt force trauma absorbed by the earth had cracked its thin gravelly terrain which rested only on a sewer system, and it was starting to break.

"Everyone, move!" Ebony yelled but there was nowhere to go as the zombies closed in.

The ground gave way to Chane's sewer system.

It squelched upon impact, coating all in a thick layer of who knows what, but no one had time to complain.

"Run!" Emmanuel yelled and Caleb, Oscar, Stella, and Ebony didn't oppose. What however wasn't elucidated, was the direction in which he meant and whilst Emmanuel and Oscar sprinted to the left, Caleb grabbed Stella in one hand and Ebony in the other and they sprinted to the right. Zombies and Magma men instantly poured in after them and they were separated.

Ebony? Where are you? she heard Emmanuel yell.

We went the other way she thought back. "We need to lose them."

"Yeah, no shit," Caleb said.

"Keep going!" Stella urged, "we're out-running them." Ebony dared glance back and cried out as a zombie lunged and grabbed her leg. It climbed on top of her, its teeth bared.

Caleb yelped some incoherent warble and with mighty, studded Chelsea boots, he drop-kicked the zombie round the face. With a crunch, it crumpled.

"Come on darling. No time to stop." Stella heaved Ebony up under her arms and they turned and ran again.

"Thanks," Ebony said, clutching her side. The zombies were on their heels, but their eagerness slowed them down as they barged into each other and Ebony, Caleb and Stella got far enough ahead, until they were briefly out of sight of the zombies. From a nearby wall, light shone. It illuminated a graffitied opposing wall and Ebony hoped for the sake of those who graffitied the tunnels that they weren't in there now.

"In the gap, quickly!" She wedged herself into a crack which had opened up, the armour protecting her skin from the protruding rock, and Stella and Caleb clambered in quickly behind. It led into one of the many underground shopping centres in Chane, which had been exposed to the sewer by Magma men using it as a route under the roads. But it was starting to flood with sullage and as Ebony, Caleb and Stella rushed down a faulty escalator which offered to take them both up and down of its own volition, the lights flickered and dulled. With another step, Ebony's foot was soaked in cold water, and she couldn't go further.

"We can't go this way," she said but the sounds of zombies and Magma men behind them meant they couldn't go back through the gap, either.

"We'll be safe from the Magma men in the water, right?" Stella tried to scientifically predict the actions of a magical being. "They'll solidify."

The three of them waded into the water. It was dangerously acidic, but their armour withstood the burns.

Ebony stood, Caleb and Stella a few feet behind, waiting with bated breaths as the zombies cluelessly rushed past the gap in the wall. Caleb squeaked as one stopped and stuck its head through the gap to see what was there, but Stella wrapped her hand round his mouth. The zombie, who clearly when being resurrected had forgotten to bring its nose, didn't see nor smell them and continued.

Several Magma men, however, did go through the gap and Ebony stared fearfully as one descended the escalator, glowing with anticipation of a potential kill. One, she could handle. But if more came, they were screwed. Tentacles traced the floor in front of it like a walking cane but as predicted, the magma man stopped short of the water and when the tip of its limb crackled and steamed, hastily left.

"Are they gone?" Caleb asked uneasily. His eye could see through the wall but seeing the dead wasn't built into its programming.

"I think so." Ebony squinted into the darkness. Once the rumbling of the masses ceased, they carefully climbed the escalator. The path through the shopping centre had been ruined by water and rubble but they didn't want to go back through the sewer.

"I can't see a thing," Stella frowned.

"I think I can do something about that," Ebony realised. Cupping her hands together, she rested them in the air in front of her and willed a flame to grow. Telepathy seemed easy enough; all she had to do was think, but pyrokinesis, she didn't know where to begin. But with no easy feat, and such concentration that she could feel physical strain clogging her veins, a small flame grew in her hands. Stella gasped and leant down to admire it, holding her hair back.

"Now that's incredible."

"Did we miss something? You were a telepath a minute ago," Caleb stated, his eyes widened in the flickering light. "Can it find us the way out?" Ebony shrugged.

"Long story. There are shopping centre entrances across the city, we have to find one eventually." With the small light to guide them and the pungent smell from the sewers spurring them on, they traipsed through the halls but fell silent as a growl echoed across the room.

"Light off," Stella demanded. Ebony squeezed her hands together and the flame was gone in a minuscule puff of smoke.

"Down here." Caleb put his ear to a staircase. "Seems safe." They splashed down the saturated treads, but it was a wrong choice.

Caleb wailed, as, despite his eye, he skulked directly into a wall.

Ebony, without thinking nearly as hard, summoned back the flame, and held it towards Caleb, who's nose was bleeding heavily. A whistle of air escaped her pursed lips. "You'll be fine."

"Ebony." Stella tapped her shoulder and followed her eyes. From the staircase from which they came, came grunting and shuffling.

"We're trapped," Caleb whispered, pushing at the walls of the shops. His nose was the least of his worries as claustrophobia grasped him like an icy hand. He buried his chin in the jumper he had on over the armour, breathing in the smell to find a sense of comfort and familiarity.

"Ebony, can't you do something?" Stella breathed but Ebony was overcome with fright and found it impossible to do anything.

"I'm trying." She was clicking her fingers, but couldn't focus enough with the oncoming threat to conjure anything of use. "Just be quiet, they won't find us." A zombie rounded the corner, trying to sniff them out like a dog.

"I need to sneeze," Caleb whispered as he sniffed deeply.

"Caleb, darling, with respect, if you sneeze, I will feed you to the zombies myself." Stella instilled the fear of God in him. He struggled for a moment but twitching his nose like a mouse, the urge disappeared, and the Zombie walked past.

"Welcome to Chane mall." The electric advertisement board behind them lit up brilliantly. "Welcome ttttttttttt ch-ch-ch-ch-chaaneeeeeee m-m-m-malllll." As the water rose around Ebony, Stella, and Caleb's legs, it washed over the electronics. The sign fused and broke but not before making an ungodly noise. The zombie worked out where they were. It wasn't hard, even for a creature without a brain. On spotting them, saliva dripped from its mouth, and it clawed the ground like a bull ready to charge.

"Ebony," Caleb said urgently. "Ebony!" He raised his voice as the zombie charged. Ebony held out her palm and a burst of air fired from it. She fired again. The zombie stumbled back but another one replaced it and Ebony's bursts of air were rendered inoffensive.

The zombie lurched forward, and they all ducked. But the pain of a zombie clawing into their insides never came. Ebony, who had squeezed her eyes firmly shut, dared open one.

The zombie before them was completely paralysed. Caleb gambled uncovering his face but was left untouched. He waved his hand in front of the zombie's stretched gob, but it didn't react. Ebony and Stella unshielded themselves.

"Are they dead?" Stella asked. "Like, dead dead?"

"Don't know," Caleb said.

"Can you check?"

"No."

"Why not?"

"Cause they might be dead and I don't want to touch a dead body with my bare hands."

Stella rolled her eyes. "Ebony, was that you?"

"I don't know," Ebony said. Then, with an almighty groan, the ceiling above them began to crack.

"Is this you?"

"No!" Ebony cried and they covered their heads as rubble started to fall. But, contrary to their expectancy that the ground was about to collapse on them, it instead flew upwards until their tunnel was drowned in daylight. Ebony saw Oscar help Emmanuel clamber out of the rubble and whilst she wanted to run to them, she paused as a shadow covered her and the ground was thrown carelessly into a nearby skyscraper.

Ebony turned to see who'd saved them, but she would have felt safer with the zombies who now poured away as Atlas landed. With a click of his fingers, Caleb and Stella yelled out in pain and dropped to the floor. Atlas yanked his hand upwards, and they became entangled in the same snare that Stella had been caught in before.

"Atlas, stop!" Ebony yelled. Every weapon was pointed at him but she was still disadvantaged and as Caleb and Stella struggled against the tendrils, Atlas gained the upper hand. He adjusted the corroded metal crown he'd refused to take off and smirked.

"Ebony, I'm so glad you came."

"Cut the crap Atlas, this isn't a family reunion."

Atlas raised an eyebrow. "So, you know?" He stroked the air where his beard would be if he'd had one. "Come with me, we can talk in private."

Ebony don't test him Emmanuel whispered in her head. *He'll kill you.*

I know Ebony replied, but she couldn't oppose his request without putting Stella and Caleb at risk. She took a tentative step towards him as he offered a path through the rubble, bricks parting as he waved his hands. The silence that had befallen Chane was one not heard since Drognir had been an undiscovered planet of mere bacterial life. It was as though even the birds had stopped to witness the confrontation on the bleak shores.

"Let them go and I'll come with you," she bartered. Atlas rolled his head back with a single spat out laugh.

"You still dare to negotiate your terms?" he thundered. "They'll be freed once you've come with me."

Ebony, if you're his daughter you can do anything Emmanuel reminded her. Atlas narrowed his eyes at Emmanuel, sensing telepathy but unable to hear it. He wasn't yet restored to his former glory, and Emmanuel kept his mind well shielded.

"Okay," Ebony agreed aloud, talking to both of them. She boldly walked forward, the zombie crowd gnashing their teeth, held back by some intangible force of Atlas' doing. She found herself hoping his power was strong, if only to keep them at bay for long enough.

"Ebony don't." Oscar started forward but the smoke whipped out like snakes, and he stepped back into place. Atlas grinned as Ebony moved, falsely believing he had won her over.

"See, we're not so different, you and I," he said. Ebony was halted by his riling words, clenching her fists. She had no inclination to bond with her supposed father.

"We are nothing alike." Ebony stood defiantly. "Our differences are monumental."

"How so?" Atlas was thoroughly entertained.

"You want to destroy this universe," she said, "and all I want is to save it."

"It's much simpler than that," Atlas scoffed. "You and I want the same thing. Power. Once you've tasted the power you can command, you'll never have enough. you're like an open book!"

"And what do the pages say?" Ebony yelled.

"They say—" Atlas began but Ebony cut him off.

"—They say that everyone in this entire bloody universe craves power whether it be the power to run a country or the power just to get out of bed in the morning. So yes, I want power. But I want the power to do my part and make the universe a better place!" Atlas growled at her lampooning outburst.

Ebony's eyes watered and her voice broke as Caleb and Stella's lives hung in the balance behind her.

She had to do something.

Clicking her fingers, she remembered how Noah had summoned a portal. Small sparks erupted from the tension between her thumb and middle finger, and when she looked into her palm, she no longer saw the calloused, pale skin of her hands, but a view of Atlas from behind, and herself walking towards him. The question was now not how to make a portal, but how to use it. To free Caleb and Stella or to attack Atlas.

Attack Atlas.

At a closer range, she envisioned herself appearing behind Atlas, gun in hand, aimed for his head preferably. Touching the small of her back, Ebony stepped over a gun, and it floated into her hand, pulled from Atlas' parting rocks.

You can do this Ebony Emmanuel thought.

But suddenly an almighty roar scotched Ebony's train of thought and her portal fizzled out. Noah was riding towards them on the back of Jeff, who was now a dragon, burning the zombies below with an everlasting fiery breath.

"Noah, get out of here!" Ebony screamed, as he unwittingly began the catastrophic accident that Cascia had foreshadowed. But he, on a violent rampage, soared from the back of Jeff and dived towards Atlas.

Ebony conjured a portal and without thinking jumped through, appearing in a dive next to Noah.

"Belize, get them out of there!" Emmanuel shouted.

"Noah, get out of here," Ebony cried. Atlas had daggers of dark magic pointed at them. The element of surprise was lost. "Noah! He'll kill you!"

Belize? Emmanuel couldn't find her thoughts. Noah, who's confidence quickly faded, tried to teleport but he was panicked and couldn't.

Calm down Ebony told him. What she meant was that she would create a portal instead for both of them to fall through. But Noah mistook her meaning and assumed she meant try again.

Two portals were simultaneously created.

As they grew, they merged and spasmed out of control, colliding until Ebony and Noah could no longer get to safety through them but instead, saw an unknown world. Noah, being the more professional teleporter tried to make a new portal but in the air neither could control themselves. Tumbling downwards, they flew straight into the portal, and it snapped shut behind them with an explosion that rocked Drognir to its core.

Chapter 14

Atlas sat on his throne, his body bound in a series of bandages, lotions, potions, and herbal remedies. The nurses who had applied said medicines now lay dead, or close to it, in a pool of blood across the floor, accompanied by the woman who, twenty-one years ago had stolen Ebony away and sealed their fate.

Atlas winced as he moved and then winced as he winced, a nasty scar running down from the peak of his singed brow, through his eye and to his cheek. He had faced the explosion caused by Ebony head on and was forced to leave. His body was badly wounded, his pride even more so.

"I want her found."

"My Lord..."

"Daegel!" Atlas yelled. He clenched his jaw and the whimpering of the nurses ceased, and the man who was once confidently Atlas' right-hand man shuffled meekly towards him. "You have failed to capture Ebony and now she has escaped."

"CCTV caught the incident. Her and the other teleporter's portals collided, and they fell through to an unspecified world. We've been searching the universe but have yet to find her." Atlas raised his hand and Daegel fell silent.

"Her portal?" he questioned. Daegel gulped, scratching the back of his neck.

"Yes, sire, it seems she is discovering what she can do with the help of the other Enchanteds," Daegel explained, "and those-" he gagged, "-humans." Atlas fell silent and Daegel gormlessly felt it appropriate to continue talking. "It's not surprising. She is your daughter." Atlas snapped his fingers and Daegel instantly dropped to the floor, clutching his neck. He choked and Atlas took pleasure in watching for a moment before he clicked his fingers again and Daegel was released. The reapers in the room watched on, wearing the same vacant expression as they had when Atlas had done the same minutes earlier.

"Ebony is only just discovering what she can do. It won't be long before she attacks."

"We don't know if she's still alive." Daegel tried to make things better.

"She is. If her amount of magic was to fade, I would feel it. But I want her dead." Shock spread across Daegel's face and there was a cry of protest as Joplin stepped forward from the darkest corner of the room, treading lightly over the bodies of what were her only friends on the ghastly island.

"My darling, we still need her to revive Sonneillon. And you promised—" Atlas interrupted and glared at her; lips curled back in anger.

"—I promised? I promised she would remain alive, and you could have her when I was done with her. But you promised me twenty-one years ago that the daughter you gave birth to wasn't an Enchanted-" he turned his anger to Daegel, "-and that she had been disposed of! None of this would have occurred if you hadn't lied." Joplin's face fell, Daegel's further with the thought that his idol would hate him so. "So, Joplin, I promise you can have her dead body," Atlas said conclusively, spitting at the floor. Joplin held back her tears.

"I am sorry my Lord." Daegel dropped to a knee. "I humbly beg for your gracious forgiveness, although I am not deserving of such a reward." Atlas' eyes narrowed.

"You believe that your admittance of Ebony's existence, twenty years after it began, warrants my forgiveness?"

"You were angry sire," Daegel fumbled. "You had the chest, but the key was gone, and I knew where. I thought if I told you about her, you would be pleased."

"I would have been delighted if only the words had spilled from your wretched mouth twenty years earlier!" Atlas screeched. "You are not forgiven. You are alive only because your service to hunt Ebony down is still required. Don't mistake your usefulness for my sentiment."

"Yes, my lord." Daegel bowed. Atlas sat back in his throne.

"You shouldn't have named her," he further berated Joplin. "You get too attached to the children you name. That's why we number them."

"I understand," Joplin said, rubbing her stomach with a hand as the baby within kicked. "What about Sonneillon?" she asked timidly.

"He was weak." Atlas stood and from a table placed to the left of the throne, picked up the box containing Sonneillon's magic. "And the weak are not deserving of such power." He held out his hand and a new, identical key came flying into it.

He shoved it into the box.

It clicked.

"I don't need to rely on Sonneillon to—"

"--This much power could kill you," Joplin warned. Atlas' body went rigid and even Daegel drew a sharp intake of breath.

"I'm sorry? Did the middle of my sentence interrupt the beginning of yours?" Atlas spun round and stared at her, eyes like a snake and saliva dripping from his open mouth. He was hungry for the magic and Joplin saw something change within him. A new evil, a darker evil, one she neither supported nor loved. "Screw Sonneillon, that Ancient was nothing without me." Atlas clenched his fists. "My days of being second best are over." He paused and watched Joplin with a sick smile which made her step back. "Belphegor and Adremelech's strength combined with Sonneillon's magic, it's all we need," he said. "We have to kill Ebony, before she becomes an even bigger threat." Atlas knew he could become powerful again but him and his kin had been beaten before by their daughters and he dare not take any risks.

"What would you have me do?" Joplin asked.

"Nothing. By the last light of the day, I'll be powerful enough to kill Ebony, like a child tramples a bug. She, those Enchanteds and the human scum following her around will beg for death when I'm through with them. But only when the last piece of muscle is peeled from their bones, the last bone smashed beneath my fist, will they feel that sweet release." Atlas threatened. "Daegel, assemble the armies together. We're going to war." The command cheered Daegel up; after all, he was a man who thrived on combat.

He bowed deeply, before walking out with Joplin. As the door crashed shut, Atlas knelt with the box in front of him. With only a moment's hesitation, he opened it. Power surged out, in the form of smoke and light and pain and Atlas howled as he began to absorb it. The whole process lasted less than ten seconds but when it was over, Atlas was a different man.

Was he even a man anymore?

He stood, visibly tired but also stronger. The bestial monster roared; serpentine eyes transfixed on the door.

"Joplin, I did not say you could leave." It quickly opened and she reappeared.

"Yes, Atlas?" she asked, bowing deeply. His reddened eyes marked her with a deathly stare.

"I no longer require children."

Joplin knew what it meant for her.

"Did I ever mean anything to you?" She asked.

"You were a womb," Atlas answered, raising a hand. Rather than try and run, Joplin stood steadfast and stared deeply into his eyes.

"I pray for my daughter. I pray for her friends. And I pray that you burn under her hand," she cursed.

"That will never happen," Atlas said simply. He admired his own hand as a green spark surrounded it, lighting his veins. "Did you know, one of Sonneillon's favourite magic tricks was his acid? Gave an agonising death but neat to clean, because by the time the person was dead, they were nothing but a puddle on the floor. The only reason people knew someone had died, were the screams." Joplin adjusted her dress and savoured her last breath.

"I shall not give you such pleasure." With a tap of his finger against the throne, Atlas sent a wave of acid flooding into Joplin.

Nothing could be heard throughout the corridors.

When the deed was done, Atlas waved his hand and the reapers grabbed the muck, reaping the two souls left lingering in the air and throwing the remains into the lava to dispose of it. Atlas smelt the stench of death as though it was ecstasy to him. And then he faced the corner of the room where two men stood, tied in iron chains to the wall and staring in horror.

"You bow to me now." The light of the lava flickered dully across the faces of the two men who were obliged to sink on to one knee. "We will kill Ebony. Belphegor. Adremelech. Brothers. Soon, we will be restored to our former glory, and the world will burn."

Chapter 15

The surroundings Ebony found herself in were unfamiliar and somewhat menacing. Clouds of claret red and a rolling thunderstorm made her think she hadn't landed in the nicest place but thankfully, Noah had crashed with her. She was comforted by his company despite only knowing him for a short while. They were squatting cautiously at the entrance of the small cave they had found, warily watching the environment for any hostility.

Noah's leg was outstretched as he pulled his trousers tightly around the cut down his calf. The atmosphere was rich with nitrous oxide, which helped with the pain.

"How you feeling?" asked Ebony, as Noah rolled his shoulder.

"Like I've been slapped by a bus, sliced by a skyscraper... I think inanimate objects have it in for me." Ebony chuckled.

"We haven't landed in the friendliest of places," she commented.

"I don't think you're strong enough to teleport yet, so we'll have to stay for a bit."

"Can't you take us home?"

"I can't teleport that great a distance. I've barely been practising my powers a month and it was an immensely strong portal you summoned," Noah praised.

"Believe me, I didn't mean to," she muttered. "A month?"

"Well, I've been able to teleport for years, but never wanted to."

"Why?"

"Dad thinks I'm a freak. He disowned me, banned me from seeing my sister Leana. I hoped that not using my skills would somehow change his mind about me. But alas..." Noah trailed off, slapping his hands against his thighs. "So recently I thought, screw it. I might as well make the most of what I can do." He seemed light-hearted despite the sadness of the tale.

"Sorry."

"Nah, don't be."

Ebony watched him, bewildered and jealous of his relaxed attitude.

"Is this an average Monday for you? Fighting zombies, using skyscrapers as slip n' slides and teleporting to creepy planets?"

"Nah, normally that's on a Tuesday. Mondays are my days off," he grinned.

Ebony chortled. "Sure." And then she took a more serious tone. "Noah, how could Atlas possibly know I'm his daughter?"

"He sounded sure but… I guess that doesn't mean much."

"All he had to go on was a necklace." Ebony wanted him to be wrong.

"There is a way of making sure but I'm not sure how good an idea it is." Ebony sat up straight.

"Tell me."

"Enchanteds tend to have a cluster of related powers, i.e.: Emmanuel is telepathic, but he is also somewhat telekinetic. Jeff can shapeshift but he can also talk to animals."

"So, what's your collection of skills?" Ebony asked.

"I can teleport, but I can also dream walk i.e.: teleport into people's minds, and I can travel backwards in time."

Ebony admired his skills. "So technically we could go back to see when I was born?"

"If Atlas sees us, we're screwed," Noah said.

"But we don't have to go near him." Ebony was getting excited. "We can go to the orphanage where I was dropped off and talk to the person who left me there!" She jumped up.

"Are you sure?" Noah asked. "What if Atlas was the one who left you there?"

"You think he'd take the time out of his day to take care of a baby?"

"Fair point."

"I'll get us back to Drognir if you'll take me to the orphanage," she traded.

"Deal." They shook hands and after a moment of regaining her composure, Ebony made a portal, still stunned by her own ability, and the two of them stepped through and into an alleyway of present day Chane. The orphanage was on the outskirts of town, so they were safe enough but even from afar, Ebony could see the damage done. Alarms wailed, their noise unheard of since the last galactic war, and an evacuation zone was being set up just east of where Ebony and Noah stood.

"Right, a deal's a deal," Noah said and with more effort than a normal portal required, he summoned one of a different calibre, shakier and much more unstable. Its physical appearance seemed to warp in and out of reality. "Through, quickly," he urged, and they jumped into the past.

It was now a cold and nostalgic December 2nd, 2568; the year 2592 could only be dreamt about. Their first activity in the past was to take cover from the intense storm brewing. Beneath some scaffolding, Ebony stared at the orphanage with a degree of contempt. It was as she recollected. Since she'd left it had been renovated but, in this year, it was the same rustic shithole she remembered it to be.

Stella had been raised alongside her in this very same orphanage until she had been fortunate enough to be adopted. She was the closest thing Ebony had to a family and still was, despite now knowing her real relatives. Growing up in the same orphanage, they were equally inseparable as kids and adults; even ending up looking similar. And neither of them had looked back once leaving. It was obvious as to why.

"You lived here?" Noah remarked as water ran down both sides of the windows. The whole building was in a dilapidated condition, bathed in a shaft of moonlight which revealed only its flaws. A broken window, an overflowing gutter, and a roof which didn't seem to cover the whole ceiling, meaning that whoever slept on the top floor was in for a wet night when it rained and a cold night when it didn't.

"Yep," she sighed. She was one of the forgotten orphans of Chane. Noah cringed.

"So, now what?"

"Now, we wait," she said.

They sat out of the rain and in an air of lethargy, watching for any movement. Noah technically hadn't even been born yet; his birth was to come six days later on a planet on the other side of the universe.

It hit midnight before something happened.

"Ebony." A pointy elbow nudged her ribs and she jolted from her half-asleep state, where nightmares of Atlas plagued her conscience.

"There." Noah pointed to where a woman was rushing towards the orphanage, flinching at every noise whether it be the loud cars on the highway or the buzz of the fluorescent street lamps overhead. She was carrying a bundle of cloth and as she lay it at the door, it squirmed and moved and Ebony and Noah watched as a small baby fist emerged from it, reaching for someone to hold her.

"That's me?" Ebony was shocked. She watched intently as the woman rang the bell and sprinted away, luckily in their direction. As she rounded the corner, she yelped as Noah and Ebony stopped her and shovelled her into the alley.

"What do you want from me?" she cried. "I don't have any money, please."

"We're not here to hurt you." Ebony put her mind at ease. "We just want to ask you a few questions."

"We won't keep you long," Noah said. The woman relaxed a little, her shoulders sagging as he let go, but she still wore an expression of apprehension.

"I can't take the child back," she said hastily. "It's not mine."

"That's not what we want. Were you sent here by a man called Atlas? Or a woman named Joplin?" Ebony asked and the colour drained from the woman's face.

"I really must be going," she said, successfully barging past Ebony but not Noah, who blocked her way.

"Please. Answer the question," he said, his demeanour kind but stern. The woman exhaled and checked over her shoulder, wrapping her shawl tighter around her.

"Joplin sent me. Atlas doesn't know I've come. If he did, he'd kill me, and her, and the baby too, and probably everyone else for good measure."

"Why, why did she send you?" Ebony asked.

"Joplin lied to Atlas, told him the baby wasn't capable of possessing magic, so to him she was useless. He sent Daegel to kill her, but a mother's love is stronger than Atlas' orders. She told me to take her as far away from him as I could," she said. Ebony's jaw dropped.

"So, Joplin is my... the baby's mother and Atlas is her father?" Ebony confirmed.

"Yes," the woman said, Ebony was speechless.

"Thank you." Noah shook the woman's hand but she pulled it away. "Sorry for scaring you." The woman flashed a half-hearted smile and rushed off into the darkness. Ebony turned to him.

"I've met her — Joplin," Ebony said. "Twice. I spoke to my mother, and I didn't even know it." Her eyes stared past Noah and to the baby on the doorstep. No one had answered yet, but Ebony wasn't surprised. The matron was a heavy sleeper and cared more for her bed than for the children.

"We should go," Noah said, but Ebony shook her head. She gulped.

"Give me a minute," she said, and wandered over towards the stairs with a strange sense of Déjà vu. She was rewriting her past and could almost recollect herself as a baby seeing a stranger walk towards her.

"Ebony, you shouldn't interact with your past self," Noah warned.

"I'm not even a day old, it's not going to hurt," she answered. Noah stayed back, standing idly by with a portal should trouble present itself, but smiled warmly at the child as Ebony picked herself up. She nudged the blanket from the baby's face and a pitiful sigh left her lips as she revealed the fateful necklace hanging from her neck.

"Hey baby me," she said, holding out her finger. "Bet you weren't expecting to see me, were you?" The baby clasped it with a tiny fist and yawned and Ebony beamed. "You're gonna have a lot of shit ahead of you," she said, "then when you get out of the orphanage, it's going to be even worse. But you've got this." Little Ebony gawked back at her and gurgled profusely in her own strange language. "I'm sorry all this happens to you. I wish I could take you away and keep you safe from all of this…"

Dull lights in the window above their heads clicked on and footsteps could be heard making their way to the door. "Ebony we need to go," Noah warned. He reassuringly put a hand on her shoulder as she held herself closely.

"I'm coming." Ebony carefully put the baby down, kissing its forehead. "And remember, don't feel shit about being an orphan, parents are overrated, especially ours." Noah laughed.

Ebony smiled sadly and regretfully walked away, wishing she could save herself. If she gave the necklace to another random child, maybe

Daegel would never find her. But she didn't want to burden anyone else with what she had to do.

As they rounded the corner, they heard a squeak and Ebony couldn't help but veer back towards the orphanage. The matron had finally opened the door and viewed the baby in utter scorn.

"Mistress Giles," she called, "we've got another one." With sausage-like fingers and face blushing like a tomato from the effort of walking, the much-disliked matron hauled Ebony up and took her inside, slamming the door. Ebony heard a baby cry from the noise and imagined it was herself.

"She's pleasant," Noah said sarcastically. "We've got another one. You're a baby not a piece of trash."

"She was a lovely woman if you like skunk-smelling, God-complexed assholes," Ebony said in response. "She didn't much like the job." Noah observed her pitifully.

"Clearly," he said, unimpressed. "Come on, "let's get out of here."

"Can't we go back further?" Ebony asked. "Take out Atlas before all of this happens."

"Ebony. For one, I can't go back in time that far. And secondly, going back in time to change things won't change the future." Noah concentrated on making a portal back to their current time. "I don't know how it works, but those are the rules. Otherwise, historians would have ruined history."

"Historians?"

"Yeah," Noah said. "How d'you think we know so much about the past? It wasn't all dug up from a hole in the ground." Ebony smiled as Noah wiggled his eyebrows. He extended the portal towards Ebony but before she could step into it, he gently touched her arm. "Ebony, one thing," Noah said quietly. "Remember what Cascia said; if we stuck together something bad would happen? Be prepared for it not to be okay on the other side of the portal." Ebony slipped her arm through his. She gulped.

"We'll manage," she said, and they stepped through.

Noah crafted several consecutive portals as they planet hopped away from Chane in increments he could manage, and through the final portal Ebony found herself in a place she'd never been to.

An asteroid.

"Where are we?" She marvelled.

"Welcome to Alchemacier, the home of the Enchanteds, where we've lived since the bloodline began," Noah introduced. If Ebony's jaw could have dropped to the floor, it would have done. There were so many things to behold, Ebony didn't know where to begin but she was utterly captivated by what lay before her.

Herself and Noah had landed at the end of a paved viaduct stretching across the sky. It ended abruptly a few metres behind the portal they'd come through, with broken rocks falling from the precipice, some hanging from ivy which wormed its way through the cement and precariously dangled the rocks in mid-air. Water poured from drain openings in the side of the walkway and plummeted down the moss-covered wall, whilst above their heads the ruins of ancient archways provided a little shade from the closest star.

The walkway originated from the structure before them, the most prominent feature of the asteroid; a fantastical castle which challenged the gravitational pull of the rock, floating above a waterfall that poured through a mountain and deep into the heart of the asteroid. It was anachronistic of early 21st century, or perhaps late 20th, Ebony wasn't sure, but it was nevertheless magnificent. Large towers upsurged into the sky, heavily fortified turrets guarding each corner and a luscious garden surrounded the entire building. To ensure it didn't float away, bulky chains covered with scandent vines secured the castle to the mountainside.

As well as paths, Ebony noticed several floating islands leading to the castle and beyond, ascending in increments with rope bridges and floating stepping-stones attaching them. Some housed long piers for ships to dock, whilst others held towers on them for a view of the asteroid as a whole. But one thing was for certain, the castle was undeniably the designated centre of the asteroid and everything else built around it.

A town, technologically advanced although one would never guess looking at the cottage design, climbed the mountain from several angles and cascaded into a valley below. Pseudo old buildings packed closely together similarly to Drognir but with half the height. Cobbled streets protruded from the edges of the walled municipal and disappeared into several different otherworldly biomes, which Ebony assumed had been mimicked to cater for all Enchanteds on the asteroid.

"It's nothing like Bract," Noah commented. Ebony couldn't draw her eyes away from the surroundings to answer.

"You were raised on the pit stop?"

"Yep. Not a single piece of nature to be seen." Bract was humanities first stop between leaving Earth and finding a second home, a planet of dirt. But despite the unattractiveness of it, many people chose never to leave and so it became known as the pit stop. And Noah was right; Alchemacier was nothing like it.

An antediluvian jungle stretched beyond the horizon of the asteroid. A dense thicket shaded the self-sustainable food rich fields lying to the side of it. Peeking out from the leaves were properly engineered treehouses and on the forest floor, supersized mushrooms made unique homes for the Enchanteds living there. With lanterns dangling from every tree and branches grown to intertwine, creating pathways, the whole forest had a fairylike feel.

To the right of Ebony and Noah, the waterfalls consolidated within a deep river flowing through the city and into a lake on its outskirts. The lake was crystal clear and below the surface the city continued; glass domes filled with houses were intercepted by vibrant coral reefs stretching across the lake floor. Ebony also noticed several large holes scattered about, which led into underground cave systems, yet another habitat on the asteroid. It was a utopia.

However, Ebony's favourite part of the asteroid wasn't the homely city, nor the futuristic underwater housing; it was the animals. As Ebony had tried to take in the vista, she'd noticed animals walking across the rolling fields below them. Some of them didn't faze her, such as the elephants who wandered without restriction across the plains, but others did and once again, her jaw dropped as she gawked at an animal close by.

"Uh, Noah… is that Jeff…?" Ebony trailed off as she watched a majestic, prehistoric creature walk through the undergrowth of the forest which sat atop the western hill.

"Nope, Arnold, our male Hua… huecathlu… huehuehuecathanltus… Huehuecanauhtlus?" He scratched his head.

186

"Easy for you to say," Ebony said. She felt like a giddy child watching the Santonian dinosaur saunter by. "How?"

"We have a male and female of almost every animal ever to live in our universe. They live in harmony across this asteroid, so we can always preserve at least two of every species. Sort of like Noah's ark but without killing people."

"Wait, was Noah real?"

"Oh yeah, he was a great Enchanted too apparently, had the ability to talk to animals." Noah winked as Ebony's smile brightened.

Above their heads, two birds Ebony couldn't name sat chirping at each other. For her, it was nice to see a real bird, not one with a camera lens for an eye like many on Drognir. As they walked, a grizzly bear traipsed by, grunting at them but in a docile manner. Ebony's first instinct was to take a step back, but Noah kept on walking and bobbed his head to the bear as he walked past.

"The animals here are nothing to be afraid of," he told Ebony. The bear stared at her. Harnessing a mixture of Jeff's unique power and Emmanuel's brief lesson in telepathy, she grunted but in her ears, it didn't sound like a grunt.

"Hi," she said, surprising herself.

"Hello," he said. "I didn't know a new shapeshifter had arrived." Ebony's eyes widened and her mouth opened in delight.

"I'm Ebony."

"Odwic." He walked to Ebony and held out a paw, which Ebony took in both hands and shook. "It's a pleasure to meet you."

Ebony, Noah. Emmanuel's voice filled their heads suddenly with a stiff expression. *We need you in the castle.* There was no, 'we're glad to have you back', no, 'thank goodness you're all right' and Ebony didn't know what could have happened for Emmanuel's thoughts to be so dampened.

"We should head up," Noah suggested. Ebony nodded.

"Nice to meet you Odwic," she said. The bear bowed his head majestically and continued on his way, as Noah and Ebony headed towards the castle. They walked as opposed to teleporting. Ebony wanted to watch the animals, but the two of them were also apprehensive about the situation they were headed towards, so much so that Noah preferred to walk on an injured leg than take the easy route.

Across the path before them a horned horse cantered towards the grasslands, and a skip was added to Ebony's step.

"Is that a unicorn? I didn't know unicorns ever existed." Her excitement quickly crumpled as Noah tutted.

"They don't. Jeff, stop messing about!" Noah yelled, throwing a rock playfully in his direction. The unicorn snorted, air coming from its nostrils as it ponied away.

"Huh." Noah raised his eyebrows. "Guess they do."

"Good to see you're okay." The door was open when Noah and Ebony reached it, opened by Cascia. She was still standing with her weight propped on one leg, shoulders hunched and utterly defeated by the basic chore of opening the door.

"You too," Ebony said but she received a nasty glare.

"You got Belize killed," Cascia spat. "I couldn't care less how you are." She refused to make eye contact as she limped off. Cascia was hotheaded and maybe it was the way she swung the heavy door on Ebony, or the way she looked at her as though she was a piece of filth, or the fact that they'd exchanged few words but Cascia contradicted everything Ebony said, but Ebony was sure Cascia disliked her greatly.

Ebony's blood boiled, her nostrils flared and if it weren't for Noah holding the door open for her, she would have yelled a stream of curse words. He offered for her to walk indoors before him. The chivalry soothed her slightly. The door shut with a mighty bang that left in its wake a graveyard silence as Cascia disappeared from view.

The castle's interior was spacious, with arched ceilings and grand marble floors stretching from outrageously huge rooms. Chandeliers hung from the ceiling and statues of figures Ebony didn't recognise but would one day learn were famous Enchanteds, guarded the entrance to each room.

"Ebony?" From a grand staircase at the end of the entrance hall she saw Oscar. He was frail and the colour was washed from his face. But he was alive.

"Oscar!" She took the stairs two at a time, nearly knocking him off his feet as they embraced. "You're okay," she cried, tears flushing down her cheeks. She buried her face safely into his chest, the familiar smell of bread still lingering on his clothes that dampened with her tears.

"We thought we'd lost you," Oscar said. His nails were bitten raw from anxiety and his whole body was shaking.

"Where's Caleb and Stella and Emmanuel?"

"Emmanuel's upstairs… Listen Ebony…" Oscar's words stopped Ebony in her tracks. One foot on the stair above, she turned to him. His poker face was abysmal.

"What?" she asked. Oscar was a near impossible person to make cry. He could be overwhelmingly emotional, but she'd only ever seen tears from him at Ignis and so her heart plummeted in time with the tear that rolled down his cheek.

"Ebony…" His voice was brittle, and as he shook his head, ash fell from his hair despite having had a shower.

"Tell me, what happened?" She braced herself as Oscar brought her in for another hug. He remained quiet, so she leant her forehead against his. Rather than him speak, Ebony found herself slowly delving into his mind.

"Ebony!" Oscar screamed. He watched as her and Noah fell in unison through the sky, struggling to keep control. "Emmanuel, do something," he begged.

Jeff, catch them! Emmanuel ordered but Jeff had pulled up like a jet to avoid crashing into the ground and wasn't close enough. Without understanding what had happened, a huge hole opened in the sky and Ebony and Noah were gone. As Atlas fired at them, the hole closed up, deflecting his power back at him. He was clearly too weak to fight himself off and as the magic soared back towards him, he tried to destroy it with another surge of energy. "Get down!" Cascia yelled and grabbing Oscar who was nearest, she shoved the two of them into a manhole. There was a painful bang, so loud that as Oscar recalled it Ebony recoiled. An engulfing shadow of smoke and fire blasted across the manhole at such force the ladder snapped and Oscar and Cascia yelped as they fell back into the sewer.

"Oscar. Where are Stella and Caleb?" Ebony stopped reading his mind momentarily. He bowed his head.

"I wanted to save them." Ebony gazed into his puffy eyes, but he looked away. The words 'I'm sorry' replayed over and over in his head as he recollected what had happened and the more pain he felt, the more piercing and vivid the memories got.

"Oscar… Oscar?" As smoke slowly left the sewer, he saw Cascia in front of him. She grabbed his shoulder and shook him violently. "Can you hear me?" she yelled, fingertips pressing into the torn armour he wore.

"Yeah, yeah I can hear you," he said as he banged his hand against his head. Gunk fell from his ear and he gagged, revolted. He couldn't see properly and his memories from the moment were shaky, but Cascia spoke.

"Stay here a minute, I'll see what's going on." She propped the broken ladder against the slimy walls.

"I'm coming," Oscar said defiantly. She gave him a stern frown but didn't argue and they both climbed the ladder into an empty city. Ashes of the zombies floated in the soughing wind and Atlas was nowhere to be seen; he was, after all, in the heart of the explosion. It was as though a nuclear bomb had gone off, shadows of the zombies scarred the floor and stained the walls. Oscar caught sight of Jeff, sitting on the ground, still in the form of a dragon but curled around something.

"Jeff?" Cascia cried and on opening his golden reptilian eyes and seeing her, he shifted back to human form, his clothes torn and soot covered. He revealed Emmanuel lying next to him. "Emmanuel?" Cascia was beginning to panic but bruised, bloody and alive, he stood from where he was being protected by Jeff's fireproof wing. Mentally, he was lost. He had witnessed the deaths of the obliterated as though he had not just heard but felt everyone die.

"What happened?" Oscar asked.

"Ebony and Atlas' powers combined caused an explosion. Her and Noah could be anywhere, and Atlas is gone," Emmanuel said. *Killed Belize and fled like a coward!* he screamed suddenly, and his voice rung in everyone's head as he kicked the ground. Jeff cautiously approached, putting a firm hand on his shoulders as they drooped.

"Where's Stella? And Caleb?" Oscar asked, looking to the sky with

190

dusty tears crusting his eyelashes. Jeff shook his head as he recounted what he saw.

"We all ran for cover. I think they hid behind the ship." The Hyperion was still in the sky. Oscar sought to find to where Cascia had landed the launch ship, but it was no longer there.

"What ship?"

"It was destroyed in the explosion." Reduced to ash, as well as the buildings and everything else in the area, the only evidence the ship was there was the memory they had of seeing it. Oscar dropped to his knees and crawled over to the spot, where the shadow of a crouched figure blemished the tarmac.

"You can't be gone." He dropped his head to the ground, banging his fists until he drew blood. "No!" Tears fell in torrents down his face as he stared at the shadow. A single, trembling finger traced its outline, the permanent reminder that his friends were dead. Cascia hobbled over to him and knelt by his body, clutching his hand in hers. She ignored her own pain to try and sooth his.

"There's only one shadow," she said. "There's a chance one of them is still alive."

As if on cue, a noise made them start.

Somewhere, someone had survived.

"Oscar…" It was a faint whimper but someone was calling his name.

"Did you hear that?" He paused and so did the others. The noise of sirens was drawing closer and could easily be mistaken for a yell, but Oscar was adamant. "Someone said my name. Emmanuel, you can read minds, who was it?"

"It doesn't really work like that; I have to know who I'm talking to…"

"Make it work!" Oscar yelled, rage brewing inside him. Emmanuel, tired and broken over Belize, grimaced angrily. Nevertheless, he shut his eyes and concentrated. After a moment, he looked at Oscar, with a powerful hint of hope in his eyes.

"I think… Caleb?" he questioned. Oscar stood and yelled, his voice hoarse but unwavering.

"Caleb? Caleb!" No one else spoke and the feeling of hopelessness spread through Oscar but as he was about to give up, he noticed a second manhole, further back.

"Caleb?"

Oscar pulled away from Ebony, rubbing together his bloodied knuckles anxiously.

"He's upstairs." Oscar shut off his thoughts as Ebony tried to force herself further into them. He worried about how she would react. Ebony had a tendency to be too harsh on herself. She would pin Stella's death on herself.

"Stella…" Ebony said numbly. "My Stella." The physical breaking of her heart in two was a more prevalent pain than any she had felt. She clutched at her chest. Oscar bowed his head grievously. He'd cried his tears dry, left only to sniffle.

"Caleb's alive. Third degree burns over most of his back and he's lost his original eye but he's alive."

And he's asleep. Emmanuel had appeared on the balcony, observing the hall as Ebony was learning what had happened. He had caught Noah up on the accident and the two stood solemnly, Emmanuel at the top of the stairs and Noah at the bottom, guilt ridden by the knowledge that it was his fault. "You can see him when he wakes but for now, we need to talk. All of us." The vexation in his voice was unnerving. He was mad.

Noah said something that could have been, "I'll get Cascia," but the whisper was nearly inaudible. He took the same route as Cascia had done earlier.

"Ebony?" Oscar offered her to walk in front of him, but she didn't move.

"I thought I was saving her," Ebony told him, "but I killed her." Before she could attack herself in a frenzy of self-loathing and mourning, Oscar rushed forward and cradled Ebony in his arms. She screamed into his shirt and Oscar winced at the pain she was in. She crashed her fists against his chest, letting her emotions run freely. She'd been strong, but with the thought of Stella gone, there was no strength left in her.

"I'm so sorry Ebony," Oscar cooed into her hair. "I'm so sorry."

Ebony and Oscar followed several hallways until they reached a modernised conference room. On display screens were pictures of where Atlas had been sighted, what he was scheming and if there were any ideas on what he'd do next. But following the explosion the trail had gone dark.

Jeff was sitting amongst a crowd of computers, typing away chaotically. When Ebony entered, he gave a casual salute and a cheery hello despite his eyes giving away the tears that had fallen from them.

"I was the unicorn," he told her, before getting back to work. Ebony forced a small laugh; she appreciated the effort to make her feel better. A moment later Cascia appeared, with Noah behind. Keeping her head down she sat across from everyone and spun on her chair until she was facing the window. Ebony watched her reflection; she was inconsolable as she stared in angst into the sunset. Finally, Emmanuel appeared. He sat at the head of the table and looked at everyone.

"We've lost Belize. We've lost Stella. What do we do?" Emmanuel's strength was leadership but at the moment he was crumbling. He had found Belize several years prior when she'd first come to discover her magic. Her father, Louis, had just passed and her powers had flourished uncontrollably in her grief. Coerced by others into an underground fight club, she was rescued by Emmanuel after nearly drowning the room. He felt guilty, not for saving her, but for the fate it led her to.

The question was left unanswered for a good minute. Eyes glanced unceremoniously about the room. Ebony spoke.

"Atlas is coming for me. If I'm not around you all then he won't hurt you."

"Good idea," Cascia spat.

"Out of the question," Oscar threatened. Emmanuel remained quiet as a silent battle of stares raged across the room.

"We need to find out what he's planning," said Jeff.

"How?" Emmanuel posed another impossible question, and another minute went by before Noah, who was happy to stay quiet in the conversation and merely listen as he nursed leg, spoke.

"I dream walk, take you with me and whilst I'm inside his head, you read his mind?" Sounded simple.

"Woah, I was thinking the exact same thing," Emmanuel clapped.

"Really?"

"Of course not. That's a terrible idea." He ruled it out instantly. "Atlas may not be at full power, but he senses us in his head, and he'll trap our consciences inside."

"He could do that?" Ebony asked.

"He can and he will," Emmanuel answered, sliding his elbows onto the table and resting his head in his hands.

"It's a good idea," said Noah.

"No," said Cascia, firmly fighting against it. "We're not losing anyone else on any of these half-arsed, suicide missions," she said, staring intentionally at Ebony. Ebony felt it best to keep her mouth shut. She was aware she wasn't the smartest person in the room and didn't understand exactly what was being discussed but nodded along with a façade of knowledge.

"Whatever we do won't be half-arsed," Emmanuel said defensively.

"It will — it always is." Cascia was stroppy and slammed her hands on the table as she stood, sending the chair rolling away. "How about we do nothing and wait for him to make the first move before we put anyone else's life on the line?" The sly remark about Belize's death rose like a wall that further separated Cascia from her friends as she became increasingly agitated.

"Or how about you tell us about what you can see in the future? Anything important?" Noah leapt to Ebony's defence. Cascia's eyes were misty as she blinked back tears.

"I can't see a future!" she yelled. Swinging her chair around she turned her back to everyone, trying to compose herself. Her back rose and fell heavily, and Noah put a hand on her shoulder, but she shrugged it away.

"We'll figure something out," Emmanuel said unconvincingly. A shortage of words donned the room and brains could be heard whirring. Ebony tried to find a plan where no one would get hurt but she couldn't think of an idea without involving possible casualties.

Jeff spoke. "I've had a thought?"

"Did it hurt?" The air was thick with oppressive tension, but Jeff ignored Cascia's remark and addressed the others.

"Can you send a human into a dream walk?" They all stared at him, and he elaborated. "Dream walkers are detected by their magic. A human would be undetectable." He may as well have suggested suicide, but Noah was warm to the idea.

"Theoretically, -" Noah hesitated, "-but I can't guarantee it."

"And even if he could, they'd have to dig dangerously deep to find out what Atlas is planning without the help of a telepath," Emmanuel pointed out.

"It's too dangerous," Cascia said, trying to draw the discussion to a close.

"Not necessarily," Jeff said and with a startling jump, he rushed to the smartboard planted helpfully in the centre of the room. "We have Noah, but we also have Ebony who is technically capable of dream walking." Ebony leant forward as he wrote in a barely legible scraggly handwriting. "Because Ebony is inexperienced, she takes herself and Emmanuel inside the human's head, then Noah sends the human into Atlas' head with Emmanuel and Ebony's magic perfectly concealed, because her subconscious is inside someone else's subconscious. Emmanuel can safely read Atlas' mind and find out what he's doing without him ever knowing we were there." Jeff paused and gave everyone a moment to work out exactly what he'd said. Oscar piped up first.

"I'll do it." Before Ebony could object, Jeff did.

"Not you Oscar. This is only theoretical but even if we could pull this off, we couldn't send you."

"Why not?"

"You've had many encounters with Atlas for us to be one hundred percent sure he won't detect you."

"So, who?" Emmanuel asked. Jeff looked uneasy for putting Caleb in the spotlight.

"Atlas has only met Caleb once and for a short period of time," he said, fidgeting. The room instantly came to Caleb's defence.

"Have you seen the state he's in?" Emmanuel pounded his fist on the table, fond of the boy in the short time they'd known each other. "He is in no fit condition to do this."

"I know. But technically, he doesn't have to be physically fit, only mentally," Jeff argued his case.

"Absolutely not," Ebony joined in. "Caleb's hardly a part of this, I don't want to drag him in now and risk hurting him beyond repair!"

"I'm not losing another friend," Oscar said. "We're humans, not spare parts." Jeff dropped the pen in surrender, but it was both Cascia and Noah who came to his rescue.

"It's the safest and best thought-out plan we have," Cascia said, all in favour of a thought through plan that risked Ebony's friends over hers.

195

"The risk of death is small."

"But the risk of Caleb being lost inside Atlas' mind until the day he dies is huge," Emmanuel fought back.

"Emmanuel, have faith in us," Noah begged. "My powers aren't the greatest, but I wouldn't do it unless I was fully confident everyone would be okay. And I can teach Ebony," he added. The room was at a stalemate and both parties were discontented with the other's mentality.

"The bottom line is we need to know what Atlas' play is, because without Ebony he's got to have a plan B and we don't know what said plan is," Jeff argued. "Better ideas are welcome." But sorry was Ebony to say that there were no better ideas.

"Fine. We ask Caleb. But if he says no then no is the final answer," Ebony compromised. "We stop all of this and find another way. That's the deal everyone's got to agree with."

"Fine by me," Jeff said.

"Fine," said Cascia.

"Anything to keep everyone safe," Noah said. Emmanuel remained unsure and Oscar was visibly upset he couldn't offer himself in Caleb's place but the two of them also agreed.

"Any questions?" Ebony asked.

All hands were raised.

"That aren't stupid or sarcastic?"

All hands dropped.

"That settles it then," Ebony said. "We'll dream walk."

Chapter 16

The older halls of the castle resembled a museum. Famous art pieces ornamented the walls and precious artifacts were suspended in glass boxes along the centre of the room. Plush benches were scattered between for Enchanteds to rest. The glass ceiling flung shards of light across the floor. Ebony had followed these halls until she found the bedroom where Caleb was. He had a machine hovering above him, lasering prosthetic muscle into his back to try and aid his recovery.

"I'm sorry this happened to you." She sat on the chair beside his bed, resting her head on the mattress as Caleb slept. The ridges of the crumpled bed sheet formed a riverbank where Ebony's tears dropped onto the material. She cried as she gently stroked his tousled hair, grieving over Stella. She didn't have a body to bury. She didn't have someone to confide in. She no longer had one of her best friends and she was in physical and emotional agony. She had known Stella for longer than she could remember; her face was so familiar that Ebony could picture it as though she was still in the room. But whenever she reached out for her, Stella was gone.

Caleb slowly awoke and despite the pain he was withstanding, he smiled widely in seeing Ebony. "Hi," he mumbled.

Ebony smiled. "How're you feeling?"

"Like a fried chicken," he answered, and she chuckled. Despite everything, his sense of humour hadn't faded. "Is Atlas dead yet?" he asked. Ebony winced; she didn't want to lie but his injuries were too major for his effort to have been for nothing. his back was void of skin and his organic eye had glazed over whilst the other was struggling to repair itself.

"He will be," she wished, and Caleb valued her not saying no. It gave him hope.

"Every cloud has a silver lining."

"And what's the silver lining to this?"

"Uh, I get to wear an eye patch," he said proudly.

That's your silver lining? she thought, but answered him aloud with, "you're ridiculous."

"I know — isn't it wonderful?" Ebony stood from the chair; despite the personality, she could see how much pain Caleb was in. He was clenching the sheets, dripping in sweat and the burns were severely deep. The laser was doing a good job but doing it painfully, but then an idea crossed her mind and she bent over, viewing his burns.

"Sexy, aren't they," he joked. She shook her head, dismissing his comment.

"Can I try something?"

"Go for your life." Ebony held her hand over Caleb's back and squinted her eyes as she concentrated.

"Humans are sixty-four percent water, right?"

"You're the biologist."

He buried his face in the pillow as Ebony took a moment to steady her hand. At first nothing happened but after a moment, the burns on his back almost moved. Caleb's muscles flexed and he grunted into the pillow as the dead skin was washed away. Then, slowly but surely his skin began to regenerate. It was a modest effort but what were gnarly, muscle tissue deep burns were suddenly shallower wounds with a chance of healing with minimal scarring and suffering.

"I don't know how much more I can do." She stepped back. The fact that Caleb even had the strength and ability to roll onto his side and swing his head over his shoulder showed the progress Ebony had made. He examined his back in the mirror standing in the corner of the room.

"It feels a whole lot better than it did," he said merrily. "Thank you Eb."

"You're welcome." Ebony turned to go and stepped into Emmanuel who had silently entered the room.

He admired her work with wonder. "Ebony your power is incredible," he praised.

"I hope it will be enough," she doubted.

"Well, we're about to find out. Have you asked him?"

"Not yet."

"Asked me what?" Caleb said curiously.

"We think we've found a way of working out what Atlas is doing, what he's planning." Ebony faltered. "But we need your help."

"Yes. One hundred percent yes. Whatever you need," he said earnestly. Ebony was moved by his bravery but stopped him.

"It's dangerous, and there's a small chance you could get trapped inside Atlas' mind," she said, wincing in the expectation of a bad reaction. Caleb stayed quiet. "Emmanuel and I will be with you the whole time and you won't be there for more than a minute." Caleb scoffed and Ebony worried he would change his mind.

"Honestly, Ebony, you're always trying to dissuade me from the fun stuff," he said. "Of course. Anything it to avenge… Stella." Mentioning her name was the first time his smile faded as he settled himself back down on his stomach.

"Thank you, Caleb," Emmanuel said. "We appreciate it."

"Yeah," he said dejectedly.

"Right, well-" Emmanuel opened the door, "-Jeff's got some quasi-scientific magicky machine thing running in the basement."

"I'll bring Caleb down." Ebony nodded to him and like the gesture released him from the spot, Emmanuel rushed from the room. She heard him give the good news to the others, and suddenly their minds were aglow with thought, optimistic and pessimistic.

Caleb winced as she helped him stand. He limped through the portal that Ebony made to the basement, shoulders hunched as he stood.

The contraption Jeff had built in such a short amount of time was mindboggling. Four beds collected in a group in the centre of the room and the walling was built from electrical panels conducting electricity to a strange contraption tucked to the left of the beds.

"See, magic may be amazing on its own but science and magic combined? That's out of this world," Oscar awed. He reached for a wire, but Jeff slapped his hand away.

"Don't touch," he warned, brandishing a screwdriver. Oscar surrendered the wire and backed away.

"How did you build all of this?" Ebony asked. Her and Caleb walked jointly to the beds and Jeff tapped his nose knowingly.

"Had some help from some friends," he said, and he grunted wildly. Ebony was at a loss as to why until two gorilla looking animals that Ebony had never seen passed the doorway, responding to what Ebony supposed was Jeff saying, 'thank you'.

"Of course," she said. She helped Caleb lie down and hopped into the high set bed next to him, swinging her feet about nervously. Jeff had a bundle of wires in his hands, which sparked when they touched, and Emmanuel looked disgruntled as Jeff came at his face with them.

"And what exactly does this machine do?" he asked, as Jeff taped a wire to his forehead. He frowned and Jeff sighed as the tape wrinkled.

"These wires relay the information from your cerebral cortex to the screen so we're able to see what your detached mind is seeing. And this wire-" he clipped a wire to Emmanuel's ear lobe with a snap, "-means we can communicate with you despite your unconscious state." Jeff promoted the machine like a businessman; confident words, lengthy sentences; Ebony was sold. "Essentially, we can keep an eye on Atlas' mind. If he randomly starts thinking about one of you whilst you're busy sifting through his other thoughts, we'll see it and let you know," Jeff said. "This machine is your insurance."

"Brilliant," Noah commended, and Jeff beamed smartly.

"Better work." Cascia was pessimistic.

"It will." Oscar tried to bring confidence to the room. Himself and Cascia were of no current use, and found themselves standing uselessly, avidly watching the screens even though nothing was yet showing.

"Ebony, whenever you're ready," Jeff invited, patting the tape on Ebony's head. Ebony squeezed her eyes shut and clenched her fists, and as Noah had spent the day teaching her, envisioned her mind transferring from one body to another.

There was a sensation unlike anything Ebony had felt before.

Then she was inside Caleb's head.

Her physical body went limp, a hand rolling from the side of the bed. But instantly, the room from her perspective through Caleb's eye flashed on the screens and there were gasps.

"This is weird," Caleb stuttered.

"Emmanuel, I'm bringing you in." Ebony's physical body didn't speak but her voice from a microphone attached to the machine did. Quickly, Emmanuel's body slumped, and he was with Ebony. But it didn't have the greatest effect on Caleb. Having a telepath in his mind brought some of his memories forward, and the more prominent, the quicker they appeared. Everyone watched in sympathetic horror as the almost tactile memory in the forefront of Caleb's mind was him watching Stella die.

Don't think about it Ebony urged from inside Caleb's head and with some encouragement, the nightmarish memory subsided. He smiled bravely and clenched her cold hand.

"Noah, send him in," Jeff said. "Carefully." Noah shivered and he dug his nails into the palm of his hands in concentration. Whilst Noah remained conscious, Caleb too slipped under and after a moment, his taut voice whispered from the mic. The screens were an eery blur of black and red, with tormented shadow figures flying by.

"I'm inside."

"Stay put, let Emmanuel find what he needs to," Noah warned, muscles flexing as he held Caleb's mind in place.

"Wait," Oscar said instantly, watching the screens as Atlas' thoughts popped up. "He's thinking of Ebony." Everyone froze.

"Do you think he knows we're here?" she panicked as Emmanuel stopped his mind-reading.

"Don't think so. He's thinking of when you blew him to kingdom come." Jeff said. "He's just remembering his failings."

Emmanuel continued to dig but Caleb's mind was distractingly loud and as Emmanuel tried to work, his mind was overridden with Caleb's fear of Atlas.

"Caleb, you're safe," he soothed. "Please try to clear your mind." Caleb tried but Atlas' head wasn't a pleasant place to be, and his constant evil thoughts were a pain inducing burden to bear.

"Update?" Ebony asked. She was holding Emmanuel and herself steadily in Caleb's mind, and was blind to anything that Oscar, Cascia or Jeff could see.

"He's still thinking about your fight," Cascia said, "but don't worry, he's not so focused on you now." She meant the comment to put Ebony's mind at ease, but it did the polar opposite.

"Who's he thinking about?"

"It's like he's searching for someone," Jeff said. The images across the screen whipped by with such clarity they could be watching drone footage instead of memories as Atlas searched the port.

"Who?" Ebony asked. No one responded for a moment and suddenly, Atlas' mind was filled with the tanned and not so chipper face of Caleb. The room seemed to darken.

Oscar yelled at Noah. "Get them out!" he cried but suddenly, Noah's body lurched forward, and he convulsed as Caleb's mind was torn away from his. Oscar caught him as he fell from the bed, his head hanging low on his chest.

"Noah?" Noah turned the whitest shade of pale and locked eyes with Oscar.

"I've lost him."

"Caleb. Nice to put a name to a face, especially when it's trespassing in my mind," Atlas said. The screens filled with a murky black as they watched Atlas' thoughts descend on the helpless boy in his head. Caleb was frozen.

"Noah," he squeaked.

"No one's coming to help you," Atlas said. "You're trapped here." Atlas let dark thoughts cross his mind of the torture Caleb would suffer and Caleb backed away. But as merely a conscience without a body, there was nowhere to back away too. Everywhere he turned, Atlas' mind taunted him.

"Emmanuel, we have to do something," Ebony cried. "We're in Caleb's head, we're not getting out if he's not getting out." She turned to him but his conscience, present in the form of a version of his human body was crouched on the floor, clutching his head. "Emmanuel." She tried to grab him but there was nothing physical to get a hold of.

"Too many thoughts," he yelped, clawing at his head. He gripped his hair and pulled at it in pain, knotted clumps coming away in his hands.

"Emmanuel, try to block it out!"

"I can't," he whimpered helplessly.

Ebony made an executive decision. "I'm leaving Caleb's head."

"You can't," Emmanuel grunted, unsure he heard her correctly over the noise. "You'll be condemned to a life of eternal torture!"

"Thanks for making me feel better," Ebony said, "but I have to get Caleb and you out and I'd argue he wants me more than Caleb."

"Ebony, don't," Emmanuel pleaded but the voices grew and his conscience weakly flickered. Ebony's stubbornness again shone through when her friend least wanted it. With a war cry, she left Emmanuel in Caleb's mind and appeared in Atlas'.

"Ebony, no!" Oscar yelled, as Atlas' mind flared in glee. The screens lit up in an array of colour at his joy.

"Ebony," he hissed.

"You've got me, let my friend go," she demanded.

The third time bargaining with Atlas worked a charm.

There was no way for her to worm her way out of his mind unless he chose to let her go, and he wouldn't.

"Anything for my daughter," he taunted and with a simple blink, Emmanuel and Caleb woke with a start in the basement of Alchemacier castle. Ebony was all he wanted and now he had her.

"Caleb." Jeff clicked his fingers in front of his face, and he struggled to respond. "Can you hear me?" Caleb was weak at the knees, back arched with a pain that rocketed through his spine, and as Jeff juddered his shoulders he stared blindly, unresponsive to touch.

"Mhmm," was his only reply. His cyber eye dulled as he retreated into the comfort of his own mind and Jeff could have sworn he saw flashes of Atlas' leering face blink in the reflective material.

"His mental cognition is fried," Jeff worried.

"Caleb I am so sorry, he pushed me out." Noah was distraught.

"Emmanuel?" Cascia hesitantly approached the bed. He was clutching his head between his legs, wires ripped off and scattering the floor as he waited for the raging images in his mind to subside. They were whirring by at nauseating speeds, and he could only bring himself to wave a hand at her.

"Guys, can you still hear me?" Ebony asked.

"You have friends listening?" Atlas asked. "How quaint." Maybe it was the threat of being inside Atlas' head that made her feel a certain way, but Ebony felt Atlas was somehow eviller than during their first encounter.

"Yeah, we can hear you," Oscar said. He pressed his lips to the mic as Jeff tended to Caleb. "Ebony, get the hell out of there."

"Give me a second."

"What's this? Do I get an audience with my daughter?" Atlas asked. Ebony ignored his snarky comments.

"Why are you doing this, Atlas? Why try and destroy the universe?" Atlas laughed.

"My dear child, I'm not trying to destroy the universe, I'm trying to save it." Ebony was taken aback.

"What?"

"This universe is dying, and humans cannot save it. But I can."

"What do you mean?"

"What humankind calls revolutionary, I call a slow day at the office," Atlas sighed. "Human aspirations are nugatory. These pathetic technological and scientific enhancements humans herald as miracles, are not enough. When two planets collide, science can't stop it, but magic can. When a black hole appears and swallows galaxies, science can't stop it, but magic can. But the plague of humanity has forced Enchanteds into hiding; Ancients are myths and magic doesn't exist. They must be cleansed of this universe so it can be rebuilt. You see Ebony, I am trying to save this universe."

"By wiping out the human race?"

"Precisely."

"You're a bigoted mad man," Ebony cried. "Science and magic can work together. You don't have to eradicate one to have the other. You're insane."

Atlas smirked. "Insane or divine."

"Oh brilliant." Ebony was only her subconscious, but she imagined face-palming. "You have a God complex." She gulped. "Better not be a Zeus kind of God."

Atlas growled. "Say what you like about me. A new universe will be born, and you, Ebony, won't be around to see it." Inside his own head, Atlas screamed, expecting it to have some torturous effect upon Ebony. But Ebony imagined the noise getting quieter and quieter and it worked. Not letting her conscience succumb to Atlas, the scream soon quieted to a whisper.

Atlas stopped.

In his lair on Ignis he stood from his throne, baring his teeth.

"You dare try and manipulate my own thoughts?" He was ferociously angry. His temper flared into a ball of rage which he threw across the room, cracking the obsidian from floor to ceiling. "You'll pay!"

"Not if I can help it," said Ebony and with an ability never before seen by Atlas or the others, who were intently watching the screens, she summoned a portal in Atlas' subconscious and willed her own subconscious to jump through it.

She was gone.

With a deafening crash, the machine imploded. Oscar ducked from the sparking wires and the lights flickered before steadying themselves with the same clinical white glow. Everyone was left in a stunned silence.

Noah stuttered at Ebony's empty body. Caleb cried quietly in the corner and Emmanuel mustered the strength in his somewhat displaced mind, to stand and walk over to him. They sat in a huddle, fearful of Ebony's fate.

"Jeff, where is she?" Oscar said.

"I don't know, Noah's the expert." Jeff backed away as Oscar loomed over him, seething with an anger that threatened to boil over and explode at Noah..

"Where. Is. She?" he snarled.

"I don't know," Noah said as Jeff tried to get the machine up and running. "I didn't know it was possible for a portal to be created whilst in a dream walking state. Her subconscious has gone into freefall somewhere." It wasn't the answer Oscar was searching for.

"Get her back," he demanded but no one in the room knew where to begin. Cascia glimpsed at Ebony's body. She thought her mind might be playing tricks on her.

"Did her hand move?" She rushed over. It lay motionless and limp and she wasn't sure what she'd seen. Attention was drawn to the vacant body and suddenly, Ebony jerked like electricity had been passed through her. As though she was never even gone, she sat up, unaware of the panic she had engendered.

"Is everyone okay?" she asked.

"Are you serious?" Oscar asked, marching back towards her. "Is everyone okay?" he mocked, before throwing his arms around her. "Are *you* okay?" She hugged him back tightly.

"I'm fine."

"How the hell did you manage to create a portal when you were nothing but a subconscious? And how did you get through it? And how did you get into your own mind?" Noah had so many questions.

"I didn't make a portal," Ebony said. "I managed to manipulate what he thought by being inside his head and I guess once he saw the portal and thought I was gone, he stopped trying to trap me."

"You manipulated his own thoughts from inside his head?" Cascia asked. "Surely he'd sense you were still there?"

"I don't know?"

"We didn't need to send Caleb in. In fact, having a human was what got us caught," Emmanuel said unexpectedly. Attention turned to him.

"How?"

"I saw Atlas' plan. He's coming for Ebony. He hasn't revived Sonneillon, he's absorbed his magic as a means to kill her and he's planning on bringing an army to do it." Eyebrows were raised. "He has so much magic inside him it's doubtful he would have noticed a little more, but the small blip of humanity caught his attention immediately." Emmanuel eyed Caleb who gave him a tenuous smile, his lips twitching at the strain to curve upwards.

"So, in short, he has literally scrapped his entire plan to kill me?" Ebony's stomach twisted in knots.

Emmanuel raised his hand like he felt left out. They looked at him. "Us," he corrected. "Kill *us*."

"So, what do we do?" Noah asked.

"He's a demon, right?" Oscar said.

"Yeah."

"Can't we just exorcise him?" Oscar asked.

Emmanuel smacked his head against the closest wall.

Cascia lost the will to live.

Ebony laughed humourlessly.

"That's brilliant. Why didn't I think of that? Oscar, you get the salt for sprinkling over him, I'll find a quick recipe on how to throw demons back in the oven and Noah, do you mind quickly diving back into his mind and asking him to sit real still whilst we chant incantations around his head like some ooga booga cult? We're trying to kill an Ancient not bake a cake!" Ebony screamed. The room fell quiet as she stood, thinking.

"Let me do something to help," Oscar mumbled.

"You're not doing anything," Ebony told him. "You know what happened to Stella, you've seen the state of Caleb."

"But I can help!"

"No," Ebony decided authoritatively, "and as for you all-" she addressed the room, "-I get it if you don't want to help after this shitstorm of a plan, but I think the best shot we have is to take the fight to Atlas on an abandoned planet. No casualties, quick fight."

"It's suicide," Oscar argued. Ebony's sad eyes bore into his.

"Better ideas are welcome."

Jeff spoke up. "I'm in. If we're all gonna die whether we fight him now or later, we might as well get it over and done with."

"We're doing it together," Emmanuel decided. "We have a better shot if we work as a team."

"Thanks for the optimism, Jeff," Noah rolled his eyes, "but…" he stood and headed over to Emmanuel and slung his arm over his shoulder, "I'm in too Manny. 'Til the end." Emmanuel patted him on the back.

"Cascia, you've been uncharacteristically quiet," he pointed out. "Thoughts?"

"I'm in," she said, although her sudden pale complexion spoke otherwise.

"Sweet," Jeff said. "Nothing says friendship like premeditated murder."

Chapter 17

"This mind stuff has well and truly scrambled my eggs," Caleb announced as Ebony entered the kitchen. "You going somewhere?" His memory retention was suffering since his conscience was yanked from his head and although he was in the room when their plan was decided, he'd mostly forgotten. He did however remember how much he enjoyed bacon as he shovelled it in his gob.

There are talking pigs outside Emmanuel thought as he walked by, and Caleb swiftly opened his mouth and let the bacon fall back into the pan.

"We're going to fight Atlas," Ebony reminded him.

"Without me?" Caleb pouted his lips, shovelling down eggs and hoping the chickens wouldn't hate him for it.

"And without Oscar," Ebony added. "You've already done more than enough, giving us a head start on his plan. You two are staying here where it's safe." Ebony was devastated to leave him; she expected it was the last time she'd ever see him. She not so successfully hid her face before her eyes watered and Caleb stopped her.

"Ebony." with a pandemonium of moans he got to his feet, holding the dining table as a crutch. He was struggling to straighten up as the scarring skin on his back pulled awkwardly, and his top was merely an untied apron to avoid anything touching it. "I miss Stella. I miss her a lot," he stuttered, "so you better come back." Ebony hugged him carefully, and both of their forced smiles faded into the crooks of each other's necks. But when they pulled away the smiles were back, at least for a moment until Caleb pulled a stern face. "Promise me you'll come back." His burning stare filled Ebony with guilt.

Five minutes Emmanuel said. Ebony nodded at Caleb.

"I will."

She left the room, unable to offer any more consolation.

In the hall, she was greeted by Oscar blocking her way to the door. He didn't say anything, so Ebony hugged him tightly.

She opted for, "see you later." A façade of optimism hid her fear. Saying goodbye was too hard. He brushed a strand of hair from her face, cupping her cheek in his hand. "What are you doing?"

"Remembering your face." Sadness clouded his features. "See you later," he replied, letting his hand fall to the other where he wrung them vigorously. Turning away before she could cry and taint his final memory of her, Ebony walked away from Oscar for the last time.

There was no singular weather pattern on Alchemacier. Each day sustained a crisp season dependant on the biome. But if there was one, it would be raining. The day was solemn and quiet, with a sense of impending doom and the vibrancy of the world dampened. Day didn't bring the joy Ebony searched for, but rather acted only as an interlude between one darkness after another.

Morale was low and it was a struggle for Ebony to accept that she was leading herself and her friends to their deaths. Stella wasn't there. If she had been she would have perhaps talked some sense into everyone. But she wasn't. Ebony's world was coming apart at the seams and no amount of magic could fix it and perhaps fighting Atlas would be the only way to assuage the grief that hung over her.

"I've found a moon. Population of about 1000, known as the Poseidon Settlers," Jeff announced. "They're deeply religious. The moon's water comes from vast, free roaming, bubbles floating in the atmosphere that are full of marine life, some even home to whales. Only documented place in the universe where it occurs, which is why the bubbles are hallowed." He showed Ebony a hologram on his band. "Oh, and they don't believe in avid space travel, so as long as we land out of their line of sight and don't pop a sacred bubble on the way, they'll never know we were there. Unless they find our dead bodies." When nervous, Jeff tended to speak until something stopped him.

Ebony shut the door of the castle. Her hand lingered on the lock before she twisted it. The physical barrier between her and her friends destroyed what was left of her good mood.

"That's good." She climbed aboard the ship.

"It'll take a couple of hours from here," he estimated. "The moon's on the edge of the outlands." The outlands were the fringes of the universe, where colonies settled outside of government control and wars over land rampaged. Jeff tried to lighten the mood with the news that they wouldn't have to go through dangerous territories, but it was like trying to shine a broken torch through murky waters. When Ebony didn't reciprocate in good spirits, his sunny disposition faded, and they silently parted ways.

Ebony kept walking. They were back on the Hyperion with plenty of room for no one to be near her. As Emmanuel busied himself readying the ship for take-off, Cascia, Jeff and Noah finished filling the ship with weapons and armour. The engines roared to life and Ebony absorbed the beauty of Alchemacier for the final time. From the window of the castle, Caleb was waving but Oscar was nowhere in sight.

Ebony's body was covered in bruises; new wounds and old scars formed a pattern across her rough skin, but it was the mental fight she was battling that traumatised her more than anything else. Being the reason for a thousand deaths was hard but being the reason for the death of her best friend was unbearable. She was still labouring to come to terms with it. It made leaving Caleb and Oscar so much harder.

Cascia appeared in the doorway of Hyperion's lobby, her hair braided and pinned, ready for a fight. She stopped when she saw Ebony. An instant 'ugh' feeling came upon Ebony. She didn't have the energy to fight with Cascia and got up to leave under the assumption that Cascia was just as thrilled at seeing Ebony as Ebony was seeing her. But Cascia outstretched her hand and took a few quick paces towards her.

"Don't leave," she called. Ebony stopped. "I came to apologise." She got straight to the point. "You weren't responsible for Belize's death. I told her to stay clear of Atlas and she didn't. I'm sorry. And I'm sorry about Stella. I was so busy focusing on my grieving that I forgot you were too." Ebony was taken aback but warmly accepted the apology.

"Thank you," she said with the most sincerity they had yet shared between them. Truth be told, she hadn't considered how badly Cascia was affected by Belize's death and a discreet glance into her mind told Ebony they'd been best friends for as long as herself and Stella had been.

"I'm sorry about Belize too." Cascia smiled as the two of them spoke properly for the first time. "Did you mean what you said? You couldn't see a future?" Ebony asked. Cascia, who set herself upon the other end of the upholstered bench, twiddled with her fingers.

"I shouldn't have said that. It's not true, not exactly. I'm just missing a lot of details."

"What can you see?" Ebony asked inquisitively. Cascia shut her eyes and rubbed her temple with her fingers as a lengthy breath escaped her lips. She was searching through the future and Ebony watched on eagerly.

"I can see us getting close to the moon. But we never make it."

"Why not?"

"We're interrupted by something and decide to change course, but I can't see by who or where we choose to go."

"Why can't you see?"

"Normally I can't see past a moment where I help change the fate of the future."

"You can actually do that?" Ebony was impressed.

"Only on a small scale." Cascia radiated off of Ebony's eagerness to see what she could do. A cracked smile wore into her hardened face and her hands glowed a royal purple as she lifted them up, and in the air, mimed plucking a leaf from a tree.

"What did you do?" Ebony asked.

"One of the Enchanteds who lives on Alchemacier is an avid gardener; keeps the place spotless. I knocked a leaf from one of his prize plants. He'll stumble across the leaf and stop for a moment to tend to the plant from which it came, which will slow his journey to the woodland, thus triggering a whole new series of events. Good ones, I might add," she assured Ebony.

"And now the futures changed? That's amazing," Ebony applauded.

She was relieved they'd made amends; that they were getting on. They chatted for a while longer and Ebony found herself warming to Cascia and vice versa. When Cascia made an excuse to leave and busy herself elsewhere, Ebony believed it was actually because she had something to do, not because she no longer wanted to be in her company.

For a while longer, Ebony watched the windows. The ships were coming further and further apart; a sign that both pleased and terrified her as they headed towards an unpopulated area of the universe. Suddenly needing company, she stood and was wandering the halls of Hyperion back to the flight deck when she heard something she didn't expect.

"What the?" she blurted out as an adventitious noise startled her. Then it happened again: a knock? She paused in the ship's entrance hall. Technology was good but not as good as to have people walking around in deep space. The banging happened again; this time more urgently which made Ebony less willing to open the door. But curiosity got the better of her and she reached for the handle.

From his seat in the captain's chair, Emmanuel stood, motioning the others to follow the noise of Ebony's loud thoughts.

She grasped the door handle and opened it cautiously. Two complete strangers were drifting alongside the ship. They had no protective gear, no oxygen masks or technology in sight; torn trousers barely covered them. Soot and filth clung to their skin, dirt sat in their foot long beards and under their overgrown nails. They were coated in the scars of mistakes they would only make once; posture hunched and vulnerable. Their eyes were lifelessly dark, but when Ebony looked into them, they changed, one to an ashen grey and the other a fresh green. She held the door firmly, opening it no more than necessary.

"Ebony? Is it you?" One of them spoke in a way that sounded like a hundred combined accents, thickened by the forgotten memory of where they were raised and the years of travelling across the universe.

"Who's asking?" she said untrustingly.

"We know you're her, please let us in." The other man sounded more well-spoken. They both were thin and pale and one of them was sweating under the pressure of standing unaided.

Behind Ebony, Emmanuel wandered over curiously. He'd brought a gun with him, tucked in the back of his trousers but with a hand tightly grasped around the handle.

"How can we help you?" he asked. He sounded kind but his eyes narrowed, and he acted with extreme hostility, approaching with calculated footsteps.

Ebony, I can't read his mind.

Neither can I.

"Please. We've been tortured, we've been attacked, and now we've come to you for help." The one who was shaking had no choice to grab the door as his legs buckled. "Let us in." They reached for the door but Ebony's hand shot out, using a wave of air to push them back. The stronger one braced himself against it but the frailer one crumpled to his knees, nearly falling out of the ships orbit.

"Who are you?" she growled as her eyes narrowed.

"Ebony don't be afraid," the standing man started. "We're your uncles." Ebony took a moment to realise what they meant.

"Uncles? I don't have any un—" Her eyes widened and she screamed, rushing to slam the door.

"I'm sorry for this," one of them apologised pre-emptively and as Ebony tried to close the door, instantly the stronger man was pushing back, air flying from his hands. He sent Ebony and Emmanuel sliding across the floor much like Atlas had done on Egoran and they crashed into the fountain, the star feature of the hallway.

"Sorry," he called again, dragging in the weak one and setting him gently on the floor. He shut the door behind and locked it.

"What's going on?" Cascia and Noah hurried into the room and Noah dropped to Ebony's side, helping her up as he noticed the two men. Cascia reached for her knives, standing protectively over Emmanuel.

"Uncles?" Emmanuel questioned, flying swiftly into a sitting position, and aiming his gun with marksman accuracy, a lasered dot on the standing man's forehead.

"Please Ebony, we didn't come to hurt you, we're not what the stories say," they begged.

"Whose uncles?" Noah tried to catch up.

Your uncles? Jeff too appeared in the room but sensing the hostility, hadn't appeared in his own form but had opted for a tiger, claws clacking on the ground as he crouched, back legs ready to pounce at a second's notice. He growled and whilst the standing one took a respectful step back, the one on the floor scoffed.

"You can't hurt us," he reminded them.

"Ebony, whoever they are I couldn't see them in my vision," Cascia worried. "They're the ones who make us change course. Who are they?"

"My uncles," she gulped, hair on end.

"You're an orphan," Noah stated the obvious.

"My uncles," Ebony repeated. "Belphegor and Adremelech." The colour drained from Emmanuel's face and for the first time, Ebony watched him as he scurried backwards, away from the situation. Jeff too took a step back and she heard Noah let out a small squeal of fear as he hunched his shoulders as though trying to collapse in on himself. The only one who stood steadfast was Cascia, although she was visibly shaking. She was more prepared for the intrusion than anyone else with the prior knowledge that something would happen, but her chest still tightened, and she suddenly wished she had Jeff's ability to turn into a mouse.

"We aren't here to hurt you," the one still standing said.

"You're demons who escaped from hell for a homicidal road trip across the universe," Ebony reminded them. "You're here for some villainous intent."

"We're not," one of them said. Ebony couldn't distinguish who was who. "Atlas revived us. He tortured us for information and allegiance."

"Allegiance?" Ebony scoffed. "Bullshit. You three worked together under Sonneillon, if you're loyal to anyone it's him."

"It wasn't out of choice. We were Sonneillon's henchmen because we were smart. In the darker days, it was kill or be killed," they explained hurriedly.

"So rather than die you chose to kill millions?" Ebony crossed her arms.

"It was hardly a choice. But this time we made one, the right one."

"How did you escape Atlas?"

"Adremelech attacked him, I went for the door," Belphegor mumbled. Adremelech, clutching his side, definitely seemed to have gone through a battle.

"We don't stand with Atlas, we stand with you," he added.

"Please, how do we get you to trust us?" Belphegor begged. "My brother is ill, our power is drained, we can't harm you."

"But you can push us across the floor," Emmanuel hissed. The laser shining between Belphegor's eyes hadn't moved.

"I apologise for that. We need somewhere to lay low and get our power back." Ebony wasn't convinced and Belphegor knew it. "We'll swear allegiance to you. We'll help you kill Atlas," he promised. Jeff snarled; he couldn't speak but the hair on the back of his neck was on end, and he bared his teeth threateningly. He didn't like them.

"Ebony-" Noah added to the debate, "-they could help us if they're telling the truth."

"And if they're lying, they could kill us."

"They have the power to kill Atlas."

"So, they equally have the power to kill us."

"How do we know Atlas didn't send you?" Cascia barked.

"You think Atlas would send someone to kill the only threat he's had in the last several millennia? If Atlas has a personal vendetta, he handles it himself," Belphegor said.

It was true; the second Ebony had become a big threat on Chane, he himself tried to kill her.

"I need more," Ebony said. Her intuition was telling her to push them into deep space and leave them there, but her desperation stopped her. "You can stay. But for a price."

"Name it," Adremelech said willingly.

"Information." Belphegor and Adremelech traded glances at each other and their bedraggled appearances.

"How about a shower first?"

Chapter 18

Belphegor was pacing the room like he owned it. He held the undivided attention of everyone within it but not because they suddenly liked him. He had something they were all eager for. Information. Adremelech sat, peeling off strips of chipping paint from the wall, much to Emmanuel's ire.

"So, you're saying your old home planet is now the most heavily guarded prison in the outlands of Andromeda?" Jeff's enthusiastic interest didn't match the atmosphere of the room. He'd shifted back from a tiger after settling into the situation and was now massively enthused by what Belphegor was telling them.

Ebony was not.

She steeled herself against Adremelech's leering gaze every time she looked at him. In her opinion, there were few upsides to them being on board and she guarded herself carefully against their inimical powers.

"If by a prison you mean the planet Nibiru then yes," Belphegor clarified, projecting his voice across the room.

"Yes, Nibiru but it's known as 'The Prison'," Jeff said. "Only the worst of the universe are thrown in there and once you're in, you're never getting out." He was teeming with knowledge. "The prisoners are thrown onto the planet which is laid out as a combat game; originally used to train ground armies, it's now used to psychologically taunt, deliberately degrade and humiliate and eventually kill the inmates by segmenting the planet into different deathly situations and seeing how well they handle them."

"Sounds lovely," Ebony commented.

"How?" Adremelech asked curiously, still picking the paint. Emmanuel scowled.

"Do you have to?" he decided to ask, hoping Adremelech wouldn't turn his knees into flowerpots.
"You told us 'no murder' so I've had to resort to the smaller things," Adremelech replied snarkily.

"The prison makes them think they have a chance of escape," Jeff said loudly, recapturing the room's attention. "In the centre of the planet is a mountain all inmates are told to go towards. It is said if you reach the prize in the middle, you are given a second chance," he explained, "which of course you're not. You're teleported out and into a prison cell on another planet, where a jury decides whether to send you back in for more fun or deliver a fate worse than death."

"What's the fate worse than death?" Adremelech asked keenly. Ebony shot him a cold glare.

"What's the prize?" asked Cascia, sitting on the table, twisting a gun around in her hand.

"Allegedly it's an expensive weapon. A sword, I think," Jeff told them. Adremelech and Belphegor gave each other a knowing nod.

"So, it does still exist," Belphegor said.

"What does?"

"The sword of Sonneillon," Adremelech said. "The most powerful object ever created, and humans have made a game out of it for the scum of the universe," he scowled.

"The what?" Ebony asked.

"The sword of Sonneillon," Belphegor said. "You requested information, it's the best we have."

"What does this sword do?" Noah asked. He was standing in the doorway, arms folded, sternly watching in case one of the Ancients stopped cooperating.

"It kills Ancients," Belphegor answered. "If you get the sword, you actually have a fighting chance of stopping Atlas rather than running in blind and killing yourself."

"I thought no such thing existed," Emmanuel said.

"Ignorance must be glorious," Adremelech commented, and Emmanuel glared at him. "Ancients can be killed by the sword which is imbued with an Ancient's power. How do you think our daughters killed Sonneillon?"

"So, what are we waiting for?" Noah exclaimed. "Let's go get it."

"Easier said than done," Jeff and Adremelech said in unison. Jeff sank back in his seat as Adremelech stared him down.

"You go first," he offered and Adremelech grinned smugly. He had a naturally pretentious air about him, and Ebony found herself warming more to Belphegor than him.

"Sonneillon was smart enough not to leave a weapon that powerful lying around. The planet is surrounded by a magic repellent shield," he said. "We can't use our magic on Nibiru."

"Which leads on to the second problem," Jeff continued. "This planet isn't only guarded magically; it's guarded by some of the most heavy-duty technology to date. One-way forcefield. You can get in but not out. So, getting the sword is going to be hard enough but getting off the planet with it is going to be near impossible."

"So, we can get in easily enough?"

"Yeah. They figured that anyone is stupid enough to try and get onto Nibiru, then they deserve to stay there."

"There's a third problem," Belphegor added. "When an Enchanted or Ancient gets close to the sword it detects their magic, warning the owner. And, because Atlas has absorbed Sonneillon's power..." he trailed off.

"...Atlas is technically the owner. He'll know what we're doing," Ebony finished, "and therefore your information is useless." She stood up, fists clenched. "So, what else can you offer me, before I throw you off this ship?"

Noah, attempting to be the voice of reason, stopped her. "They can help. They know where the sword is." Ebony stared at him.

"He's right," Adremelech said. "If this shapeshifter is correct and the planet is now some absurd prison game-" he spat the words bitterly, "-it doesn't stop us from leading you to the sword. Dear niece, trust us." Ebony drew flames to her hands.

"Don't call me your niece," she cautioned. "As far as I'm concerned, we are of no relation. And I don't trust you. At all."

"Fine," Adremelech said. "We can send in your spare Enchanteds to try and find the sword alone if you prefer."

Noah scoffed. "Spare Enchanteds?"

"Your death would be nothing but a minor inconvenience. We're here for Ebony, not you," Adremelech said. Belphegor sighed at his brother's hostility and Emmanuel came to Noah's defence.

"Adremelech. Have you ever tried sticking a knife in a toaster?"

"No."

"You should try it sometime."

Adremelech, clueless as to what a toaster was but liking the sound of a knife, nodded. "I will."

"Emmanuel." Cascia looked at him and he sighed resentfully.

"What?"

"You've got a big mouth."

"Shocking revelation."

Jeff sniggered. "Shocking."

"Enough of this," Belphegor said. "Ebony, let us help you. Atlas is an arbitrarily lethal tyrant; we cannot risk the sword falling into his hands." Ebony was irritated. She debated the options. Continue on their path to the moon and almost definitely die or try and get the sword for an advantage but trust Atlas' brothers.

"let's get the sword," she begrudgingly decided.

"Aye, aye captain." Emmanuel leapt at the chance to be away from Adremelech and rushed for the Hyperion's controls, swinging it around and aiming for their new destination.

"Tell me," Belphegor asked, keeping the peace. "Which one of you is human? You may come in handy when getting closer to the sword." Eyebrows were raised.

"We're all Enchanteds," Cascia said. "I see the future, Emmanuel reads minds, Noah is a teleporter and well, you saw what Jeff can do."

"I can sense a human," Belphegor pressed.

"No…" Ebony put her head in her hands. "Oscar, this ship isn't for stowaways!" she yelled. There was silence but footsteps could be heard and Oscar guilty rounded the door.

"I didn't want to leave you alone," he apologised but he didn't get told off. In fact, seeing Oscar caused Ebony to grin from ear to ear.

"I'm glad to have you here." She clutched his hand. He felt a warmth in thinking she smiled because of him but cowered away as Adremelech gave him daggers. He was clearly unhappy about a human in their midst. To Adremelech, he was pepperoni on a vegetarian pizza.

"Why is the human here?"

"Because we want him to be." Emmanuel defended him instantly.

"He'll waste supplies," Adremelech scowled. "He's unneeded baggage."

Waste supplies? The Hyperion has enough for thousands of people Emmanuel thought angrily.

"Brother," Belphegor scolded. "If he's here, he must be a valuable asset. Somehow." He tried to ease the tension.

Ebony heard Oscar whisper to Jeff. "If I wanted to listen to an asshole I'd fart." Adremelech whipped his head in their direction.

"Sorry, what was that? I don't speak plebeian." Oscar tried to find something clever to say but was reduced to silence as he stared.

"Oscar's here and he's staying and that's final. If you're not happy you can leave," Ebony said before a fight Oscar wouldn't win broke out. Adremelech quieted with his mouth drawn in a thin line.

"The prison isn't far, under an hour away." Emmanuel changed the conversation. "We could try and lead Atlas there to fight?"

"He'd never fight without magic on his side," Adremelech said. "That idea is pointless."

"Okay…" Emmanuel trailed off and decided to focus more on steering the ship.

Adremelech cleared his throat. "If you don't mind, I'm going to stretch my legs." Irked by Oscar's very being, he stood. Ebony hesitated to let him go alone.

"I'll watch him," Cascia offered.

"Not alone you won't," Noah said, and Ebony was grateful as they stalked out the door behind him. Oscar was uncomfortable in the presence of an Ancient and he and Jeff quickly busied themselves too. Ebony was left unnervingly with Belphegor watching her, and Emmanuel flying the Hyperion in the background.

"Why did it have to be Nibiru?" Emmanuel asked, in an attempt to clear the fog of awkwardness. "There are so many abandoned planets around here, like Scoplya for example."

"Scoplya?" Belphegor asked.

"Dedicated to gaming," he scowled. "Why couldn't the sword be there, where all we have to do is play a little game, win a little race." Ebony shrugged and Belphegor blanked his whining. Emmanuel shut up.

Ebony and Belphegor caught each other's eye. In his lifetime, Belphegor had never been one for small talk, but Ebony didn't enjoy the silence.

"You don't look like the scary Ancient being your reputation gives you," she commented.

Belphegor raised an eyebrow. "I haven't killed anyone recently enough to make clothes out of their skin."

"Oh." The breath in Ebony's throat hitched. Belphegor's mouth twisted into what Ebony supposed was an attempted smile.

"I didn't do that," he assured. "My reputation precedes me." He made no attempt to keep talking. Ebony scratched the back of her neck. She noticed he was twitching slightly.

"Did Atlas hurt you badly?"

Belphegor grunted. "I saw what was coming," he said solemnly. "The moment we were revived I could see something different in Atlas' eyes. More animalistic. Hungry. But it was nothing I didn't deserve." Ebony was surprised at Belphegor's acceptance of torture. She didn't expect remorse from him but to feel slight pity for him was more unanticipated.

Ebony didn't show her sympathies. "We'll all get our revenge."

"I don't want revenge for me," Belphegor said. "I don't deserve it."

"Why are you helping us then?" His motives were unclear, and Ebony didn't trust him.

"I want revenge on behalf of everyone who died under the hand of an Ancient."

"And what does Adremelech want?" Ebony asked. She flinched as Belphegor stood menacingly. From his seat in the captain's chair, Emmanuel quietly reached for a gun holstered to the underneath of the table. His telekinesis wasn't strong, but he raised another gun that was rested on the shelving behind Belphegor and silently aimed it at him.

"We want the same thing. Do not doubt me or my brother," he warned. His chest heaved up and down as he breathed heavily, and his large hands threatened to take Ebony's head off with a single punch. She nodded. Belphegor sat back down, grabbing the gun from the air, and snapping it in half. "And don't take me for a fool," he told Emmanuel. Emmanuel's grip on the gun loosened.

Ebony had nothing else to say. She sat timidly, wary of Belphegor until she drifted off into a dreamlike state. Her mind flickered abruptly from staring at the white walls of the control room, to seeing a huge mountain. She could see herself sitting on a cliff face with other people, although their faces were blurred beyond recognition. Rocks were tumbling over them. In the daydream, she tried to move but was rooted to the spot as rocks hurtled past her until suddenly—

"—We're here!" Jeff barged into the room with Oscar on his tail and Ebony jumped with a start from her daydream. She'd never had such a vivid daydream but perhaps it was a vision like the ones Cascia had. But said vision had provided no information and so she shifted the unhelpful hallucination to the back of her mind and watched as Jeff and Oscar pressed themselves against the window.

Outside, a vast expanse of planets, too far from Andromeda's presidential planet Altuse to be governed by the dictator, hung in the sky. They were part of the outland planets. Below them, a jungle planet filled a vast expanse, but it looked abandoned. Adremelech appeared at the doorway with Cascia by his side and Noah following behind, brows furrowed.

"Adremelech found out what a toaster is," he whispered, and Ebony gulped.

"It has been a long time since I've seen this place," Belphegor recalled, looking out the window.

"What have they done to it?" Adremelech asked.

"It's been commercialised brother," Belphegor said blatantly as advertising bombarded the shield around it.

"I don't like it."

"Me neither."

Belphegor suddenly staggered forward. Adremelech caught him as he cried out in apparent pain.

"Brother?" He thumped him on the back. "Snap out of it." He clicked his fingers in front of his face. Belphegor blinked a couple of times before clutching his head. His eyes unclouded but he remained fearful, and Ancients weren't ones to be easily spooked. Him and Adremelech exchanged another glance.

"Your father knows we're here. We don't have much time," Belphegor informed everyone. "It's now or never." Ebony felt chills caress her spine as Belphegor referred to Atlas as 'father'.

Cascia piped up suddenly. She had been closely watching the

222

planet's terrain. "We have a small window of opportunity here. The section below us is pretty close to the mountain. If we land there, we can work our way to the centre," she said.

"I agree," Adremelech said. "The planet may have changed but I know the layout."

"We can't land," Jeff said.

"Pardon?" Adremelech placed a hand on Jeff's shoulder and swivelled him and the chair around, the weight of his hand nearly crushing Jeff's shoulder. Half of his body sagged as he tried to ignore the mounting pressure.

"The forcefield doesn't let heavy duty materials through. Otherwise, co-conspirators of Nibiru's inmates could casually fly by and drop weapons in," he explained. Adremelech released his grip.

"Can we parachute in then?" Noah asked.

"If the material isn't seen by the forcefield as a threat then yes." Jeff wasn't instilling much confidence.

"In which case -" Ebony stretched her neck from left to right until it produced a satisfying click, "-I'll get the armour, and someone get some parachutes."

"I'm not jumping without one," Noah said. He rushed to the door in anticipation, but Emmanuel barred him from proceeding with a yell in his head. Noah winced.

"Um, lads. We have a small problem. Probably nothing. Could be something." He gestured to the ship's radar which had detected several red blips coming towards them. It didn't tell Emmanuel what the red blips were, but they were small and travelling fast.

"What is that?" Ebony asked. A lump rose to her throat. The last time she was on a large ship for a long period of time, it ended up in several million pieces.

"It looks like a—" a loud bang echoed through the ship and there was a chorus of yells as the Hyperion lurched to the side. Everyone was thrown across the deck and as the ship settled itself, no one was left standing. Ebony rolled over into a pool of arterial blood, glossy, warm, and thick along the reflective floor.

"Shit." She scoured the room. Another stain of blood was smeared across the cracked radar where the impacting blow to Emmanuel's head had occurred. Blood trickled across the floor into the grooves of the tiles as the ship moved, and Emmanuel lay face down, body outspread in the centre of it all.

"Emmanuel! Emmanuel, can you hear me?" Ebony pulled him onto her lap, and he flopped unconsciously over her, his blood coating her hands. She pulled up an eyelid and his eyes were rolled back in his head. She checked his pulse, neck and wrist.

It was there.

Jeff crawled out from beneath the control panel and Ebony looked at him, aghast.

"What's damaged?" She cried. He hauled himself up, cradling his arm and heaved himself into the chair, mopping the blood from the radar with his sleeve.

"Back engines offline, stabilisers are struggling," he said, "and we're being hacked."

"By who?" Jeff's answer was overpowered by another group of beeps as the radar sensed more missiles. But the screen was broken beyond repair so Jeff could only hear that they were under attack.

Noah sidled towards Ebony, staying close to the floor as to not be thrown about as Jeff guided the ship. "Is he alive?"

Ebony answered with no solace. "Pass me the med kit." It was hung on the wall behind Belphegor and Adremelech who had both rushed to grab it. Belphegor tossed it her way, but she fumbled to open it, the greasy blood on her hand gaining no traction on the clasps.

"Here. Let me." Impatience was a virtue for Adremelech as he snatched the kit from Ebony's hands and ignored the clasp as he tore it open with fingers of stone and retrieved a thick bandage.

"Thank you." Ebony unwound it. The ship jolted again.

"Jeff, hold her steady," Noah called as he found himself slipping across the floor.

"I'm trying," Jeff groaned. He grabbed the joystick and the Hyperion creaked as he tried to manoeuvre the beast of a ship agilely through the sky. The beeping became more frantic, and he quickly buckled his belt.

"Find something to hold on to!" he shouted. Another missile rocked the ship and Ebony looked around in panic; Emmanuel was in her arms, Oscar and Cascia were holding on to the fixed table. Adremelech and

Belphegor were like sitting ducks as the smooth textured walls didn't provide much to hold on to, and as much as Ebony didn't want to, she offered her hand to them. Adremelech took it gratefully and she pulled them to the table. In return, Belphegor allowed a thick stem of air to flow from his hands to try and steady the ship.

Ebony looped her arm around the table leg and pressed the bandage to Emmanuel's head with her free hand. The Hyperion wasn't yet on fire, but a strong smell of exhaust fumes and gasoline suggested it would be a charcoaled mess within minutes and it wasn't helped as Jeff's driving became more erratic.

Suddenly, the radio crackled, and a disembodied voice came through. "Ebony, it's been a while. I've missed our encounters. How have you been?" Daegel cackled.

"Daegel," Adremelech roared. "Leave us before you regret being born!" But Daegel let out a guffaw.

"Didn't enjoy our little torture sessions then?" he sneered.

"Pardon?" Belphegor said.

"I said, didn't enjoy our little torture sessions then?"

"Pardon?"

"Didn't enjoy our…" Daegel trailed off and put his hand to the hole in his head where his ear once was. "You piece of shit," he yelled. Twenty-one years and he still wasn't over it.

"Pardon?"

Daegel gave up talking to Belphegor. "Ebony, you've abandoned your father to work with your uncles," he tutted, disgustingly sloppy mouth noises coming through the speakers. "This family is remarkably screwed up. But I tell you what, hand yourself over to me now and you and I can go and make amends with Atlas. Sound good?"

Ebony chose her next words carefully. "Pardon?" Belphegor smirked and folded his arms and felt a feeling he'd never felt before. Pride.

Daegel spat on the mic. He sounded stressed. But little did Ebony know that Atlas had granted Daegel an ultimatum. If he didn't retrieve Ebony, his head would be slowly pulled from his shoulders, fibre by fibre, and used as a scarecrow on the crop fields of Ignis. He wasn't worthy of the bone throne.

"Your friends will die a slow and painful death and only after you have watched each of them suffer, will I run my blade along your throat." Daegel's was a man of loutish speech, but Ebony was over his threats.

"How about you go screw yourself!" she yelled as the ship engines began to stutter. Jeff had pushed the Hyperion to its limit, and the missiles had totalled the engines. Black smoke poured into the room like water into every nook and cranny and visibility was becoming an increasingly precious commodity as the seconds passed. Ebony tried to push away the smoke, but she didn't know how to draw air from elsewhere and ended up recycling the smoke back into the room.

"Shapeshifter, get us back over the drop point, we're going to have to jump," Adremelech hollered, yanking at the joystick.

"Are you insane?" Cascia yelled.

"You got a better idea Enchanted?" he spat. "We'll be blown up before we can get the parachutes. Listen to me!" Jeff gulped but complied fearfully. With a harsh wrench of the stick, they headed in the opposite direction.

"Give it up Adremelech," Daegel jeered.

"Jeff, get the door open. Everyone, hold on until my cue," Ebony ordered. She wrapped her hand tightly around Emmanuel's waist. Alarms sounded as the doors glided open and gale force wind whipped around the room.

"I can't hold on," Noah cried. His sweaty fingers slipped and in a gut-wrenching moment, he fell.

"Noah!" Oscar lunged to catch him and caught his shirt sleeve. In one slick move, he swung his leg around the table leg of the control panel and dangled there precariously, holding on to Noah as he swung perilously in the air. Ebony tried to calm the wind, but her panicking did little to fight the gale and Adremelech and Belphegor were in no state to help.

"Get ready to jump," Jeff yelled, unbuckling his belt. Ebony braced herself as he counted. They were jumping without parachutes. They had nothing to break their fall.

"Three... two... one!" he screamed and she let go.

Everything went to shit for the millionth time.

Another missile whacked the Hyperion to the tune of Daegel's laughter. As everyone leapt towards the door, the ship rolled and only half of them fell. The rest were thrown off course. Ebony curled her body around Emmanuel as she collided with the side of the ship, the open door mocking her as she was flung against the sealed windows. Cascia locked eyes with her momentarily before she also fell out, Adremelech close behind. Ebony aimed for the door, but the ship had no intent on cooperating. Her main focus was holding on to Emmanuel as she felt for the pilot's seat. Hoping the ship wouldn't roll again, she pushed off the leathery seat and followed the jet stream of air out the door.

It was so cold in the atmosphere and Ebony felt numb to the touch, which was bad on the pneumonia side of things but good for crashing into stabbing pine trees, as the pain was only slightly unbearable. As she fell, it was as though someone vacuumed the magic from her body. For a second, she was able to slow her decent but through the shield layer, her magic was blown out like a candle. Being mundane had never been such an inconvenience.

Chapter 19

Ebony could hear other screams and watched as the Hyperion, which had helped them so greatly, fulminated in the sky, raining fire and metal above the planet in a blinding flash. It was a ghastly sight but one she didn't watch as she hit the trees and closed her eyes to avoid the needle pointed pines stabbing at her pupils. It was impossible to hold on to Emmanuel any longer as his arm slid from her clenched fist. Both fell freely through the trees, landing painfully on the ground where little lay to break her fall but dead shreds of grass in the dry packed dirt and scattered pebbles. How she'd survived, Ebony didn't know, but she wasn't unscathed.

She was seeing triple but could see well enough the tree branch sticking out of her leg and Emmanuel lying stilly in the grass only three or four metres away. Behind him was another body; Ebony couldn't make out who in the long grass. But as long as they were unharmed, she didn't care who it was.

"Okay, okay, okay." She braced herself and slowly straightened her leg in front of her. Hissing in pain, she clutched both hands around the nut-brown branch. It was cultivating fungus, a confused beetle sat on the splintered top and moss climbed down the sprouting twig. If she didn't get it out, she would have a miniature ecosystem growing from her leg.

"Like ripping off a plaster," she convinced herself, "but the plaster's a tree branch and it might make my leg fall off." She shook the upper half of her body, rinsing away the doubt. "Can't be that bad."

She tugged.

The top half of the branch came out. The other half stubbornly snapped off and remained lodged inside her. Ebony made a noise like a boiling kettle before tossing out a litany of swear words. She tore off her shirt sleeve and started dabbing profusely. She'd deal with the 'splinter' later.

"Gonna have to do," she mumbled and bracing herself, she stood with some sort of contorted one legged squat to help her up. The pain was impressive, a solid seven out of ten, but sitting a tier above the agony of her leg on an unbearable ten was the possibility of Emmanuel lying dead. She bit her lip and dug her nails so far into her hand it left a mark as she hobbled over, falling short as her leg succumbed to the searing pain and gave out on her. She could see the nasty gash on the side of Emmanuel's face, cutting deep but not through to the skull. He was covered in small scratches from the trees; as was Ebony, but otherwise looked relatively unscathed. She reached out and put a finger to his wrist. There was a slow but discernible rhythm.

"You're breathing. That's a start." As she sat there with him, watching advertisements cover the sky, there was movement from the trees. Trunks as wide as buses with low hanging boughs hid hostile criminals roaming the planet and Ebony wielded the other half of her 'splinter' at the trees. But a person whose worst and only crime was stealing his neighbours Wi-Fi emerged.

"Oscar. Are you okay?" Ebony asked. He jogged over, baggy shirt billowing in the breeze.

"Pretty sure my finger wasn't meant to be sticking out the way it was." He held out his hand and Ebony cringed at the swelling joint on his pinky that forced the tip of his finger ninety degrees. "Are you hurt?" he asked, gaping at the stump sticking from her leg. She stared at him.

"No."

"No?"

"No. I'm dandy. In fact, I regularly stab myself with tree branches for pleasure. Better than cocaine."

"Sorry," Oscar said. "You want me to get it out?"

"If you can." Ebony braced herself as Oscar leant down by her. Her eyes watered as he wrapped both hands around the branch, twisting it slightly as he reinforced his grip. His face was contorted, and he winced at the injury and Ebony spoke up.

"You know this is worse for me, right?"

"Debatable," Oscar mumbled. He let out a sigh and made fleeting eye contact with Ebony. She nodded.

"Get it over with." She sunk her fingernails into the ground and gritted her teeth.

"One. Two…" Oscar missed three and yanked as hard as he could, and Ebony let free a harrowing scream as the branch came away in Oscar's hand.

"Thanks," she panted heavily. She blocked the hole with her sleeve and ripped the other one off to tie it firmly in place.

Now wearing a makeshift tank top in the burning sun, Ebony turned back to Emmanuel and Oscar knelt beside him in the arid grass, holding a cloth to his head. He stirred but wasn't conscious. Two bloody handprints marked his face. They were Ebony's handprints, dried and crusty on his otherwise unblemished skin.

"You see anyone else?" Oscar asked. He rested his fingers on Emmanuel's wrist and counted a steady pulse, or what he thought was one. He'd never been good at anthropology which is why he spent his professional life staring at plants instead.

"There's someone else in the grass," Ebony suddenly told Oscar. "Adremelech or Belphegor, or an inmate?" Her attention was focused on the body facing away from them in the long grass. It moved slightly; muscular build reflective of an Ancient.

"Maybe." With their attention held by the figure in the grass, it came as a surprise and relief when Ebony felt Emmanuel's hand prod hers and the both of them were momentarily distracted by him as he let out a pained moan.

"Hey bud," Oscar grinned. Ebony's sigh softly deflated, and she casually peered over her shoulder and back to the stranger. Recognition dawned on her face.

It was Daegel.

Grunting like an angry pig, chest rising and falling like he'd just sprinted a marathon, he whipped a knife from either side of his belt and stalked towards them. His guns had been destroyed through the forcefield, but apparently knives were still allowed.

"Oscar, run." Ebony pushed his arm roughly and he looked at her and then to what she was staring at. Daegel waved and clanged the knives together above his head as his approach quickened.

"Get him up, get him up!" Ebony panicked as her and Oscar desperately tried to carry Emmanuel. Daegel's remorseless green eyes stared Ebony down as she tried to force Emmanuel to walk. He wasn't far from them, but he took his time, skipping daintily, stopping to brush his hands in the genetically engineered flowers, because between Ebony, Emmanuel, and Oscar, only Oscar could move fast enough to outrun him.

"Oscar, take Emmanuel and run," Ebony forced.

"Never." Oscar stood steadfast over the two of them as Daegel approached. He was barely ten steps away.

"Oscar!"

"I love you Ebony," Oscar said. She pulled him into a hug and quickly span their bodies, so her back was facing Daegel like a human shield. She squeezed her eyes shut and braced for impact. But a shadow flickered over them, and she never felt a thing.

"That's for torturing me," Belphegor snarled, snapping Daegel's arm backwards from the elbow and plunging his own precious knife deeply into his chest. He held him by his neck as Daegel choked on the blood pouring from his mouth, still gripping the knife buried within him. Then, throwing him to the ground roughly, Belphegor stood on his chest, smiling as he heard several ribs crack under his boots. Daegel gurgled, unable to speak. "And this, is for hurting my niece." With one sweeping movement, as if putting a golf ball, Belphegor pulled the knife from Daegel's chest and sliced through his neck. The life faded from his eyes in seconds.

"Belphegor," Ebony said in disbelief. He wiped his new blade clean on his arm.

"Update on the boy?" he asked. Ebony shook herself from her shock.

"He's uh… he'll be fine."

"Good. I won't have any Enchanteds dying under my watch," he said, more fondly than expected. "Have you found anyone else, friend of foe?"

"No," Oscar said, surprised at the demon's kindness.

"I'm sure they'll be along," Belphegor said. He turned around and took several paces into the grass and bent down to the flowers. Ebony watched as he took one in his hand, a lilac blossom with a bunch of broad, saucer shaped petals. Careful not to pull the roots from the ground, he sniffed it. A slight smile graced his lips. Ebony watched the curious behaviour and realised that he'd probably never had a chance to experience a moment of serenity.

"Where are we?" Emmanuel grumbled from the floor. "I feel like

I've been thrown through a blender."

"We're on Nibiru," Oscar informed him. "You were."

"Will you be all right for a moment?" Ebony asked. "I need to speak with Belphegor." Oscar raised his eyebrows with a 'be careful' expression and she nodded to him, before her and Belphegor took a brief walk around the perimeter of the clearing.

"What is it?" he asked, matching her shuffle of a pace as she limped along.

"Thank you for ridding us of Daegel. It was long overdue," she said but she looked weary, and he noticed her hesitancy.

"There is something more bothering you?"

"Why do you care Belphegor? You spent your life murdering people, now you've changed and suddenly become the good guy? Forgive me but I don't trust it," she said, fiddling with the hem of her T-shirt nervously. Belphegor raised his face to the three stars above Nibiru and savoured the light. When he spoke, his words were slow and deliberate.

"You have every reason not to trust me. But when I killed, I did it under threat of death, and because Sonneillon blinded us to the possibility that the universe could thrive and blossom into something as incredible as it has become. I have fallen in love with it and cannot allow Atlas' intentions to destroy it come to fruition." He looked at her, chalky grey eyes passionate and candid to what he was saying. "Many of the Enchanteds in this universe are my descendants and I'm so proud of that. I've never had anything to be proud of before, nothing to cherish." Belphegor acted almost upset as he glanced towards Emmanuel and back. "I never got to see my daughter and nieces grow up. So, when Atlas mentioned he had another daughter, I realised I had a chance."

"A chance?"

"At redemption. To find a family I belong to." He poked at the ground with his foot and words failed Ebony for a moment. She worried that he was just trying to propitiate her with flowery words.

"I'm glad that you see the universe for what it is." Belphegor well disguised his happiness. "But family is a powerful word," Ebony said, "and I already have mine." She pointed at Oscar and Emmanuel and Oscar waved back cheerily as he noticed. Belphegor smiled wistfully but shook off the emotions he had spent so long bottling away. Inside, he was experiencing another emotion he'd failed to feel before.

Heartbreak.

As they finished their conversation and lapped Oscar, Emmanuel cautiously got to his feet, hand dabbing the side of his head. He flinched but placed a surely smile on his face.

"I'm only seeing one of each of you." He squinted. "Maybe one and a half. Let's go."

"Belphegor, which way?" Ebony asked.

"North," he said, pointing towards a towering mountain in the distance. He looked at her, perceiving her as slightly dumb in the moment.

Ebony pouted, hands on hips. "Makes sense."

She stooped over Daegel's body to see if he had anything useful. He had a backpack strapped to him, but Ebony didn't want the extra weight with the long trek ahead of them. Grabbing a tree branch, she used it as a makeshift crutch and grinded the butt into the ground as Belphegor rolled Daegel's body face down into a ditch, leaving him for whatever creatures lurked around.

Oscar walked by Emmanuel's side, watching him take a few shaky steps before he settled into a steady rhythm, his head bobbing up and down contrary to his steps to minimise the movement of his head and nauseating sensation that came with it. Belphegor led the way, carrying a knife in each hand, stalking through the vegetation like the predator he was.

"Where do you think the others are?" Oscar asked, as the jungle grew thick and their pace slowed. There were no footsteps, no evidence the others were around.

Adremelech will look out for them," Belphegor replied. He continued to hack away at the vines growing thickly in front of them.

If they're together Ebony thought but of course, no one heard her.

The jungle, in spite of the things lurking in the shadow's hell bent on killing them, was remarkably beautiful. Small, freshwater streams trickled through mossy rocks, offering reprieve from the thirsty walk, and grand old willow trees blew above their heads, caressing their surroundings with lance shaped leaves. The remains of long-forgotten pathways and crumbling archways could be seen buried under the leaf litter and the light from the stars warming the planet danced through the swaying tree branches, creating complex patterns across the floor.

As Belphegor slashed at an intricately woven wall of impenetrable vines, Ebony lowered herself onto a log and stretched her leg out in front of her. A red stain had grown through the cloth and a numbness trailed up her thigh. But she tried to not let it get to her and sought distraction in Emmanuel.

"Shoot," he sulked. Ebony let out a burst of laughter but clapped her hand round her mouth as Emmanuel shot her a glare. He'd sat absentmindedly in a puddle and was now wiping a stain from his trouser leg.

"Aww, ickle Manny's had an accident," Oscar joked. Emmanuel hurled a rock and Oscar ducked. It hit Belphegor's back and the three of them froze but Belphegor, so ensconced in the vines, didn't acknowledge it. Or maybe he did but he used the plants as a quickly sought and therapeutic anger management session. They breathed again.

Ebony looked at the puddle below Emmanuel and watched as it settled but as the ripples slowed, they were jarred again by an unknown force, water particles bouncing across the earth. She put her hand on the ground to investigate closer.

"No one move," she said.

"What?"

"Shh." She held a finger to her lips. The ground was vibrating and as it got more violent, a faint rumble could be heard in the distance. It was growing exponentially.

"Where exactly did we land? Do any of you know?" Ebony asked.

"Well, back in my day this was—" Belphegor began.

"--No. What part of the world?" Ebony urged. "What's coming for us?"

"That is Jeff's department," Emmanuel said. A sudden yell relieved anyone of the need to answer. Ebony aimed her walking stick at the trees; but if it was a person, would they be deterred by the threat of an incapacitated girl with a stick? Unlikely, but Belphegor took the first stand, marching past her and standing defensively in front. The treetops in the near distance started to shake. Like in a horror film, birds squawked and soared high into the sky, away from the noise.

"Mind out lads." There was a bang. "Timber!" the voice called as a tree groaned. Ebony hobbled out the way as the trunk smashed against the ground, revealing Jeff, who was standing on it proudly. He smiled down at everyone and gasped at the rusting knives they were wielding, and the simple stick Ebony held.

"What are you doing?" he asked, flabbergasted as he descended the tree trunk and landed gracefully at the bottom.

"Us? How about you? What the hell is going on over there?" Emmanuel exclaimed.

"I'm great. Never been better. Nibiru is such an interesting planet. Never seen it from this perspective." Jeff was packing an exhausted weapon into his belt as he spoke. "There's a pack of SID's coming towards us, they come in waves with a half-hour grace period for the prisoners to collect as many weapons as possible but-" he took note of the lack of weapons, "-you didn't know that." He heaved a sigh. "Here." Pressing two fingers behind his ear, from his body came a pixelated light, which quickly formed into what looked like a menu screen. It was filled to the brim with weapons and medicine bottles and Jeff marvelled at it proudly. "Collected them all myself," he boasted. He looked over his shoulder and the vegetation had now also begun to shiver in trepidation of the mysterious SID's.

"How are we meant to fight with holograms?" Belphegor questioned.

"And what exactly are we fighting? What are SIDs?" Ebony added. Jeff rolled his eyes.

"SIDs. Self-Inflicted Damned," he said, as though it was meant to mean something to them.

"Who?"

Jeff tutted. "I'll explain everything once we're safe." Reaching into the pixels he grabbed a gun. It materialised instantly in his hand, and he grinned, cocking the barrel. "But for now, help yourselves." The four of them rushed forward, grabbing all the guns they could hold. "Here, for the leg and the head." Jeff threw two medical bottles at Ebony and Emmanuel who hastily opened them.

"Bottles up." They clinked and chugged. The medicine had the taste and consistency of acrid soupy glop with a purple colouring, and it invoked an immense pain. It soared through Ebony's leg, and she gripped her thigh tightly. Emmanuel nearly collapsed as a white burning rocked his head but in a brief moment, it was over. Ebony stood, firmly on both feet and Emmanuel stood up without the world swaying around him. Both were healthy as though they hadn't ever been hurt.

"What is this stuff?" Ebony marvelled. "Why is this not standard medicine?"

"Science profits off mortality," Jeff reminded her. She grimaced. "Now let's get this party started. To the mountain!" He winked and took off at a run and jumping from one rock to another, he swung himself into the tree, perching on it gracefully. His scrawny figure misled everyone into believing that when not an animal, he was of average ability. But they were greatly deceived. Jeff's strength and agility was hidden ambiguously behind the guise, muscle disguised beneath baggy clothes.

"Pace yourselves, it's a long way to the base of the mountain and a long climb through a cave system once we're there," he told them.

"How do you know that?" Belphegor asked.

"Adremelech told me. Haven't you seen them?" he wondered curiously.

"Them? Were Cascia and Noah with you too?" Ebony asked.

"Yeah, I saw you from across the clearing, told them to catch up whilst I gave them a head start against the SIDS."

"We haven't seen them," Emmanuel clarified, "but they probably went past without realising it. We'll catch up."

"Gotta fight off the SIDs first," Jeff said as he fired at a well-camouflaged body in the trees. A SID fell to one knee and Jeff didn't hesitate to shoot it again and once more until it was on the floor. With the noise of a hundred trampling footsteps, SIDs began to appear from all directions.

The SIDs were lethally weaponized cyborgs. With bladed horns, metallic claws, a mash of robotic limbs ranging from chainsaws to bludgeons and teeth shaved into daggers, they struck fear into everyone's hearts as they rushed forward. Propelled by the springs on their legs and spurred on with manipulated arm and leg joints which allowed them to navigate the jungle with ease, they were a mortifying enemy.

"Jeff, I thought you said they were behind us?" Oscar cried out as he did the limbo to avoid his chest being sliced open.

"They were but because we've left them behind, they've despawned and they're respawning here," Jeff explained. "Have you never played a game?" he scoffed, as he aimed his gun and fired.

"Everyone into the trees," Ebony ordered, giving Oscar a leg up. He tugged her onto the branch, and she held out her hand for either Emmanuel or Belphegor to take. But they didn't.

"Fleeing is for the weak," Belphegor answered, teeth flashing with a devilish grin. For a man who had thrived on combat and then been deprived of it for several millennia, it was hardly surprising and as the SIDs charged, he gleefully charged back, choosing his knives over the guns he'd packed on his back.

"Or we could do that," Jeff grinned, backflipping off the high branches and scurrying along the low ones. One of the major flaws of the SIDs was their struggle to climb, so as Jeff shot them from above, they could do nothing but snarl at him. Inspired, Emmanuel grabbed a gun and stood close to Belphegor, shooting the SIDs as they came from the other direction. They moved in sequence, Enchanted and Ancient dancing in circles of perfect synchronicity, shooting every SID they saw with a good enough aim as to miss Jeff as he darted about the trees.

"I didn't see you as the pro fighter type," Ebony said to Emmanuel. He faced her, raised his gun to the left and without looking, shot a SID perfectly between the eyes.

"Really?" he said cheekily.

"He's our loveable killing machine," Jeff smirked, cartwheeling over their heads and ruffling Emmanuel's hair as he did so.

Oscar too was shooting ferociously, copper alloy coated steel bullets flying through the gun and into everything that moved with a robotic mechanism, although his shots were nowhere near as precise. As a SID with a chainsaw arm attacked the base of the tree, he jumped down but was quickly swamped. From behind, an unexpected rogue SID slipped through Belphegor and Emmanuel's massacre and lurched forward, its robotic hand grabbing Oscar's leg. He yelped as its claws raked his calf and yanked him to the forest floor, showing no restraint until Ebony's boot collided with the side of its head, crunching its skull against a rock with another rock she hauled from the ground. Oscar looked up and she

237

held out her hand for him to take, helping him into the tree for a second time.

"Stay here," she warned, and he nodded in embarrassment.

"I will," he said humbly. But instead of reprimanding him, Ebony grinned and with a smirk, she pulled two machine guns from her back, handing him one.

"Bet I can shoot more than you," she wagered and with a shared glance, they both open fired. The noise was painfully loud, but it was an effective method and as the bullets ran out and the last shell hit the floor, smoke from the guns dissipated from the forest and revealed a sea of dead SIDs scattered ungracefully across the flattened mud.

"Is that it?" Ebony asked wearily, as Belphegor pulled his knife from a body and wiped the blood along his sleeve, the same place where Daegel's blood had now dried in the humidity. He was relishing in the combat, and it made Ebony nervous. Emmanuel dabbed his forehead from the sweat and sat down.

"For now, yeah. One wave per area but they get harder as we get closer to the mountain," Jeff said as he dipped his hands in the river and drank thirstily, cautious to drink upstream of the bodies.

"How many more waves between here and the mountain?"

"Two, but the gaps between are fleshed out by randomised events to keep prisoners on their toes."

"In which case, if we're vaguely safe, let's make camp here for tonight," Ebony suggested, noting the three stars hanging in the sky disappearing below the horizon and the moon beginning to swell above them.

"Agreed," Jeff said, settling on the ground. "We'll get going tomorrow."

"SIDs used to be prisoners of the planet. They're the ones who made it to the mountain and the jury decided to not put back in," Jeff explained. "They're called the Self-Inflicted Damned because apparently, a fancy title warrants the experiments Nibiru's scientists perform on them. They committed a crime and therefore they deserved damnation."

"What did they do to them?"

"Everything unethical and more." Jeff snuggled deeper into his jacket. "Buried in the outlands so the Altusien government can deny its involvement. Removed limbs and added robotic enhancements without anaesthetics. Rewired their brains until they no longer had freewill. And then had the audacity to call them all Sid."

"As you do," Oscar scoffed sarcastically. Belphegor's eyebrows arched.

"I don't."

"It's a figure of speech... never mind."

Jeff continued. "They're coded by the prison guards to attack incessantly; I doubt they even know they're doing it." Jeff's story sent a cold shiver round the campfire and suddenly, Ebony wasn't proud to call herself a scientist.

"That's awful," Oscar said.

"A fate worse than death, like I said." Jeff rubbed his own arms to warm himself as he lay across the logs. He settled to sleep as the clouds parted and the gorgeous night sky was almost visible past the adverts.

"Why was Nibiru chosen to become a prison?" Emmanuel asked as he stoked the fire.

"I would assume it's because we kept all of our treasure on it," said Belphegor. "What we had hidden in the mountain, could easily topple your galactic empires. It's the perfect goal and in a place like this, protected from all who seek to steal it." Belphegor made polite conversation with Emmanuel who relished the heat of the flames, creeping closer to them. They all listened to him, save Jeff who had fallen asleep remarkably quickly atop a pillow of dirt. A loud snore from him interrupted their chatter and Belphegor excused himself, sitting comfortably in the moss.

The flames flickered, creating shadows that danced together across the trees, spreading a warm glow around the makeshift camp. A few logs had been rolled to make less than comfortable seats above the wet ground and whilst the one thing none of them had considered bringing was food, Oscar had stocked up on biscuits which hadn't been crumbled to dust in his fall. He passed them round, much to the appreciation of everyone.

"Jeff," he whispered, and Jeff awoke to eat one before falling back into his slumber.

"Thanks." Ebony took one and munched on it quickly before

clutching her hands together, holding them out to the fire.

"You cold?" Oscar asked.

"Little bit," Ebony replied, shivering.

"Here." He tapped Jeff's neck as he slept and from his digital backpack of wonders, Oscar pulled out a blanket. He stood and relocated next to Ebony, and she smiled faintly as he wrapped it around both their shoulders, leaving his arm over her shoulder as he did so. They sat and watched the fire and the cold subsided, but Ebony didn't try to sleep. She was gently tapping her foot against the ground, rapping her knuckles together until they went red.

Oscar noticed. "What's up?"

Ebony looked to the sky. "The never-ending darkness of an empty void looming upon us which will one day destroy us all if we don't all die first."

"… Are you okay?"

"Fine," Ebony fibbed plainly. "Just thinking about Noah and Cascia."

"I'm sure they're probably as worried about us as we are about them. Belphegor is keeping us safe, isn't he?" Ebony glanced at Belphegor, knife in hand, beady eyes darting about the surroundings. She was afraid for the leaves that dared blow in the wind in case he spotted the movement and flung a knife.

"I guess," she answered, although knowing Oscar and Emmanuel had offered to keep watch alleviated her woes.

"I'm sure Adremelech is doing the same."

"I'm sure he is." Ebony put her fears to the back of her mind. She leant into Oscar's side as the fire crackled in front of them and found herself slowly drifting off to sleep, lulled into unconsciousness by the steady beating of his heart.

Chapter 20

Ebony awoke for no particular reason, wishing she was in the comfort of her own home. Opening her eyes slowly she nearly lashed out as she felt something on her head, but it was Oscar's hand. She was resting across his lap, and he was idly stroking her hair as he spoke with Emmanuel who was lying across the wood, lazily prodding the fire with a stick. She smiled and stirred as morning came over the horizon accompanied by a crisp rolling bar of fog. Stretching her arms out she yawned loudly. A sticky dew clung to her jacket, and her legs had stiffened in the cold where the bedewed trousers had frozen around them. She looked up hazily and Oscar leaned forward.

"Good morning," he said. Ebony sat.

"Morning."

"We're heading off as soon as Belphegor's awake."

"Wake him now, we should get going."

"If you want to wake an Ancient demon who sleeps with knives in his hands, by all means, be my guest," Oscar invited with a swooping hand gesture in Belphegor's direction.

Ebony's cheeks puffed with air. "I think we should just let him wake up in his own time," she decided. Picking up a gun, Ebony walked over to the other side of the campfire which now smouldered as a pile of stony ash. Her trousers crunched as the material freed itself of icy droplets. Looking at Emmanuel on the way past, his brow was furrowed in concerned and Ebony suspected he was thinking about Noah and Cascia. She was thinking of them too.

Noah, where are you? Her imagination ran awry. *You and Cascia better be watching out for each other.* She took a seat by the tree and noticed Belphegor who, as Oscar had pointed out, had two knives sealed tightly in his hands as he slept. His eyes were closed but Ebony was convinced he was awake, listening to everything going on. She trusted him a little, but Adremelech was a different story.

"Good morning." Jeff was a spritely morning person, contradicting with the entire company as he stretched his way in deep lunges around the fire pit. "How did everyone sleep?" There was a mixed mumble of 'barely', 'uncomfortably' and 'not at all' and Jeff rolled his eyes.

"Well, you better get some energy in you. Today isn't going to be fun, I'm warning you now." Ebony yawned, tucking into the biscuits which were erring on the side of stale. They weren't as comforting as the night before. She yawned through a mouthful and let the crumbs fall to the floor.

Emmanuel extinguished what was left of the fire; Jeff had demanded no trace of their camp be left behind in case inmates followed their tracks, and Ebony and Oscar rolled their log back into the thicket, turning in time to see Belphegor carry one on each shoulder and lob them into the trees.

"Show off," Emmanuel grumbled, missing his telekinesis.

As the warmth of the day grew exponentially and the muggy heat rosed their skin before they'd left the makeshift camp, they relinquished several layers of clothing. As Jeff had explained to them, everything on the planet was controllable, including the weather, and the controllers orbiting Nibiru from their space station had decided to hand them a heat stroke threatening day.

The trek was a never-ending uphill struggle, which, accompanied with the sweltering, soupy air, and dense, unforgiving forestry, slowed their progress significantly. But on the rare occasion that the mountain stream flowed overground, they stopped for but a minute to drink, and then they persevered. Ebony sometimes enjoyed the walking. She found that when walking, she didn't have time to think about Noah and Cascia and the intrusive thoughts kept themselves at bay.

Hours into their climb, when the stars in the sky made their way around Nibiru, they were relieved by the looming shadow of the mountain before them and whilst for Belphegor, Ebony, Emmanuel, and Oscar, the closer they got the happier they became, Jeff became increasingly agitated. In the dense thicket, where wet mud swamped their shoes and they were fused to the ground, Jeff threw down his walking stick, splattering mud up his legs.

"We're stopping," he said categorically, coming to a halt.

"We need to keep going," Belphegor countered.

"We need to stop."

"What's wrong?"

"All of this," he exclaimed. "We're less than a day's walk away from a treasure so heavily guarded, it is near impossible to get to and there hasn't been a thing stopping us. It's too easy."

"Maybe it's luck?" Oscar suggested. "It's not like we haven't been struggling," he said as he fought the mud for custody of his boot.

"When have we ever been lucky since starting all this?" was Ebony's answer. "Jeff, what's meant to happen in this area of the planet?"

"It's an apocalyptic warfare area, so SID raids, combat with other players and increasingly hard, randomised events."

"So, what should be killing us here?" Emmanuel asked as he tied his hair back with a paper-thin vine in anticipation of combat.

"I have no idea," Jeff answered. "That's what randomised means."

"But we won't find out if we don't keep moving," Ebony said. "We've got to get to the mountain and stopping isn't going to get us there." She went to keep walking where the earth below her seemed dry when Belphegor grabbed her, yanking her back as the ground crumbled away below her and her feet dangled above an extensively dark pit. The shiny blade of one of Belphegor's knives was out of sight in an instant as it dropped from his hands and into the bottomless trench.

"You had to say something," he grumbled.

"What the hell?" Ebony's heart pounded in her chest. Belphegor steadied her. The crack barred their way; it was just wide enough to be impassable. Then more cracks opened around them, small and insignificant fissure at first but then the ground opened with an urgent need to swallow them up.

"Up the trees," Emmanuel demanded. The others followed suit, clinging on to low hanging branches as large canyons in the ground opened up. It wasn't only the depth of the holes that was of concern but the billowing ash, powerful heat and glowing light rising from it. Then the ground stopped trying to devour them and a low rumble took the place of crumbling dirt, the sound originating from the bottom of the cracks. Ebony was sure it was Magma men.

"Smells like Atlas' doing," she feared.

"Stay still," Belphegor ordered as she went to get down and

investigate. He lowered himself from the top branches and ran skilfully across the lower ones. For a well-built man, he had well-polished agility. Everyone waited as he jumped to the ground, but no more cracks appeared.

"What's in them?" Oscar worried. "It looks like Magma men." He feared the same as Ebony. Belphegor peered over the side of one, his face illuminated by the amber glow.

"It's the oldest game in the book," he said. His stomach twisted into knots as he lightly touched the floor beneath his feet. It was heating up.

"What?" the others demanded simultaneously.

"The floor is lava."

The controllers of Nibiru had a sadistic sense of fun.

Suddenly, an air bubble of lava exploded, rupturing through the crack and mounting into the sky as though it could climb the air. Belphegor roared as it splattered over him, burning holes into his clothes and skin. He sank to his knees as the viscous lava ran down the back of his leg, melting a channel through his skin.

"Belphegor!" Ebony didn't hesitate to jump from the branches, and she covered her face with her hand as she grabbed him and pulled him out of harm's way. The jet of lava sprayed liberally across the ground and abated once it had too struck Ebony. She gagged at the smell of burning flesh, trying to ignore the sizzling sound or fleshy bubbles that rose on her arm. She hauled Belphegor to the closest tree and from above, Emmanuel dropped down. He tapped behind his ear and pulled from the hologram a medicine bottle.

"Last one. Take it quickly." He handed to Ebony who unscrewed it with trembling hands. Belphegor was twisting in pain as the lava solidified. A smattering had landed on his face and he tore at his skin but the magma had latched on like a leech. Ebony tried to give him the medicine but it was prevented by his writhing movements, and he clenched his jaw shut.

"Help me!" she demanded desperately as Oscar and Jeff rushed over. They grabbed Belphegor's arms and legs, fighting with him as Ebony grabbed his jaw, forcing his mouth open. She poured the liquid inside and smothered his mouth with her hand, holding his nose and forcing him to swallow. The pain increased momentarily, but then the wounds closed up and Belphegor stopped struggling, his scarred skin no more disfigured than it was.

"Thank you." His chest rose and fell rapidly as they helped him up and he regained his uncompromising countenance.

"Ebony, your arm." Oscar clutched her hand as she tried to pull a jacket over it. She wrenched her hands away, protecting the bubbly skin from sight.

"We'll gather more first aid along the way."

Emmanuel, who was back up in the trees and watching the lava from a sheltered distance, descended the trunk like a pole. "The lava's still rising, we've got to go," he urged. The faint smell of sulphur filled his nostrils and he spread his arms wide, gesturing them towards the mountain.

They ran.

Vaulting over cracks, they sprinted through the trees as lava propelled upwards in jet streams around them, burning into the earth channels of lava. Ebony couldn't help but think that Atlas, with his affinity to lava, had something to do with the calamitous situation. But it got significantly worse as the lava began to spill over the cracks and suddenly, the floor was slowly engulfed. After all, it was the name of the game.

"We've got to get to higher ground!" Ebony yelled as she found herself running on tiptoes.

"There is no higher ground," replied Belphegor. The trees may have been synthetic models of the real thing, but they were just as flammable. Whether they were engulfed by the flames or swallowed up by the earth, they fell in every direction, destroying all higher ground. They continued to run, Jeff leading the charge and Belphegor coming up the rear but soon collided with an even bigger problem. As they cleared an especially large crack, someone flew into Belphegor, knocking him off his course. He stumbled, grabbed the SID, smashed its skull in with a rock hard fist and pushed it into the lava. Ebony turned to him as he wiped his brow of sweat.

"This day could not get any worse," she groaned. All of them were slowly running out of stamina but with the added threat of SIDs they couldn't afford to stop. As they got to the top of a small hill, they were barred from going any further. Lava was gushing in a stream, blocking their paths, and from behind the familiar growls of blood thirsty hordes of SIDs grew louder.

"Now what?" Oscar cried. "The base of the mountain is right there!" he pointed. Through the trees, a rocky cliff side could be seen, but it was out of reach.

"We're trapped," Ebony cried.

"No. Not if we're smart," Emmanuel piped up. "Everyone up the trees." They followed his instruction on one of the few remaining trees that fought to stay standing. As Belphegor followed Ebony, Emmanuel stopped him. "Belphegor, see the branch over the lava?" Belphegor narrowed his eyes at the snapping branch.

"Yes?"

"Climb it."

"If you want me dead just tell me. I won't be offended."

"Just do it."

"It's not going to hold me," he warned.

"It's going to have to," Emmanuel said. Belphegor frowned and shuffled along the branch tentatively slowly as it groaned and arched under his weight.

"Emmanuel what are you doing?" Ebony watched him wearily, clutching the tree until her fingers went white. He winked at her.

"I'm building a bridge," he said, stretching his arms wide. Ebony, Jeff, and Oscar began to fire on the SIDs as they climbed the hill, but Jeff was right when he said the encounters would only get worse. Not only were they quicker, more sporadic, and much more terrifying to behold, they had nearly doubled in size as the human part of them had all but disappeared. A single bullet was no longer enough to take them down.

"Belphegor." Emmanuel looked up. "Be ready to catch me." Belphegor's hands were at the ready, but the branch was begging him to get off as it bowed and creaked. Emmanuel stood steadfast as the SIDs approached. He was a mouth-watering meal in their eyes, and they took the bait.

"Come get me assholes!" he yelled. As though waiting to be embraced, Emmanuel stood with his knees bent and arms wide, and the SIDs charged, full steam ahead.

"Emmanuel jump." Belphegor was a hairs width away from being able to grab him. His fingers waggled in the air.

"Not yet." He readied himself. His arms were stretched rigidly and the heat from the lava behind stuck his shirt to his back.

"Emmanuel," Belphegor warned.

"Wait for it."

"Emmanuel!"

"Now!" he bellowed and sprung into the air, linking hands with Belphegor who hauled him into the boughs with ease.

The branch held.

The shock on their faces was rapidly replaced with a joyful disgust as the SIDs, who were so riled in the anticipation of killing someone, neglected to notice Emmanuel's disappearance, and continued to charge into the lava. And once they did notice, they couldn't stop. The SIDs behind, so desperate for the kill, pushed forwards, plunging more of their own to a gnarly death. It was an utter blood bath but a path through the lava comprised of hot metal and modified plastic flesh was created.

"Emmanuel, that was sick," Oscar commented.

"Sick epic or sick disgusting?"

Oscar gave a singular firm nod. "Yes."

"Come on, the lava's not going to stop," Belphegor said. With adrenaline pumping through his veins and caution thrown to the wind, he jumped onto the scrap heap of SIDs to discover they held his weight, with the disadvantage of coating his boots in fleshy remains. The others followed suit and treading lightly, they jogged over the metal before it could burn through their shoes, reaching the jagged mountain cliff.

"Here." Belphegor took a knee and held his hands out, to which Jeff scoffed and scaled the cliff whilst Oscar, Ebony and Emmanuel graciously took the help.

Ebony swung her leg over the side of the cliff, muscles aching, and could finally pause and breathe without the fear of SIDs.

"Could have been a lot worse," Oscar commented, pointing into the distance, "look." From the vantage point they had, they could see a vast expanse of the world. Pockets of fire were dotted across the planet; a favourite way to kill the inmates Ebony assumed. But there were other ways. The woods were moving in the distance as SIDs marched through them and even further back, storm clouds were smashing the ground with lightning at a deadly pace. But over Ebony, the sun was shining, the breeze was tranquil and for a small moment, it was peaceful. Belphegor grunted as the last to climb the cliff, and when he was securely up, she lay back and put her hand in something cold and wet. She pulled her hand away. It was ensanguined with fresh, thick blood. She inspected everyone briskly and they seemed fine.

"Who's bleeding?" she asked. Emmanuel arched his brow.

"None of us?" Ebony studied the fresh blood.

"Then whose is this?"

"An animal?" Oscar hazarded a guess.

"Maybe." She felt a familiar sickly feeling rake through her body and settle in her stomach and as though he knew what she was thinking, Belphegor sat himself next to her.

"Adremelech may be hard to tolerate, let alone get along with but you can trust him," Belphegor said. "He won't do anything to your friends."

"Did they even survive?" she asked, acknowledging the fire.

"Cascia is a hardcore survivalist, always has been, and Noah knows to listen to her. They're fine," Emmanuel said confidently. However, his optimistic exterior was hypocritical of his pessimism. He would never doubt Cascia and Noah's strength pitted against Enchanteds but against an Ancient, even without power? He had no faith in what he'd said and even less faith in Adremelech.

Chapter 21

Belphegor dangled a branch over the side of the cliff, and it caught alight in the remains of the lava. He twirled it around in his hands like a fire performer as he strolled absentmindedly, and neatly propped it in the centre of a tepee of branches he had built. Another campfire was built. Days on Nibiru were short despite the three stars above it, and nights long and cold, but at least the ads across the energy field surrounding the planet gave them light to see by. Further up the mountain they had settled for the night.

"Jeff, how come you know so much about this planet?" Ebony asked, sitting with him where the rock was smooth and tolerable against her legs. He dropped his head shamefully, revealing a tattoo on the back of his neck. It spelled 'Wyatt'.

"I worked here many years ago in the body disposal unit." He looked sad.

"Oh," Ebony answered.

"I didn't want the job," he explained. "I was looking for my brother, told my parents I'd bring him home for their peace of mind."

"Wyatt?" Ebony asked. Jeff rubbed the back of his neck and pulled his collar tight. "Did you find him?"

"Mhmm," Jeff hummed. "What was left anyway." He fell silent and raked his fingers up and down his upper arms.

"I'm sorry," she said, linking her arm through his.

"Don't be. He was insane. Like, all the craziness in the galaxy with a cherry on top insane. He deserved to be here." The inconsistency of the way Jeff spoke of his brother, first softly and then with a casual and disregarding tone seemed wrong to Ebony. Jeff didn't believe that Wyatt deserved to be on Nibiru, but it was something his family had forced him to say to the extent that it was now drilled into his mind as a natural response.

"I see… was he an Enchanted?"

"Shapeshifter too, a great one actually. Better than me. But he didn't use it for good. He committed a lot of crimes, which wasn't his fault…" Jeff stopped himself from saying more. "The one that got him thrown in here was stealing nuclear codes from the Altuse presidential planet and selling them to the deep space rebels." Ebony's mouth stood agape.

"That was your brother?" she gasped. "It was always a mystery how the thief got in and out of the safe."

"Shapeshifting into bacteria," Jeff said. "Yeah, like I said, he deserved to be in here." He looked ashamed.

"You have any other siblings?" Ebony asked.

"I'm not at liberty to say."

"You're not… What?"

"Witness protection. People were pissed at Wyatt and we were in the line of fire."

"We?"

Jeff scowled at his slip up. "Me. Legally, I have no home planet, no extended family, no surname etc… My real name might not even be Jeff." Jeff couldn't help but grin as Ebony's face broadened in wonderment, and grinned further as Oscar revealed yet more biscuits. "Thank you!" He scoffed five and then crammed another three in, crunching loudly.

"At least someone doesn't get bored of them," Oscar said, as Ebony kindly declined. He dropped the last few into Jeff's lap. "Goodnight," he said.

"Night," Ebony smiled. Darkness blanketed the sky quickly, but they fell asleep quicker; as the adrenaline from the day wore off, tiredness consumed them all. But it wasn't a restful sleep nor an uninterrupted one as nightmares of Atlas berated her brain.

She was woken suddenly when the moon had reached its peak.

"Emmanuel!" Ebony jolted awake, sitting up as Emmanuel's name rung around the mountain from an unknown source.

"You heard it too?" Emmanuel asked. He and Belphegor were sat bolt upright. Oscar and Jeff innocently snored, undisturbed in their slumber.

"Was that…" Ebony trailed off as there was another yell.

"Jeff! Ebony! Help!" It was Noah, his voice cracking as he screamed out across the jagged mountain.

"Noah! No-" Belphegor slammed his hand around Ebony's mouth as she woke the other two up.

"Don't yell," he advised but it was too late.

"Ebony!" Noah cried out hopefully and Jeff and Oscar also stood, reaching for weapons, "Eb—" there was an echo of a blunt object cracking something and it fell silent. Ebony shoved Belphegor away and spun frantically in circles, searching for anything pointing to where he was.

"I think the yells came from higher up the mountain?" she guessed. "We need to go." Her breathing heaved and she felt her head pound. Her cheeks were soaked with glistening tears. Oscar wiped them away.

"Ebony stop." He gripped her shoulders. "He's alive, okay? We heard him, he's alive." He tried to knock some sense into her, but she wasn't the only one panicking.

"We should go," Jeff said hysterically.

"I agree." Emmanuel's hands were shaking as he briskly packed his belongings.

"Emmanuel," Belphegor started but Emmanuel turned to him with a gun aimed squarely at his chest.

"He's not okay," he said plainly, "because people don't scream help if they're okay. People don't suddenly stop screaming for help when they need it," he spat, nostrils flaring, "and if he's hurt because of Adremelech, I will kill him and then I will kill you. He's family." Emmanuel made his position perfectly clear as he marched towards Ebony. "I'm coming with you."

"I understand your concern," Belphegor accepted, hands raised in surrender, "but you must be quiet." He untrustingly eyeballed the mountain and to the loose rocks which were beginning to slide. It was only pebbles at first, but he watched in concern as some larger rocks began to move. Ebony's vision of the rockfall grazed her memories for but a second as she shared in his concern.

"We can't go now. We won't be able to see where we're climbing," Oscar argued, to which Ebony turned on him, ignoring the falling rocks.

"Stay here then Oscar." she raised her voice, and he narrowed his eyes at her.

"We don't have time for this bullshit bickering. We're all going, we can't split up now," Emmanuel decided.

"Fine," said Ebony.

"Fine," said Oscar.

"Fine," said Belphegor.

…

"Jeff?" Ebony asked.

He didn't respond.

In the darkness, he appeared normal, just oddly quiet for such a character, but as he stumbled closer to the fire and his figure was illuminated, they could see he was anything but okay. Thick blood was running down the side of his face and sticking out from the side of his head was a huge rock.

He gargled blood and fell.

"Jeff!" Emmanuel screamed and ran over to him. "Jeff, Jeff can you hear me?" He fell to his knees, hugging Jeff's head. Blood soaked their clothes as Emmanuel twisted his face gently to the side. The rock had embedded itself in his skull, smashing it to pieces and Emmanuel's hands were scratched with shards of bone as he hurried to help him.

"We need medicine now," he demanded, choking on tears as he panicked.

Oscar froze up.

"We used the last one on Belphegor," he said accusingly. Ebony tried to move but she was pegged to the spot, unable to utter the word.

"There's got to be something we can do." Emmanuel refused to believe it as Jeff stared into his eyes, limply grabbing his shirt. "I've got you," he promised. "Stay with me Jeff, stay with me. You're not dying here."

"My… brother." Jeff was staring blankly as his muffled whisper swept up to Ebony's ears.

"His only chance is up. I can heal him the second we're out of here," Belphegor promised. He rushed over to Jeff, but Emmanuel barred his way.

"He'd be okay if you hadn't taken the last medicine," Emmanuel croaked, body a convulsing fusion of shock and upset, as tears soaked his skin.

"Let him go, I'll carry him up."

"You won't touch him!" Emmanuel lunged for Belphegor, punching at his chest and wailing. His fingers bruised on impact as Belphegor took the beating.

"Emmanuel, stop!" Ebony cried. "Please stop." She vaulted the smouldering campfire and rushed Emmanuel from behind, cast her arms around him and locked her hands together. He struggled as she pinned his arms by his side.

"Ebony let go," Emmanuel begged. Belphegor seized the opportunity and quickly wrapped Jeff's head in a blanket to cushion the rock, before carrying him over his shoulders.

"Quickly." Belphegor nodded to Ebony who released Emmanuel from her grip. He spun round and Ebony flinched, thinking he would lash out, but his arms snaked around her neck and he hugged her tightly, knees buckled until she was the only thing holding him up.

"He's going to die," Emmanuel sobbed, his body slack. "I thought we were going to be okay but he's going to die." Ebony was in shock as Emmanuel wept on her arm.

"No. He won't." She forced him to look her square in the eyes. "We will save him."

"Come on!" Oscar hurried them along, throwing each of them a backpack as they started running after Belphegor.

"Belphegor, do you remember where you're going?" Ebony worried as she hurled herself recklessly over unstable rocks in pursuit.

"I never forgot," Belphegor said. "Hurry." He continued up the steeper and more winding paths with the others following behind, until they got to a cave opening. It was lit with miniature floodlights buried in the walls, beckoning them inside to a huge cavern.

Mountains of treasures climbed the sides of the cave. Crates of riches carelessly littered the floor, enough to tempt even the most jaded millionaires. Armour stood proudly, if a little covered in dust and cobwebs, in cases along the walls. Belphegor rushed in confidently, the others followed bravely, although intimidated by the noises that lurched from deeper within the cave. They ran for a short time, which felt like a painstaking year, until they arrived inside a huge chamber, more splendorous than anything they'd seen.

A rounded, crystal encrusted geode illuminated by a shaft of an advert light was positioned in the middle of a bed of bones. Next to it, on a gold engraved lectern of stone, was a button, one which teleported the survivors off the planet and to the next prison cell. It didn't sound like much of a way out but for Enchanteds, they could teleport out of the prison immediately. Yet it didn't exactly fill them with hope. Belphegor gently lay Jeff down and started forward but he stopped, eyes darting about the room.

"Something's wrong." He pulled out his knife. From the unlit corner of the room there was movement and shadows flickered across the wall.

Ebony agreed. "Isn't there meant to be something here? A final trial? It shouldn't be this easy."

"Not that," Belphegor said, hand waving them to stay put as he placed a foot in the field of bones. "Where's the sword?"

"Here." A voice echoed from the corner of the room and into the beam of light waltzed Adremelech. The sword of Sonneillon, a blade of meteorite and diamond, hilt of solid gold, was engraved with jewels and strange markings. He held it in his hand.

"Brother," Belphegor exclaimed, rushing forward. "You succeeded," he hailed. But Adremelech pointed the sword threateningly and his tone changed. "Adremelech? What's going on?"

"Where's Noah and Cascia? What have you done with them?" Emmanuel's finger was tapping the gun trigger. From behind Adremelech there was more movement. Cascia appeared and with her, dragged a gagged and bound Noah. She had her knife to his throat, shoving him around guiltily. He had tear streaks ploughing through the dirt on his face.

Emmanuel and Ebony advanced as muffled shouts bounced off the gag and back into his mouth.

"Nah ah, back up." Adremelech brandished the sword. He shoved Noah to the floor and Noah yelped in pain, grimacing as Cascia yanked his head back by his hair. He was in an awful state, bleeding to the extent where it couldn't be pinpointed as to where the blood was coming from. He had wounds across his chest and down the arm he was using to cradle a broken hand, he had the same bubbling sores Ebony had. Through two black eyes he noticed it too, smiling weakly at Ebony as he wiggled his head, so the gag fell loose.

"Snap," he mumbled. Adremelech, without even looking, whipped out his fist and punched him across the face.

"Shut it," he snarled, as Noah spat blood across the floor. "Cascia, you said the rock fall would stall them, yet here they are." Cascia's dirty cheeks visibly flushed red.

"That was you?" Emmanuel said in disbelief.

"It was only to slow you down. I never meant to hurt any of you," Cascia protested.

"Yeah well, tell that to Jeff." Emmanuel stood to the side, revealing Jeff's deteriorating state. Oscar touched his neck, as pale as his skull, searching for a pulse. He gulped.

"He's not gonna make it."

Noah's heart sunk as he wriggled against Cascia's grasp. Cascia didn't give the courtesy of looking at him.

"You can't even look at him. Traitor!" Emmanuel screamed. "That's why you claimed you couldn't see the future. It's because you were too ashamed to admit how much of a traitorous bitch you are!" He charged forward but Belphegor held him back by the scruff of his collar, letting his limps flail feebly.

"Don't," he warned. "He won't hesitate to hurt you."

"She's not a traitor. She's been smart. Picked the winning side," Adremelech praised.

"How could you brother?" Belphegor asked. "Siding with Atlas? I thought we were of the same mind."

"We have never been of the same mind," Adremelech spat. "You're weak and insignificant. Those aren't traits of which I associate myself." Belphegor took a slow step forward towards Adremelech and they faced off each other in the spotlight.

"So that's how we escaped Atlas. You didn't fight him, you bargained with him, then dressed yourself up in a sorry state," Belphegor said. Adremelech's lack of reply was tantamount to an admission of guilt, and he let silence befall to let the realisation settle.

"Well done," he ridiculed. "Atlas knew the first thing you'd want to do was help his unfaithful daughter kill him. All I had to do was follow your plan and it led me straight to the sword." He waved it around. "So, for that I owe you a debt of gratitude. But we really must be going."

"Cascia's not going with you," Oscar said defiantly, "and neither's the sword."

"Aw, the little ape's trying to get involved," Adremelech chortled. "She's coming of her own free will," he said. "Needed no convincing."

"That's not true," Emmanuel argued.

"It is," Cascia said to his surprise. "Atlas is going to win. It's the clearest vision I've ever had. I'm supporting the winning side and you should too," she said cynically. "It's the right thing to do." Ebony practically keeled over with fake laughter, before looking at her with a straight face and a gun pointing at her head.

"The right thing. The right thing? I'd rather have the honour of death than betray my friends," she spat but Adremelech whipped out a gun with his other hand and aimed it at Oscar. Ebony lowered the gun instantly.

"All right, let's wrap it up. Roamers will be here soon and they're not happy with you lot," Adremelech said. Belphegor cocked his head.

"What did you do?"

"Come on, brother?" Adremelech was exasperated. "Did you never wonder why Roamers didn't come after you? This is the most heavily guarded planet in the outlands and we didn't exactly crash through quietly. But I sorted them out," Adremelech grinned. "About a hundred followed us down in a silencer ship and were unfortunate enough to find me before you. I told the one I left alive that I slaughtered them for you, Belphegor, and that they'll find you in the mountain. I'm sure they're flying from across the galaxy as we speak."

"You really are despicable," Ebony insulted but he put his hands to his cheek, grinning.

"Thank you." He took it as a compliment. "Cascia, we're leaving." He walked to the button with his gun still trained on Belphegor. "Kill the boy."

Ebony instantly re-aimed the gun from the floor to Adremelech. She fired it, hitting him square in the chest and he yelled out as he fell backwards. Ebony sprinted for Noah, Emmanuel to the button and Belphegor to Adremelech but within a matter of seconds, Adremelech was back up. He threw an empty medicine bottle to the side and with a grand swing of his sword, sliced the air in front of Belphegor's throat. Belphegor stood back. A single hair from his trimmed beard floated through the air where it caught on the sword and turned to dust. Emmanuel dropped the button as Adremelech fired a gun inches from his hand and he swiped the button from the stone slab for himself.

"Cascia don't do this," Ebony begged as Cascia wielded her knife. Ebony didn't have confidence that she could shoot without taking out Noah too.

Adremelech advanced on Ebony. She fired again but the weapon was empty. He grabbed her collar and Belphegor grabbed his arm, but Adremelech raised the sword and held it inches from Belphegor's eye. He simpered at the situation that entertained him greatly.

"You're so lucky Atlas wants to have some fun before he has the pleasure of killing you himself." Adremelech threw Ebony roughly across the room and she went skidding across the stone, shredding the skin on her arm. "Belphegor, if you would be so kind." Adremelech eyed Belphegor's tourniquet of a grip and snarled like an untamed beast as he let go. The grip was sure to leave finger marks, but Adremelech wore them proudly.

"Adremelech, you said you'd let Noah go." It was Cascia's turn to speak. He scratched at his stubble whilst pretending to give a damn, before roughly grabbing Noah by the neck. He squirmed and gagged as Adremelech began to squeeze, animosity raging behind his dilated pupils. Noah's eyes bulged, blood trickled from the side of his mouth and the veins in his neck popped.

"Stop it!" Emmanuel screamed. Cascia had to intervene, but she wasn't.

"Leave him alone!" Oscar fought against Belphegor who held him back firmly. He knew the dangers of the sword in the hands of someone like Adremelech.

Cascia shouted, and then shook her head in disbelief that she'd decided to shout at Adremelech. She quieted slightly. "Stop hurting him, please," she panicked.

"I don't want him to suffer," Adremelech said. "You can stop his suffering." He glanced to her knife. "End it quickly."

"Stop it," Emmanuel begged. "Leave him alone!"

"I'm getting impatient," Adremelech forewarned.

"Cascia…" Noah's eyed rolled back in his head. A tear rolled down

Cascia's cheek.

She raised the knife.

Like Noah had never been anything to her, Cascia plunged it into his chest.

Ebony screamed as Adremelech discarded Noah's body on the floor. Emmanuel's feet gave way from beneath him as his world was destroyed. One best friend was dead, the other on the brink and the third betrayed him like their friendship was nothing.

"See you soon," Adremelech promised and with a whack of the button, him and Cascia were gone.

"Noah." Ebony half ran, half crawled to his body. "Don't be dead, you can't be dead," she cried out. She grabbed his wrist and after a second, yelled out, "he's alive, he's still alive!"

"We're gonna fix you," Emmanuel said, tears washing his face of the last blood stains, as yet again he knelt beside the body of a best friend, nursing the wound. Belphegor carried Jeff over and lay him next to Noah.

"What are we going to do?" Ebony asked Belphegor who paced around like a lost and injured puppy, burdened by the betrayal of his brother. He turned away, unable to answer the question and watched as Oscar went through Cascia and Adremelech's bag.

"Noah, please wake up." Emmanuel put his head on Noah's chest, cradling his body.

"They have medicine," Oscar called victoriously. He rooted through the bags, but his face fell. "Only one left." He held it up. Ebony beamed.

"So, they get half each," she said. She snatched it from him and began to unscrew it, but Oscar pulled the bottle away and flipped it over. A half year abroad during school learning about the medical properties of plants taught him to always read the label.

"This bottle contains the exact dosage to cure one person," he read. "The entire bottle must be taken for any effects to take hold." His body sagged. "We have to choose." The room fell silent.

"We'll go back down the mountain and find another," Ebony said, clutching the bottle.

"Look at them, Ebony. They'd be dead by the time we got back," Belphegor said.

"There's got to be something. We get them out of here and cure them

258

when we're back in the air?" Emmanuel begged.

"And how do we get out? The teleport's been used, the Hyperion is permanently grounded and there are hundreds of Roamers coming for us," Belphegor reasoned. "If we can save one of them, we need to do it now."

"You're asking me to choose between two best friends?" Emmanuel asked. His head lolled from side to side as he tried to comprehend it. "I can't choose." He stood slowly and backed away.

"Emmanuel," Ebony tried but he held up a hand to silence her.

"I can't sit here and watch you debate with their lives. I'll be outside."

He turned away.

Ebony watched as his figure disappeared.

"Ebony?" Oscar turned to her.

"I can't," she said, taken aback. "I can't do it."

"Why not?" he asked. She sniffed and gently placed her hand on the side of his face, wiping away the dirt.

"I've ruined one too many lives."

"But it's you. It's always you. You make the decisions, you choose what we do," Oscar said. Dropping the medicine in his hands, Ebony refused to make eye contact.

"I made the decision to camp on the mountain where the rocks were unstable. I made the decision to run up the mountain," she said. "Cascia would have had no reason to stab Noah if we hadn't interrupted them."

The little faith Ebony reserved for herself had drained and to the sound of Oscar's cry of protest, she followed Emmanuel out of the cave. She found Emmanuel sitting at the entrance, looking out at the sunrise, and sat quietly next to him. He held out his hand and she gripped it tightly.

"Why did we ever trust Adremelech?" she whispered.

"I don't know," Emmanuel said cluelessly. "It was stupid to think this could ever end with all of us surviving." The two of them fell silent. It felt so alien to Ebony, somewhere in the cave behind her a friend was dying but she didn't rush to help. Instead, for the first time in a long time, she let someone else deal with it. Belphegor was dealing with it. The brother of two murderers. A murderer himself. She wanted to run back into that cave, to slaughter Belphegor where he stood. But Adremelech's betrayal had collapsed his hard shell. The emotions she saw within him, the compassion and the heartbreak and the sympathy told her that he was different to them. And if he wasn't; if her misplaced trust in him ended up hurting someone else, then she told herself that she would be the first to end his life.

Time passed like paint dried. Ebony checked the time every hour yet only a minute had passed. She fidgeted impatiently, Emmanuel sitting beside her like a statue. He appeared patient but the cracks in his stillness became apparent as time continued. She couldn't imagine his suffering. Two friends lost, nearly three.

"It's done," Oscar whispered. He emerged at the cave entrance, blond hair stained red. Ebony's heart pined, knowing one of her friends had been sacrificed. "We did what we had to." He walked past her, not in the mood for talking. Emmanuel and Ebony turned, stony faced and ruminative, and braced themselves for who would walk out the cave behind him.

"Hey." Ebony knew the voice before he'd appeared.

Noah limped out.

"Noah!" Emmanuel was hard to read, his face was contorted in joy and anguish. Noah rushed over to him, and they embraced in a bone crushing hug over the loss of someone they both considered to be a brother. Noah was visibly shaking, and Emmanuel could barely hold himself together as his face reddened from the emotion.

"Noah?" Ebony stuttered. He smiled at Emmanuel and patted his cheek, before turning to Ebony. She leapt into an embrace. He wrapped his arms around her, burying his bloodied and muddy face into her neck as she squeezed him tightly. She pulled her face away.

"I thought you were gone." Her eyes glazed over with tears again, but she smiled them away.

"So did I," he said. His stab wound had healed although his shirt was so torn from the knife it hung uselessly around his neck and he was still clearly injured by the way he held himself. The bruising around his eyes continued despite the medicine.

"I'm glad you're here," she said. The corner of his lips strained to curve upwards as he tried to smile. Emmanuel took a step forward and Ebony thought it best to let the two of them console each other. She treaded slowly to Oscar who was standing on the cliff edge, surveying the planet.

"Not going to jump, are you?" Ebony half joked and Oscar looked at her.

"Who would take care of you if I did," he pondered.

Ebony smiled sincerely. "Thank you for making the decision," she said. "… Why did you choose the way you did?"

"The confrontation with Adremelech took too long. Jeff was dead before I could give him the medicine," Oscar said. "I had no choice."

"And if he was alive, who would you have chosen?" Ebony asked.

"I don't know," Oscar said sharply. His distress at being made to choose between two people's lives was obvious as his nostrils flared aggressively, and he refused to catch Ebony's eye. "Just be happy Noah's with us."

"I am. Of course, I am." Ebony didn't want to aggravate him further. "Where's Belphegor?"

"He's burying the body."

Chapter 22

Belphegor emerged from the cave. His sleeves were rolled back, hands dirty where he'd dug the grave with nothing but his fingers to haul the dirt. He picked at the remnants under his nails. Ebony and Emmanuel stood on his arrival and Ebony could feel the anger and hatred radiating from Emmanuel. But Emmanuel, lips pursed in a tight line, held his tongue.

"He's been buried," Belphegor said. Emmanuel's jaw tightened. Oscar noticed and he addressed the company as a whole, changing the conversation from its bleak beginnings.

"Noah and I think, maybe, we've found a way off Nibiru," he called, piquing their interest.

"We have a lot of Roamers coming for us," Noah said. "When they come to arrest us, they'll have to deactivate the shields around the planet to fly us out of here. So, when they do, I'll teleport us from the cells to the flight deck."

"We'll take control and make our escape," Oscar said.

"When is anything ever that simple?" Emmanuel asked.

"We just have to hope for the best," Belphegor answered. Emmanuel turned on his heels and walked away from the group before he was tempted to swing a punch at Belphegor and send him over the side of the mountain.

"Don't mind him."

"He hates me."

"He hates Adremelech, but Adremelech isn't here to take the brunt of his anger," Ebony said. "He'll cool off." Belphegor sighed unsurely. He didn't think Emmanuel would ever forgive him.

They sat impatiently and waited for the Roamer ships to arrive. It was a sombre silence concocted of overwhelming guilt, frustration, and desolation. Atlas might as well have already won. Ebony pulled at the singed grass on the side of the mountain. She'd had a vision of Jeff's death and maybe she could have prevented it. Now, the only thing they had attained from Nibiru was a deceased friend.

Noah was lying next to her, drumming his fingers on his chest as he breathed purposefully. He wasn't much his cheerful self, and with a gaping yawn sounded like he was about to fall asleep. Then another yawn followed as he cherished every breath that left his lungs.

Oscar had his legs dangled over the side of the mountain and Belphegor was sitting close by, staring unblinkingly at the woods below. Secluded on a sharp ledge above the cave entrance sat Emmanuel. Ebony could hear him muttering to himself as he wiped his eyes clean of rheum. The lack of magic which normally energised an Enchanted was exhausting.

"Ebony." Noah had sat up.

"Mhmm?" She glanced his way.

"Those stars look a bit bright for stars." Ebony followed his line of sight through an intrusively obnoxious ad for prosthetic hearts.

"I think you're right," Ebony agreed. She jumped up and held out a hand for Noah who stood beside her. "We've got company." The lights from the ship grazed the woods and travelled up the mountain towards them. No one made any extra effort to be seen as the ships could clearly spot them with their thermal imaging cameras. But the ships didn't try and land, their wheels remaining firmly tucked away, and suddenly they were aiming guns at the mountain.

"Into the cave," Emmanuel warned, and they tucked themselves in the corner of the entrance, buried behind a boulder. Belphegor dared peek out as more ships arrived, powerful headlights focused in a cylindrical beam on the cave entrance.

A baritone voice swamped the sky. "Surrender now or we will shoot to kill. This is your only warning."

Ebony cried out. "I thought they would arrest us?"

"Apparently not people like us," Belphegor said. The ships stopped just short of the forcefield, and he worried briefly they wouldn't deactivate it.

"Come on, turn it off," he willed. From the mothership, a camouflaged beast of costly metal, the voice spoke ruthlessly.

"Fire!" it declared. From the sky, bullets and missiles rained upon them and the adverts shimmered out. Fractured chips of rock decimated the cliff but as Oscar crouched in fear, fingers in ears at the popping, the others inhaled as magic flooded back into their veins. Belphegor bared his teeth as for the first time in too many millennia to count, his magic was at full capacity. Ebony, nervous and excited to see what he could do, shrieked as a bullet ripped into his back.

"Belphegor get back!" Noah cried as he readied a portal. But Belphegor took the bullet like only a butterfly had landed on him and laughed in a slightly haughty manner, eyes wildly bouncing from person to person.

Ebony could see some of Atlas in his eyes.

With a snap of Belphegor's fingers, they were on the deck of the Roamer mothership with such speed that they never even saw the portal that engulfed them. Everyone snuck clandestinely to the turquoise door of the control room, crouching behind it.

"How many people on board?" Noah asked.

"Eighteen," answered Emmanuel, Ebony, and Belphegor simultaneously. They looked at each other.

"Sorry," Ebony said to Emmanuel. "We'll leave the telepathy to you."

"I'll take out the crew," Belphegor offered eagerly. Ebony cocked her head with a harsh stare. "Gently." The door opened with a creak. Nearly the entire crew was in the room, watching intently as the mountain was reshaped into a cratered hole. "Be right back." He closed the door behind him with a wink. Ebony knew invisibility was something Belphegor was capable of, but he didn't opt for subtly.

"Oi!" Through the door there was a muffled yell from one of the Roamers. There was several shouts and thuds. Ebony thought she even heard a cat screech. The Enchanteds and Oscar dropped to the floor as stray bullets from a fearful Roamer fired at the door, which caught the ammunition, forcing bumps into the metal. It went silent for but a second, before the door bent with the force of a body being thrown at it. With an almighty groan, the hinge gave way and the door fell outwards to the floor.

Ebony peered in. Belphegor swept his arm upwards and all eighteen unconscious crew members flew into the ship's escape pod. He slammed the door and kicked it, his strength enough to send the pod flying into space.

"Like I said. Gently." Belphegor was chuffed with his work. His definition of the word was clearly disparate to theirs.

Emmanuel rushed the controls. Flipping a series of buttons, he grabbed the wheel tightly and accelerated at full speed. As they fled the scene, the ships around them slowly rotated, realising their mother ship had been hijacked. They aimed impeccably and fired mercilessly but none of the bullets made target.

Belphegor was stopping them.

He strained as he held his hands outstretched; he was forcing a shield of air around the ship, deflecting the bullets, and aiming them elsewhere. Then, he bellowed as he conjured a portal in the space in front of them. It was bigger than anyone had ever seen, and Noah watched jealously, unable to conjure one so great. As Emmanuel agilely flew the ship through, it closed on the nose of another ship, leaving them free from Nibiru and the angered Roamers.

Oscar had sat below deck, searching mindlessly through the Roamer database to amuse himself. Belphegor had decided they should stay on board for a while, in case Atlas came for them, and Oscar had decided to avoid Emmanuel and Noah, who had been numbly listening to heartbreak ballads on repeat for half an hour, so he was left bored and curious. But his boredom ended when a voice came through the radio system. It was a broken connection at first but after fiddling with the touch screen, he tuned the system precisely and what, or rather who he heard was remarkable.

"Hello? Guys hello? Can you hear me?" Caleb's voice came through the speaker.

"Caleb?"

Caleb's voice was joyous to hear although he sounded agitated. "What happened to you? Last thing I saw was the Hyperion hovering over Nibiru, then I lost all connection. Had to hack and track your bands to find you."

"The ship blew up." Oscar caught him up to speed.

"What?"

"It's a long story," Oscar said. "We found Ebony's uncles, Belphegor and Adremelech, went to retrieve a sword capable of killing Atlas but Adremelech and Cascia betrayed us, stole the weapon and… we lost Jeff," he said, a hint of pain lingering in his wobbling voice. The connection went silent for a moment.

"I'm sorry," Caleb said dolefully. "I was tracking his band too. Life signs went off about twenty minutes ago, but I hoped he'd just misplaced the band." Oscar gulped.

"Twenty minutes ago?" he repeated. His face whitened like a sheet.

"Yeah. Why?"

"No reason." Oscar changed the topic nervously. "Daegel's dead too."

"That's some good news at least, because I've got some bad," Caleb said. "But listen, I also think I've found something to stop Atlas." Oscar punched the air. "But—" Oscar interrupted him.

"--Hold that thought." He rushed upstairs to the flight deck where the others were lounging about, bashing his head on a low hanging pipe in his eagerness.

"Guys." He burst into the room. "Guess who's showed up?" He rushed over to the main console, whacked a few buttons and in the centre of the room a holographic Caleb appeared.

"Is he too an Enchanted?" Belphegor asked, currently unimpressed.

"I'm not," Caleb responded, wide-eyed at the handsome man. "You're Belphegor?"

"Yes."

"Caleb, how are you?" Ebony asked but he brushed off her question.

"Turn on the news."

"Which channel?"

"Any channel; all of them are reporting, live coverage." Noah switched on the pilot's screen.

It was utter carnage.

The news reporter squashed in the corner of the screen spoke frantically as she reiterated what was happening.

"…thousands of ships have been taking off in an attempt to flee the destruction whilst ships from the neighbouring planets and passenger ships passing through Solar System 12 have diverted paths to help. It is currently unclear as to what has caused this disaster but one thing we know for sure; Drognir and Farnir are on an unforeseen, unstoppable collision course."

"Atlas?" Ebony choked.

"Who else?" Caleb said.

They watched on in horror.

Drognir and Farnir grew closer to each other. As they did, the gravitational force of Farnir, which was larger than Drognir began to pull structures and ships towards it. Skyscrapers were ripped from the ground and javelined into the opposing planet and fleeing ships were trapped between the two, slowly dragged into Farnir as the two got closer. An accident, the reporter called it, but it was no accident.

"This can't be happening," Oscar watched in disbelief. "My family! My family's in Chane!"

"They're safe," Caleb said. "I found a teleporter on Alchemacier. Your family is safe. So is mine and so is Esso." Oscar body swelled with relief.

"How do we stop this?" Noah said.

"We can't stop him without the sword," Belphegor answered. He clicked his fingers, and the ship flew through another portal, and they no longer needed the TV screen.

They were amongst the hundreds of other ships who were all watching on, helplessly.

Bang!

With an explosion sending shockwaves across space, the two planets collided.

Rock fragments the size of continents spread in a wave across both of the planets, obliterating the surface until both planets were engulfed. large bodies of water instantly evaporated. Every object on the planet's surfaces simply ceased to exist. Drognir and Farnir were nothing more than two fireballs, with no evidence life ever existed on them.

As the pressure mounted to unquantifiable levels, Drognir, now lodged in the side of Farnir, cracked.

The pressure was released.

The planet fell apart.

Ships fled as chunks of rock spun off uncontrollably into space. The reporter on the news channel wrestled to keep up with the situation as it unfolded.

"…The population of Drognir was roughly twelve billion, Farnir just ahead but it's been estimated so far nearly nineteen billion lives have been lost. Body collectors are arriving on scene to help clear the surrounding skies of people, but this mass clean-up effort seems futile as Drognir and Farnir continues to break into smaller pieces and-" the journalist paused as the cameras began to shake, "-the source of this catastrophe has been located. It's a… a person?" She disappeared from the screen as the cameras zoomed into the nexus of the wreckage.

"He was never this strong," Belphegor muttered. Flying on thick, black smoke, with charred eyes of scarlet red as opposed to his recognisable, soulless black was Atlas. He was wielding the sword proudly. On his right stood Adremelech, who leered rapturously as he helped wreak havoc in his new status following Daegel's death. On his left, looking painfully at the bodies floating by but with no thought to rescue them, was Cascia.

"Why has he done this?" Oscar asked.

"I was raised on Drognir," Ebony said flatly. "Adremelech said it himself, Atlas wants to have fun." Ebony watched as her home was destroyed, piece by piece. "Billions are dead." She sat down heavily in a chair, putting her head in her hands.

"It's not your fault." Belphegor knelt in front of her and gently pulled her hands from her face. "This is purely Atlas' doing."

"He's always one step ahead," Ebony grimaced. "I want him dead!" she cried. "We could jump through a portal. Kill him now and it would be over."

"Wouldn't work," Emmanuel said. "I tried to hear his thoughts, but I can't. I think he's warded himself against us. And we would need something equally, if not more powerful than him, to kill him," he said, "and the only thing as powerful is the sword."

"Which leads me on to my next point," Caleb reminded them, "which is perhaps a slight controversial opinion… This isn't so bad." If looks could kill he'd be on the floor.

"Not so bad?" Ebony scoffed, "Caleb Calwyn Erisroth, you better have a damn good explanation." She looked at the hologram bitterly. But

Caleb looked hopeful; the day could yet be salvaged if he could get his weary friends to listen to him.

"I compared the massive power surge coming from Atlas to other similar activities from the past with the exception of natural collisions, black holes, supernovas, etc… and only one power surge in recorded history has ever come close to being stronger than this," Caleb explained. "On this asteroid, there is a lot of lore concerning Vesper, Orabella and Lorelei, and one particular story explains what happened before their deaths."

"Orabella." Belphegor said her name with fondness and affection. "Tell me she died peacefully." He looked at the hologram and Caleb eased his mind.

"The database suggests the three of them made a pact, because after millennia of living they would rather die than turn bitter towards the universe. So, nearly two thousand years ago, the three of them took cyanide capsules and passed away."

"Impossible," Belphegor contradicted him. "Something as simple as cyanide could never kill an original Enchanted."

"Exactly," Caleb said, "because the magic would prevent death. But they died, which means they no longer had their power at the time of death."

"What are you insinuating?"

"I'm saying, hours before killing themselves, a planet called Tcheeva experienced a major power surge, larger than Atlas'. However, no fault lines moved, no volcanoes erupted. And bear in mind this planet is in deep space, it has unexplainable days and nights and a consistently warm temperature. Now, I did some more digging and discovered that the Papaloawu space rebels of the Cygnus constellation pilgrimage there, as in their local dialect the name Tcheeva means, 'rested power' and I found out, if you trace the blood line far enough back, the original member of the tribe was an Enchanted who apparently knew the three daughters well." Caleb leant back in his chair, visibly impressed with himself.

"So, you think they stored their magic inside the planet?" Belphegor clarified.

"I do." Caleb had done his research well.

"It's possible," Belphegor mused. "Magic can't be destroyed, it just dissipates."

"I think their magic still exists and if Atlas absorbed Sonneillon's when they weren't even related, what's to stop Ebony from doing the same with her cousins and sister?" Ebony gasped. When Vesper, Lorelei and Orabella had been mentioned, they were referred to as the original Enchanteds; people who lived in the past and nothing more. Ebony had only just considered that they were more than related.

She had a sister.

"If you had their power, your magic would level the playing field, if not give us the upper hand," Emmanuel added excitedly.

"It could work," Belphegor encouraged. "They beat Atlas once; it can be done again. And this time, you have the help of an Ancient." Ebony looked to Caleb, and everyone looked to Ebony. The burning remains of her home and neighbouring planet reflected in her hollow, sleep deprived eyes. But she looked at the others with confidence.

"I'm in. How do we get there?"

"Portal," Caleb said simply. "It's not guarded by anything because no one knows what's there." Ebony, without speaking, conjured a portal but not to Tcheeva. She stuck her arm through, and Caleb's hologram disintegrated as he was on the ship with them.

"Hey." She pulled him in for a hug and he groaned as she did, causing her to pull away with an aghast expression. She didn't want to cause more pain to his back.

"It's fine," he joked. "All healed up and ready for duty."

"All right Caleb?" Oscar held out his hand and Caleb rushed over. The others watched in mind boggling confusion as they carried out an intricate handshake, ending with an elaborate high-five. He saluted to everyone else, except Belphegor, who he dropped to one knee in front of, dramatically.

"I am but a humble, trash bag floating in the wind of life compared to you," he prosed melodramatically.

"He's an Ancient, not a God," Ebony said with a second-hand embarrassment driven nudge in the ribs.

"Oh." He stood.

"It's good to meet you, Caleb. Thank you for giving us another way."

Belphegor shook his hand strongly. Caleb beamed, ignoring the grip that almost crushed his hand.

"Caleb, all I need is the location of Tcheeva, and I can get us there," Noah interrupted, and Caleb cringed.

"Love your enthusiasm but hold your horses for a second there. We might want to be smart about this," he suggested. "For a start, I'm all for grabbing the magic and smoking Atlas' ugly ass but we need to protect ourselves. Atlas and Adremelech can both read minds and Cascia can see parts of the future so the last thing we need is for them to know our every move."

"Atlas could already know what we're planning?" Ebony asked.

"I don't think so," Belphegor said. "The warding he's using, I've seen it before. It works well but comes at a price. We can't get close to him but to the same extent, he can't get close to us."

"So, he screwed himself over?"

"That was always Atlas' weak point," Belphegor remembered. "Act first, asks questions later." He shook his head. "We'll have to work fast. He'll come for Ebony the second she absorbs Vesper, Orabella, and Lorelei's magic. That power will be felt by Enchanteds across the galaxy."

"So, we use it to our advantage," Emmanuel said. "If the power will be felt everywhere, we send a message with it? Reach out telepathically to every Enchanted, telling them Atlas is back and we need help."

"There's no harm in trying," Ebony said.

"Right," Caleb agreed, turning to Noah. "You can let those horses go now!" he cried. "Let's get this show on the road."

Chapter 23

Alchemacier was busier than anyone had ever seen. Belphegor had sent out a distress signal to those Enchanteds who were closest to hear it and after some persuasion that he was no longer a black-hearted, stone cold murderer, many came to Alchemacier to help. It had transformed from a land housing a few hundred Enchanteds to a land housing all who lived within several lightyears, including several influential figures, and then some. Seeing them strengthened Ebony's resolve.

"I've never seen these powers," Ebony marvelled as she spotted an Enchanted with the above-average number of limbs. Ebony waved and she waved back with a third hand protruding from her ribs.

"It's spectacular, isn't it?" Belphegor said. They wandered slowly throughout Alchemacier town, admiring the work of their kin as they fought in friendly combat, honing their skills for the vicious fight against Atlas. Enchanteds whose abilities were flight, soared through the air with angelic, feathery wings sprouting from their back. One of them paused whilst airborne and twirled to face Ebony's direction. He flapped his heavy wings, creating a blast of air which nearly knocked Ebony off her feet, even though it wasn't aimed at her.

"Wow." She made a mental note to try and grow wings when she had the chance. The Enchanted who had been knocked down by the winged Enchanted was carrying whips of electricity, lashing them at the feet of anyone who ran past as she parkoured across the tiled rooftops. But she was pulled to Ebony and Belphegor's level by tree roots that held her to the floor. Ebony was nearly startled by an Enchanted who proceeded to climb stealthily from a nearby bush. Her arms were covered by twisted branches, her hair a fern green.

"Camouflage?" she asked.

"Botanokenesis," Belphegor corrected quietly. "The girl by your feet is camouflaged." Ebony took a quick step back as the ground moulded from cobblestone to wood and the Enchanted sprinted off to an oak tree, fading into it with ease as her skin changed colour.

Belphegor and Ebony found Oscar beneath one of the mushroom houses, with an Enchanted who's powers didn't physically manifest, but he was skilled in unarmed combat to the extent where he could dodge a bullet with ease. Ebony listened in to their conversation as they wandered by.

"So out of all two hundred and six bones in the human body, the easiest one to break is the clavicle whilst the most painful one is the fibula. To break them you…" As he kept talking, Belphegor and Ebony exchanged a disgruntled look. They didn't want Oscar fighting and had tried to press upon him the importance of his role of working on communications between everyone from a safe distance. Ebony tilted her head and sent Belphegor to deal with the situation. His shadow loomed over the two of them and the fearful Enchanted cowered slightly in his muscled appearance.

"What are you doing?" Belphegor asked.

"My sincerest apologies sir." The Enchanted cringed at Belphegor's sternly set jaw.

"If we're fighting against child zombies which Atlas will use to turn your paternal instincts against you, there's upwards of another sixty bones to consider." Ebony smacked her forehead. It wasn't what she meant.

"Sorted," Belphegor said proudly. Ebony gave him a brief thumbs up and they kept walking. They passed Esso in the background, who's new home was Alchemacier. Physical sparks flew from him as his science-wired brain tried to comprehend an Enchanted who drove past him on the track to the forest atop a stegosaurus. Mentally unhinged, Esso went and did what Esso did best. Cook.

Oscar caught up with them a short while after. "I just got off the phone with Stella's father," he announced.

"Who?" Belphegor asked.

"A friend of ours killed by Atlas."

"I'm sorry."

"Why?" Ebony asked Oscar.

"Because it's sad to lose a friend," Belphegor said.

Ebony sighed. "No, not you Belphegor."

"Because Simon is the five stars rank general of the Milky Way

Alpha quadrant army. It took a lot of explaining but he saw the Atlas on the news and on Chane and he wants revenge for the death of, well, everyone."

"So, he's going to Tcheeva?" Ebony asked.

"Yes."

"With whom?"

"Everyone."

"Everyone?" Ebony repeated.

"Everyone," Oscar said. "Ebony, add on the deaths on the Transtar ships to the deaths on Drognir and Farnir and it's the biggest massacre since Space War I and I've given an army chief the location of where the person who caused it will be. He's informed the Milky Way quadrant masters and all legions are involved, as well as fleets from Andromeda. I also told him Atlas' second in command was Daegel, so he said he'd call the Roamers in, with an added personal apology to Caleb for their ignoring him." He paused and drummed his fingertips against his chin, raising an eyebrow. "Do we need anyone else?"

"Oscar it's more than enough. It's brilliant. Thank you," Ebony said sincerely.

"Well, you guys have got your magic, I'll stick with good old-fashioned technology." He waved the phone in the air. "He said he'll be at Tcheeva whenever we call." Oscar didn't look nearly as happy as he should have been, but they were interrupted before Ebony could enquire.

"I've requested the help of a few more people." Unbeknownst to them, Caleb had walked into the conversation through the acasia trees and was listening eagerly.

"Caleb, who else could we possibly need?"

"Well…" Caleb trailed off. "I put in a call. You might want to come back to the castle."

Ebony, Oscar, and Belphegor rushed over rope bridges and out of the jungle. They passed a group of Enchanteds who were talking in whispers too low to hear and gawking at Caleb as he led them swiftly by. Then another group of Enchanteds passed by where the same thing occurred, and another. And another.

"What has he done?" Oscar thought. When they left the shady shrubbery adorning the edge of the jungle, they were prevented from walking the path to the castle by an army of robots and a man, sitting atop a throne, levitating above them.

"Who is that?" Belphegor asked.

"The King of Foro," Caleb said. "I call him Xavier. Bit tyrannical but a nice enough guy." Upon recognising Caleb in the crowd, the king's face went from a stern frown to a delighted grin and the throne flew to the ground.

"Bakewell boy," he cried with a look of wonder. Caleb smiled shyly.

"Hi," he said. The king let out a bellowing laugh and to the relief of the party, his guards dropped their weapons with a wave of the king's hand. Ebony and Oscar both turned to each other in surprise.

"Good to see you lad. I didn't recognise you under your eyepatch." Xavier ignored the others and brought Caleb into a bone-crushing hug and Caleb reciprocated, though his arms barely went round the king's sides.

"Bakewell boy?" Belphegor raised an eyebrow.

"It's a long story," Ebony said.

"We don't know most of it," Oscar added.

"For what reason did you call me here?" Xavier asked, leaning back on his throne, his disproportionate body leaving his stubby hairy legs to dangle above the platform. Caleb scratched the back of his neck.

"King Xavier. I've called to collect my debt. We are in need of your assistance, with regards to your red guard." Xavier's face dropped. The robots around stood to attention when their name was mentioned.

"My guard is elite, I'm afraid I don't send them on missions of more minor importance."

"Forgive me but you miss my point," Caleb said. "We need them to fight a man called Atlas. He's the man who destroyed the Transtar ships, Chane and then Drognir and Farnir." Xavier's back straightened. "You must have seen the destruction? We need your help."

Xavier's attitude changed instantaneously. "Anything you need to end him I will supply to the best of my ability."

"We need your guard. Robots would put us at an advantage to Atlas," Caleb said. "He underestimates technology." The king was silent and for a minute he worried the answer would be no.

"If that's what you need, then they are yours for this conflict." He tapped the arm of his throne, where from his perspective a touch screen appeared. With the touch of several buttons, he looked at Caleb. "Say a word."

"Jellybean." Caleb didn't know if he was hungry or not as he blurted out the first word that came to mind. A couple more taps of the screen and Xavier lent back in his seat. It wavered under his weight and the stabilisers beneath the chair flickered.

"They answer to you now. To send them into battle, say the name of the target and the specific word. They will fight until there is nothing left of them to fight with."

"Woah." Caleb grinned from ear to ear and Oscar pinched the bridge of his nose.

"Caleb in charge of a robot army?" he said. "We're doomed."

"Hey," Ebony nudged his arm. "He's given us another major advantage."

"Exactly," Caleb said. "Thank you, your majesty, I appreciate it." The king bowed his head into his perpetual third chin.

"They will return to me when the battle is over. I wish you good luck," he said and with merely two robots leaving with him, he climbed back aboard his ship and left the asteroid, a mural of his likeness staring at them from the underbelly as it flew away.

"Salute!" Caleb yelled, and every robot saluted him. Giddy with excitement, Caleb rubbed his hands together gleefully, a look of mischief spreading across his face.

"What is Bakewell?" Belphegor was still confused. "How does it warrant giving you an army?"

"What is Bakewell? What is Bakewell? My man, you haven't lived if you haven't had Bakewell." Caleb beckoned for Belphegor to follow him and assuming they were headed straight for the castle kitchen, Ebony chuckled.

"It's good to see you smile," Oscar said.

"I'm trying to," she said confidently. "Where's yours?" Oscar shifted his weight back and forth uncomfortably. He gulped and Ebony found him avoiding eye contact. A strained look. An awkward shuffle. He was hiding something. "Oscar? What's wrong?"

"I… I can't…" He didn't want to tell her but the guilt on his mind was weighing him down.

"Oscar, you know you can tell me anything," Ebony encouraged, as she sat them on a hovering bench that flew itself over, sensing Ebony begin to sit. Oscar gulped. Were his hands always so sweaty? His limbs went taut as he tried to contain his anxiety.

He spoke slowly. "I think Jeff was still alive when we left Nibiru." Ebony's exuberance had been valuable and short lived. The spark of hope left her eyes as her face fell.

"Why?"

"Caleb hacked our bands to find us." Oscar was trembling.

"The band transmitters didn't work on Nibiru." Ebony said sharply. Her heartrate was rising.

"They did when the forcefield was taken down."

Ebony took a moment. Her mouth went dry. "He was alive?"

"Caleb said he saw Jeff's heart rate stop at least ten minutes after we stole the Roamer ship." Oscar bowed his head.

"Didn't you check he was dead?" she cried. Oscar was in a state of panic.

"I did. I could have sworn I did."

"Well, did Belphegor check before he buried him?"

"I don't know!"

Ebony's head was spinning. "I need to find Belphegor." Remembering the Enchanted from not ten minutes prior, Ebony's hands balled into fists as she concentrated, and wings sprouted from her back. They weren't majestic falcon wings, merely those of a new-born bird which is all she could conjure.

Oscar's cries of protest fell on deaf ears as she left him to run back to the castle. She arrived swiftly, if not with a turbulent landing. Blasting into the kitchen, she found Caleb eating through a Bakewell tart. Belphegor wasn't there.

"Apparently Belize made this?" Caleb looked up as she walked in. "I'm sorry, you can do all the magic you want but nothing is going to impress me more than this tart. Girls are great at this, I could neve —" In a fury, Ebony marched over to him, slamming her hands on the table like an interrogation. "Want some?" he offered. Ebony slapped it from his hand.

"Is it true? Jeff died after you started tracking our bands?"

"I—" Caleb stuttered like he'd forgotten his dentures.

"Answer the question!" she screamed.

"Bloody hell, yes!" Caleb held his hands up.

"Where's Belphegor?"

"Upstairs. In his room." Ebony's face went red. She screamed telepathically for the whole island to hear.

Belphegor! The building nearly shuddered.

Ebony, what's going on? Emmanuel thought from across the asteroid. She ignored him and made a new portal. Jumping through, she left a confused Caleb with an out of breath Oscar, who had arrived in time to see her leave.

Belphegor was sitting on his bed, quietly reading, an empty plate with scattered crumbs of Bakewell tart beside him when Ebony raged in.

"You called?" he said calmly.

"Did you check that Jeff was one hundred percent dead before you buried him."

Belphegor closed the cork book and stood. "Of course, I did."

"Because he wasn't." Ebony broke the news to him. "You buried him alive." Belphegor hadn't shown much emotion before this point. His grey eyes grew turbulent at the possibility he could have left Jeff to die. He gulped.

"He didn't have a pulse," Belphegor assured her.

"He did have a pulse. And you killed him."

"He was alive?" Emmanuel had arrived to see what the commotion was, followed closely by Noah. He careened against the doorframe.

"He was alive," Ebony choked. She was furious but in keeping a level-head, knew she couldn't blame Belphegor entirely. That was until she turned to march away. There was a small, white bottle, glaringly out of place on Belphegor's oak table. He saw her focusing on it and froze.

She picked it up.

She flipped it over in her hands.

She shook it to make sure it was full.

"This is a medicine bottle. From Nibiru," she said. Belphegor's mouth hung open at the realisation of the fatal mistake he had made. "Belphegor, where did you get this?" Belphegor didn't reply. "Where did you get this!"

"You killed him on purpose," Emmanuel muttered, stepping forward and speaking on Belphegor's behalf. "You killed him on purpose, didn't you? You're working with Atlas, aren't you? Trying to pick us off from the inside!" he roared.

"Never." Belphegor vehemently denied the accusation. "I swear to you I didn't know Jeff was alive," he said. "I found it in his pocket before I buried him."

"And you didn't think to give it to him?" Emmanuel shouted.

"I thought he was dead!"

"You should have tried it anyway!" Ebony's eyes went from brown to black. Rage built inside her like a bomb ready to explode. And it did. Belphegor shrunk away, cowering in the corner as Ebony released a wrath of pent-up energy, blasting it directly at Belphegor. When she stopped, he staggered and fell to his knees. He clasped his hands together and grovelled as the mint green curtains settled.

"Ebony, please. I didn't mean to let him die," he whispered. Ebony couldn't bring herself to look at him.

"Leave," she said.

"Ebony, I—"

"--Get the hell off this asteroid and never come back!" she yelled with such punch that Belphegor was forced back on his heels. "Forget ever finding a family amongst us." Grabbing Emmanuel whose eyes were red from tears, she left the room, marching down the corridor. Caleb and Oscar watched as Belphegor stood. He stared at them, hoping they'd back him up but Oscar and Caleb both turned away. Noah, who owed Belphegor his life, hovered for a second longer.

"You should go." He was soft spoken but firm.

Belphegor stared at the medicine bottle. Something that saved lives had certainly just ruined his. He tried to hear Ebony's thoughts, discover if she meant what she said. But she'd blocked him from her mind. Belphegor felt a familiar sense of loneliness and loathing towards himself. He couldn't escape his monstrous reputation, no matter how hard he tried to rectify his wrongdoings.

With a final glance at the medicine bottle, he summoned a portal and left.

"Why did we ever trust him?" Ebony sobbed, falling into a chair. She had already built new walls in her mind. She told herself she was going to trust no one ever again. It saved her the pain of betrayal.

"It seemed like an acceptable idea at the time." Emmanuel reached for a whiskey bottle in the tower where they sat and took a mighty swig. They were leant against a vintage style 360-degree bar, commissioned over a year ago by Jeff. Emmanuel liked to think that he was with them in spirit, and drunk double in his name.

"Jeff was alive. Probably still aware of his surroundings," Ebony muttered. "He must have been so afraid."

"And now we have three Ancients to fight," Emmanuel said, "and Atlas knows our exact numbers because if Belphegor doesn't tell him, Cascia will. What's the point in fighting a battle we're going to lose? May as well count our losses and wait for death." The whiskey wasn't helping Emmanuel's depressed outlook.

"If we don't fight for the universe, who will?"

"Someone else," Emmanuel said firmly, raising the glass to his lips. "Don't know who. Don't care who."

Ebony's forehead creased. "Do you think Belphegor is helping Atlas?" She wondered whether he was already on his way to Atlas to divulge their plan to him. Emmanuel waved the bottle in the air, letting the alcohol fuel his answer. He didn't drink often and slurred his words as a result of the heavy intake.

"I don't think he's helping anyone but himself," Emmanuel said. "He wants redemption. He got his fill helping us get to the sword. Now he's probably buggered off to some small corner of the universe to retire."

"As long as he hasn't been playing us the whole time," Ebony mumbled. Now her temper had subsided she wished she hadn't told him to leave. Yelling was a mistake. She'd known that the second she saw the look on Belphegor's face. If Oscar had missed Jeff's pulse, Belphegor could too.

"Does it ever go away?" Emmanuel asked, the bottle empty and cold in his hands.

"Does what go away?"

"The pain of it all," he said helplessly.

Ebony regretfully shook her head. Her eyes brimmed with tears. "I don't think it will ever go away."

Chapter 24

"To Jeff, without whom we would not have survived Nibiru." Emmanuel raised a glass to his memory.

"And to Belize and Stella, who helped us get this far," Ebony said, and everyone followed suit, clanging the glasses together. They'd decided to have one last drink; the calm before the storm. None of them could guess how the fight was going to end but as discussed, they would stand by Ebony and fight Atlas until the bitter end.

That was the end of the solemn discussion. Ebony wanted what could well be their last night alive to be imbued by happy memories and celebration. Most of the talk was innocent; stories of life growing up on Drognir and other home planets were recounted, how no one could have predicted the life they were living, but on the occasion where Emmanuel brought up the idea that their recent memories were fonder without Belphegor, Ebony shut him down. In the back of her mind, a thought was clawing like an itch that Belphegor truly wasn't bad, and he had just made a mistake.

"Well-" Ebony stood as the last drop of alcohol from the bar was drunk, "-now we're stalling." She conjured a weak forced smile.

"Procrastination is a natural human trait," Caleb drawled, reaching through the portal Noah had opened to a liquor store and pulling out a bottle of wine. He popped the cork and it soared neatly into the bin. But Ebony pulled it from him, and he sniffled like a baby.

"But—"

She cut him off. "--If you're about to tell me wine is one of your five a day, I'm going to throw you out the window."

"A whole bottle is two," he grumbled in dismay. Noah shut the portal to the shop as the last drops of everyone's drinks were finished and the attention was brought to Ebony.

"Whenever you're ready," Oscar said.

She nodded. "I'm ready."

With stoic determination, Ebony walked to the window of the

lounge. World swaying far below her feet, she took a step off the windowsill and with a flourish, shifted into a dragon, the first animal she'd ever turned in to. Bold purple wings cast shadows over Enchanteds, of which many had congregated outside the castle walls, and they stared in wonder as she spoke.

We are fighting for the tomorrow of everyone in this universe. Our resistance is the future. I won't ask that you sacrifice your life to this cause. I just ask that you stand beside your friends and fight to make the universe a better place. Fight for your loved ones. Fight for your friends. Hell, fight for the cat that lives down the end of the street so it can continue to wind up your neighbour's dog. Fight for the rare new blossom sapling so it may grow to watch over the generations of our children and grandchildren and their grandchildren to come. Because all of it will be gone. Life as we know it will be over if Atlas wins. You know the stakes. So, we're going to kill Atlas, once and for all, and never again will humans and Enchanteds alike, have to live in fear that they will never have a tomorrow. Who's with me? A huge chorus of cries echoed amongst the riotous crowd, and she yelled again, *who's with me?* and the asteroid moved with the force of the stomps and cheers and tumultuous applause. Whooping yells of comradery and spirit echoed into the atmosphere.

The ships were filled. Animals roared in the excitement as Enchanteds strapped saddles on the back of dinosaurs, their size and strength, as Jeff had once demonstrated, a perfect zombie battering ram.

"Inspirational," Noah said. He was hovering close by with Emmanuel, Oscar, and Caleb next to him. They were ready to lead the charge.

Let's go kill ourselves an Ancient or two Ebony said. She shifted back to human form, hands remaining a slight scaled purple, and landed by her own ship that Esso had been rescued in from Chane. Herself and Noah instantly clambered to the front. They were several lightyears away from Tcheeva and making a portal of such a distance took a combined effort of not just their power, but of other teleporters who joined them. With the teamwork of seven Enchanteds, a portal grew. Tcheeva was just beyond.

"We'll bring you all through when the battle begins," Ebony said to the Enchanteds standing by. "Keep the portal open." They waved them

282

off with cheers as Ebony's ship glided through and travelled lightyears in seconds.

They were on Tcheeva.

"Looks like a beautiful place," Oscar commented.

"It's the magic of Orabella, Vesper and Lorelei, giving the place life," Noah said. "Let's hope we can still breath after we steal it."

"Not steal," Ebony said. "Permanently borrow."

"You'll be fine." Caleb smacked his hand camply through the air.

"We'll be here, helping from the skies," Oscar promised.

"Good luck." Ebony gave him a thumbs up and one portal later, Ebony, Emmanuel and Noah were off the ship and standing amongst the greenery of Tcheeva. Looking around, the planet gave the impression of being magical whether one knew of the existence of magic or not, filled with luscious greenery, indescribably vivid coloured plants, exotic animals that Ebony couldn't hope to name, and rich, flowing rivers of mulberry water.

"So, what now?" Emmanuel asked. "Where do we find the magic?"

"Everywhere," Ebony said. "This is so brilliantly magical, the whole planet's a metaphorical box of it."

"So, how do we metaphorically crack open said box and harness the power?"

"Guys?" Oscar's voice echoed around them. Ebony tapped her wristband and he materialised in a hologram.

"Got anything?" she asked and watched as Caleb collided his chair into Oscar's, sending Oscar skidding out of reach of the hologram's coverage.

"I've taken a reading of the geology of the planet." Caleb was cut off as Oscar rolled back into frame.

"Who took the reading?"

"Fine. Oscar took the reading," Caleb corrected, "but *I* found something. The inside of the planet is hollow, and it's being powered on the inside by one tiny ball of energy and by tiny, I mean watermelon sized."

"That's got to be it." Ebony crouched to the ground. Putting her palm to the earth, she started to push but before they could descend into the planet, Oscar and Caleb piped up again.

"Ebony," Oscar stopped her.

"What?"

"Belphegor has entered the atmosphere." Ebony's first action was to look at Emmanuel. He looked back. He looked disgusted at her wide, sympathetic eyes.

"He killed Jeff," Emmanuel said. Ebony's face softened.

"He didn't mean to."

"Murder is murder," he said but Ebony's opinion had completely changed.

"In which case, condemn me and Noah and Oscar too." His face conveyed an expression of surprise.

"Why would I—"

"--Oscar also didn't feel his pulse, I..." Ebony trailed off. She didn't want to tell them that she'd seen his death coming and blatantly ignored it. "...I gave Belphegor the last medicine, and Noah was revived instead. We all had a hand in his death."

"Oh, by all means, make me feel worse about my existence," Noah said. Ebony's eyebrows slanted apologetically.

"Sorry."

"I'm sorry too."

They turned.

Belphegor landed a distance away so as to not come across as a threat. He didn't know how Ebony and Emmanuel would act.

Emmanuel growled.

Ebony didn't act exactly thrilled by his appearance, but she was secretly glad of his arrival.

"Really?" Emmanuel asked. Belphegor buried his foot in the dirt as he found the words.

"I would never intentionally hurt any of you." He locked eyes with Emmanuel. "And despite what you think, I would never side with Atlas." He faced Ebony compassionately. "I know you said you wanted me gone. I understand your anger. I'm not asking you to trust me, I'm asking you to let me help." He dropped on one knee and bowed his head shamefully. "Please forgive me." Ebony and Emmanuel exchanged eye contact again, a battle of thoughts raging from mind to mind. Eventually, Emmanuel acquiesced.

"It was a mistake," he admitted, "and under the circumstances, anyone could have made it." It was all the forgiveness Belphegor was going to get from him, but he took it appreciatively.

"Thank you."

"I'm sorry I told you to leave," Ebony said. "I was wrong." Belphegor bowed humbly, unused to such kindness.

"Thank you, niece," he smiled, and she didn't call out the use of the word.

"Guys, we're here for a reason," Noah reminded them. "Shall we get going before or after Atlas destroys us?" Ebony collected herself and knelt on the ground, mud soaking her knees as it had just done Belphegor's.

"Before," she said. Belphegor raised his hands, creating a ball of ice around them as they sunk through the earth.

"Belphegor, it's a bit cold in here," Noah commented.

"We're about to go to the power source of a planet," he said, "believe me, it'll warm up."

Noah held his tongue, widened his stance and focused on keeping his balance as they shot through the ground. Ebony parted the earth with her hands. The hologram of Caleb and Oscar flickered out as the connection was lost, so Emmanuel put a hand to his head.

Let me know when we're getting close he said into Caleb's mind as they continued to swiftly fly downwards. Caleb spoke up after a brief two minutes and Emmanuel relayed the information to the others.

"Ebony, the core is coming up. Slow down," he warned. She slowed. More cautiously she dug through the earth until the earth was no longer there and they were in a giant cavern. Their fall was gentle as Belphegor guided them to the ground.

Emmanuel stood with a start. He was still paying attention to Oscar and Caleb's voices. Nothing much had been happening, Oscar was vaguely quiet, and Caleb was inner monologing about some fantasy where he was the one who defeated Atlas. But now they'd started yelling.

"What's wrong?" he said aloud, capturing everyone's attention.

Emmanuel, we've got company they were screaming. *Adremelech has landed on Tcheeva.*

"How did they know we were here?" Emmanuel asked, again aloud. There was an undercurrent of suspicion towards Belphegor.

Cascia's with him Caleb said. Emmanuel rolled his eyes and repeated what he'd heard to Ebony.

"Adremelech and Cascia are here," Emmanuel informed her, spitting Adremelech's name through gritted teeth. Belphegor's face ballooned into a maroon complexion at the mention of his brother's name, and he swung into action, opening a portal. They were suddenly standing by a rock in the middle of the cavern from which was resonating a powerful light. Belphegor raised his arms up and small disturbances tremored in the air as he displaced the natural lead concentration and gathered it to create a shield against the radiation from Tcheeva's nucleus. The rock, the core of Tcheeva, had a single hole in it and Ebony could feel the surge of power just by standing close.

"Quickly Ebony," Emmanuel said. "I can hear them. They're coming down here."

"They're close." Belphegor faced with his back to them, watching intently the walls that enclosed them. Adremelech could appear from anywhere, and Belphegor refused to be taken by surprise.

Ebony cracked her knuckles, bounced on the balls of her feet as she shook her limbs, and took a single breath.

She slammed her hand into the rock.

The magic surged through her veins so powerfully it lit them up visibly through her sudden translucent skin and she sank to her knees, hand still reaching for the magic. It was a struggle to contain such power as she felt the souls of her cousins' band with hers, but she could hear them in her head, pushing her to dig deep. Vesper's magic surged through her last, clawing at every inch of her being as it bound and rewired every last strand of DNA, every atom and every molecule that was Ebony Echnovarria.

Do what I never could Vesper whispered. *I believe in you.* Ebony's eyes burnt a lustre of satin gold as the last drop of magic from the planet drained into her and Vesper and her became one. There was a moment's pause and her body slouched before a surge of energy blasted from her. She threw her hands in the air, arching her back as a transparent power was released like a nuclear bomb, shooting through Tcheeva, blowing Oscar and Caleb out of the atmosphere, and travelling beyond the universe. Ebony yelled out for her brethren to listen.

Enchanteds, I need your help. Atlas has come to destroy the universe and he must be stopped! she bellowed; her voice amplified until it rocked the room around them.

Emmanuel, what's happening? Oscar thought as back in the ship, him and Caleb were being battered by unprecedented winds rising from the ground.

She's done it! he yelled back, bracing himself as the gale slowed. Ebony dropped onto one knee, wiped out.

"Ebony?" Noah said hesitantly. She looked at him and he took a step back as she blinked, and her eyes faded back to brown.

"I think it worked," she laughed, standing up. "It worked!" she shouted, and they joined in her celebration. Ebony felt a new lease of life surge through her, at least for a moment.

"It worked!" Caleb and Oscar chanted happily from the ship. The celebrations were, however, short-lived.

Ebony felt her breath taken from her as a sharp pain shot through her back. She had never handled the type of magic coursing through her and put the source of the pain down to a side effect. She looked to her friends, but they weren't looking at her. They were staring in horror at the thing that lurked behind.

Noah was paralysed. Belphegor's face dropped as he started forward with his knife out but was stopped as the rocks beneath him grabbed his legs. He fought them as they tried to drag him into the ground with suffocating consequences as they reached for his face.

"What?" Ebony tried to speak but choked as she felt warm blood flood into her throat. The tip of a knife poked through the fabric of her top. She grasped her fingers around the wound as deep red blood trickled over her hands, staining her shirt and the floor.

Adremelech stood beside Ebony, admiring his work. Cascia shivered in his shadow, giving Noah a sorrowful look that he turned away from angrily.

"Atlas will be here shortly to finish all of you off," he announced. "Any last words?"

"Leave, before I rip your head from your body," Belphegor chose.

"And how, brother would you do that?" he sniggered, gesturing to Ebony who was motionless. "Your weapon is indisposed."

"You should have chosen the right side when you had the chance," Cascia said sympathetically.

"They did," Ebony said.

Adremelech flinched. "What?"

Ebony turned to him.

She grinned and pulled the knife from her chest.

She held it out to Adremelech who stared in shock.

"I think you dropped this."

"No," Adremelech backed away.

"Well, the technical term is stab."

"How are you okay?"

"If you don't want it back, I'll keep it," Ebony said. He snatched it from her and watched in shock as clutching her hands to her chest, a blue glow shone from Ebony's wound. Before their eyes, she began to heal herself. Both wounds closed like they were never made. Adremelech lost his nerve and lunged for Ebony, but she flicked her hand, and the knife flew across the room.

"You should have chosen the right side when you had the chance," she mimicked and that was enough for the coward. He dived through a portal before Ebony could grab him.

"Adremelech," the fickle Cascia said timidly. Ebony turned to her, rage burning in her soul. "Adremelech get me out of here," she called but Adremelech was long gone. Ebony held out her hand and Cascia's feet were frozen to the spot.

"What was your problem with me?" Ebony grilled. "Why did you choose his side?" Cascia had the audacity to let out a laugh.

"Uh, maybe it was the fact that you got Belize killed!" Cascia yelled, "or maybe it's the fact that you waltzed in here and it's taken less than a week for you to take my friends and turn them into puppets, willing to throw down their life for you!"

Ebony was livid. "Do you think I wanted Belize to die? If anything, all of this is your fault because you should have seen it coming."

"I couldn't see her death because you and your magic interrupted our fight," Cascia argued. "If you hadn't been born, this wouldn't have happened."

"Well, at least my life is important. What's the point of you?" That was the last straw for Cascia; she let out a scream as she drew her knife and lunged at Ebony, but Ebony clicked her fingers and she stopped.

"This is what you get for betraying us," Ebony said flatly, and the water began to drain from Cascia's body. She started to shrivel.

"Ebony, stop," Emmanuel said, horror stricken. Cascia's body sagged, and cheeks hollowed as she tried to speak. From her mouth, Ebony drew a steady stream of water.

"Leave her alone!" Belphegor commanded. "Don't let the power turn you into your father."

The words stopped her in her tracks.

Ebony released Cascia from her suffering. Without any motion save a harrowing glare, Ebony sucked the air from her insides, and Cascia crippled to the ground, permanently subdued.

"Ebony, what did you do?" Emmanuel said. His feelings for Cascia were hateful but the history they had couldn't be forgotten and he didn't think she deserved the torture she was in. He twitched at the sight of her. Noah's mouth hung agape. Ebony wasn't the same person she was when they landed on Tcheeva.

Ebony, you're scaring them Belphegor warned as he kicked off the rocks around his legs. *This was how Atlas succumbed to his magic. He tasted power and then all he wanted was more.* His words stung Ebony's ears and guilt flooded her. *Don't become your father's daughter. Be better than us.* Ebony was disgusted by the fact that she could be compared to Atlas.

The fog of anger parted from her mind and Ebony's fingers splayed. Water rushed back into Cascia, enough to keep her alive. Ebony turned to Emmanuel and Noah. "I'm not like Atlas," she promised. "I won't ever be like him." Waving her hand, the earth dragged Cascia's body into it and towards the surface, hiding the evidence of the dark side of her power.

"We know you won't," Noah said kindly, although he was apprehensive to take a step towards her.

"Be like Belphegor instead," Emmanuel said. Belphegor grew an extra ear on his forehead.

"What?" he asked, stunned.

"You heard me. I'm only saying it once," Emmanuel said, but a smile played on his lips, a rare spark of the personality he once had.

Caleb interrupted the moment, voice riddled with fear as a crashing noise came from the surface earth. *Atlas… he's here.* A glance was shared between the four of them. Ebony shut her eyes. Lorelei, Orabella, and Vesper were in the helm of her mind, encouraging her onwards.

"Ready?" she asked.

"As we'll ever be," Noah said. With no help from Belphegor, Ebony, who was now stronger than him burrowed to the surface of Tcheeva. It was no longer the paradise they'd landed in. Stealing the power of the daughters of Ancients had drained the life from the planet and it was now a barren and dusty wasteland, cold to the touch.

Ebony turned to Belphegor. "Are you sure you're ready for this? Our goal is to kill you brother," she reminded him.

"I could ask you the same, niece. You're about to kill your father."

Chapter 25

On the plains of Tcheeva, where once lived a thriving ecosystem, now rotted a wasteland of such a vast expanse it seemed to have no end. Even the sky had greyed, hiding itself behind clouds in fear of the fight ahead. Ebony's hair floated slightly as the gravity of the planet altered, but her feet remained firm to the rimy ground.

"My daughter." Ebony swung round. "No hugs for your old father?" There was no meaning behind Atlas' words as he sought only to rile her up. He was floating in the air amidst tendrils of black smoke, the sword of Sonneillon in his hand. A blackened cape rested on his back and thick impenetrable armour adorned his war relishing body. He still wore the crown. Undead and Magma men flooded the plains around him, and he grinned, throwing a bolt of lightning across the sky. Surely, he had the upper hand. He was confident. But Ebony gave away nothing of the power she possessed as she turned to him, and he revelled in his misplaced self-assurance.

"You're worn out and pathetic, sending in your lap dog to kill me." Ebony addressed Adremelech who stood below Atlas in trepidation. "You failed miserably."

"Yes, *he* did," Atlas answered, swiping the air. Adremelech ducked to avoid a face full of green acid which spewed its way across the ground. "It doesn't change the inevitable though. I'm going to win." Ebony folded her arms as her face crinkled.

"Eh," she said. "I'd agree with you but then we'd both be wrong." Atlas found her unbearably upbeat and snarled.

"I will take great satisfaction in wiping that smirk off your face. The satisfaction in killing you and your friends will be … inimitable."

"You won't touch them old man," she told him savagely. "Your days of hurting people are over." Ebony walked forward surely.

"Such spirit, such a waste," Atlas sighed. "You would have been such an asset if your humanity hadn't got in the way," he toyed.

"My humanity?" Ebony scoffed. "At least without magic I still have common decency. Without magic, you are nothing. You're like a door handle without a door; absolutely useless and a complete and utter knob."

"It's a good thing I have magic then." His eyes flickered red as he flew closer. Belphegor nudged Noah and Emmanuel backwards and Ebony ascended in a circle of golden light to meet Atlas, until she could feel his breath on her face. "I have Sonneillon's power coursing through me. One Ancient against a couple of Enchanteds? Hardly a fight."

"Because it worked so well the last time an Ancient fought an Enchanted," Ebony reminded him. He drew back, not in intimidation but in anticipation.

"You will die on this planet Ebony, there's nothing you can do about it. Your resting place will mark the coming age of Atlas." He addressed everyone around to hear. "You will all die on this planet. I have Sonneillon's magic, I have his sword and-" he waved his arms, "-I have an army," he boasted as his soldiers started to march forward.

"Yeah?" Ebony raised her eyebrows, unwavering. "So do I." Ebony hadn't timed anything but as if they were waiting in concealed wings, ships inundated the sky over the planet. And not several hundred but several thousand lined the skies, each filled with platoons ready to fight and kill for their galaxy.

"Atlas!" The voice of Simon Braxton rung across the sky. "You have been charged with the murder of twenty-three billion known innocent people. You will not be leaving this planet alive." Portals appeared across the sky and ships of Enchanteds flooded through from Alchemacier.

"Atlas!" Caleb's voice echoed across the sky. His moment had come. "Jellybean!"

From behind the mountain, robots soared upwards. Ebony locked eyes with Atlas.

"Having fun yet?" she asked. Atlas' patience was tested. The results were negative. He was void of all patience.

"You're dead," he spat. He waved his arm and Ebony went flying across the sky, skidding across the dusty ground. Everyone else took the move as a signal.

The war had begun.

Bullets pelted from the sky as soldiers and Enchanteds alike jumped from their ships. Ebony stood and marched forward, deflecting the next attack Atlas threw, spinning it and sending it back to him. She hit him hard and fast, and Atlas become more furious in his moves as she forced him down, lashing him with whips of fire.

Noah appeared on her left and Emmanuel on her right and they fought off the surrounding enemies as Ebony focused on the fight. stomping her feet created waves of power, scorching the earth and torching the zombies running at her. Holding her hands to the sky, she felt for an electrical charge and pulled lightning down on Atlas. He covered himself and launched a counterattack. Using his smoke as blades, he whipped them at her, cutting into her skin but she healed immediately. Ebony feigned pain and used the distraction to whack Atlas with an almighty blow when he slowed to bask in the glory of her supposed injury.

"Give it up Ebony!" he taunted. "You know you can't win." From the nearby mountain he hurled boulders at her until she was enclosed inside a circle of solid rock. But again, it didn't stop her, and she broke free with a powerful punch. As she did, Atlas lunged forward and swiped her across her stomach with Sonneillon's sword. It was barely a scratch but travelled the extent of her waist, and Ebony tried to heal the wound, but she couldn't.

Atlas gleamed.

Ebony panicked. She threw everything she had at him, but he deflected the attacks with the blade. The fight had become dangerously unbalanced in favour of Atlas and she feared the worst as his attacks with the sword became bolder. The two of them were caught in a flurry of portals as Ebony tried to dodge them. Out of the corner of her eye, she spotted Adremelech, and further along the battle ground, Belphegor.

He's coming for you she said, sending the thought sailing across Tcheeva and into Belphegor's head.

"Thanks." He spotted Adremelech who was leant over a corpse. Belphegor slowed. It was Cascia, killed not by Ebony but by a fatal tear along her throat. Adremelech caught sight of him and gleamed. He raised his thorn covered knuckles. "So, this is how it ends brother," Belphegor sighed.

"Killing you will be an honour," Adremelech said, hopping from one foot to another in keenness of battle. A trail of dead Enchanteds littered the floor in his wake and Belphegor's blood boiled as he walked slowly to meet him.

"You wish," Belphegor spat, and they ran at each other. Their collision caused a monumental bang as they fought, pure rage and hatred fuelling each side.

"You're weak!" Adremelech screamed as he forced Belphegor to his knees, dodging a retaliating blow. "You're out of practise." he punched him round the face and Belphegor shuffled back as thorns pierced his cheek. Adremelech grabbed the back of his neck with a knife to his throat. "And you have always been the lesser Ancient," he insulted. Belphegor laughed. He hadn't taken a beating because he couldn't fight. He just wanted to see the best Adremelech had. The thorns popped from his cheek.

"I may be weaker," he mumbled, locking eyes with his brother, "but I have always been smarter, and you show off too much for your own good." He spat blood into Adremelech's eyes which quickly turned into tiny beetles that crawled behind his sclera and into his head, and Adremelech reeled as he clawed at his face, giving Belphegor a chance to stand.

Grabbing Adremelech's hair, he yanked him forwards and held him in place with several limbs protruding from his body to do so. He created a portal and shoved Adremelech's head through.

"You always counted physical strength and force over imagination and brains, so I guess you don't need them."

"Brother!" Adremelech cried out. As the portal surrounded his neck, Belphegor snapped it shut.

"Spineless crap bag," he muttered. The decapitated body of Adremelech flopped to the floor, squirming lifelessly as the beetles fed on his innards.

"Ebony, heads up," Belphegor said. Ebony looked up, and so did Atlas and they both paused for a second as Belphegor dropkicked Adremelech's head through the portal above their heads and it bounced to the floor between them.

"You're screwed," Ebony said as Atlas panicked. Suddenly, a bright light appeared from the sky and slammed into the planet, evaporating miles of undead and Magma men around them and sending both her and Atlas flying. As the light faded, people began to rush out of it, screaming a war cry as they charged.

"Ebony?" She had been momentarily stunned, as had Atlas who rolled to a stop on the ground. Someone offered her a hand and she took it, standing up.

It was Coraline.

"Coral? What are you doing here?" She hugged her tightly.

"Turns out, I'm an Enchanted," she smiled, as a tattoo glided across her arm. It was of a compass and was currently glowing an angry red, whilst pointing directly at Atlas. "And we heard your call."

"I have waited a lifetime for your demise, Atlas," Belphegor yelled as he marched forward. Atlas stood and tried to rid himself of Belphegor as he redirected the Magma men around him. With Belphegor busy riding tidal waves to wash them away, Atlas' attention was back on Ebony.

"Enough of this!" he screamed. He stood, and drawing all his power, fired a stream of pure energy at Ebony. She retaliated quickly with the same thing, shielding herself and Coraline as their powers clashed.

"Ebony!" Noah, Emmanuel, and Belphegor stood behind her and she protected them as they came to her aid. Emmanuel screamed in Atlas' mind and Noah created two portals, one which absorbed half of Ebony's magic and the other which opened behind Atlas, shooting him in the back. But Atlas quickly held an arm out behind himself too, fighting power from both directions. However, Belphegor added to the power attacking Atlas, and it began to push him over the edge. Atlas couldn't fight another Ancient too.

"Never underestimate an Enchanted!" Ebony screamed, as other Enchanteds stood with her. The elementals joined their powers together with Ebony, firing at Atlas with everything they had. Teleporters helped Noah, expanding the portal until Ebony's power surrounded Atlas from all sides. The screaming from the telepaths was so powerful that Atlas cried out, shaking his head as they filled his mind with enough noise to match a rocket engine.

There were others around too; many of the shapeshifters had opted for dragons and as Jeff had done, were swooping over the battle ground, burning enemies, and collecting wounded allies to take to the ships. Several Enchanteds chose to bowl, lobbing Magma men through fields of Undead. Illusionist Enchanteds blinded Atlas so he couldn't see where the attacks were coming from. From above, Simon rained hell fire upon him, and the robots that Caleb commanded did their part in sheltering the innocents from the bullets as they concentrated their abilities into destroying Atlas. It didn't matter who they were or what power they had; they had banded together, and Atlas was nearly dead.

"Ebony, I'm your father!" he screamed. "You wouldn't kill your father."

"I would," she said, willing every ounce of her being to keep fighting. But Atlas had a trick up his sleeve that no one saw coming except for Cascia, who was too dead to warn them. In the space of a second, he went from fearing for his life to utterly complacent.

He shrugged.

"Have it your way," he said and shot into the air. Ebony followed so closely she could see the patterning on the sole of his combat boots. She couldn't lose him, not when he was so vulnerable.

Where the air thinned in unbreathable territories, Atlas smirked at Ebony and flipped over her head in a sudden change of direction, and plunging back to the ground, collided with the earth. Ebony felt all hope leave her body. Magma men and undead felt the tremor he had created and began to melt into pools of flesh and blood. Shapeless masses of flesh and bone and magma and magic merged as it raced towards Atlas. Ebony landed beside Belphegor.

"What do I do? Belphegor, I don't know how to do this type of magic. This is necromancy," Ebony cried desperately, as Atlas' body was swarmed and shielded. Surrounding them, all attempts at a fight had ceased as people stared in bewilderment, and Belphegor realised all too late that the confusion is exactly what Atlas had needed.

"Kill him!" Belphegor screamed. "Kill him! Quickly!" The attack was relaunched but futile, and Ebony was unable to take her eyes off Atlas who was quickly consumed by the flesh that had no reaction to magic and bullets alike. It piled up and slowed only after it broke the height of the atmosphere, to which the ships reacted by cowering a safe distance away, conserving their ammunition for something that would be affected by it.

Once the fleshy mountain had stopped growing, it slowly mutated itself, forming and reforming, and Ebony summoned a portal to the mountain top as the flesh reshaped into some ghastly configuration of Atlas. With more limbs than the population of a small country, sharpened teeth layered down his throat and a mangled body with joints dispersed randomly along his arms and legs, he laughed piercingly and with one swing of his hand, took out several ships, sending them crashing into each other in an explosion that lit the sky.

"Pull back, pull back!" Simon cried as Atlas marched across the planet, stomping on the Enchanteds and soldiers as though they were ants. His morbid form was of no detriment to his speed, despite the sagging weight of excess flesh.

Ebony! She heard Emmanuel in the crowd of screams as he fled Atlas and teleported him to the mountain where he wouldn't be trampled.

"You see Ebony, you cannot defeat me!" Atlas cackled. "Your humanity makes you weak and my ambition is far too superior!"

Atlas, this has to end. Belphegor penetrated his mind. *Stop!* But it became clear Atlas had barely begun. Despite sagging eyelids and matted eyelashes that overgrew his eyes, Atlas saw Belphegor and Emmanuel standing with Ebony, and watched gleefully as they were plucked from the mountain, dragged against their will towards him. Never before had Ebony seen an Ancient look so puny and helpless. Belphegor attacked Atlas unyieldingly, burning holes through his flesh which carelessly remoulded itself. Emmanuel continued to yell powerlessly, the little telekinesis he had failing him.

"Brother." Atlas greeted him at eye level and then looked at Emmanuel, recognising the limply hanging figure. "And the pathetic Enchanted who stole Ebony away from me," he growled, leaning in.

"You do not deserve to call me brother, and you will never win," Belphegor said defiantly, attracting the attention back to himself as Emmanuel curled into a ball.

"But I will." He grinned. "Just ask Cascia. Oh, wait." He grabbed Belphegor between two fingers and even the gentlest squeeze nearly deflated him. Ebony flung herself off of the mountain and onto Atlas' hand. She plunged her hands into his flesh, trying to get him to drop Belphegor but Atlas flicked her away like she was a bug. She tried again, this time aiming for Emmanuel who was suspended in mid-air, but Atlas wrapped a shield of impenetrable wind around him, leaving Ebony to do nothing but watch as he was battered by the hurricane. Whatever she did, Atlas had a counterattack to leave her powerless in his wake.

"Go away, insect." Atlas, unphased, pushed Ebony back again and she feared he was going to crush Belphegor between his fingers.

But what he did was worse.

So much worse.

Raising his hand up high with a slow deliberation that struck fear into Belphegor and Emmanuel as they realised his intentions, he dangled them in the air above his head and opened his mouth. Ebony launched herself forwards. Atlas knocked her back.

They locked eyes as he dropped the two of them into his gob.

Atlas swallowed dramatically, licking his lips.

Ebony wept uncontrollably. She tried to fight through the gale force winds but it swept up her magic like a flower in a tornado.

"I told you Ebony, your friends die first. It's the price they pay for helping you." He showed no remorse as he scanned the ships and looked directly through the front screen of Caleb and Oscar's one.

"Don't you dare!" Ebony screamed, reading in his mind raging thoughts that sickened her to the core. She teleported again but Atlas changed the location of her egress and she appeared beneath a pile of his sentient fleshy entrails who lashed at her as she fought them off. Atlas grabbed the ship and Oscar and Caleb held each other tight as he closed an eye and squinted with another into it.

"Shake well before opening," he pretended to read. Like tossing a coin, he pitched the ship into the air and caught it with a harsh shake.

Ebony got up from the ground to watch Atlas rip off the top of the ship. She may have been far away, but she clearly saw as he inverted it and tapped the bottom until Caleb and Oscar, who had been clinging on for dear life, lost their grip and fell into his mouth. He snapped his mouth shut and again, made a point to exaggerate the swallow, making direct eye contact with Ebony as he did.

"Ebony." Noah appeared next to her, but she didn't notice. "Ebony, snap out of it!" He shook her shoulders roughly and she turned to him. His body was bruised and bloody, his eyes bloodshot from tears but he maintained one last shred of hope.

"The sword," he urged. "Atlas dropped the sword. Help me find it!" Without showing a scrap of fear Noah dived through a portal, appearing by Atlas' feet. Using a group of strategically placed portals he darted around the ground, searching frantically until he saw it. Discarded carelessly following Atlas' newfound power, the gold hilted sword of

Sonneillon stuck out from a pile of bodies and Noah lunged for it but Atlas saw what was coming, vaporising Noah's portal. He didn't have time to make a new one and crashed painfully into the pile.

"Noah!" Ebony flew to him and as he blinked in a dizzy haze. Atlas lifted and separated the two of them into the air, and as Ebony fought to be free of his grip, he squeezed and she yelped as her ribs began to crack.

"I tell you what. Since I'm your father and I care," Atlas lied, "I'll allow you to die together." His eyes lit up as Ebony struggled. She tried to hurl ship debris from the ground into his body, but it was unphased.

Ebony, do what I couldn't. Normally, Ebony would ignore voices in her head, but in her mind's eye she could see Vesper, telling her what to do. Ebony nodded.

"Screw you Atlas!" She yelled and to the best of her ability she aimed her hands at his eye and launched a beam of gunky green acid, the very same that had killed her mother. Had he blinked in time, the tough skin of his eyelids would have been impassable, but Atlas howled as the acid penetrated his pupil, instantly blinding him. He stumbled backwards, holding his eye in pain.

Take him down! Ebony yelled into the minds of the remaining ships. They didn't need telling twice, taking advantage of Atlas' ruined eyesight to fly around and fire missiles.

He yelled out, snapping his fingers as he was engulfed into a ball of fire and smoke. Ebony felt pressure building around her as Atlas' grip tightened and focused all her magic in saving herself and Noah from suffocating, pushing his fingers away as he tried to crush her. But as more missiles flew and he realised he had bigger issues than Ebony, he lifted her and Noah into the air.

She screamed.

She struggled against his magic.

She tried to push her and Noah out of the way as he dangled them above his mouth.

"Goodbye Ebony." Atlas said.

He opened his fist.

They fell.

His jaw closed behind them.

Chapter 26

It was the worst slip n' slide of Ebony's life.

The inside of the human body was dark. Very dark. She had never really considered it. She didn't think she was going to survive long enough to have to think about it as she slid down Atlas' throat and landed on a mess of muscle, flesh, and ship debris. She wasn't sure how long she'd been lying unconscious in the pile but came awake alone.

Noah wasn't anywhere to be seen.

She opened her eyes and couldn't see a thing.

That was probably why.

She tried to summon a flame to her hand but all that came was a measly spark the size of a lighter. She turned to her band, but it had seriously malfunctioned and was blinking with a red warning light that caught someone's attention as she stumbled around a corner.

"Hey... Ebony?" Her head jerked up as Caleb rushed towards her, skidding on the slippery floor like a comical penguin. "Are you okay?" He clicked his fingers in front of her eyes and she looked at him dizzily. "You looked concussed; how many fingers am I holding up?" he asked, shoving three fingers in her face.

"Twenty," she said sarcastically but she looked at him in concern as his cyber eye flickered on and off. "How many fingers am I holding up?"

Caleb huffed. "It's like I'm involuntarily blinking."

"I see," Ebony said distastefully. She put her hand out to steady herself, but it slipped down a disgusting wall and as she pulled it away, a slimy gunk came with it. "What the hell is that?" She wiped it down her trousers.

"Mucus," Caleb said dead seriously and like a brick wall, all of Ebony's memories flooded back to her. The emotion shot through her like adrenaline.

"Oh my God, you're alive?" she cried out, hugging him tightly. But she regretted it and pulled away as her ribs stung.

"Bit of a delayed reaction but yes," Caleb said. "You sure you're not concussed?"

"Caleb I'm fine," Ebony insisted, despite the throbbing in her head and sharp pinch in her sides that came with every deep breath. "Where are we?"

"Atlas' oesophagus?" Caleb guided her to the edge of the inlet where they were standing. "Although his insides are weird." Looking up, there was a huge hole disappearing into nothingness and looking down, Ebony could faintly see what looked like a green river of acid and bile. Not typical of the human anatomy. The air tasted of copper.

"Are the others, okay?"

"Emmanuel and Oscar are fine, Noah's a bit dazed but Belphegor..."

"What happened to him?"

"Emmanuel said Belphegor pushed him down Atlas' throat and out the way."

"Out the way of what?" Ebony said. Caleb wasn't finishing his sentences and it concerned her. He led her away from the edge and towards the back of the cavity.

"Ebony... Atlas chewed him." Caleb didn't look her in the eye but stood to the side to let her through. She lumbered forward, a small flame in her hand.

"Ebony? We need light over here now." Emmanuel's voice was shaking, and he choked back tears. "Hurry up," he urged. She saw his pale face in light cast by the flame and knelt by him.

"Hold the light this way," Oscar ordered. "Noah, keep pressure." He was fumbling with a med kit which had fallen with other supplies into Atlas' mouth along with them. Noah caught Ebony's eyes.

"Magic is dulled to practically nothing in here," he told her. "Our bands are wrecked. We can't do any more."

"Belphegor?" Ebony stuttered. She looked over at what was left of him. One of his arms was amputated cleanly through the forearm and Noah was struggling to stop the blood surging from it as he clogged the gaping hole with clothes and rags. If it wasn't for magic being so vital to his life force, he'd be dead.

"He's been unconscious for the last minute or so." Oscar caught Ebony up. "We don't know what to do." Ebony held out her hand over Belphegor's body in a desperate attempt to fix him but in the same way as she couldn't summon more than a small flame, the wound barely healed Before Ebony was exhausted by the attempt and her body refused to give more.

"He's not going to survive this," Ebony panicked, "not at this rate. Noah, move the rags." The sour scent of septicaemia filled Ebony's nostrils as he did and she quickly concentrated the flame into more of a laser and tried to cauterise the stump of his arm. It was sleepily inefficient progress and despite vigorous concentration, she managed a dismal display of magic.

"How do we get out of this one?" Emmanuel said. "We have nothing."

"We have one thing," Noah said. From the mushy floor behind him he pulled out a sword.

"The sword of Sonneillon," Ebony gasped. "You stole it from him?"

"May have crash landed but I crash landed on top of it," he said. "If we're inside Atlas, maybe we can reach his heart?"

"He doesn't have one," Caleb interrupted.

"I know he metaphorically doesn't," Noah said, "but regardless of his questionable morphology he physically does and if we could reach it, we could kill him."

Ebony asked, "can we get to his heart from here?" There was a round of shrugging and she decided to take charge. "Noah, help me sort Belphegor out. You three; find us a way there." They followed her orders and Caleb, Oscar and Emmanuel shuffled to the edge of the oesophagus to work out a plan.

"Noah, can you not teleport at all?" Ebony questioned. Noah summoned a portal, but it was the size of a ring, and led to more of Atlas' insides.

"It's the best I can do, I'm sorry." He pulled fresh bandages from the kit, winding them around Belphegor's arm. Ebony continued to push air into his lungs to keep him breathing. She leant forward and gently wiped the grime away from his face. He looked peaceful almost. A blanket on top of him and no one would be able to tell the torture he was going through.

"You're going to be all right Uncle, I promise," she said, before she let her head lull into her lap. Running her hands through her hair, she pulled at it angrily, digging her nails into her scalp.

"Hey, hey-" Noah crouched in front of her, "-don't." He gently coiled his fingers around her wrists, pulling them into her lap. Holding them with one hand, he put a finger under her chin and lifted her head until she was looking at him. "We've got this," he promised. Caleb waltzed in and they turned to him.

"Any progress?" They stood up.

"Sort of," he said. He inclined his head and the two of them followed, displeased to leave Belphegor.

"We can't leave him," Ebony worried.

"We'll only be a minute." Caleb led them to the edge of the oesophagus where it looked like they could go no further, and Oscar and Emmanuel weren't there.

"I think I've discovered a new definition of madness," Oscar called from an unknown location. "Come down." They looked down. He was hanging from a bone poking out through the muscle.

Clinging on to the mucus and using indents in Atlas' skin, they followed Oscar down, cautious of the pool of acid below.

"I know I'm no anatomist but I'm pretty sure this isn't what the insides of a living thing looks like," Caleb said, as he jumped onto a mass of flesh. Ebony followed. In front of them, the beginnings of a rickety rope bridge led out over a deathly drop in a green fog.

"I would agree."

"How is this even here?" Noah touched it, checking if it was real. It was. A real solid rope bridge, carved from bone and cartilage and tied together with dead veins.

"Evil." The voice no one expected to hear caused them to jump.

They turned to the darkness where his figure appeared from.

Instantly, hands were drawn into fists and aimed at the figure.

"Atlas," Ebony gasped. He covered his face with his scrawny freckled arms.

"No, please!" he pleaded. "Don't hurt me! I'm not him. Well, I am but I'm not!" He fumbled with his words and looked a shrivelled mess. Wearing a casual shirt and ragged trousers that hung loosely from his form, with messy hair and large bags under his eyes, he looked like less of a threat and more like a deer in headlights.

303

"Explain," Ebony ordered.

"I'm the angel on Atlas' shoulder, except I fell off," he said hurriedly, watching the knife Oscar was pointing at his face. "Atlas' evil is so powerful it's grown its own conscience and built itself inside him like a nest. I'm the only thing left of the good conscience, so I am him… well, I was him once," Atlas said, feeble in his movements as he wrung his wrists.

"How do we know you're telling the truth?"

"I can help you cure Belphegor and take you to Atlas' heart."

"Why would you do that?" Ebony asked. "Our plan is to kill Atlas, ergo, kill you." Atlas looked at her in defeat.

"I'm hardly living," he said. "I just want this to be over." Ebony lowered her hand. She told herself she would never trust someone again. The exact thought crossed Oscar's mind.

"Trusting him could be our downfall."

"How can you save Belphegor?" Ebony quizzed.

"I'm still Atlas; I have all the good magic he doesn't use." Ebony listened to Oscar's advice but didn't follow it.

"Save him, then we'll talk." With Noah untrustingly bringing up the rear with the sword pointed at Atlas' balding, chalky head, Ebony led him to where Belphegor was laying.

"Oh, brother." Atlas took a knee by his side. "What have I done to you?" He heaved a sigh. Shutting his eyes, he held his frail and bony hand out over Belphegor's arm and its glowed blue, shaking from the trauma of climbing the oesophagus. Atlas had no muscles, something the evil had stolen from him.

"You've done a good job Ebony," he praised, although she'd done very little. "I can't get the arm back, but I can heal what's left." He allowed blue energy to transfer tranquilly from his hand and it swirled calmly around Belphegor's body. It wound like a river bend around his arm, healing the wound. After a moment, Belphegor stirred as if waking from a reposeful slumber, disoriented and confrontational from the remnants of his mood before Atlas had eaten him.

"He's not gonna be happy," Noah whispered, shuffling backwards. The others chose to do the same as Belphegor glanced their way.

"Where are we?"

"Inside Atlas," Ebony said.

"Inside…" Belphegor hesitated as he saw Atlas sitting in front of him and tried to push himself up on his non-existent arm, falling clumsily to the side.

He stared downwards.

He froze.

Then he screamed.

"What did you do to me!" he yelled, staring in shock at the stump where his arm once was. He lunged for Atlas, grabbing him by the neck. "What did you do?" He shook the enfeebled Atlas like a limp ragdoll, threatening to snap his neck. He may have been incapacitated but was still deadly.

"Belphegor it wasn't him." Ebony spoke calmly, not overly bothered that Atlas was choking. "This isn't Atlas, this is a manifestation of the good in him. He saved your life." With a grunt she tore his good arm away. Atlas coughed and shuffled behind Ebony, cowering in fear.

"I'm sorry about your arm Belphegor," he said.

"I can still feel it," Belphegor moaned, staring at the space where his arm would be. He clutched the stump as a phantom pain struck him, and realised quickly that he had no magic to make it better. "How am I meant to help you kill Atlas with one arm?" he whined.

"The exact same way you've helped us so far," Ebony said, "except this time we have a plan. Take the sword of Sonneillon, shove it through Atlas' heart."

"You make it sound so simple." Atlas wiped his brow. "It's really not."

"It can be the hardest I ever have to do but I'm doing it." Ebony's defiance grew from her anger and pain. "I don't care if it kills me, I'm killing him." Atlas frowned.

"Evil has taken hold of every nook and cranny of his body. Walking to the heart won't be hard, it will be damn near impossible."

"We've done impossible things before," Emmanuel said.

Atlas wasn't convinced but he pushed himself up weakly on trembling arms. His body was debilitated as the controlling Atlas' power embedded itself deeply within him.

"Follow me," he said, doddering back towards the bridge, "and stay close. It's a long and dangerous journey and I don't want to be responsible for any more deaths." He cast a guilty look and hurried on, eager to prove his use.

"Here." Emmanuel and Caleb stooped down to help Belphegor, but he snarled, pushing them away in agitation.

"I don't need your help. I'm not some helpless old man," he insulted, standing up. He was fine until he tried to take a step but his body, who for the past couple of millennia had grown accustomed to having an arm, was awfully unbalanced and he staggered to the side. Ebony reached out to help but Atlas knocked on her arm gently.

"What?" she barked. His mouth moved silently as he looked for words and he clutched his hands together, summoning the courage to talk to her.

"I want to apologise. That's all. I was an awful father. I could see through Atlas' eyes like a TV screen. I hated seeing how he treated you." Ebony's eyes widened. She watched sorrowfully as he began to climb down the oesophagus, his face full of nothing but guilt and regret. She said nothing. Behind Ebony, Belphegor was still coming to terms with the new struggles he was facing.

"Belphegor," Noah offered. "Let me help you." Belphegor was hanging onto Atlas' muscle tissue with the glare of a raging bull as he worked out how to get down.

"I'm fine."

"Take my hand."

Belphegor scowled at his hand with disgust. "No."

"Seriously? I'm not coming onto you, I'm trying to help, so stop being a stuck-up prick, and take my damn hand." Belphegor was speechless.

With a sizable eye roll, he leant towards Noah, who grabbed his good arm whilst Oscar helped from behind. Ebony's powers may have been dulled but she could still hear Emmanuel slightly, even though it was barely a whisper.

We're never going to make it like this he thought to Caleb.

I know Caleb thought back.

"Oi, curly haired boys," Atlas called. "Come on." He too had obviously read their minds.

"It's Emmanuel," Emmanuel corrected.

"Caleb." Caleb waved.

"I've already forgotten," Atlas commented and Ebony, as much as she distrusted the man in front of her, hid a smile within a yawn.

Dick they both thought, climbing down in unison, and following Atlas back towards the rope bridge. He paused.

"Everyone link hands," he said. "The fog across the bridge is hallucinogenic."

"Of course it is." Caleb, out of everyone in the group, was still impressed by the magic he saw around, whether good or bad. From the others, Atlas received a collective sigh. He held out his hand and Ebony took it; Oscar took hers, then, Caleb, Emmanuel, Noah, and Belphegor, without another choice, went at the back.

"Nothing you see in the fog is real. Keep holding hands and whatever you do, don't stop walking." Atlas laid out clear and strict instructions. "The fog feeds off people's regrets. It will try and keep you in its grasp by any means. It will give you whatever you want or break your spirit until you don't see a point in leaving," he said. "Everyone ready?"

"We don't have much of a choice if we aren't," Oscar replied.

Atlas began to walk, and they followed him into the mist. It was a sickly shade of green and so thick no one could see their own body, let alone the person in front or behind.

As Emmanuel strode confidently, he started to hear voices which wasn't uncommon to him, but strange when the voices didn't have a body to them.

"Can anyone else hear that?" he asked.

"Ignore it," Atlas called from the front as he marched on persistently.

You're insane. You don't have powers, you have problems a honeyed voice whispered, and Emmanuel turned, staring in fear at the shadows growing around him. As the voices grew louder, his vision went black, and he loosened his grip as all sensation in his hands numbed and he couldn't tell if he was still clinging on to Caleb and Noah.

"Guys, I can't see," he worried but the fog had separated him visually and audibly.

They don't care. You're blinded by your self-righteousness, trying to do the right thing the mangled voice heckled as Emmanuel sightlessly felt for his next step. *You thought getting your friends involved would kill Atlas, but it got me killed instead!*

"Me?"

"Me." He spun round as the voice blew down his neck. Eyes wide and lips trembling, he braced himself as in the black he was seeing, someone appeared.

"Belize?" His mouth hung agape, and he fought back tears. "Don't use her against me."

"It's me," Belize said, standing before him, clothes sliced by the force that killed her. "I was killed by Atlas. I was thrown in here to suffer for all eternity. It was your fault," she accused and instantly she had Emmanuel hooked as he pleaded for forgiveness. Her body was absorbed by Atlas' power. Who wasn't to say it wasn't actually her?

"Belize," he sobbed. "Please, I didn't know you were going to die!"

"You could have read Atlas' mind, to see what he was going to do." Emmanuel's heart dropped.

"Please forgive me. If I could die in your place, I would," he swore.

"Oh, Emmanuel." Her personality changed as she floated closer to him and he held out his hand to her. Without a single word spoken, she gently put her hand around the back of his neck as if reaching for a hug, but suddenly yanked his hair back. "I would love for you to die in my place." Her eyes, now empty white sockets bore into his as from thin air she plucked a spear of rock. With immense precision, she plunged it into Emmanuel's chest, sending it through at an angle so it pierced his heart and shot through the back of his spine, pinning him to the ground.

"We need to keep moving!" Ebony called but suddenly there was no one around her to talk to. "Hello?" she called but again, there was no answer, and she narrowed her eyes. "Your tactics won't work on me," she said to the fog. "I get it; isolate me, try and scare me. Well, it's not going to work." There was an uncomfortable chuckle from amidst the fog and it transformed into a person. It was Cascia. But not the healthy, lively Cascia who Ebony held memories of. It was the Cascia moments before death, skin shrivelled, body lanky and sagging.

"You did this to me," she hissed.

"Your information is wrong!" Ebony yelled into the fog. "Cascia is alive!"

"Not anymore," Cascia said. "You killed me."

"I didn't." Ebony backed away and stumbled as her foot slipped on the damp bone.

"You did. You left me to die on the plains of Tcheeva." An image of Adremelech appeared behind Cascia; he violently stabbed at her body. Ebony looked away.

"I'm sorry." She didn't want to indulge the fog, but it stood in her path.

"You're not sorry. You took your time, you enjoyed torturing me," it sneered. Ebony remained in a sombre silence. "Did it ever occur to you I didn't want to betray you?" she asked. "Did it occur to you Adremelech threatened to torture and kill me and my family if I didn't side with him?"

"It did," Ebony lied, "but Noah didn't give in, so why did you?"

"Noah had no one to lose, I have a family." She paused and corrected herself with a bitter laugh. "*Had* a family. Two sisters, Renee and Ezeli. Neither were Enchanteds and neither would stand a chance if Adremelech decided to pay them a visit, which he promised he would do if I stood against him. And then I died knowing that they, and my friends, would never see me as anything but a traitor. I died feeling nothing but hatred. I died and no one will ever care."

"I'm sorry," Ebony said, and she barged by. But the fog was persistent and didn't want to lose a prize such as Ebony.

"Maybe this form isn't getting through to you," she said and before Ebony's eyes she divided in two and the other form amalgamated into Stella.

"What happened to you?" Stella asked. "I thought I could trust you, but you got me killed." Ebony tried to keep going but Stella stopped her.

"Please stop."

"It hurt you know. Being vaporised only took a second but the feeling was more agonising than anything I've ever felt. Like ripping off all of my skin at once." Stella melted away and Ebony felt relief until Jeff replaced her, head cracked from temple to crown.

"I suffocated in a mound of dirt, alone and afraid and thinking you all had abandoned me. If you hadn't given the medicine to Belphegor, I would still be here!"

"Stop," Ebony whispered but they had formed a circle that she wouldn't be getting through. They had barely begun. From the fog, more figures appeared. One of them was someone Ebony had only ever seen twice but could never forget the face of.

"Mum?" The word was foreign to her.

"I am so ashamed of the woman you've become," Joplin said. "I'm dead because of you; Atlas' patience finally wore out. You were the one who pushed him over the edge, yet I was the one to take the fall. Just like your friends, taking the responsibility for your actions with their lives." Ebony's jaw hung loosely.

"You're dead?" she asked but the fog had already morphed onto its next figure.

"You took our magic, our power and wasted it," Vesper said.

"You let my father be killed," Lorelei accused, "when all he was doing was trying to survive!"

"And look what you've done to my father," Orabella said. "He's been tortured, burned, shot at, chewed, knocked down again and again, and for what? For you to berate him. For him to lose an arm because you can't step up to the plate," she ridiculed. "You can't save anyone. Billions are dead because of you, and they all have something to say about it." As figures began to swarm her, Ebony crouched into a ball, rocking backwards and forwards. At first it was only a few and Ebony felt as though she could fight them as they approached, swinging punches into a gas that couldn't be touched. But as more of Atlas' victims appeared over the side of the bridge, beating her down, kicking, punching, doing whatever they could to hurt her in a blind frenzy driven by revenge, Ebony felt the weight of the world fall on her shoulders, and she gave up.

Belphegor stumbled slightly as the shadows, rather than take on someone's form, swirled around his shoulder and grew back a new arm before his eyes. For a moment he celebrated but his arm came at a hefty price, and he howled as his legs dematerialised from under him and he fell to the floor. A shadow towered over him, and he dug his fingers into the path angrily.

"You always were the worst brother," Adremelech said, blocking the path on which he was pulling himself. Belphegor growled.

"You're dead," he spat.

"You're dead," Adremelech jeered. "You wish. You never could beat me, could you?" He laughed and casually removed his head from his neck, holding it towards Belphegor's face. "And you never will," he taunted, his words echoing inside Belphegor's head as he disappeared. Belphegor could hear someone behind him but kept trying to move forward, crawling with his arms along the wood.

"How can you even call yourself a father?" His eyes widened but he didn't look back. After so many years, the creamy voice was still familiar to him. But he was too ashamed to look into his daughter's eyes.

"Orabella," he murmured.

"You were never good enough for Sonneillon and weak in the eyes of your brothers, but me? I loathed you."

"Please Orabella, you have to understand, everything I've done I did out of love for you."

"Bullshit." She put a foot on his back and rolled him over like a football. "You never did anything for anyone but yourself," she said through gritted teeth. "I detest you! There is only one person in this universe who hates you more than me." Belphegor tried to get into a sitting position, but Orabella kicked him resentfully and he rolled over. She kicked him again and he cried out as he began to slip over the edge of the bridge. With no legs to stop him and his arm beginning to disappear again, he had only one hand on which to hold with as he hung precariously over the side. Orabella smiled sweetly and put a booted foot on his hand, and he bit his tongue as he felt his fingers breaking.

"No one hates me more than you," he said sadly.

"Dear old daddy, the only person who hates you more than me, is Ebony."

"No." Belphegor fought to hold on. "I was there for her. She forgave me!"

"And still she is revolted by you. Thus, my point is proven. You will never be good enough." Orabella sniggered and, with Belphegor staring into her eyes with a broken soul, one by one she pushed his fingers off the bridge.

Noah, unlike the others, could see the end of the path through the fog but as he walked the rope bridge confidently, between him and the end grew a huge chasm of nothingness.

"What the hell?" He peered over the edge. Clawing up the walls of the never-ending pit of despair were the souls of the damned, writhing in agony as their bodies were swallowed by the fire fuelling the fog.

"You've hidden behind your power to overcome every obstacle, but you can't defeat this one," a voice said. Noah let neither the voice nor the chasm bother him as he watched Ebony stride by. He waited for her to slow close to the edge, but she didn't.

"Ebony, look out!" He went to grab her, but his hand went through her body like she was a mere apparition. He watched her reach the broken end of the bridge. She gave him an ugly smile, mouth stretched open past the corner of her lips and all the way up to her ears. Then she turned and dropped off the edge. He screamed and screamed harder as the others followed, all except Oscar.

"Why are you here Noah?" Oscar asked. "What help have you been?"

"I… Oscar, why are you saying this?" Noah asked, confused, and frightened.

"You don't belong with us." Noah backed away, wary of the precarious end of the bridge.

"You don't mean it," he said defiantly.

"I do. You don't belong with us," Oscar repeated. "You don't belong anywhere. It's why your father disowned you for your power. You travel from place to place, one portal at a time because you know you don't belong."

"It's not true."

"Maybe not," Oscar said, "but there's one thing I know for certain." He grabbed Noah by the collar and Noah fought back, thrashing out and kicking as he was dragged closer to the edge by the fog. But he was still unable to touch Oscar, despite Oscar's fingers being pressed around his shirt.

Noah was thrown onto his stomach and rolled, to see it was no longer Oscar standing over him but Jeff.

"It should've been you who died, not me!" Jeff thundered. "I was a valuable asset, but you were the one who got to live!" As Noah watched, Jeff's head began to crumble and bleed. His skull became dust and a rock took its place.

"You did this." Oscar dragged him to his feet. "I wish I'd chosen Jeff! This is what you deserve!" Jeff, with a bloody hand, dislodged the rock from his brain with a spine-chilling crunch.

"Jeff, I'm sorry," Noah cried. Oscar twisted his arm behind his back in response and he fell to his knees.

"An eye for an eye," Jeff said. Noah squeezed his eyes shut.

Jeff raised the rock above his head and swung it like a golf club into Noah's head.

Silence.

Noah flinched as he awaited the impact, but the rock didn't hurt him. In fact, it didn't do more than give him a momentary headache. He lifted his head to Jeff and Oscar.

It was only the fog.

"You're not real," Noah realised. How could he have forgotten it was fake? The fog wavered. Jeff took another blow with the rock but this time it practically bounced off Noah's face like a pebble.

"You did this!" Oscar yelled again, lunging for him. But Noah sidestepped him, put his foot out and Oscar tripped. Noah's fingers connected firmly with Oscar's back, and it sent him plummeting into the chasm below.

"You're not real!" Noah yelled into the fog. He turned to the end of the bridge. "It's not real." He psyched himself up, jumping and shaking his limbs as he stared at the gap between him and the edge of the fog. "It's not real, it's not real," he cried out and with reckless abandon, he sprinted off the edge.

Before the fog had totally lost its grasp, he had landed by Atlas' feet in a heap on the soft, squidgy insides of Atlas, away from the bridge. The fog receded. Atlas, eyes shaded beneath the tip of a hat he had manifested, tipped it towards Noah.

"I told you all to keep walking."

"Sorry," was all Noah could think to say.

"I don't know how your friends are going to get out." Through the fog, he could see them stumbling around but was helpless to do anything but watch them and pray they got to the end.

Emmanuel was pinned to the ground but not by the spear. By his own shock. After a moment of staring into Belize's eyes, he came to another realisation.

"I should be dead," he told her. "And this should definitely hurt more." He grabbed the spear and yanked, and it didn't even come out of him before it disappeared. He lifted his shirt, checking for a wound and there was none and as he pulled his shirt down, there wasn't a blood stain in sight.

"I'm sorry the real Belize is dead," he said, as the foggy apparition of Belize backed away, "but I'm going to be a damn sight more excited when you die." He grabbed the smoke and it didn't wait around, coiling into the air and disappearing into the darkness. As it did, his sight came back to him and with a little grunt of impressiveness, he dusted his shirt and continued to walk until he found Ebony rocking back and forth and Belphegor, barely five metres away, hanging from the bridge. He rushed over and grabbed his hand.

"Belphegor it's not real!" he cried, holding on to his arm with such tenacity he almost formed a tourniquet. Whilst the situation was normal from Emmanuel's point of view, for Belphegor it was a different story. Emmanuel had thrown both hands through Orabella's leg and his face was sticking through her chest.

"You're not real!" Belphegor yelled, spittle flicking into Emmanuel's face. "You can't control me!"

"I am real!" Emmanuel cried, pulling on his arm. Belphegor rolled his eyes.

"I know you are," he said. Orabella narrowed her eyes and tried to push Belphegor but with one powerful swing, he lifted a leg which from his perspective had suddenly grown back, and clobbered her around the face, barely missing Emmanuel in the process. Emmanuel ducked and Belphegor grunted as with one good arm but two great legs, he heaved himself over the side.

"You all right?" Emmanuel asked.

"Daughters. Am I right?" he sighed, happily taking the hand Emmanuel offered.

Emmanuel shrugged. "I guess?" Belphegor could now see what was real and what wasn't and looked to Ebony who was cradling her knees to her chest as she cried. Her body was spasming as though she was being kicked and punched and unbeknownst to the two of them, she was. From her eyes, Belphegor and Emmanuel were two small beings in a group of millions, all converging on her.

"Ebony!" Emmanuel pinned her wrists to the floor as she tried to lash out, clawing at his face. "Ebony, look at me, it's not real!" he called but his words were lost in the screams of the mob, and she had her eyes clenched shut. She was trying to fight it, repeating to herself it was nothing but a hallucination, but the evil within Atlas was being especially cruel to her and it clung on diligently.

"Ebony," Belphegor tried. "Open your eyes; it's us." Emmanuel shut his eyes and concentrated hard, trying to worm his way into her mind but as he did, he hit an unpleasantly loud wall.

"Emmanuel?" Belphegor caught him as he fell back.

"So many voices," he gasped as his heart rate sky-rocketed. "I can't get through." He struggled to pace his breathing.

"Stop, stop," Belphegor said. "Let go before you hurt yourself." Emmanuel's face which was twisted in pain, relaxed as he ceased to push further. But it had almost been enough. Ebony opened her eyes and although to her there were other people holding her down, she could see Belphegor through the crowd.

"Belphegor?" her eyes glistened with tears. "Help. There are so many," she cried, "so many…"

"I'm here," he cooed, pulling her into a sitting position. "I've got you. They can't hurt you anymore." Suddenly, she pounced at him but not to attack. She wrapped her arms around Belphegor's neck and hugged him tightly and Belphegor, who had never had a hug before, was humbled, if a bit unsure how to react.

"You're meant to do the same back," Emmanuel whispered, receiving a harsh but fairly deserved glare. As Belphegor held her into his chest, the people around started to disappear, unable to hurt Ebony through him. He wouldn't let them.

"You're okay, I've got you."

"There were so many people," Ebony said. "So many dead."

"We know." Emmanuel tapped his head.

Belphegor helped her to her feet, and Ebony, reluctant to let go, stood with him. "Let's get out of this fog." They half jogged, half carried each other out of the fog and were greeted by Noah, who had worry plastered across his face in the form of sweat and flushed cheeks.

"Didn't think you were gonna make it for a second there," he said. "Where are Caleb and Oscar?"

"You mean they're not out yet?" Ebony lost her nerve. They hadn't seen the two of them and looking back couldn't see anyone in the thick fog.

"How is this happening?" Ebony turned to her father. "They've got to be in there somewhere, haven't they?" she asked. Atlas shrugged.

"I don't know. Normally only pure humans can be completely swallowed by the fog."

"They are pure humans!" Ebony bellowed. Atlas face palmed.

"You're joking?" he questioned rhetorically. "Humans are one hundred times more susceptible to the fog than Enchanteds are."

"So why the hell didn't you tell us?" Ebony demanded, towering over him.

"I didn't know they were pure human!" he exclaimed. "What madman brings humans into a fight against me?" Ebony clenched her fists. The lack of noise coming from the fog was a million times worse than if they were at least able to hear them. Ebony feared the worst; they could have fallen over the edge of the bridge.

"We have to go back for them."

"You can't. The more times you go into the fog the stronger its hold on you becomes," Atlas explained. "You go in now and you'll be sucked into whatever disturbing vision Caleb and Oscar are trapped in." He urged her to stay put.

"I don't care. I love the two of them and I'm not leaving them in there," she said and without further comment, she charged back into the fog.

Chapter 27

Ebony was sitting in the first-class cabin of a private passenger train. Two rows of plush grey sofas lined each wall, pressed against double glazed windows. The walls were made of a faux wooden vinyl, and a fake budding plant sat in a dry pot atop a table affixed to the ground.

Oscar was dozing, his head resting atop hers. She was engrossed in a book, until the chapter ended, and she slid the tablet into her bag. She'd been reading about the adventures of a magical group of friends. Thrilling, but wildly unbelievable. Gazing out the window, Ebony squinted as she saw a planet filling the sunrise, embellished with its cities floating in bubbles around it. They were headed to the Milky Way presidential planet, Debrene, for a science convention, sitting in a traffic jam of passenger ships queueing to get there. Suddenly, a crisp hit her head and she saw Caleb giggling foolishly with a hand over his mouth on the seats opposite them.

"What?" she laughed. She grabbed it and threw it back and he rammed it in his mouth, regardless of the fact it had landed on the floor.

"I was trying to get it in his mouth," Caleb admitted. Oscar's jaw hung open as he slept.

"Ladies, gentlemen, robots and all, we shall be landing on Debrene in twenty minutes," the captain said over the loud intercom. Settling back into her seat, Ebony wound her fingers through Oscars, and he woke to her touch, squeezing her hand.

"We're arriving soon," she informed him and he stretched out, yawning dramatically.

"I'm excited," he commented, straightening his pinstripe suit.

"For what? The award Ebony's getting or for a chance to meet sexy physicist Gloria Merika?" Caleb teased, making kissy noises as he smacked his lips together into a pout.

"Probably Gloria." Ebony laughed as Oscar nudged her in the ribs. She looked over to Caleb and he smirked but as Ebony blinked, he appeared as though he was glitching. His eye flickered rapidly at her and his other disappeared into his head. But Ebony blinked again, and Caleb faced her with a normal face and puzzled frown.

"You all right Ebony? You look like you've seen a ghost," he chuckled. She laughed along with him.

"Yeah, I'm fine," she said but she couldn't shake the feeling that something about the journey wasn't right. "Where's Stella got to?" she mentioned, noticing the empty seat beside Caleb.

"She's gone to the toilet," he said, absentmindedly fiddling with the chair seat as he waited for her to get back. "I'm going to do it you know. Ask her out this time, without being a chicken." He tapped his foot impatiently. "Where is she?" He was getting nervous, and sweat was threatening to displace his perfectly combed and overly gelled electric blue hair.

"She's probably dead," Ebony said, and her face contorted in confusion at her own random outburst. Oscar looked at her oddly.

"Say what?" Caleb asked.

"Nothing," Ebony said quickly before turning to Oscar. She panicked for a moment but put on a false smile. "I'm joking. Sorry."

"Funny," he said but a warm relief still flooded over him as Stella returned, taking her seat in a slim fitting floral dress.

"They'll be good together." Ebony watched them through the reflection in the window as Caleb nervously began to speak. The reflection was slightly off; Caleb's face looked to have a smudge over it, and she couldn't see Stella's reflection at all, but Ebony put it down to the warped angle of the glass as the train sped along.

"As good as we are," Oscar said, wrapping his arm around her shoulder. He leant over to kiss her, and she happily kissed him back, butterflies rising in her stomach. His bristly moustache tickled her upper lip and she pulled away and smiled at him. He looked weird with a moustache; rather out of place, she thought.

"Feels like the first time we've done that," she said. An absurd memory tried to push its way into the forefront of her mind.

"It's not." Oscar brushed her cheek with his fingers. "You sure you're okay?" He checked her over. "Nervous? Maybe some food will do you good." He reached for the button above his head and a server promptly appeared.

"What can I get for you today?"

"How about an arm," Ebony burst, before clapping her hands around her mouth. "Sorry, I don't quite know why I said that." She got flustered.

"It's quite all right." The server, dressed in a comical red and yellow striped shirt and matching red bow tie too looked confused. "I don't know why I checked," he said, rolling down his sleeve. "What can I get you?" He presented them with an extensive list of food and Ebony scrolled through, once whilst looking at the options but completely distracted by the server's arm, and then a second time to actually read them.

"We have to escape," the server said. Ebony's eyebrows furrowed more than she thought possible as he stared intently at her.

"What did you say?"

"I said we've got some good rates." But he was also second guessing his speech. "Stellar rates on the food…" he trailed off. "It's cheap," he clarified with a laugh.

"I'll have the peanut mellow whirl." Oscar dropped some money in the tin at the front of the cart for both him and Ebony.

"And I will have the-" she paused to think, and the server's expression changed from content to concerned, and there was a subtle but definite shift in his posture, "-the Chocotoff please."

"Of course," he said, rummaging through the cart. "Oh shoot." He clutched his stripy hat. "I haven't got any more of those on the cart but if you'd like to accompany me to the food cabin, I will get you another one."

"Sure." Ebony stood. "I'll be back in a sec." She patted Oscar's knee and followed the server out the door. The second it was closed he turned to her.

"Ebony Echnovarria," he said, pulling off the bus boy hat.

"Have we met?" she asked sweetly.

"It's me, Belphegor." Ebony cringed.

"I apologise if you're a fan of mine. Thank you, I really do appreciate it, but I don't remember everyone I meet," she admitted. "Don't worry about the Chocotoff." She reached for the door, but he put his hand on it, slamming it shut. She took a step back. In her jacket she carried a small pocketknife, and she swiftly dug her hand inside, fishing for it at the bottom of the pocket.

"I can't let you leave Ebony. This isn't real." He didn't realise how his words sounded until utterly petrified, Ebony backed up against the wall and quickly pressed an alarm module on her band. Belphegor put his hands up and softened his voice, taking a step back as Ebony raised the knife. "I'm not going to hurt you, but you need to listen. Everything around you, it's one big hallucination."

"You're crazy," she said but she doubted he was, and he sensed her doubt.

"You know I'm not." He pursed his lips. "I don't know how to get you to trust me but right now, we're inside Atlas, we're trying to get to his heart to kill him. Oscar and Caleb are with you."

"What about Stella?" Ebony asked. Belphegor looked at her with an expression of sorrow. Ebony looked at the world around her, and suddenly it didn't seem as real. She looked to the clock mounted on the wall, and for some reason couldn't read the time. Then she looked out of the window of the dreamlike train and at the sky which looked like a blurred oil painting.

"I knew she was dead," Ebony said. "I don't know why, but I knew she was dead."

"Exactly. Like you knew I only had one arm!"

"I don't know," Ebony hesitated, and Belphegor groaned in frustration.

"Ebony, Caleb and Oscar are going to die without your help. Emmanuel and Noah are counting on you to get them back."

"Noah. Emmanuel." The names lingered on Ebony's lips, and she ran her fingertips across them. She could picture their faces, but they were unfamiliar, like someone she'd bumped into once before, not old friends. Belphegor was staring at her, urgency behind his eyes, mouth twitching at the thought of what more he could say without scaring Ebony further into the illusion. His eyes flickered passed her chest, and instantly recognised the necklace she wore.

"That," he pointed. Ebony looked down.

"My necklace? It's worthless. Sentimental value only."

"No, I'm not trying to steal it," Belphegor said exasperatedly. "It's what started all this." Ebony trailed her fingers up the satin collar and touched the necklace.

"It didn't feel right. The train didn't feel right," she mumbled. "I don't remember getting on this train… I—" she gasped. "Belphegor? Why did you go back in the fog?"

"You remember?" He looked to the skies in thanks.

"Yes, I remember! Why are you here?"

"Because we were waiting for you to come back, and you didn't!" he exclaimed. "We're trapped in Oscar and Caleb's vision."

"Aren't the visions based on regret though? Surely they'd have different visions if it were the case? What do they regret about this?" Ebony said. Belphegor had already figured out the answer and he sucked his teeth as he winced.

"They regret not having a normal life." He gently touched her shoulders and pivoted her to face the window. "That would be you right now if you'd never discovered magic," Belphegor said. Ebony stared at her friends. Their smart outfits, fancy briefcases and first-class cabin suggested the success of their lives. She looked to her own satin dress and fur coat.

"I messed them up, didn't I?" Ebony regretted.

"Not you. Atlas. So, the sooner we kill him the better," Belphegor hinted.

"Right, yes, let's do it… How do we do it?"

"The fog is giving them what they want to get them to stay, so we mess it up, match the fiction to the facts," he said, "and in theory, they'll snap out of it."

"Wait. does that mean…?" Ebony trailed off. Caleb had finished ranting to Stella and they were now sitting contentedly in their seats, holding hands across the arm rest. Caleb's face was a wash of pink and he caught Ebony's eye through the glass and did a less than discreet thumbs up.

"Stella has to die, Oscar has to know you and him aren't a couple, and we have to flood this illusion with all the magic we have left," Belphegor said. "Beginning with this." He grabbed his arm and pulled hard until the fog came away and dissipated into the train air vents. His flappy sleeve was left wanting an arm to fill it.

"I don't know if I can do it."

"I know you don't want Stella to die again but it's got to be done.

Remember, it's not her," Belphegor reminded her. She didn't want to tell him that she felt it would be harder for her to tell Oscar she didn't love him than it would be to kill a version of Stella.

Ebony walked back through the glass door, signalling for Belphegor to stay put and she retook her seat by Oscar.

"Where's the Chocotoff?" he asked.

"They didn't have any in the food cabin either," she said. "Can you come with me to the other one to see if they have any?"

"Ebony, that's on the other side of the train. Can't you have something else?" Oscar sighed as she pouted her quivering lips, her eyes open wide, batting her eyelashes.

"Please?" she whimpered. Oscar shook his head with a chuckle.

"How could I say no to that face?"

"Come on," she said, tugging his wrist as she stood. He looked at her with loving eyes and followed her through the carriage. Glancing back quickly, she felt guilty as she watched Belphegor walk back through the door without the cart and stop by Caleb and Stella. The plan started promisingly but as the door closed behind them, Oscar stopped.

"Shoot, I've forgotten my change," he said, patting his pockets, "hang on a second." He circled around and Ebony had never hated anything more than the glass door connecting the carriages. It all happened too quickly to react; Oscar and Ebony watched through the glass as Belphegor grabbed Stella. He would, had he still had two hands, made a quick and painless kill with a snap of the neck, because whilst he knew it was the fog, he still didn't want to hurt a friend of Ebony's. But he didn't have the luxury, so he pushed her back in her seat, wrapped his hand around her mouth and with the power he had left, quickly sucked the air from her brain. She was dead before Caleb could even rise from his seat.

"Stella!" Oscar and Caleb both yelled, Caleb striking Belphegor across the face as he let go. Ebony grabbed Oscar and pulled him back, trying to stop him from going through the door.

"What did you do!" Caleb screamed, punching aggressively as Belphegor grabbed the spasming fog before it could rebuild itself. He put his hand against the glass which smashed under the pressure he was applying and with a strong throw, he threw Stella's body out of the window and it faded into the fake scenery as it fell. The rushing wind outside the train didn't come in. The fog didn't understand air resistance.

"Oscar!" Ebony tore her eyes away from the sight and grabbed both of his arms, dragging him away as he dug his heels into the carpet.

"We have to help. What the hell happened?" Oscar fought against her.

"It's not real Oscar, none of this is real! Stella was never here; we aren't together!" Ebony shouted in his face. Admittedly she could have been more delicate, but she didn't have the time. Oscar froze and stared at her.

"What?" he choked.

"I'm sorry to be so blunt but everything around us is an illusion, it's not real!" Ebony said. "Don't you remember? We're inside Atlas, trying to find a way to kill him!" He flung his hands to his head, door taking a beating as he kicked it angrily.

"You're insane Ebony!" He barged past and rushed into the carriage where Caleb and Belphegor were. They were both sitting silently. "You murderer!" Oscar moved in with the intent of killing Belphegor, but it was Caleb who jumped in the way, eyes sunken and blemished with redness.

"Stop!" he cried, tears staining his face. "I remember!" He lowered himself into the train seat like an old man as he rubbed his one eye dry.

"Remember what?"

"I know how much you want this to be real but it's not," Caleb told him. "Believe me, I wanted this to be real too but Stella... she's gone, and we can't get out of this illusion until you realise everything around us right now is a lie." His speech was brief, and he ripped at his nails anxiously as he spoke.

"Oscar, please believe us," Ebony said.

"Why would I want to?" he asked. "Why would I want to believe that?" Ebony didn't know what to say. The awkward pause was filled by Belphegor.

"We need to leave."

"Oscar, I love you as a best friend and I couldn't imagine my life without you but I'm sorry. I wish I could give you what you want," Ebony said, "but I don't love you," she reiterated, hoping he would wake up. He stared at her blankly and she raised her voice, "I don't lo—" he cut her off.

"--I remember. You don't have to say it again," he said quietly. A single tear trailed down his cheek as the illusion around them faded, the malevolent fog retreating as it lost its final grip on them. It didn't take long for their old surroundings to take hold and the bridge appeared beneath their feet, instead of the carpeted floors of the first-class cabin.

They rushed through the remaining fog and breathed a collective sigh of relief as they felt the bounce of muscle beneath their feet. Noah and Emmanuel greeted them with jubilation, Atlas with the temperament of a mother watching her naughty children.

"Can we all agree to stay together this time?" Noah requested as they were all reunited.

"Whatever. Let's get this done." Oscar barged passed his smiling face, hitting his shoulder as he stormed off and breaking Noah's one request immediately.

"What's his problem?" Emmanuel asked.

"Don't ask," Ebony advised. "Atlas, where now?"

"Onwards and upwards as they say," he said. "We have a climb ahead, through Atlas' lungs and then into his heart." He caught up with Oscar who was conveniently headed in the right direction. "But the fog was like the barbed wire before the landmines," he metaphorized.

It was a long and harsh walk between where they were and where they were going, and the endless dark and fleshy walls drained the spirit from everyone. Noah decided to start a conversation in his boredom. He turned to Belphegor who had spent the entirety of their walk staring at his arm and wishing for it to reappear.

"Who is descended from who?" he asked. "Is there a way of knowing?"

Belphegor tucked his lip between his teeth as he thought and went to scratch his ear with the arm that wasn't there. "It's hard to tell since there are so many abilities. But I assume the Enchanteds who have our most powerful traits are definitely related to whoever the magic correlates to."

"So, what were your best powers?"

"My speciality was mind reading," he said, "to the extent I could control what people saw, control things with my mind and see what people saw. Atlas' was necromancy and energy manipulation and Adremelech was a skilled elemental and teleporter."

"Nice," Emmanuel commented.

"Shit," Noah said.

"Don't even go there," Ebony said to Noah.

"Fair."

"So, Emmanuel, you're probably one of mine," Belphegor said to him proudly. Emmanuel nearly blushed, proud of his heritage even if the others weren't so much and Belphegor smiled. They finally seemed to be getting along.

Chapter 28

No one was worried about walking into unexpected company whilst headed through Atlas' body. It wasn't the kind of place where one expected to bump into someone they knew. Thus it came as quite the surprise when they did.

"Ebony, Belphegor, worthless vermin," a voice hissed out of the blue. "Wherever you think you're going, you won't make it there," it threatened, stopping everyone in their tracks.

"Who the hell is calling me worthless vermin?" Caleb was instantly pissed off.

"Who are you? Atlas?" Ebony asked and the voice cackled.

"You take me for such a low life? He is nothing," it hinted, "although he shows more initiative than you, Belphegor." Belphegor growled.

"Atlas, do you know who this is?" Ebony asked. Atlas was leading them through several pathways; he was unusually quiet and refused to answer Ebony's question as he buried his head in his shoulders, pulling the hat down over his eyebrows.

"Atlas may own the exterior of his meat suit but in here, you're mine. And as much as I would love to see Atlas dead across the floor, I can't have you shoving the sword through his heart."

"Why not?" Ebony asked.

"Because, due to your negligence of responsibility, he's the one keeping me alive," it bellowed, winds barrelling down the tunnel as its rage swept by. Ebony gulped as she finally put the voice to a name.

"Sonneillon?" She wouldn't have been so afraid had Belphegor not yelped and taken a cowardly step back.

"Hello darling. And Belphegor," he sniggered. "Whilst I appreciate you are Enchanteds, and a pitiful excuse for an Ancient, I have grown to learn that the universe has become… infested." He chose his words carefully. "Overrun with the disease that is humanity, and my descendants have done nothing but watch as they have been forced to hide their power in the shadows. This universe needs to be purified, cleansed of the disease and rebuilt."

"Kill us and rebuild the world?" Ebony said fearfully.

"Kill you myself? It's not worth the time of day. I've created a warding; call it insurance, around whatever life source I possess to finish you for me. Try reaching Atlas' heart if you wish but you'll have to face an emotional, physical and mental challenge to do so." If they could see Sonneillon they knew he'd be smiling. "None of you will make it," he said. "So, enjoy your final moments. I'll be watching."

His voice stopped.

"What the hell was that?" Emmanuel whined. "Atlas, what challenges is he talking about?"

"His emotional challenge is the fog we just cleared. But I'm unaware of what else Sonneillon has in store for us."

"But I still don't understand how all of this is inside Atlas. He's been supersized for what? An hour?" Oscar said, "and all of a sudden, he's got rope bridges and conscious evil beings inside him? It makes no sense."

"Evil doesn't have a specific size, neither does conscience," Atlas said. "I've lived here for millennia, the rope bridge back there was made by me longer ago than I care to admit," he explained. "The creatures are simply evil entities taking on whatever form they want, some of which are unexplainable creatures. If you could change your permanent form into something stronger, wouldn't you?"

"I guess," Oscar said. Atlas chose to end the conversation as he turned away. The presence of Sonneillon had reduced him to a shaking shell of a man, and even Belphegor was silent.

They continued walking. The passage was narrow and the ground uneven, designed to trip up and injure those who found themselves inside. But barely fifty paces following Sonneillon's threats, Caleb faltered.

"Uh, guys," he stalled.

"What's wrong?"

"I can't see." He tried to remain calm but there was a cold dread behind his voice as it hitched in his throat.

"What?"

"My eye. It's gone out." He stumbled forward a step, his arms stretched out in front of him and fingers twitching as they searched for something. Ebony grabbed him and he flinched because he didn't see her coming.

"You can't see at all?" she asked, looking into his cyber eye. It had dulled completely, and the pupil had a miniature red error sign cast across it.

"Nothing."

"How are we going to guide him through this blindly?" Emmanuel feared.

"He can go on my shoulders," Oscar offered.

"Terrain isn't going to be easy," Emmanuel said, peeking around the corner they'd come to. "We've reached Atlas' lungs." Helping Caleb take a few steps forward as he clung to Ebony, they appeared in a thin stretch of room. Barely five metres in width, but in length and height it was impossible to see the end. It was Atlas' lungs. The waving motion they made and accompanying echoing noise was sickening, drilling into everyone's head and causing bouts of sea sickness as they watched it. Belphegor looked up at the towering rib cage soaring above them and rested his remaining hand on his hip.

"Up there?"

"Unless his heart has fallen through the floor," Atlas said sarcastically. Belphegor gave a passive aggressive side glance.

"I'm too old for this," he remarked, grabbing a dingy lung with a hand, and swinging skilfully. Atlas' lungs looked like he'd smoked ten packs a day since birth and whilst it was repulsive to cling on to, the tar coated rot gave good handholds to use. But Belphegor didn't get far before he stopped, dangled momentarily and dropped to the floor.

"I can't," he said. "I can't climb this with one arm."

"And how can we expect Caleb to climb it?" Noah said.

"Wait-" Caleb's eye flickered briefly and for a couple of seconds his nose crinkled as he grinned, "-I can see!"

"Really?" But his eye flickered off again and he groaned.

"Nope."

Ebony punched the lung furiously. "What do we do?"

"Leave me and Caleb here?" Belphegor suggested.

"No!" There was a unanimous agreement.

"I think not," Caleb said. "I'm not the self-sacrificing type."

"We'll get you both up there. We just have to work out how." Ebony tapped her chin and after a moment's pondering, cogs whirring in her head to create a plan, clicked her fingers. "Noah, give me the sword."

"Here." He removed it from its snug position inside his trouser leg. Ebony turned to her uncle.

"Hold still." She pushed it inside the remaining shirt material and paused. "Anyone have anything to tie it?" she asked and a couple of belts were unbuckled. But Caleb blindly rummaged through his rucksack from which he hauled a length of rope.

"Will this do?" He dropped it, thinking Ebony's hands were ready to catch.

"Why do you even have that?" Ebony asked and he shrugged but before she could pick it up, Atlas stepped in and pushed the hilt of the sword against Belphegor's arm. Belphegor hissed as the smell of burning filled his nostrils, and a strange sensation gripped his elbow like someone was tugging on his funny bone.

"It's in," Atlas said.

"In?" Belphegor repeated. He turned back the sleeve and the sword was sticking out of his arm like a cutlass. He swung it. Mild concern diminished to childish glee as it sliced the heavy air.

Belphegor charged at the lung again and this time scaled it effortlessly, using his good arm to pull himself up and the sword to hold his position.

"That's one of us sorted. What about Caleb?" he asked. Without Caleb realising, they all turned to him.

"I can fix the eye to an extent," Atlas announced.

Ebony didn't trust him to touch Caleb, but Caleb's trust was unwavering.

"Anything that helps."

Atlas nodded.

"I said anything that helps," Caleb repeated.

"I nod- oh. Sorry." Atlas pointed a dirty finger at his eye and the technology slowly came back to life, forced into rebooting by Atlas' power.

"Thanks man," Caleb said.

"Careful," Atlas warned as he cheered up. "I'm not strong enough to fix you completely. Your eye will stay on for longer but will have to shut down for a minute every so often to recharge. It's the best I can do."

Caleb shrugged. "It's better than it was."

"Thank you, brother." Belphegor touched Atlas' shoulder and he beamed at the compliment.

They began the ascent.

The throbbing lungs made climbing terrifying; they pulsated like a vertical trampoline, attempting to throw off anything that held on to them. Every so often there was a welcome break as they reached a rib and Ebony paused once with Caleb as his eye recharged, but they were driven by the idea that the longer they took, the more chance there was for something to go horrendously wrong. Hardly a word was exchanged between them except the occasional, 'do you need a hand?' or 'are you okay?' as they fatigued.

"This is exhausting." Emmanuel dropped onto a rib.

"It wouldn't be a physical challenge if we weren't struggling," Ebony said, trying to be light-hearted. Emmanuel swung his legs a little as they sat for a moment on the discoloured rib. The others were ahead by a little way, being shepherded up by Belphegor.

"You all right down there?" he asked.

"We're fine," Ebony called, before turning back to Emmanuel. "I think he's pretty chuffed to have you as a descendant," she commented.

"I'd rather have an ancestor like him than like you."

"Ouch," Ebony joked. As she watched Emmanuel get back to climbing she drooped her head to look how far they'd come. They were about half-way and Ebony couldn't see the bottom at all. What she could see though was movement, which she was certain hadn't been there before.

"Emmanuel." She gripped his scrawny ankle before he could get any further and he stopped.

"What is that?" he asked, looking straight past her. There was something rising upwards from the darkness, clawing at the lungs as though it was climbing in a humanlike form. Emmanuel immediately held out his hand.

"Ebony, come on." She took his hand, giving her a bit of a boost upwards. "Guys!" he called upwards. "Keep moving, we've got company," and of course they did the complete opposite, all pausing in curiosity to look. Glitching entities, raven black in colour and of a multitude of shapes and limbs were crawling up the lung with absolute ease.

"It's the evil!" Atlas yelled. "Don't let it take you!"

"Go!" Ebony ordered and they began to climb again. But climbing fast wasn't climbing safe and as they went, Noah misplaced a foot and as he reached a hand to the next fleshy outcrop he slipped.

"Noah!"

Belphegor reached down reflexively to try and grab him but the only arm he had free was the one with the sword and as Noah reached out, the sword sliced through his hand, deep into his palm. He went plummeting down and if it wasn't for Emmanuel and Ebony below who had jumped back onto the rib to catch him, he would have fallen the whole way. It would have been the end of Noah.

"Pull him up!" Ebony yelled as she held onto his shirt. Her and Emmanuel tugged and heaved him successfully onto the rib, but they weren't out of the water by a long stretch. Ebony grabbed his hand, held in an awkward claw shape as Noah tried to ease the pain, and tried to heal the cut. Tiny compared to what she'd healed before, it didn't work.

"I can't heal him!" Ebony called, struggling the same as when Atlas had scraped her stomach.

"You can't heal a wound caused by the sword of Sonneillon," Belphegor said.

"Noah, can you climb?" she asked but it was a brainless question. His hand was bleeding profusely, and he could barely wiggle his fingers. The nerves were damaged, completely severed in places.

"That would be a no," he said, the pallor of his skin showing through his blushed cheeks.

"I have rope," Caleb called as Noah cradled his hand. He too jumped onto the rib, and it bowed under the pressure. "Tie this around you. We'll pull you up," he said, acknowledging that the idea was hairbrained with a shrug but reaching for the rope anyway.

The evil was closing in.

He unwound it from his shoulder and Noah fastened it round his waist. Ebony took one side, Caleb took the other and they tied it around themselves too as Emmanuel headed off to the others.

"Let's see if this works," Ebony said and her and Caleb started to climb. Noah used his feet and one hand to stabilise himself, but he kept his other hand tucked firmly under his armpit. Ebony winced but hid the strain as she pulled. Caleb too, struggled with the strenuous effort; the pain grew as the rope rubbed on his back where new and tender flesh grew.

"We'll get you up," he grunted, tensing against the rope.

"Guys hurry!" Oscar said, staring with wide eyes. The evil was climbing the walls at nearly double the speed they were, and it looked hungry, salivating with appetite as it grew closer.

"Atlas how far is it?" Ebony called.

"Not much further." Ebony fought determinedly; clutching the lung and refusing to yield despite the ache of her muscles.

Then a yell from below made her stop and look back. The evil had caught up to Noah. He thrashed about and Ebony and Caleb grunted against his weight as he dangled in mid-air to defend himself. He didn't look heavy but Noah was muscular and came close to weighing the same as Ebony and Caleb combined.

"Belphegor, the sword," Ebony called and without a moment's hesitation he jumped from above them, using the blade to slash down the lung and slow himself. Noah yelped as his foot was yanked downwards but as Belphegor reached him, he rammed the sword into the evil and it screeched, falling into the inky darkness. He stayed below, climbing parallel to Noah to prevent the attack but the evil soared past them until it was climbing on top of the others too. Emmanuel hollered as one grabbed his hair and yanked his neck back with an unsatisfying click, but he clung on for dear life and Atlas kicked it off with his boot.

Ebony shouted from below. The evil was targeting her especially; she was Sonneillon's biggest threat and he couldn't have her surviving. It pulled on the rope around her, dragging her past Noah's feet and as a result pulling Noah with her, Belphegor who was fighting on his behalf and Caleb who was now the only thing holding the two of them above the precipice.

"Caleb, pull us up!"

"I can't!" he replied with a screech, digging his nails firmly into the flesh. "I can't see." His dull eye stared unseeingly into the lung as he strained against the pressure of two people. He lifted a hand and tried to climb sightlessly but couldn't find a sturdy hold without risking falling and taking Noah and Ebony with him. His body shook and his grip was feeble, more so as the rope between him and Ebony was mauled.

The evil wasn't mindless like Zombies, or incapable of free will like SIDs, or unable to form a coherent thought like the Magma men, and they knew that the thin rope was the quickest way to Ebony's demise.

But Belphegor wasn't about to let that happen as he approached Noah. "Climb on." He turned his back and Noah grabbed his shoulders, tucking his legs around his waist like a small child. With unfathomable strength and agility, Belphegor began to climb as though there was nothing on his back. As he soared up the side, Ebony was pulled with them and Oscar cut the rope between her and Caleb so he could climb quickly before he lost his sight again. In a thin line along the lung, they climbed in unison, stabbing and punching evil as they slaughtered it. There was no mercy for the entities who would show no mercy themselves.

"Above the next rib there's the pulmonary vein," Atlas announced. "Once we climb in, we're going to have to swim until we find the heart."

"How long does it take?" Ebony asked.

"Three minutes of strong, fast swimming," Atlas said.

"It's impossible," Noah said from Belphegor's back. "We've been climbing for forever, we're already out of breath."

"You can talk," puffed Belphegor.

"He's right though," Oscar said.

"Belphegor and I aren't completely drained," Ebony said as she swung away from an incoming evil and smashed its head into the lung with her elbow, "but I have another idea."

"Now's the time to share," Atlas urged. Sitting on a ledge to their right was the cylindrical opening of the vein. In sync, everyone moved diagonally towards it.

"Noah, how much power you got left for a portal?" Noah clicked his fingers thrice before a small portal sparked. It wasn't much, about the size of a matchbox leading to the bottom of the lungs.

"About this much."

"How many can you muster up?" Noah focused and managed one more before the third one dissipated all three.

"Two."

"Belphegor, how many?" He conjured two. Ebony produced the same and a third, identical to Noah, was too much and caused a chain reaction which destroyed all three.

"What's the point of this?" Belphegor asked.

"We need a way to breathe. We use the portals as oxygen tanks. It might just work."

"'Might' being the operative word," Belphegor said. "We only have six."

"So, we share. No one gets left behind," Noah said as they reached the hole. Looking in, they saw a well of inky blood.

"We're swimming in that?" Emmanuel gagged. "Exceptional."

"Be thankful it's not the colon," Atlas said. "I don't remember the last time a vegetable passed through there." Emmanuel's face contorted in disgust, but he still wasn't convinced the vein was a better option.

"I'm so glad I can't see," Caleb commented. His eye had gone out again as they reached the top; Noah had a hand on his shoulder to help him balance.

"I don't want to," Emmanuel groaned but as an evil grabbed his foot and he kicked it in the jaw, he changed his mind.

"I'll take Emmanuel," Noah said.

"I've got Caleb and Oscar," Ebony bagsied, and Belphegor sighed, looking at Atlas reluctantly.

"Fine." He dipped a toe in the blood and stuck his tongue out in disgust, but the evil hadn't stopped chasing them and the only way was forward. "See you lot on the other side," he said and the two of them took the first plunge into the blood.

"That's disgusting," Noah said as they disappeared into the opaque gloop. He looked to his slashed-open hand and back to the blood. The diseases he feared were uncountable. He flinched as the blood sloshed around.

"We've come this far." Emmanuel patted him on the back with vigour and he slipped in.

"You asshole!" Noah yelled as he surfaced, blood coating his face.

He wiped it from his eyes as Emmanuel jumped in next to him, spilling more over his head. "I might actually let you drown now. I'm tempted," Noah warned as he flailed. With a deep breath taken, they disappeared too.

"Right, you two, in," Ebony commanded.

She felt disgusting.

The blood was thick and tacky and large blood clots from the oxygenated blood were coagulating in several floating buoy-like masses.

"Caleb, you get your own portal," she said, creating one by his mouth. "If your eyesight goes again whilst we're in there, the portal will still be in front of your mouth."

"Thanks."

"Oscar, you and I are sharing," Ebony said. Caleb's eyesight returned and he grimaced at the blood, preferring to go in blind, but with the evil behind them there was no time to waste and the three of them dived.

Swimming in water with clothes was hard enough but swimming in blood was debilitating. The thick liquid pushed back against their limbs. Blood wasn't meant to be swam in.

Their sight became massively impaired. Ebony tapped Oscar and could see the outline of a thumbs up, so she stuck her nose inside the portal, breathing deeply before giving it back to him. They continued in this cycle, Ebony looking back every so often to see if Caleb was all right. His illuminated eye made it easier to keep track of him. It all seemed to be going as well as swimming through an artery could until...

"That's cheating."

Sonneillon's voice vibrated through the liquid.

Ebony turned her head erratically and stretched her limbs as she felt for Caleb and Oscar, not wanting to lose either of them with a presence like Sonneillon's lurking nearby. A pressure mounted on her brain and she squealed, squeezing her mouth firmly shut as she was unable to hold the portals open.

"You better hurry," Sonneillon said. "I've heard that drowning can be rather painful." Ebony yanked at Caleb's shirt as Oscar swam in front, body working overtime to make the heart. She looked back. Caleb's eye was still on and he batted his hand at her, telling her to keep going.

As they swam in utter terror, Ebony saw a shoe in front of her and swam alongside the body.

Oscar had stopped.

She prodded his ribs but he was out cold; she was the one who had had the portal before Sonneillon had stolen it and so Oscar hadn't taken a breath in too long. She snaked her arm around his chest and heaved, forcing herself not to breathe. She felt as though her lungs were collapsing and her muscles were stripped of their strength. She banged on the side of the vein to see if it was weak enough to break through, but it was tough skin and muscle. Before she knew it, the desperation was too much and with a huge scream, she breathed out and quickly held her nose to prevent herself from breathing back in.

Behind her, Caleb was scrabbling at her feet. His eye was dull. He couldn't see and didn't know where to go. Bubbles were shooting from his nose.

Ebony kept swimming to where she thought she'd seen a foot leave the blood. Odds stacked against them, she swam and clung onto Oscar as he began to hypoxically convulse, his body searching for oxygen whilst he was unconscious. Dark spots formed around her vision and the more she blinked, the darker the world became until everything was a red blur.

Unable to hold on any longer, Ebony did the worst thing she could and breathed in deeply through her nose. It burnt as blood flooded her windpipe and lungs and she choked into the blood. But as she shut her eyes someone grabbed her, and she glided through the blood until her and Oscar were dragged upwards and into the air.

Ebony rolled onto her stomach and vomited blood onto the floor, choking as Noah wiped her hair from her face.

"Breathe. Breathe," he willed. She put her head on the cold floor as she gasped for air. Her mouth was filled with the disgusting taste of warm metal, and she smelt of rust as her clothes sagged with the weight of the blood.

"Caleb!" Belphegor dived back into the blood and hauled Caleb out as he swam past, unable to see that he had missed the exit. He crawled across the dry land, coughing as his body tried to take in oxygen faster than he could keep up with.

Oscar was unresponsive.

His body was no longer convulsing, and he had froth spilling from his mouth.

Ebony tried to rush over to him, but her arms and legs gave way before she could even stand. "Oscar, wake up," she pled as she crawled over.

"C'mon Oscar." Belphegor and Emmanuel were leaning over him. Caleb sat nearby, shivering and staring in shock as his eye came on. Atlas stood back; the concept of grief foreign but it playing on his mind that he should be sad.

"Wake up boy." Belphegor began chest compressions, pushing hard enough to crack a rib as he tried to resuscitate him. He paused for a moment, opening Oscar's mouth, and blowing air into him. When his lungs didn't accept the air, he resorted to back to chest compressions.

But Oscar didn't move. He lay there, fingers blue from hypothermia and Caleb weakly pulled off his jacket and put it over Oscar's legs to keep him warm.

The compressions weren't working.

Belphegor leant back. "Everyone let go of him," he said, and Caleb and Emmanuel removed their hands. "This might sting a little," he apologised, before hovering his hand over Oscar's chest. His hand crackled and a bolt of lightning shot from it into Oscar and for a second his body flared up in a silver lustre beneath his skin. The small strike caused his body to lurch, but he fell back limply.

"Come on Oscar." Ebony's tears soaked Noah's blood-stained shirt as she cried into his shoulder, clinging onto his arm. "You're not allowed to leave me." Belphegor tried again, lightning sparking around his body as it shot through him.

It worked.

With a ferocious cough, Oscar's body shuddered, and he took a deep breath before a mixture of blood and water spewed from his mouth. For the second time, Oscar had drowned and been brought back from near death.

"There you go." Belphegor gently rolled him on his side as he clutched at his throat.

"Oscar, you scared us," Emmanuel said, rubbing his back soothingly. Ebony sat back on her heels, hands in a prayer position against her forehead. She hadn't the words, but relief beamed through her toothy smile. She turned to Caleb who's knobbly knees were knocking against each other. He tried to stop the shaking by squeezing them to his chest, processing the ordeal. Ebony rested a supportive hand on his knee, and he smiled, grateful that for the moment he could see her.

"Belphegor, you used magic in here," Noah commented. "You think you could warm us up a little?" he requested, pulling at his clothes. He tried to wipe his bloody hands on his jeans but pulled them away with more blood and a newfound hatred of soggy denim.

"Here." Belphegor sparked a flame. Ebony added to it. Atlas, who hadn't spoken since before the tunnel tried to make a flame too, but the stronger Atlas, the real, wicked Atlas got, the less his conscience could do.

"We've got one challenge left," Atlas said, as they all huddled around the flame, Oscar particularly quiet as he thanked every breath for leaving his body. "But I don't think I'm going to make it." He rubbed his hands together and Ebony noticed the flaking skin. It was as though he was slowly melting away. He hid his hands from his own sight, pretending it wasn't happening. An obscure malaise surrounded him, and he could only guess as to why.

"Why not?"

"Atlas' malice grows forever stronger," he said. "Think of his goodness and evil as a percentage. As his evil grows his conscience shrinks. I'm down to the final one percent."

From nowhere and everywhere, someone began to clap.

"Who would have thought? Atlas had brains beneath that thick skull," Sonneillon hissed. Ebony stood, the drying blood crackling as her clothes stretched out with her movement.

"I don't see what you're so happy about, Sonneillon. We're beating you." Sonneillon laughed and the noise concentrated from an unknown location to, for the first time, a physical manifestation in front of them. Ebony could finally put a face to the voice, and his presence alone made him ten times more horrifying. If she'd seen him before speaking, she never would have opened her mouth.

Towering over even Belphegor, his robes hugged the ground that sizzled beneath each acidic step. He was swathed in a toxic green aura that clung to his skin, pale like a body drained of blood, and he had an uncanny valley about him that made his appearance unsettling.

The first noticeable unhuman thing about him were his fingers. A second set of knuckles allowed his spindly fingers to bend forwards and then backwards, and when he pressed them together his pointed fingernails curled backwards towards the back of his hands. His mouth was abnormally wide and when he grinned it opened to the corner of his eyes, something Noah had witnessed in his hallucinogenic apparitions. And finally, his hairless face was waxy, like a doll's, and the few hairs that he had rose like wires from his head, unbending and thickened.

Needless to say, everyone scooted backwards and away from him.

Ebony gulped but he wasn't so interested in her as he was Belphegor. Belphegor had a predisposition to bow in Sonneillon's presence, but he was no longer the Ancient that showed Sonneillon allegiance. He ran at him, unconcerned by the fanged mouth that curled into a cocky smile. As Belphegor's hand went around Sonneillon's neck, Sonneillon disappeared and reappeared on the other side of the room.

"You're in my domain now." He turned to Atlas who was busy burying himself amongst the fleshly walls in an attempt to evade attention. Sonneillon shook his head, hair stiff to the movement. "Atlas no longer has need for a conscience." A finger coiled back and with a bolt of unidentifiable energy, he shot a hole through Atlas' heart. No one rushed to help but everyone stared. Atlas dropped to one knee and welcomingly splayed his arms.

"Thank you," he breathed.

Like dust in the wind, he flaked away.

"Well, now." Sonneillon tapped his fingers together. "The angel has fallen off the shoulder." He clapped in a disgustingly upbeat mood.

Ebony seized her eyes away from the spot where her dead father had vanished and looked at Sonneillon. "You won't win," she threatened. With enough anger to resist the pain, Belphegor ripped from his arm the sword. He passed it to Ebony and slowly healed the hole, solidifying his loyalty to her as his eyes locked with Sonneillon's. She took it, wielding it aggressively and took a step forward. Sonneillon laughed cruelly at Ebony as though she was a toddler threatening him with a lollypop.

"I must admit, your abundance of life grieves me," he said, "but

339

don't believe you'll survive. Hope is for the ignorant." He bowed and snarled with a wide rack of fangs before disappearing. Ebony rushed forward to stab him but hit the stale, empty air.

"Shit!" she swore, stabbing the wall with the sword.

"Ugly asshole," Oscar mumbled from the ground, his first word since being revived.

"Bloody hell." Belphegor cradled his arm, letting the pain show.

"What a twat." Noah stretched his body out towards where Sonneillon had disappeared to check he wasn't still there.

"Without Atlas, how are we meant to know which way to go?" Ebony asked.

"Follow the noise?" Emmanuel said.

"What noise?" Ebony tilted her head to the side and bashed her ear, trying to get the blood clots out. She didn't realise how little she could hear until the blood dislodged and fell out with a smattering from the puddle coating her leg. She could suddenly hear a throbbing from nearby.

"Huh, he actually does have a heart," she said sarcastically. Oscar stuck his finger in his ear, wiggling it around until he too could also hear.

"God it's loud."

"It's because we're already in the heart," Belphegor said, "but we're not in the right atrium. This doesn't look very 'final frontier'-esque."

"So, we need to be in the right atrium?" Caleb asked.

"No, we need to be in the left one." Belphegor and Ebony exchanged a confused glance.

"The left one."

"Yes," Belphegor said. "This way."

Chapter 29

Noah fell into step beside Oscar. The hallway was just wide enough for the two of them and Ebony to walk in a line, but for no one else, so when Caleb squeezed in front of them, Ebony cringed as she was pressed up against the slimy, fleshy wall.

"So, I hate to bring down the mood-" Caleb walked backwards whilst his eyesight enabled him to, "-but what could be worse than what we've already dealt with?" he questioned, mournfully mentioning the task ahead.

Clowns. Nothing worse than clowns.

"Seriously?" Emmanuel said, joining him.

"What?" Caleb asked.

"You think it's going to be clowns?" he chuckled. Caleb shuddered at the word, rubbing the nape of his neck.

"I hate clowns," he admitted.

"I was thinking the same," Emmanuel joked kindly. They looked at each other and Caleb looked away, blushing.

"Could be," Ebony fuelled. "Lots of big scary clowns coming to kill you." She grabbed Caleb and he whined like a puppy.

"Not fair," he grumbled. They were, of course, joking but as they entered the left atrium, he stopped in his tracks. "Did you hear that?"

"What?"

"It sounded like a creepy clown laugh," Caleb said and everyone instantly relaxed.

"Har, har," Ebony said but he was still rigid.

"It's not a joke." He was on edge, huddling closer to Ebony who held the sword protectively in front of his chest for his comfort. He kept looking around fearfully, his lack of one and sometimes two eyes and limited peripheral vision causing him to jolt at every shadow.

"I guess that's what needs stabbing?" He turned as Emmanuel pointed upwards. Above them, a seething mass of black energy floated, enveloping the ceiling. Ebony felt the sword physically pulling her towards it. The hilt was trembling, almost painful to the touch and the heart reacted, black tendrils extending across the room.

"Sword thinks so." Ebony holstered it in her belt.

"How do we get there?" Belphegor asked. "Because if we have to climb one more thing, I might lose it."

"Portal?" Noah answered. He tried to summon one, but it didn't work. Not a single ounce of magic. He hugged his own shoulders for comfort. "The final challenge."

Ebony tied to be confident. "Everything will be fine."

…

Everything was not fine.

"What the hell…" Oscar's voice faded away as he stared ahead. "Is that a… clown?" He peered into the darkness.

"Don't. Even. Joke." Caleb's eyes tracked to where Oscar was looking. There, in the shadows, was the distinct outline of a man. He had balloons floating above his head and comically large clown shoes tapping the floor. Caleb barely stayed standing. As he walked closer, the ghastly white makeup and smudged red lipstick of the clown could be seen. An overly swollen nose produced an out of tune honk as the clown squeezed it.

"Am I seeing this right?" Caleb lifted his eyepatch. "How is that possible?" Emmanuel clutched his arm but didn't stand bravely in the face of danger for long.

"Shit." He was looking in the opposite direction and they turned to discover what he was looking at.

"What is that?" Belphegor asked.

"A spider," Emmanuel said. "I absolutely hate spiders," he shuddered, "and the smell of them too apparently." He buried his nose into his forearm as an overwhelmingly putrid smell filled their nostrils. Belphegor was the only one who took the opportunity to sniff the odour.

"He's using pheromones," he realised. "He's inducing fear amongst us."

"So, the mental challenge is fighting our fears?" Emmanuel panicked, "because I don't think I can do that." He trembled as spiders poured out of the side of the room. They were huge, legs the size of people; bodies the size of elephants and although it was predominantly

Emmanuel's fear, the others weren't exactly thrilled. "How come you get one small clown and I get a hundred huge spiders?" he groaned.

"I didn't know you had a hundred huge spiders," Caleb complained, "because this eye has got the greatest timing in the world!" He screamed as it turned off for what felt like the millionth time.

"I don't know what my fear could be," Belphegor said, racking his brains. "I don't scare easily."

"Whose fear is that?" Noah asked, looking past the clown. A hollow growl and loud footstep vibrated the ground beneath everyone, and a hound stood forward. Again, fifty times bigger than it should have been and with three times the head, it scared everyone despite only being for one of them.

"Of course," Belphegor mumbled.

"What the hell is it?" Caleb yelled blindly; arms stiff in front of him like a zombie.

"Cerberus. The dog that guards the gates of hell. It was the only thing preventing my escape for eons," he said. "The only thing demons feared when trying to escape was this dog and its pack." Ebony had seen Belphegor frightened before, but she had never seen him physically hunch his shoulders, save for being in the presence of Sonneillon, as the dog growled.

"Hate to point it out, but we're being surrounded," Oscar warned. "Magma men." He pointed fearfully into the shadows.

"Seriously? Magma men?" Caleb interjected. It was Noah's opportunity to crease in fear.

"I can't stand those things." Oscar was fully intent on supporting him with a firm hand on the shoulder, but he was too busy being terrified to find out what his fear was. And then it came at them, like a demon from above and Noah cried out and ducked as what looked like a snake descended upon them. None of them recognised it except for Oscar and Ebony, and Belphegor who watched in shock.

"Is that a kraken?" Belphegor asked. "I haven't seen one of these since I was last alive," he stuttered.

"A kraken!" Caleb shrieked.

"Ebony and I fought one on Ignis and barely escaped," Oscar said.

"And you never thought to mention that?" Caleb was close to tearing his hair out.

"I tried to tell you, but you thought I was having a laugh, remember?" Oscar reminded him. It's all too familiar orange eyes fixated on him, and it let out a rabid roar.

"I take it back. I love spiders," Emmanuel said.

"Ebony, where's your fear?" Oscar asked but she wasn't the one who answered him.

"I've been here all along," Atlas said. She whipped round and he smiled at her. No longer the weak Atlas that had helped them, the Atlas that was currently destroying Tcheeva stood in front of her, re-gifted his red eyes.

"Of course it's you," she sighed, lightly bouncing from side to side as she balled her hands into tight fists and raised them to her chest.

"Of course it's who? I wish I could see this," Caleb cried and on cue, his eye lit up. He spun 360 degrees and the colour was bleached from his face. "I take it back. I take it back."

"How do we fight this?" Emmanuel asked as the spiders began to web across the ceiling.

"Once I would have said only one of us needs to get to the top," Belphegor said, "but now I say, no man left behind."

"Pair off," Ebony added. "We can fight these things easier if we're not fighting everything at once." She looked around. "This is the final sprint. We can do this."

"Good luck everyone." Emmanuel bowed his head. "Don't get killed."

There was a second of silence before chaos ensued.

"Go!" Ebony roared and everything in the room moved. Caleb grabbed Emmanuel. With huge courage they bolted towards the clown, who was a lot less threatening than the spiders.

"Ebony, how do we defeat them?" Noah asked. Ebony watched as the all too familiar smouldering holes appeared on the ground and Noah leapt out of the path of a Magma man.

"Normally I'd flip them over, but something tells me they'll keep coming back this time."

"Brilliant."

Belphegor, who's fondness for humans had grown considerably, grabbed Oscar and took off at a sprint towards the heart, avoiding the tentacles of the kraken as it fought with a vengeance. "How did you kill it last time?" he asked, flinching at the barks of the dog on their tail.

"With the help of a self-destructive ship and absolute potluck."

"Great," Belphegor said, pessimistically sarcastic.

"Do we have to kill every single fear?" Noah asked, as he and Ebony too tumbled inelegantly beneath the kraken's tentacles.

"I don't think the challenge is going to end unless we do," Ebony said, veering to their left. There was a fleshy muscle acting as a bridge upwards and they took it. Ebony now had a bird's eye view on the arena below them.

Belphegor and Oscar had opted for the same tactic as them but on the other side of the arena, running across the side of the muscles. Cerberus followed. It was admittedly cute, with giant padded paws nearly too big for its body and fur so fluffy it was as though Satan had shampooed him before sending him Belphegor's way. But the ghostly blue collar it wore was sharply studded, and its barbed teeth were filed to a bladed point the width of a piece of paper. Its eyes were a ferocious white with the image of Belphegor stained in them. It wasn't there for a game of fetch and cuddles.

Caleb and Emmanuel had taken the risk of attacking the clown, who towered over them like a giant. But it wasn't hard to kill him. Whilst Caleb remained a step behind Emmanuel, Emmanuel whipped out a knife and for the first time since they'd been inside Atlas, he aimed it at something which it would actually kill and threw it. The clown stared, blood spilling from its mouth and into the twisted lipstick smile, and it almost took a second to recognise that a knife had flown through its brains. It took a step forward and Emmanuel and Caleb feared for a moment it hadn't worked but the giant clown fell into the muscle tissue, lying there lifelessly.

"Finally, something that dies and stays dead!" Emmanuel cried as they ran past and Caleb paused, only momentarily, to kick the clown. As he did, he kicked a concealed horn and it honked loudly. Caleb hopped back and yelped and scowled as Emmanuel chuckled.

"They've killed the clown," Oscar noted from above. "Any chance Cerberus dies from a knife wound too?" Belphegor looked at him.

"Unfortunately, not," he said, "but we do have one advantage."

"Which is?"

"You."

"I beg your pardon?" Oscar panicked as Belphegor slowed a little. He wanted to continue as Cerberus bounded after them, slowed only by the size of him compared to the path they were on.

"Cerberus may have six eyes, but he can only see the souls of the damned. You are probably invisible to him."

"Probably?"

"I don't know. Have you ever done something worthy of damnation?"

"I used to steal pieces of jigsaw puzzles so they could never be finished but I don't know! Besides, how does that help?" Oscar said, "because, for lack of a better phrase, you're still screwed." Belphegor shrugged.

"He won't hurt you, which gives you ample opportunity to keep the kraken busy without Cerberus bothering you." He didn't want to admit that he was quite enjoying the fight.

"Are you crazy? I can't fight it by myself," Oscar cried out. Belphegor looked at him, unphased.

"You've done it before," he said and without further ado, he took a deep breath and sprinted off the edge of the cliff. Cerberus howled and skidded to a halt before also leaping off the path. Oscar jumped back as its tail flicked out and barely missed pummelling him against the wall. Belphegor landed in a cringeworthy superhero stance that made Oscar groan, and ignoring the spiders as they ignored him, ran under the legs of one and away.

"What is he doing?" Noah commented, the bone he and Ebony were running along shuddering as Cerberus whacked into it.

"No idea," Ebony said, "but I have an idea about the Magma men." She watched worriedly as the kraken climbed across the ceiling, shaking spiders from its limbs. Ebony grabbed Noah's arm and yanked him to the side as a spider tumbled down and landed on its back, unable to flip itself over. The kraken grabbed it with a tentacle and in one swift motion, ripped off the spider's head. As blood soared through the air from its neck, it opened its mouth and swallowed the carcass whole.

"Tasty," Noah gagged, as the severed nerves in the leg left behind caused it to kick out reflexively. Ebony shivered and they continued forward. "What's your idea?"

"The kraken has a water bubble surrounding its head to breathe," she pointed as she dived over the Magma men, "so we douse the Magma men with the water and they solidify and hopefully we dehydrate and kill the kraken at the same time?"

"Is that going to work?"

"Ye of little faith," Ebony said. She turned around to see Atlas, who was still chasing them. He had in his hands a ball of energy. "But we have to deal with him first."

"How?"

"Hey!" There was a yell from below them and Ebony and Noah gulped as Emmanuel and Caleb rushed behind Atlas. They expected a trail of spiders to be following in their wake, but the spiders were slowed by the fear of the Kraken looming above them which gave them only Atlas to get past.

"Hey asshole!" Caleb taunted, aiming his knife at Atlas. His eye turned off and in surprise, he threw sightlessly. His aim wasn't as good as Emmanuel's but for a blind man was amazing; he threw the knife straight through his chest.

Atlas staggered.

Triumph.

Killing him was simple…

…Or was it?

Atlas' body rippled and repaired itself and the knife was pushed from his back, falling to the floor between his feet. He kicked it away and Caleb scrabbled to grab it as Atlas stood, cracking his joints as he prepared to fight.

"Shit," said Emmanuel, as Atlas threw a ball of energy at them. He jumped to the right, dragging Caleb with him. He pressed the two of them against the wall and braced against the energy as it skimmed his back and dissipated before it could do any damage to the real Atlas.

"Now what?" Noah asked.

"Old fashioned hand on hand combat?"

"Are you serious?"

"Did I stutter?" Ebony clenched her fists. "Emmanuel, Caleb, go with Noah, keep climbing."

"No way," they all said.

"Go! Otherwise, we'll have to fight off three fears at once."

"I'll stay," Caleb said, talking to the wall blindly. Emmanuel turned him to face Ebony. "My fear is dead. We can take Atlas easily, right Ebony?"

"You're literally blind."

"Not all the time." As his eye turned on, the two of them circled Atlas who snarled.

Ebony agreed. "We'll see you two at the top."

"You." Noah pointed an accusing finger at Ebony. "Be safe." He kissed her on the cheek, lingering for a moment before he reddened cheesily, and headed upwards.

"Be safe." Emmanuel copied Noah's actions with Caleb, who grinned like a fool as Emmanuel sprinted past Atlas.

"I will," he shouted. Ebony watched and Caleb winced as spiders began to run past them and the Magma men's gaze fell away from where they were, chasing Noah and Emmanuel as they began to climb yet again.

"Bring it on, you dick," Ebony said to Atlas, and she prepared to fight him, sword drawn. He glanced at it fleetingly, his emotionless face revealing nothing of his thoughts. The sword didn't dissuade him as he sprinted at her, throwing a ball of energy. To deflect the magic, Ebony whacked it with the sword and like a baseball bat to a ball, it soared into the side of the kraken, knocking if off balance. It roared but continued to lash out at Oscar whom it was created for.

Ebony had an idea.

"Okay?" Caleb was surprised by the turn of events.

"New plan," Ebony said. "Oscar!" She called as she dodged a sudden pounce from Atlas.

"What?" Oscar answered from the other side of the cavern as he parkoured his way around the kraken. His eyes followed Belphegor who had managed to get on the back of one of the dog's heads and was attempting to steer it. However, the other heads weren't too happy, and Belphegor tried to fend off their jaws without having a leg chewed off too as he rode.

"Get over here, we need the kraken facing this way!" Oscar looked confused but did as he was told.

"Coming!" Ebony turned back to Atlas who had momentarily given up throwing magic and opted for physical combat. He swung a punch. Ebony neatly dodged and returned it. Atlas howled, eyes watering, but kicked out and sent Ebony to the ground.

"Leave her alone you... you... you poo!" Caleb rushed forward and pushed Atlas. He didn't fall like Caleb expected. Caleb bounced back on the balls of his feet; hands raised into a martial arts fighting stance. "Come on then," he coaxed, as Atlas stood.

In Caleb's head, he was fighting with incredible agility, dodging punches with an air of grace. In reality however, he was running circles around Atlas until Atlas purely didn't have the energy to keep spinning in circles and chose to start hurling magic at people again instead.

Meanwhile, Oscar was waving frantically at Belphegor.

"Belphegor? Can you give me a lift?" Cerberus bucked like a raging bull, but Belphegor was slowly getting the hang of the steering.

"Easier said than done," he grimaced. His one arm was busy holding the dog's fur and whilst he yanked it in the direction of Oscar, he couldn't let go to grab him. "You're going to have to jump from there."

"Are you mad?" Oscar quaked at the height he was at. He backed away, a sickly green.

"You've thrown yourself out of two ships. Stop being a wimp and jump!" Belphegor's patience had disappeared with his arm.

"I'm not doing that!"

Ebony was still fighting Atlas when from behind she heard Oscar do that. He hollered from the other side of the cavern as he swung himself forward on one of the kraken's slimy tentacles that had tried to crush him. When the dog's multiple heads and threatening jaws were distracted, he let go. His landing was painful but fluffy and Belphegor laughed as Oscar shrieked. The action had more roused the dog whose heads were snarling viciously as it took off with a start. They headed through the Magma men and spider stragglers. As Ebony predicted, the Kraken veered sideways, following Oscar with its menacing glare.

"Come on then," she beckoned at Atlas. Caleb tried to throw the knife, but it missed, his aim worse than when he was sightless, and he gulped as Atlas turned on him. He didn't have the sword to deflect the magic but ducked agilely it as it flew at him and met an unintended target. Cerberus howled and Belphegor and Oscar were both thrown from their perch as the magic went through the dog's chest. It wailed and dropped to its knees, its three heads flopping in different directions across the ground. Using its neck as a slide, Belphegor slid down.

"Well, that's one way of killing it," he said as he stood, wiping Cerberus innards from his shirt.

"Brilliant," Oscar said grumpily, wishing he could pull the skin from his bones from the smell that stained it.

Atlas shrieked and turned back to Ebony, firing in a more rapid succession the balls of energy. She batted them away towards the kraken. All four blinding eyes stared, providing a spotlight which cast upon them an amber light.

"Emmanuel, Noah!" Caleb yelled, rushing past Ebony. "Get the Magma men beneath the kraken's head." He waved frantically for them to come back, and they paused, searching for a way to get back to them.

"They're coming from everywhere," Noah said, the daunting blocked path of Magma men and spiders providing no through road.

"We'll climb round," Emmanuel said determinedly, and they grabbed the walls and started to climb. But the fault in their plan became apparent when the spiders sprinted hungrily up the wall.

"Watch out!" Noah tried to warn but the warning came too late, and Emmanuel yelled out as a spider raised its abdomen and from its spinnerets projected a web of gluey silk at them. Instantly, Emmanuel's hand was affixed to the wall and no amount of pulling would break him free. Then another web stuck his foot and then his arm and spiders quickly gained their ground on the two of them.

"This stuff is impossible," Noah grunted. He tried to pull the sticky substance off but only risked sticking himself to the wall too.

"Go," Emmanuel said. "The Magma men will follow you, get them to the kraken."

"I'm staying here," Noah insisted.

Emmanuel pushed him away with his free hand, avoiding any glances below his feet and to his impending death. "Go!" he ordered.

"I've got him!" Belphegor promised and Noah watched him fighting through the spiders. With backup on the way, he gave Emmanuel a supportive nod and jumped, running down the path until he was swarmed by Magma men.

"You're going to die," Atlas smiled, his intent blinding him from his part in the bigger picture. With a final blow of an extortionately sized ball of energy, Ebony batted it with all her might, and they watched as it exploded like fireworks into the kraken. With a deafening roar, it pitched forward, smashing its head against the bony wall. Noah fled from the scene but was drenched anyway as the water bubble hit the ground and burst, flooding over the Magma men. They didn't make much noise, then again they never did, but as water drained between the cracks in their rocky limbs, they slowly solidified until they looked like nothing but strange statues.

Noah, bedraggled and shivering, let out a victory cry as two of their fears died. And, it had a further good impact, as many of the spiders who clambered carelessly over the Magma men in an attempt to catch Emmanuel slowly sunk, trapped inside the magma as it dried and stuck them to the floor. There were enough left to still pose a threat but with a newfound love of baseball, Ebony batted magic into them with a tremendous accuracy.

"Ebony, the sword!" Belphegor extended an arm. Caleb and Oscar ran to Belphegor who'd dunked his elbow into excess web and used it to climb higher than Emmanuel, fending off the spiders on his behalf. Sword soaring through the air, Belphegor let go, caught the sword and standing atop Emmanuel's shoulders, he sliced the webbing until it fell away. Emmanuel dropped but Oscar was ready and caught him. Caleb, on the other hand, misjudged where Emmanuel was and as his eye turned off, held his hands out underneath thin air. His hands remained out as Emmanuel and Oscar groaned in a heap on the floor.

"Thanks for the catch," Emmanuel said. Caleb laughed awkwardly, scratching the back of his neck.

"Sorry." He put his hand out to lean against the wall but missed and fell to the ground, his eye flickering on in time for him to see everyone laughing at him. "Ha, very funny, laughing at a disabled person," he sighed. Belphegor was standing closest, and he looked up at him. "Belphegor, give us a hand."

Crickets chirped.

"Sorry."

Belphegor lifted him on to his feet with one hand and then instantly ducked back down as Atlas threw magic at them. Ebony scowled.

"Don't feel left out dad," she said. "You'll be joining the others soon." Atlas was circled methodically, six versus one and as Belphegor handed Ebony the sword, he lunged for her in one last futile attempt. With the sword raised above her head, she let out a guttural scream and took his head off in a single swipe.

As though all of their fears were purely a mirage, the dead bodies shimmered and faded, leaving the black pulsating heart the only thing in the room.

"Is everyone all right?" Belphegor asked, taking a quick headcount to ensure he hadn't lost anyone.

"Mentally, I need therapy. Otherwise, I'm dandy." Emmanuel pulled spiderwebs from his hair.

"Agreed. Are we done?" Caleb panted.

"Something tells me we're not," Ebony said. The sword felt heavy in her hands, and she let it sag to the floor.

"She's right," Noah said, "I still don't feel... magical." He clicked his fingers and the same matchbox-sized portal appeared. Ebony looked to the heart which shrunk under her watch. It could feel the sword drawing closer.

"Let's get up there and change that." Ebony marched forward, heaving the sword behind her and the others followed suit. Belphegor, who climbed easier with one hand when the wall didn't pulsate and when he could use his dregs of magic to levitate, offered to take the lead, insisting he would protect everyone until the end. Ebony followed him with the sword and Oscar took the rear, careful to spot a shaken Emmanuel, Noah whose hand still had a deep cut through it and Caleb, who's tendency to go blind was slowing him down. They reached the heart, or Hell's scrotum as Caleb entitled it on the way up, and it seemed as though nothing was going to stop them from getting close.

"I don't like this, Ebony," Oscar whispered.

"Me neither."

"You think it's a trap?"

"Almost definitely."

"So, what do we do?"

"Set it off?" Ebony raised her eyebrows. She stepped forward and without warning a force field rose from the ground between her and her friends.

"Ebony!" Oscar threw himself against it, but it flung him away as an electrified pulse charged between them.

He tried to run forwards again, but Belphegor held him back. Ebony looked at them fearfully through the field, wielding the sword as she waited to see what would happen. She couldn't reach the heart. The electricity had trapped her.

"Ebony don't go near the forcefield," Belphegor instructed as Oscar's hair stood on end. "What's happening in there?" The electricity caused a shimmer like frosted glass and he could only see pixels, not details like how her bottom lip quivered, or how she reached a hand out for company, picking at the skin on the side of her thumbnail.

"Nothing right now," she murmured. Her eyes darted about the room, and Belphegor threw his hands in the air, grunting helplessly. He tried to draw the electricity from the field, but it fought against him with a life of its own.

Ebony stared at him as he failed to break the field and for the first time through Belphegor's eyes, he saw nothing but a vulnerable, young girl. And he shouldn't have let her go in alone.

"Well. This is delightful."

Ebony didn't need to see the person to know who was talking.

Sonneillon had entered the ring.

Chapter 30

"You're alive," Sonneillon said blandly, his face quite expressionless. He looked haggard but still had confidence in his ability to beat Ebony. But, after everything she'd been through and the weariness hanging in the air, at the sight of Sonneillon Ebony was suddenly and surprisingly upbeat.

"Yeah," she said casually.

"Sonneillon, let her go. If you want a fight, fight another Ancient," Belphegor warned.

"I'd rather fight someone worthy of my time," Sonneillon sneered. He glanced at Ebony and the sword. "And why, pray tell, are you so calm?" His eyes narrowed as he formed a spiral of blackness in his hand, tossing it like a ball.

"Because you're scared," Ebony had realised and Sonneillon roared with laughter, mouth splitting to his eyes with putrid saliva dripping from his gums behind the overstretched skin.

"Scared? Tell me, how did you worm your way to that preposterous conclusion?" Ebony nearly smiled.

"The elaborate traps you hide behind. That most of your power is indisposed to Atlas. The fact that I'm metres away from killing you and all you can do is make a force field. You're a deer in headlights. You have nothing left. You got too caught up in the game to realise you were losing." Belphegor's eyes widened.

"She's right," he reinforced. "Since when were you scared enough of an Enchanted you put a forcefield between them and your life?"

"Shut up," Sonneillon snarled.

"He's got a point," Ebony said.

"I said shut up," Sonneillon growled. "I could kill you with a click of my fingers." Ebony shrugged.

"Prove it," she said. "Drop the force field." But Sonneillon didn't.

"You will die here," he forewarned, before roaring and springing forward, a knife in each hand and prehensile tendrils of smoke bellowing around him. Ebony found out where Atlas got the dramatic flair from and ran to meet him as her friends screamed from the side-line.

Dodging the first tendril, Ebony winced as the second sliced across her stomach where the wound from the sword sat raw but slashed the third with the sword which worked surprisingly well. It shrivelled back but Sonneillon jumped through the smoke, knives out and Ebony rolled away fearfully. She was confident she could fight him off in terms of magical ability; what he had left he was busy using to hold the forcefields. However, his hand-to-hand combat skills were immaculate and the tactical blinding of her with smoke and subsequent random attacks was defeating her. Her eyes watered with a punch to the nose, and she nearly dropped the sword as Sonneillon kicked her shin, but tumbled away, catching it before he could swipe it from her.

"Come on Ebony!" Noah stamped his feet as he cheered her on and Oscar found himself nearly bashing on the forcefield again.

"Give up, Ebony. Death is inevitable," Sonneillon hissed.

"Tell that to yourself." She spat blood to the ground and lunged at him again, catching his arm with the sword. He roared as blood flowed from his forearm and he dropped a knife. But, replacing it with a ball of acid mass, he threw it at Ebony. She barely missed and the electricity took the brunt of the impact, but Sonneillon jumped her, forcing her to the ground. Her head made an ungodly thumping noise as it hit the flesh and Sonneillon took the opportunity to pin her down, grabbing the sword and holding it to her chest. Both of them were holding the hilt, grunting as they pushed the blade towards each other.

"Ebony!" Caleb screamed, eyeball giving him more insight to the danger she was in.

"Now what?" Sonneillon teased. "Your friends aren't going to save you. Your uncle can't save you. Who's going to save you now?" Ebony mumbled and Sonneillon leant in to hear her as she sputtered.

"I am."

With eyes glowing gold, there was a bright flash and the next thing anyone saw was Ebony pushing Sonneillon off her with such force, he flew into the forcefield.

He had the sword.

It didn't matter.

"I don't need anyone to save me," Ebony said. Like in the heart of

Tcheeva her body began to glow, a powerful and good, golden light shining from her body as she pulled herself up. Power flowed through her veins as it overpowered Sonneillon's and he yelled out, casting both hands forward and throwing everything he could at her. She absorbed his magic like it was doing nothing. The acid soaked into her skin, but she recycled it, throwing it back at him in attack after attack, relentlessly knocking him back as the power built.

"Ebony, stop!" Sonneillon tried to command, but Ebony pushed forward, the light building until he had to cover his eyes.

"I am Ebony Echnovarria." Her voice boomed through Atlas' body and for the first time she could feel his movement as his entire body shuddered. "I am an Enchanted." Sonneillon tried to stand but she clutched him by the neck, holding him high in the air as he struggled against her grip. "I am the Enchanted that ended you for good." Her eyes burnt into his and his skin cracked until it started to peel off. She held onto him with all of her might until with a bang, his magic was destroyed, and Atlas was revealed, hiding underneath his final defence, which Ebony had at last broken.

"Daughter," he choked. "Please."

Ebony lowered her voice. "Goodbye Dad," she said as ripped the sword from his grasp and held it to his chest. "It wasn't nice knowing you."

She plunged the sword into his heart. The two of them were enveloped in an explosion of bright light and Belphegor shoved everyone to the ground as the force obliterated the forcefield, sending electrically charged debris flying in all directions. Then, the room dulled, and Ebony barely managed to stay standing as the final light faded from her. She dropped Atlas' body carelessly, looking over him.

"Rot in hell."

"Ebony, you did it!" Emmanuel celebrated. He, Noah, and Belphegor flexed in unison as their powers flooded back, stronger than ever. Ebony stood as the world around her began to sway.

Her vision became fuzzy at the edges.

"Stab Atlas' heart and this will all be over," Oscar pushed but Ebony wasn't paying attention.

"Ebony, are you all right?" Caleb asked, moving towards her. He gently touched her shoulder and pulled away to see blood stuck to his hand, red and wet on his fingertips. "Ebony?" She looked up at him with cloudy eyes and he carefully peeled back her jacket to the white shirt underneath. It was stained red.

"I may or may not have been stabbed." Ebony smiled weakly. She dropped to the floor with no effort to break her fall. A painful ringing in her ears swamped the voices of her friends and she looked at them as their figures blurred. She held her hand to her chest, drew it away and on seeing the blood, squeezed her eyes shut as her breathing became more of a struggle.

"She's going to be okay. Right?" Caleb asked, trembling. Emmanuel gripped his hand and squeezed it gently.

"Hold on Ebony," Oscar said as he tried to draw the sword from her hands, but she held it firmly.

"No," she protested. "Leave."

"We're not leaving you," he cried vehemently. "I'm not going where you can't follow, remember?" he quoted her. "Can't you heal yourself?"

"She can't," Belphegor said.

"Can't you heal her?"

"The wound is from the sword. Wounds inflicted by the sword of Sonneillon don't ever heal."

"Leave," Ebony begged. "I'll kill him when you're safe."

"Ebony, you can't even stand."

"I don't need to be able to stand, I just need to be able to stab," she mumbled.

"No." Noah held his hands over the wound, but it did nothing. "Ebony please." His eyes were lined with tears which dripped down onto her face as he gently cupped her cheek with his bloody hand.

"She's right," Belphegor said.

"No, she's not." Oscar and Noah stared at him, a rage burning behind their eyes.

"If we're all in here when Atlas shrinks and dies, we're going to die with him," Belphegor said. "He's already deteriorating as it is." Oscar and Noah remained firmly sure they wouldn't leave, and Emmanuel and Caleb agreed but as the flesh around them began to heave and shake, they grew unsure.

"Look, we're not leaving her," Emmanuel said, and Belphegor turned to him.

"I don't want her to die alone," Oscar begged.

"I'm not letting any more of my relatives die than needs be," he said. Emmanuel's brow softened and Belphegor looked at him kindly. He gripped his shoulder with reassurance. "I'll stay with Ebony. I would argue my time is up in this universe."

"Please don't." Blood trickled from Ebony's mouth as she tried to argue. Belphegor interrupted; he knelt by her side.

"Someone needs to stab Atlas and the second we do; this place is going to collapse," he said. "Noah, you have enough strength to get everyone out."

"No," Noah choked. "…Yes, but no! I don't want to leave."

Emmanuel wiped his tears and tried to act sensibly. "Ebony, it was an honour to have met you and fought by your side." He kissed her hand, and Ebony smiled.

Thank you she whispered.

"Goodbye Ebony," Noah said. He clasped her hand one more time, before, with a heavy heart, he summoned a portal. Caleb dropped to Ebony's side, shaking his head roughly.

"Caleb." Belphegor softly closed his hand around Caleb's shoulder, and he looked up to him. His eye was dull.

"I can't see you," he whimpered. "I want to see you one last time." His body was shaking as he blindly felt for her. Belphegor, with his power restored, put his hand on Caleb's back. An electrical surge travelled to his eye and if he was capable of crying from said eye, he would be as he was able to look at Ebony.

"Goodbye Caleb." She locked eyes with him. Caleb broke down in a mess of heavy breathing as he hugged her tightly.

"Be brave," Belphegor said. Caleb forced a final smile before standing. Oscar remained crouched by Ebony's side for a moment longer, looking into her eyes.

"What?" she asked. Tears dripped onto her face, and he rubbed his eyes, sniffing. His mouth twitched and he smiled for her, hoping he could bring her a final piece of the happiness she deserved.

"I'm remembering your face," he whispered and lowering his head, he kissed her. It wasn't a revelation of his feelings towards her. It was a kiss between two friends who had known each other for so long and loved each other so much that nothing else showed how much they cared and how painful the thought of losing Ebony was to Oscar. Their lips parted and he dropped his head into her shoulder. They embraced, never wanting to let go. Ebony pushed her head into his neck with all the strength she had left, whimpering as he sat up.

Go.

"Come on Oscar." Caleb gently wrapped his arm around his shoulder and Oscar held Ebony's hand for as long as he could, until their fingertips parted.

He wept like she was already gone and stepped through the portal. Noah held it open for a moment, giving Belphegor a small salute. Ebony seized her chance.

I'm not letting you die either uncle she thought and with her last remaining power, summoned a gale. Belphegor could react with nothing, but a mouth hung agape as it swept him through the portal. She heard a yell from the other side and as he turned around to lunge back in, she closed the portal up.

She was alone.

Cold and alone.

Death wasn't how she imagined. She'd always pictured herself dying of old age. This was far from it.

"Just you and me dad," she said. She pushed herself upwards, arms threatening to give way as she climbed the sword hilt. Using it as a walking stick, she dragged herself over to the heart. It flinched and cowered in her presence.

"You wouldn't kill your old man." A faded image of Atlas, all the magic he had left to summon within him, appeared, trying to appeal to her humanity. But Ebony didn't have the power to talk.

"I would," she said simply and raising the sword, she plunged it deep inside his heart.

Chapter 31

"Sorry it took so long for you to die; I was stuck in traffic. Was across the galaxy. Took the soul of an atheist and sent him to hell for a hoot. Told him he should have believed harder." There was a laugh like an airhorn. "Classic. You know, I did expect to see you here eventually, but I didn't expect Atlas to be here too. Well done for killing him. I sent him to the worst depth of hell, same place as child molesters, people who put milk in a bowl before the cereal, animal abusers, people who don't break KitKats in half, rapists and worst of all, the loud chewers. I could go on. Must admit, I don't normally hold a personal vendetta but damn, Atlas was an asshole, even for an Ancient. I haven't had a weekend off since this began, been processing so many souls, day in, day out and I can't drink coffee because I'm not a physical being, so it just spills everywhere which makes the job so much more tiring. And being stuck in a box listening to his endless jabbering. I tell you it's enough to make a grown man cry. He didn't go to therapy; in case you couldn't tell."

One minute she was dying from a gaping hole through her chest, the next Ebony was standing in a room with a revitalising energy and no more holes than a human body should have and hopefully no less. A recognisable voice was monologing, coming from the mouth of a creature sitting in mid-air. There was no one like him. And in seeing him, she knew her odyssey had come to a definite close.

"Death?" she uttered.

"You remember." Had he had the ability to blush, Death would have done but he was dead and had no blood. Or body.

"Of course, I do." She faltered from her excitement and examined her own body. "I'm dead?"

"Yep," Death said cheerily. Ebony caught her bottom lip with her teeth. Normally her breathing would heavy, but there was no breath for it to happen.

"Can you tell me… you know, which way I'm going? Up or down?" she asked timidly, and Death laughed.

"Ebony, sweetheart, listen. Normally I'd have my reapers send you on your way but not this time. I owe you a debt for saving me."

"Okay?" Death owed her a debt. She was intrigued.

"You have two options," he offered. "Either you can stay here, and I'll guarantee sending you to a better place, or you can go back to the world of the living." Ebony's eyes widened.

"Really?" she asked. "I could go back."

"Really."

"I don't know what to say."

"Well, it's not hard. I only gave you two choices," Death said sarcastically. "I mean, you could go to hell if you really wanted. But I'm not sure you'd like it." Ebony gulped and straightened her shoulders. Maybe he would do her a favour. Grant her some agreed upon secret fourth option.

"Can I–" He cut her off.

"–*May I remind you I am a magical being, who like you, can also read minds?*" he informed her. She shut her mouth, her head dropping as she stopped herself from asking a favour. Death shook his head sorrowfully. "I can't revive other people Ebony," he said. "It's against company policy."

"I understand." She bowed her head sadly. "Worth a try."

Death guided her through the blackness, floating effortlessly beside her and they soon reached a set of doors.

"One sends you upstairs, the other takes you home," he said. "Choose wisely. Not many people get to."

"Others have had a choice?" Ebony asked. Death tapped his nose secretively. She stared at the two doors, one made from solid gold, the other a refined silver, and Ebony was attracted to both possibilities. Death watched curiously as she placed her hand on the handle of one door, but she hesitated.

"No," she muttered to herself and moved purposefully to the other one.

"Mind made up?"

"Yep," Ebony said surely. She turned and held out a hand. "Thank you, Death," she said, and they shook cordially. With the golden door calling her, she opened it. But, before she could walk through, Death stopped her.

Ebony?

Yes?

I make the rules here. So technically I could bend them.

Ebony grinned. "Brilliant."

Chapter 32

The smell of wet dust was earthy. It carried across the body ridden plains of Tcheeva and merged with the rancid acetone scent of death. It was a smell only Belphegor recognised. On the hillside atop Tcheeva, he breathed in deeply. It was the smell of the coming end of battle. Everywhere he looked, carnage raged. The red horizon merged into the blood-stained dirt; planet and sky as one consolidated graveyard. The remaining Enchanteds and soldiers, given something to fight for fought mercilessly against the zombies and Magma men, driven by revenge for their lost loved ones.

Still a giant but steadily crumbling, Atlas' condition deteriorated. It was a futile attempt on his part to survive. With no necromancy to keep them alive, his army slowly wilted from his misshapen body, pools of flesh and skin sagging across the floor and never regaining consciousness.

Atlas had not a shred of dignity as he died. His whole body began to age rapidly; cataracts clouded his unblinded eye and his lips folded in on his diseased gums as his teeth dropped to the floor. His hair whitened and fell in a single fleece, and then his skin too began to drop off. There was no power left to sustain him, and Atlas began to convulse. He squealed like a deflating balloon as his muscles failed him. Naileless fingertips reached out as his knees broke and gave way.

Shrunk to his normal size, with only hell awaiting him, his life drained away.

Atlas was dead.

The victory was cold.

At what cost had they won?

"She did it," Oscar said, but there was little joy behind his words.

"That's my girl," Belphegor said, swelling with pride. Palms facing the ground, he flew himself down the mountain and shook his head in disbelief as he landed gently by Atlas' crumpled skin. Impaling him was the sword, Ebony's handprint twined around the hilt. Aligning his hands where hers once was, Belphegor pulled the sword out and as he did so, Sonneillon and Atlas' magic dissipated into the ground and Tcheeva began to renew itself. With a battle cry of anger yet relief, Belphegor clenched his fist and the decapitated body of Adremelech flew to him.

"Can't have you coming back either Adremelech," he said, no longer referring to the monster before him as his brother. He dropped Adremelech's headless body roughly into the dirt and thrust the sword neatly between his ribs and into his heart.

Is Ebony... Belphegor heard a meek voice inside his head and turned to see Emmanuel standing several paces away, Noah to his right and wrapping a bandage around his hand.

She's gone he confirmed. They tried to console each other. Further behind, as a ring of flowers grew around their shoes, Caleb and Oscar too tried to be brave.

Oscar put a finger to his lips, his emotions soaring. But Ebony always wanted him to stop biting his nails. So, he pulled his fingers away and put his hand to better use in pulling Caleb in for a hug.

It was a solemn acceptance, and triumph on Tcheeva came not without its sacrifices. As the planet regenerated, trees kindly curled their roots around the bodies of the dead, zombie and Enchanted alike, and held them firmly to the ground as vibrant vegetation grew over them. Belphegor watched as Atlas' body became but a naked shrub, a stark but deserving tribute to his memory. Despite the planet's restoration to its former youth, the rivers ran black with the remains of the dead. Tcheeva would never be the same.

Oscar knelt silently in respect for the unnamed Enchanteds who had fought beside them. He kissed his fingers and touched the spongy moss, which sprung to meet his hands like a final farewell from the fallen.

Caleb stooped down to pick up a half-melted face plate jutting from the ground. He wiped off the red dust until the metal had a dull polish to it.

"Return to Xavier," he sadly requested. "Tell him I'm sorry so few of you returned." Oscar bowed next to him at the hundred remaining robots who collected their broken parts and launched towards Foro.

Many ships hung like permanent additions to the sky. They stayed for answers. Roamers wanted to know where Daegel was. Governments wanted to know how a threat like Atlas had slipped through their fingers. Everyone wanted to know who the Enchanteds were.

"The universe will know about our existence now," Noah said as Roamers and soldiers and government officials filed onto the planet.

"I think they knew about it the second Godzilla appeared in Chane." Emmanuel remembered Jeff fondly. "But we can learn to coexist peacefully with humanity."

Noah agreed. "It'll be nice not having to hide anymore," he admitted. Belphegor joined them silently; he sat down on the ground cross legged and raised his face to the sun. Beneath his fingertips that grazed the grass, he could feel the heart of Tcheeva beat through each and every blade. He smiled contentedly.

"I've never been able to just sit and be with my own thoughts." A golden glow cast down over him. "It's nice." Emmanuel's eyes crinkled; smile lines more prominent than ever.

"You'll be able to do a lot of that now," he said and him and Noah joined Belphegor to simply sit. Oscar and Caleb sauntered over. It was a strange moment of sundry emotions. They were all delighted by the death of Atlas, but the death of Ebony outweighed any obvious joy. A wall of exhaustion hit them and suddenly, the strength to even sit up straight was gone. Oscar hugged his knees to his chest.

"I miss her." He spoke with a heavy heart.

"Get a grip Oscar," Ebony laughed. "I've been gone ten minutes, if that." Oscar sprung to his feet with such force it practically dented the earth beneath him. Caleb and Emmanuel followed suit, and Noah drove himself through a portal to face her direction with such a speed that he nearly chopped himself in half. His jaw dropped to the floor and Emmanuel wiped his eyes from the tears he shed for Ebony's loss and replaced them with tumbling tears of joy for the four people standing in front of him.

"No way." Caleb was in disbelief and tapped on his cyber eye to make sure it was working. He looked at her like a miracle. "You're all here?"

Belphegor took a moment to stand and he turned slowly, as if praying whilst he swivelled that Ebony was definitely going to be behind him. Despite the breeze whipping hair around his face, the light managed to catch a tear drop hanging to his lower lashes. Ebony didn't think he had ever cried.

"It's not possible," Belphegor breathed. "No one comes back from the dead."

"Except you and Adremelech and, well-" Jeff patted himself to prove his solidity, adorning a head full of hair and a full head full stop, "-us."

"Death owed Ebony big time," Stella said, looking as beautiful and radiant as they day she died.

"So, he let four of us come back with her." Belize gave a thumbs up, sunny disposition drying any tears that were falling. "And Ebony chose us," she beamed. Ebony walked towards the stunned group and paused in front of Oscar. With a hand hesitantly raised, he dropped it until it rested gently on her cheek.

"Hello stranger," he said in awe. Ebony snorted.

"Stranger? I thought you were busy remembering my face?" Oscars eyes brightened, safe in the knowledge she was back for good. He pulled Ebony into him, laughing in glee as they embraced. The rest of the group erupted as Jeff, Belize, and Stella, along with Ebony were dragged into one huge hug. Relief and joy swept through like a tidal wave and for the first time in a long time, Ebony felt as though she'd done right by everyone.

Oscar let Ebony go. "Four people," he said, with an impressed raised eyebrow. "Who's the fourth?" Ebony tapped her nose knowingly.

"An old friend," she said. Accepting he was to get no more from her he went to greet the others and Ebony momentarily backed away from the celebration. Generating a narrow portal barely big enough to look in, she peeked through and into the living quarters aboard a Homestead ship.

A once welcoming home was appointed in black sheets. A woman in a coal dress and smudged makeup collapsed onto a sofa, a vase of dead flowers placed in front of her. Her silent laments were interrupted by a knock on the door which the woman heard with disdain. Dragging her feet, though her limbs weighed her down, she opened the door. The stillness was shattered by her scream, and she stood trembling.

"Are you real?" she asked the man who stood at the doorway. He nodded.

She didn't need proof.

She embraced the man and Ebony could feel the happiness radiating from the two of them. The woman called out and a small child came running and the man dropped to one knee, holding out his arms, beckoning to the girl. She paused as though she had met a ghost, but the man and woman assured her it was okay.

With a yell of, "dad!" she hugged him tightly. His whole body shook in overwhelming happiness as he held her to his chest. The sight was heart-warming. As he tore his eyes away from his wife and child, he noticed the small portal and glimpsed Ebony through it.

"Thank you," he mouthed. Ebony couldn't smile widely enough.

You're welcome, Jonah. She saluted him before shutting the portal.

"Jeff." Belphegor walked up to him. "Words cannot begin to express how sorry I am for leaving you on Nibiru. I thought you were dead." Oscar glanced back and forth between Belphegor and Jeff, unable to tell if Jeff was going to forgive him.

"Let's ignore the elephant in the room," he suggested, trying to avoid another conflict. Jeff giggled at his new shapeshifted form.

"Really?"

"Couldn't resist," Jeff trumpeted. He shifted back to his normal self. "No elephant in the room. And no hard feelings. All is forgiven." He held out his hand and Belphegor shook it.

"Thank you," he mumbled. Ebony watched on as the reconciliation was made. A few paces away, Emmanuel and Belize had both exploded into hysterics. Ebony didn't know why but she didn't care for the reason they were laughing. She was simply thankful they were.

Caleb and Stella were in deep discussion already; he introduced her to Belphegor and within moments, she pointed at Caleb's eye patch and her and Belphegor burst out laughing. Caleb looked mildly offended. Ebony sighed contently. They had returned to normal.

Standing apart from everyone else, Noah wandered to Ebony.

"Only been gone ten minutes," he quoted her. "We thought you were dead."

"So did I," Ebony winced. She thought he was going to scold her, but enough hatred and fights had occurred for their lifetimes. He hugged her tightly. "Besides," she said, and her eyes widened as she realised it, "I'm technically immortal. You're literally stuck with me forever." Noah sarcastically rolled his eyes.

"But we wouldn't have it any other way," Belphegor said affectionately, as he strode up behind the two of them. "Ebony–" he grasped her hand proudly, "–you outshine the stars."

"Thanks uncle B." She nudged him in the ribs with a gentle elbow and threw her head back with laughter as he frowned at her.

"Don't call me B," he said seriously, but the grin playing on his face said otherwise. Ebony pouted.

"Sorry uncle B." She jumped sideways as he playfully lunged for her, shaking his head with a hearty guffaw. Ebony raised her hands in defeat. "What can I say, family's annoying." Belphegor's military posture softened. He cocked his head to the side, ears pricked up and his smile brightened from ear to ear.

"You mean it?"

"Of course," she said. "You have officially been promoted from the role of creepy demon to weird uncle." Belphegor fell into a flurry of nervous words.

"Really? Because I understand I haven't been there for you and my past is hard to overlook. But I promise I'll be a better person, I'll do better…" Ebony cut him off with a hug and Belphegor held Ebony tightly to his chest from which his heart nearly burst. She beamed and for the first time ever, felt genuinely safe in the arms of a family member.

"So, that's it?" Oscar asked and the others fell quiet. "We won. Atlas is gone."

"He is." Emmanuel grinned victoriously as they sat together on the renewed planet. Belize and Jeff sat huddled between Emmanuel and Noah who were never going to let them out of their sights again. Ebony was glad she could reunite a family. She held onto Oscar's hand tightly, or rather it was the other way round. He didn't want to let go. There was an air of content about all of them. Emmanuel gently rested his head atop Caleb's even messier than usual mop. On the other side of him, Stella smiled at her friends with the pride of a mother and her and Ebony exchanged a wink.

Belphegor hadn't been happier in his life than he had in the couple of moments he'd spent admiring his niece and her brave friends. Beaming in the paternal pride and joy Atlas should have always had for

Ebony, he settled into a serene state and absentmindedly leant on the arm that wasn't there.

He fell to the side.

For a moment, the veins on his forehead looked like they might rupture but as laughter exploded from everyone, he laughed along with them.

Together, they watched as the stars slowly rose over the planet, signalling the start of a new day.

Ebony held out her hand; it emitted a blue gleam as she felt magic surge through her body. It was not often that she felt as though the universe was, for but a second, winning the battle of good versus evil.